MW00422779

ACT OF GRACE

ACT OF GRACE

KAREN SIMPSON

ACT OF GRACE. Copyright © 2011 by Karen Simpson.

All rights reserved. No part of this book may be reproduced or transmitted in any form or by any means without express written permission from the author.

This novel is a work of fiction. Names, characters, places, incidents, and dialogue, except for incidental references to public figures, products, places or services, are products of the author's imagination or are used fictitiously, and are not intended to refer to any persons, living or dead, or to disparage any company's products or services.

The Velveteen Rabbit, by Margery Williams is an individual work in the public domain of the United States.

"The Second Coming," by W.B. Yeats is an individual work in the public domain of the United States.

Please visit www.karensimpsonwrites.com for information about the author and special discounts.

Printed in the United States of America

To my mom, Dorothy Jean Van Catledge Simpson, who understood the true meaning of grace.

To my Dad, Willie James Simpson, who gave me James Baldwin, my first typewriter, the advice to have faith in God, and, most of all, to have faith in myself.

Author's Note

Act of Grace revolves, in part, around the mysticism, spirituality and mythology of the African-derived practice of Hoodoo. Contrary to popular belief, Hoodoo is not a religion, and it is not all about casting evil spells or making deals with the devil. The media may portray it as such, taking advantage of the public's limited knowledge of the complexity of African people and African-American culture. But when the curtains of stereotypes are pulled back, we learn that Hoodoo is an evolving, multicultural system of folkloric practices that can be used to effect positive and negative change. Hoodoo was created and used by Africans and their descendants to help fight against slavery, oppression and racism. And quiet as it's kept, Hoodoo still contributes to African-American spirituality. It is still used to fix problems, assure justice, and move people toward self-determination. My novel, Act of Grace, is steeped in this powerful African-American shamanic tradition.

RISE

MR. GILMORE WAS SUPPOSED TO have died that day at the Justice Rally, but I got in the way and now people in my hometown of Vigilant, Michigan, are either calling me an Uncle Tom hero or hissing that I'm a double-stuffed Oreo bitch. Actually, I'm neither, but I realize now that one of the reasons why people's attitudes about me are as nasty as dried snot is because there is a critical lack of information about my motives. Those who love me already understand my reasons. For them, it's enough for me to say the ancestors made me do it. Other folks, however, especially other folks of color, feel I need to testify about why I, Grace Johnson, a supposedly rational African-American high school senior and honor student, committed racial treason.

If it were up to me, I wouldn't say anything. I would just leave everyone in the dark and go on about my business. But the voices of the ancestors tell me I owe an account of my story as an example of the true meaning of my name. Now, I can blow people off, I can tell them what part of hell to go to and give them detailed directions on how to get there. The ancestors, however, cannot be ignored. They can't be told to mind their own ethereal business because we, the living, are their business. Pain and suffering have made my hindsight telescopic, so let's begin at the true beginning, a breath to prime my memory: "rise, story, rise."

1

THE ONLY WARNING OF THE coming destruction of my old life last October was sweat and a swelling sense of unease. I woke up sodden, so slick with perspiration my nightgown had formed a big, wrinkly fist and climbed up my legs. At first I thought I had the flu, but I decided I just needed to open a window because my room was so stuffy and hot. Although the calendar read autumn, the weather was still acting like summer. But I had no explanation for the sense of unease. It wasn't my usual muddy angst, and yet the nameless brand of anxiety raised crops of goose bumps on my arms and made me turn my head to check the emptiness behind my back.

Restless and damp, I stood in my bedroom doorway, scanning the hall for evidence of my so-called family. The depth and texture of the silence told me my sister Jamila was still sucking all the beauty she could from sleep, and Mama didn't have to do overtime as a clerk at city hall. If my luck wasn't stingy, the house would be my private sanctuary for one or two hours.

An unusually swift current of hunger pulled me toward the kitchen. I made a big pot of grits, which I garnished with more than the recommended daily requirement of butter and cheese, and fried a half-pound of bacon—even though for the hundredth time that year I'd sworn I would become a vegetarian. My morning nerves seemed to drive my appetite. I ate and ate, my lips smacking out a greasy melody as I crunched on crisp cords of bacon and shoveled in snowy drifts of congealed corn. All the while I kept thinking about how good it would be to escape to college next year. Anyone who has lived in the desert realm of high school unpopularity knows how eager I was to go where no one knew me as me. It looked as if Spelman College might accept me, and I was excited. But as I sat there still hungry, even after two plates of food, my joy dissipated. I think even then, I knew Spelman was being put on hold, but I didn't know how to talk about it because I had only a shadowy understanding of my true metaphysical identity.

I was thinking so hard about the future, I almost didn't hear the present pounding on the front door. I opened it to find my friends, Shanta and Nikki, standing on the porch and doubled over from laughing. They didn't reveal the joke, and I didn't think to ask what was so funny because it seemed odd that they were there so early. They were not the type of people who even knew what eleven in the morning looked like on a weekend.

They plopped on the couch, looking for all the world like dogs who had done something they knew wasn't right. Hot as it was, Shanta looked cool, her pecan-colored skin dry, as if her pores were too proud to leak. Nikki's face, on the other hand, was tinted the shade of ruby red grapefruit, and it was shiny from the sweat dribbling down from under her dense canopy of curly auburn hair.

Shanta and I had always been together. I was closer to her than I was to my own sister. What we lacked in blood kinship, we made up for in the shared DNA of dreams and experiences. We had bonded in preschool after my father died and her family had stepped in and tried to help my crazy mother raise me and Jamila. Nikki had been a more recent addition. She'd made Shanta and me her friends after falling out with the pretty white girl cliques at school because they thought she was hanging around too many black people. Nikki was fun to be around, but I always got the feeling that she liked Shanta a whole lot more than she liked me because I was a size sixteen instead of a size six.

"Okay, what brings you out this early?" I asked suspiciously. We hadn't talked before about doing anything over the weekend. Frankly, I had planned on hiding out in my room and studying calculus, the great defiler of my GPA.

"You know the Pumpkin Harvest Jazz Festival you've been talking about since I don't know when?" Nikki started to explain.

"Yeah, the one I can't afford to go to," I said.

The festival was the annual fundraiser for the exclusive Diamond Yacht Club located a few miles outside of Vigilant. Ticket prices started at one hundred dollars, putting it out of reach.

"Nikki's mother got us tickets." Shanta's voice rose in anticipation of the joy I would feel.

"You're not messing with me, are you?" I asked.

"Would we mess with you about something like this?"

I shrugged and told my hopes to lay back down. Nikki read the doubt on my face and burst out laughing. "Oh, here look." She pulled three tickets from her purse and handed them to me. I held them like the musical gold they were. If they had been food, they would have been drool-worthy.

"See, I told you," Shanta chided.

I ran my fingers across the glossy surface, taking in the legendary name of Ornette Coleman and others. I wanted to go so bad, but pride made me say, "Nikki, I can't take this. I mean, I can't even begin to pay for it."

"It's not about affording it, Grace. My mother's on one of the committees and she got some freebies."

"Shoot, Grace, you think I would be going if I couldn't get in free? I don't have that kind of cash," Shanta added.

"Come on, Grace. They'll just go to waste if you don't come, 'cause this isn't exactly what me and Shanta are into."

I chuckled to myself because Nikki was right. The tickets wouldn't be used, not even scalped. Shanta loved hip-hop, and Nikki was partial to country. Neither of them understood my need for jazz. And it was a need. More like something I couldn't live without than a subject I was just interested in.

"Actually," Nikki said, "I don't see why you want to listen to old people's music, but I'm willing to hang out with you while you do."

"I suppose it's just a matter of what you like," I offered.

Shanta sat back and slid deep into the couch cushion. I watched as her smile straightened into a serious expression. "It's more than that with you, I think, Gracie. My dad says you love jazz and blues the way macaroni loves to be with cheese, or the way beans need to be with cornbread, because you're an old soul. He says it's like you've been here before and heard it all because it comes to you so naturally."

A covey of shivers coasted out of nowhere, and my hands shook a bit. Old soul. Shanta's dad had always told me that, but I hadn't exactly known what he meant by it. I was just happy Mr. Manning was willing to let me sit around with him and listen to his wonderful collection while he talked about the acts he had seen on stage. He was the closest thing I had to a father, and I cherished the relationship.

"Your dad's just a good teacher," I finally said as I held up one of the precious tickets. "Shouldn't you be giving him one of these anyway?"

"He's got to work, and don't think he hasn't been bitching about it. You might as well go because he's going to want to know all about it. He'll be disappointed if you had a chance and didn't take it."

"Yeah, you might as well go," Nikki chimed in.

I swiftly calculated the amount of my homework against the time left in the weekend and decided I could indulge in some recreation. The term was young and I was, after all, finally a senior. I got dressed and left a note for Mama, because asking for forgiveness was easier than asking for permission.

As I walked out into the seamless heat, I turned and looked next door to see a very tall, very dark homeless man I knew only as Oba talking to our short, slightly-built neighbor, Dr. Monroe. On so many different levels—besides their contrasting physical appearances—their being together seemed odd. But I just thought it wasn't any of my business. Both men's faces held serious expressions as they nodded at me. I smiled and nodded back to be polite. Almost immediately, I had to shake off the feeling they had been talking about me in great detail. *How could they?* I asked myself. I didn't know Dr. Monroe well, and I didn't know Oba except by name and sight. But I didn't feel like I had paranoia on the brain. My suspicions felt valid.

2

NIKKI DROVE US TO THE lake because she was the only one who had a car. It was a new, apple-red convertible harnessed with more horses than Nikki could really handle. The car had been a guilt gift from her divorcing parents, who actually believed that if they gave Nikki a really nice version of something she wanted, then she wouldn't feel so bad about the fact that they were tearing her life apart.

As Nikki hit the highway, I told myself it was too pretty a day to be paranoid. The flowing landscape was a vibrant quilt of colors. Lacy patches of Christmas red, butter yellow and pumpkin orange trees were appliquéd in abundance on the hem of a cloudless blue sky. I let my head flop on the leather crown of the back seat and began to relax as warm tongues of wind licked away my worries. I wasn't even concerned that blind squirrels with lobotomies could drive better than Nikki. I let Shanta mess with that problem. Every now and then, I would hear girlfriend yelling, "damn it, Nikki, slow down."

Shanta grew more desperately prayerful when Nikki blew past the blinking warning lights of a railroad crossing. "Jesus, Jesus, Jesus," she wailed above the loud moan of the train whistle as the engine charged behind us like a crazed rhino. If Nikki was sorry, or even scared, she didn't show it. She just tossed her hair over her shoulders and laughed. I pulled my heart off the roof of my mouth and made sure I hadn't peed on myself. Reckless behavior was one of the things that made people living in the black neighborhoods of Vigilant different from those like Nikki, whose parents were rich and lived in one of the huge homes perched along the sandy beaches of Haven Lake. They felt they owned the world around them and often didn't hesitate to act like it.

The railroad tracks were considered the unofficial border between our two worlds. On a map of Vigilant, the railroad symbol cut the city into unequal, sandwich-shaped halves of a living cliché, the proverbial right and wrong sides of the track. To me, it was like the scar on Frankenstein's neck, rigid bands of steel holding two different and sometimes incompatible kinds of flesh together. The west side of Vigilant, the side where Shanta and I lived, was predominately black and had a little something. The east side of Vigilant was predominately white and had infinitely more. That Vigilant was basically segregated would have filled the town's Quaker founders with sorrow. They had established the town as a station on the Underground Railroad and had worked to make sure the black people they helped to freedom were able to live among them as equals.

"I need to stop for gas," Nikki said.

Shanta sighed. "Should have thought about that before you left home."

"Well, I didn't, so I'm going to do it now."

"Doesn't matter," I said. "I'll go get us something to drink."

Nikki pulled into a Gas Mart, barely missing a pole and a trash barrel.

Shanta's arms shot up in the air. "Girl, where the hell did you learn to drive?"

I clambered out of the car. The mart was crowded with white tourists headed to the festival, and their vibrant chatter was mostly about the music and who was in the star-studded lineup. I pulled three flavored waters from the refrigerator cases, and snapped up a Twinkie on the way up to the counter. I was going out the door, my mouth stuffed with cream and cake, when I accidentally grazed the arm of a well-dressed white man walking in the opposite direction.

Without looking up, I said, "excuse me."

"You need to watch where you're going, nigger bitch," the man said in a voice just loud enough for me to hear.

I almost choked on cake and astonishment. People rarely let their inner demons out to feed in public anymore, so I wasn't quite sure I'd heard him right. Part of me wanted to give him the benefit of some minuscule doubt, but in my head I drew out the phrase, *nigger bitch*, the way children do when they aren't quite sure about the pronunciation of the words they are reading.

Realization made me turn around to find him standing there, grinning with nothing but the purest contempt simmering in his gray eyes. He was tall and muscular. Sunny blond hair, cut neat as a church lawn, complemented his angular features. Fear made me want to run; pride made me take a stand.

We stared at each other until another well-dressed white man came up the aisle. "Hey Gilmore..." he called out. The new guy's face was all happy until he saw me. Then, what had been a wide smile morphed into annoyance. He walked up, laid a hand on Gilmore's shoulder and said, "come on, John. Not here, not now."

I stood there locked in place, but I felt my mouth move. "John Gilmore," I said aloud, as if tasting the two names together would offer some better understanding of his behavior.

"Girl," the other man warned, "you better go."

I left, struggling not to feel like a coward. *Why didn't I say anything more than his name,* I thought as I walked back to the car. Shanta would have said something, maybe even Nikki since her boyfriend was black. I repaired my pride by reminding myself that smart black folks learned to pick their battles. Nothing would have been dumber than for me to take on a hostile white guy in a store full of white folks on the white side of town.

"Either of you know a John Gilmore?" I asked as I handed out the water and took my seat.

"Jonathan Gilmore, the pervert..." Nikki said as she unscrewed the top off her bottle, plopped it in the cup holder and started the car. "You know who he is, Grace—remember? A few years back, he got the ex-mayor's daughter, Marcie Eland, pregnant when she was like seventeen and he was like thirty. And the families demanded they get married so it looked right. "

Shanta nodded. "Yeah, I remember ... also heard that back in the day, a lot of his family use to be real big in the Klan."

"I don't remember," I said, because I didn't. The Klan part, of course, suddenly made some sense.

Shanta turned in her seat. "Why you asking?"

"No reason," I lied. "A couple of people were talking about him in the store."

The stink of my dishonesty set off Shanta's B.S. detector, and her eyes shook me down for a whiff of the scent.

"Nothing happened. I was just curious."

Shanta snorted. "Yeah right. We'll talk about it later."

Nikki did have to slow down once we encountered the long snake of traffic inching its way to festival parking. Perched like a massive diamond on the long dark finger of the highway, Haven Lake shimmered in the distance. The beauty of the water took the edge off my nerves.

"We might be a little late for the beginning," Nikki said.

"No problem," I replied. I was content to watch sailboats swirl like confetti out on the lake. Drowsiness began to leaden the lids of my eyes, and I was tumbling toward a nap when I heard myself say, "doesn't the lake look like it runs on forever into eternity?"

Startled, I sat up, pricked fully aware by the fact that my mind hadn't exactly manufactured those words.

"Only if forever is about a thousand acres, and only if eternity is seventy feet at its deepest," Shanta said in her queen of math and science voice. I smiled because it was the same tone of voice she had used to tell me how close the nearest star was to Earth when we were five.

"Where the hell did you learn that shit, Shanta?" Nikki asked.

"Same classroom you should have learned that shit in," Shanta said.

"I didn't think black folks could be nerds."

"What the hell do you mean by that?"

"Ladies, it was just a poetic observation, nothing more than that, okay?" I stretched out the words to snuff the fuse of a potentially volatile argument about why Nikki thought being cool, black and intelligent couldn't go together. Nikki was a nice person, but she had never struck me as particularly deep. She didn't seem to know enough to look carefully at some of her thoughts before she let them out of her mouth. Shanta, on the other hand, was deep and then some, and she always expected everyone to be as smart and thoughtful as she was.

"Okay," Shanta said, "let's talk about something else. Like why you're having this poetic observation."

"Hell if I know," I said, but then I remembered something from the day before. "Poetry club, maybe that's where it came from," I offered. Shanta had been sick and missed the meeting on English poets. "Mrs. Watanabe made us discuss T.S. Eliot's *Four Quartets*. She said they were his meditation on the theme of time and eternity. How both the past and the future are eternally in the present, and this other idea that all possible outcomes of any event are secretly around us, unseen and unperceived."

I didn't expect an answer, but Shanta turned around. Her expression was enigmatic—a little too wide-eyed and dreamy. It was a look I had never seen her face wear before, and it left me feeling slightly unsettled. A whisper of panic fluttered up to sit with my paranoia about Monroe, and my anxiety about Gilmore.

"What do you think about those concepts, Grace?" Shanta snapped each word like she was cracking gum.

I laughed because I thought she was doing a dead-on impression of our English teacher, but when the texture of her stare didn't change, I realized she wasn't trying to be funny. "I don't know what I think about all that," I finally spit out.

Shanta turned back around and started talking with Nikki. Everything felt normal again, but something deep had gone on. I just couldn't get the whisper of panic to tell me what it was.

* * *

Think ants scrambling to feast on mounds of sugar. That's how crowded the beach was with folks trying to get down toward the marina where the stage had been set up. It was slow going, but I was content, like everyone else, to walk and talk. I can't remember what we talked about—probably guys or homework—but I do remember looking up to see Oba walking toward us. I felt my paranoia surge again, and I wondered who he really was.

Of course, I knew what everybody knew. He was homeless, and sold bundles of incense to tourists for cash. And he seemed to come out of the nowhere we think all poor people are manufactured in, except poverty couldn't make Oba invisible because he took up too much physical space. He was thick bands of muscles laid on a bone frame that leaned up against the sky at about seven feet. If his height didn't smack people at the heart of their attention, then his jellybean black skin made big holes in their awareness. Folks were either fascinated or unnerved by all that dark. Even some black folks, who should have known better, whispered about his skin color like it was some abnormality, as if their own shades of duskiness hadn't descended from the same African source.

All that tall and all that dark acted like a knife, and the crowd parted sharply to let him through. I also shifted in anticipation, but oh, he didn't pass me by. In the space between two spoken words, within that quick second of darkness when your eyes blink, Oba rose up in front of me, and it took most of my coordination not to fall up against him. Without smiling, in a voice rich with the low notes of whale songs he said, "good morning, Grace."

I was shocked he knew my name, but I was much more concerned that my friends were moving on as if I were still with them. Without looking up, I muttered, "excuse me," and attempted to duck by him. Long fingers hinged on a massive palm clutched my arm and pulled me back with little effort. I began to struggle and flail like a small creature in a large trap. My panic was audible—I yelled like I was in pain—but people walked on by. Not with the attitude that they noticed and just didn't care to get involved, but as if Oba and I weren't there to react to. As my panic grew fiercer, Oba's hand grew hot, like his palm was the soleplate of an iron. The rising heat seemed to act as a poultice, drawing out all my struggle. Only when I stopped flailing did he release me. Tamed, I stood there with fumes of exhaustion plunging out of my mouth and my arms hanging down like wet ribbons.

"Grace," he called, and all I could do was look up and up until my gaze was firmly within his, and I knew in the way I've come to know things now that I was not to speak; this wasn't to be an A and B conversation. He held out his hands, palms up, so I could see them. Then, in crisp, almost mechanical movements, he spread them apart.

The sound of waves furiously pounding on a beach grew up and out around us as if the lake had suddenly become an ocean. As loud as it was though, I heard Oba's voice saying, "rabbit real. Rabbit real. You are standing at the crossroads. Are you ready, ready, ready?"

My heart stopped, and my lungs ceased searching for air. The seams of tissues that held my muscles taut began to unravel. Shivers ran like swift currents through both arms as, against my will, they were pulled up, spread out, and pinned in place. I panicked again, spinning around and around like a broken whirligig. A hard shove at the base of my spine sent me sprawling down into a tangled mass of darkness. I fell, as if there would never be an end to the falling, and my screams rode up like streamers behind me until something—or someone unseen, yet omnipresent—yelled, "rise."

Suddenly, I ascended and began to fly. The roar of surf invaded my ears, and I opened my new eyes to a view of a sunlit ocean usually afforded only to birds strong enough to sail the wind's deeper currents. Some rich elixir of knowledge, nourished by utter awe, informed me that the ocean, like the sky above, was also a curtain separating the land of the living from the dead. What came with this knowledge was a feeling of peace so deep and complete that I still long for it like some addict in need of the ultimate fix. But this rapture was short-lived, because a mean pain rushed in to destroy the transmission and I was slapped back into consciousness. I found myself on my knees, looking deep into a greasy white puddle of grits vomit. Oba was gone, and, of course, now everybody could see me.

"Don't move." Shanta's voice flew up behind me.

"Here," Nikki said, as her trembling fingers offered me a bunch of sweaty tissues. I clumsily wiped at my face before I sat up.

A crowd had gathered at a safe distance from us. Embarrassed, I shouted, "show's over, people." Of course, no one went anywhere.

"She's all right folks, give her a little privacy," Nikki yelled, offering a smile in exchange for some sympathy as she and Shanta helped me up. Her appeal for decency worked, and people began to peel off toward the sound of horns and mellow voices accompanied by the scattered shots of drums.

After a few minutes of feeling like water spinning down a drain, I suggested the obvious. "Let's get out of here."

I wanted to go home more than I wanted the music, because what had happened to me couldn't be explained with any vocabulary I had then. Neither Shanta nor Nikki asked any questions. Instead, they attached themselves on both sides of me like splints on a weakened leg. We all understood without saying that my mother wasn't to know about what happened because she would assume we had been drinking. However, when we got to the house, Mama sensed the turmoil in me. I could read on her face that she had somehow found out what had happened.

"Nikki's mother called and said you fainted up at Haven Lake," she said.

I stuck the back of my lips between my teeth to keep from commenting on how she could of at least asked how I was doing. I couldn't risk acting disrespectful, or I would have to listen to an hour of hellish ranting instead of a few minutes of icy mad. Mama moved close to me so I would have to look her dead in her face. She was as tall as I was but that's about all we had in common as far as looks. Mama was thin, with small, sharp features covered in skin the color of cinnamon. I am much heavier, flat-featured and dark. That I looked more like my father was something I knew my mother held against me.

"I didn't give you permission to leave the house, let alone go out to Haven Lake."

I reminded myself to keep my head down and my voice low. "Yes, Mama. I know. It was just that Nikki had some tickets, that's all. "

"That's all," Mama mimicked. "Grace, you went up there with those white folks and showed your ass. I bet you and Shanta were acting up. You're grounded, you know."

"Mama, I fainted ..." I started to explain, but then realized I couldn't tell her what had happened, and it didn't feel right to lie about it. I started again. "I'm really sorry, Mama. I'm going upstairs to study."

I was almost out of the room, almost free and clear, but I got to the head of the stairs and felt the need to turn around. I looked at Mama. Looked at her hard and said in a voice filled more with longing than sarcasm, "I know you didn't ask, but I'm really feeling much better."

I expected her to howl that I was being a smartass, and I was more than a little surprised when only silence followed me up the stairs. I went up to study but couldn't, because how can math make any sense when your life no longer adds up? I didn't know what to think, except to ask over and over again if what had happened with Oba was real. It was easy to dismiss the flying because flying was impossible, and I convinced myself that I had gotten so scared I'd imagined the part where I had risen above the earth.

Actually, little else about my experience with Oba had been unreal or intangible. The map of his immense grasp had tinted my arm bluish black, and the skin complained when I stroked it. Oba's voice still boomed along with the sound of the ocean inside my head. *Rabbit*, he had called me. Rabbit was the nickname my father had given me. A name I hadn't heard since I was little. And what had he meant when he said I was standing at the crossroad and asked if I was ready to go on a journey? The only thing I understood about the crossroads back then was that Robert Johnson sang about it on one of my favorite blues CDs. All I could fathom after hours of frantic contemplation was that God was speaking, but it was all gibberish to me.

* * *

Shanta came over the next day to help me with my calculus homework. I was deep off into not understanding a problem when she shifted a few papers to get my attention.

"Grace, do you understand what happened to you yesterday? I mean it was more than just your being physically sick. Something else was going on, wasn't it?" she asked.

I looked down at the indecipherable math equation and thought it seemed like an appropriate symbol for my life. I decided to answer her questions with one of my own. "Shanta, did you see Oba yesterday?"

Shanta smiled, and a thick, weird silence grew up around us. I looked at the face of a person I had known since preschool, and I could see she was no longer behind her eyes. Shanta, who was no longer Shanta, put her hands on the table and unfurled them, palms up, the same way Oba had done in the park.

"The waters have been troubled, Rabbit. The way has been opened," she said.

All kinds of fear made me get up and flee into the bathroom. For ten minutes, I stood there looking at myself in the mirror, trying to find the hole in the base of my skull where I thought my sanity must have leaked out. I tried to tranquilize my flailing heart with raggedy bits of breathing and failing logic.

God and I had not been on speaking terms for a long time, but I began to pray what I could remember of Psalms 23. I expected the solace of green pastures and still waters, but I didn't get what I wanted. I got what God and the ancestors thought I needed.

The prayer cut through a thick skin of denial, and what erupted from the rent was a memory of myself as a child, scared out of my mind because the darkness around my bed had quickened with presences I couldn't identify, but knew enough not to call monsters. Fear had smacked the back of my legs as I ran down the hall and into the arms of a mother who would only give me more to worry about by saying God didn't like ugly, and he especially didn't like little girls who lied about seeing things that weren't there. I had gone back to bed scared of what was living in my dark, but more afraid of a God who had made such things but didn't want you to believe in them. So I had prayed to my mother's angry God: *"Lord please make what I feel imaginary. Please make what I feel not real."* God had answered my prayers back then, but now I was no longer a child. Real was real.

I stumbled out of the bathroom to find that Shanta was Shanta again. She had gone ahead and done the rest of my homework and was acting like the whole Oba discussion had never happened. I didn't know what to do except wait for the next revelation, but I wouldn't have to wait long. My Nana Grace was coming and nobody short of God could stop her.

3

MY GREAT-GRANDMOTHER, NANA GRACE, was a powerful woman in life. In death, where I have come to know her best, she is no less formidable. When I first met her on this breathing side of our existence, she was over ninety years old. However, the words feeble or frail should not come to mind, because even then she was like the coiled fist of a heavyweight fighter. Always elegantly decorated in petite designer suits and haute couture dresses, she appeared to be the very essence of decorum, but hidden behind a mask of cream smooth manners was a volatile mix of upper class ambition and just plain street. She was, and is not to be, taken lightly and only stupid people do it more than once.

No one can say she didn't deserve the respect she demanded. She had worked her way through Tuskegee Institute in the early 1900s and graduated hell-bent on becoming rich even beyond the wildest dreams of the white men of her time here on Earth. She married well—a doctor—and when left a widow with three small girls, she used stingy thrift and cutthroat business tactics in the stock market and real estate industry to accumulate the bulk of her wealth.

Word in the family was she was a better entrepreneur than she was a mother, and God had chosen to punish her by killing her three daughters. Pneumonia smothered her first children, a set of twins. Her last daughter, Anna Marie, would survive until adulthood only to die giving birth to the baby boy who would grow up to be my father. Rumor had it that all that death had left her with was the need to talk to the dead, and depending on whose tongue mixed the gossip, she was either blessed or cursed with the ability to do it.

I was curious about this, but I knew better than to ask questions people in my family didn't want to answer. Nobody in his or her right mind wanted to be at the top of my mother's shit list, and everybody knew my mother despised my Nana Grace. As far back as I can remember, I was forbidden to speak to her and her sisters, Casmil and Peaches. All I understood about the situation back then was that Mama and Nana Grace had fallen out about something to do with my father's death. I had no clue that the something they were arguing about was me.

All this changed several months to the day after the Oba incident, just a week after my eighteenth birthday in April. I had gotten up very early that morning because another calculus test loomed in my future. Despite Shanta's best efforts to tutor me, I didn't feel prepared and was engrossed in last minute studying when the phone rang. I reached for the receiver, convinced it had to be either Nikki or Shanta. Instead, I found Mama had already answered, and Nana Grace's voice had smacked back a terse greeting. The same curiosity that kills cats made me stay on the line.

"Miriam, I need to visit with Grace today," Nana Grace said crisply. She framed it as a polite request, but I sensed it was really a command.

I expected Mama to end the conversation. Instead, a long ribbon of silence unrolled itself.

"When?" Mama finally said.

"Today at ten?"

Mama grunted. "You do know this means Grace will have to miss school."

"Oh, I know what it means, Miriam."

In my mind's eye, I pictured Mama's body stiffening for a fight. I imagined her gathering up swear words that could be flung like verbal sticks and stones, but all that came out of her mouth was, "okay."

No goodbyes. Mama just slammed the phone down hard. I was about to hang up when I heard a soft chuckle, and Nana Grace's voice jumped out of hiding. "I'll see you in a few hours, Grace."

"Damn," I hissed as I dropped the receiver back into its cradle. Red-hot beams of embarrassment shot through my body. I was mortified, not so much that I had done something sneaky and impolite, but because I had been caught doing it in such a creepy way. It occurred to me I should have been happy that I was getting out of a math test, but some new sense stirring to life in the pit of my stomach told me I was going to pay for the privilege.

I couldn't begin to imagine what Nana Grace wanted with me, and I was trying to tease out some logic when Mama started banging on the door like it was a punching bag with Nana Grace's face on it.

"Grace, put on something decent. We're going to visit your great-grandmother."

Even if I hadn't known what the up and up was, I wouldn't have bothered to ask why. The tone in her voice told me it was going to be a do as she said, no question asked kind of morning.

After a shower, I stuffed myself into an all-purpose black skirt and a frilly white blouse that had been a cast off of an older cousin who had even less fashion sense than I did. I attempted to smear on some lipstick and dabbed on a fragrance from the scented paper strip of a perfume advertisement in an old magazine. With short flicks of my comb, I backed my hair down around my ears and playfully barked, "stay," at some recalcitrant strands that wanted to escape from hair slavery and follow their own path to freedom.

My sister glared at me as I walked downstairs to sit in the living room to wait for Mama. Jamila was pissed because she wasn't getting out of school. I wanted to explain I hadn't exactly asked to go, but nothing I said would dissolve any of the envy she was feeling, so I left her alone.

There was increasing evidence my sister and I shared only a few strands of common genetic code. Folks have said often enough that we don't look anything alike, and mirrors don't call them liars. Jamila was tall, slender and shaped like one of those health and fitness models you see in magazines. Her skin was the pale golden brown that appears on the bottoms and edges of good sugar cookies, and her delicate features were well-framed by thick waves of chestnut colored hair that falls without coaxing down the flowing coastline of her slender shoulders. She was as intelligent as she was beautiful, and she had the kind of personality that was not infected with shyness or a lack of confidence. A lot of women loved her image and wanted to be just like her. Men, young and old, wanted to date her. Yet Jamila was like the moon, beautiful to look at out the window, but when you land on her true emotional landscape, she can be barren and extremely cold.

When I look in the mirror, I see a plain brown woman. I am what the fashion industry politely calls "full-figured." Until recently, my hair was a defiant mass of naps that refused to be completely beaten down by a hot comb or relaxed by chemical straighteners. Women don't want to be like me, and men—well, men, young and old—ask me about my sister.

Mama had already showered and dressed. She wore her black pantsuit unadorned by its usual "Birthstone of Jesus Cross" she had ordered off of some religious program on TV. Jamila began to whine about having to go to school almost as soon as Mama hit the stair landing. The girl seemed oblivious to the fact that Mama was in no mood to hear her. I sat there and willed myself to match the couch cover as Jamila picked and picked. Mama blew up like a bottle of Coke left too long in the freezer. She cussed out Jamila the way she usually cussed me out, and Jamila looked hurt, like some special promise had been broken. I wanted to say, "now you know how I feel," but I kept that sweet little nugget of revenge on my tongue. Jamila didn't say goodbye to either of us as she rushed out the door to catch the bus to school.

I listened to Mama on the phone in the kitchen clearing our calendars with the same lie that we were sick. Truth was, I felt nervous enough to be ill, so it really wasn't a lie. While Mama was yelling at Jamila, I had begun to understand that I was involved in something so serious my normally blunt mother had acquiesced to a relative she despised. Hell had frozen over, and I was skating shakily on top. I almost told her I didn't want to go. With a few words, I could buy my freedom, and those words were about to tumble off my lips when some inner voice that didn't belong to me said, "you leave this alone."

4

I HAD NO MORE IDEA where Nana Grace lived than I had about why she wanted to see me. Semi-obedient daughter that I was then, I just crawled into the car's front seat, slumped down, and pulled the hood of my jacket up over my head as protection against the spring cold and my mother's stare.

"You look stupid doing that. Sit up," my mother ordered as we pulled out.

I pretended I didn't hear her, and I made the door a bed and the window a hard pillow. Outside, the sky was peeling back the darkness to reveal a watery blue. I counted the naked torsos of trees and prayed for sleep to come, but sleep was off helping needier people in more desperate places.

When the silence got too gummy, Mama threw on the radio and pressed the buttons until she found a station that messed up some jazz by removing all the fat and spice provided by improvisation and vocals. No sleep, no conversation, no tunes worth listening to, so I thought about how the day would have been if Nana Grace hadn't called. I thought about how in English, Mrs. Watanabe had been pushing us to memorize the poem, "The Second Coming" by Yeats. Even though she's Japanese, she loves all things Irish, and Yeats was a favorite of hers. I thought about how he had written that things fall apart, and how I was stuck in the process of memorization, on the line, "Surely some revelation is at hand." I'd wondered why this line in this poem seemed to resonate so deep with me when Yeats had been talking about something greater than my sorry little life. Maybe some revelation was at hand, and maybe Nana Grace would bring some understanding about why my life was the way it was.

Something was up because Mama was bent over the steering wheel like the car was dragging her by the collar of her jacket down the road. Some secret Nana Grace had was making her nervous and afraid. I was the one who usually wore the fear in the family, and it was odd to see how it looked on her.

"Where are we going?" I finally mumbled.

"Fort Wayne, Indiana."

Hunger storms rolled across the atmosphere of my stomach, and I wished I had eaten breakfast. But if wishes were nuts, I could have made a jar of peanut butter. Even if I had asked, Mama wouldn't have stopped anywhere. She wasn't thinking about food, and if she wasn't hungry for breakfast, then I wasn't supposed to be hungry either. With only my curiosity half-fed, I finally drifted off.

I woke as Mama brought the car to a jerky stop in the asphalt parking lot of a set of large buildings lined up like opulently dressed women lounging on the shore of a lake. A small sign out front read: Lost Lake Retirement Community.

I waited to take my cue from Mama as the engine hummed along to some smooth jazz version of a Stevie Wonder classic. After a few moments, she left the engine running but turned the radio off.

"You know, you shouldn't believe anything Nana Grace says," she said softly.

I sat up, pulled the hood off my head, and waited a good thirty seconds for a better explanation, but Mama kept looking straight out the windshield.

"What is she going to say?"

The question sat useless between us. The engine's humming accented the fact that she couldn't give me an answer because it wasn't her answer to give.

"Go on and talk to her, but you remember I'm the one that raised you. I'm the one that put food on your plate and clothes on your back."

Something in me, something newly born and hungry for its place in the world wanted to spit out, "but you don't care about me." Fear, however, dammed the words up inside of me. I could imagine Mama's bladelike eyes swinging around to cut me down because I was being a thankless child. I was supposed to be grateful I had a roof over my head, food on my plate, and clothes on my back. As long as my visible body was free of purple-mouthed bruises, I couldn't accuse her of not taking care of me. That my soul had welts on it from the lash of her insults, or that I was starved down to the skin and bone of my self esteem because she refused me the milk of affection didn't seem to matter to her.

I shoved myself out of the car without saying goodbye. I could feel Mama watching me as I trotted toward the door. She hoped I would lose my nerve and turn around. But I didn't want to turn around. As I crossed the threshold from one life into another, she drove off, the engine expressing her disbelief in a harsh roar.

A desk attendant with big eyes and big hair squealed hello as if she had been expecting me to show up all her life. In a walk as jaunty as her voice, she led me down quiet halls decorated with brocaded wallpaper and oil paintings that said, "rich people live here." I expected to be ushered into a room like you find in hospitals. Instead, I was led into an atrium decorated with couches, chairs, and an amazing variety of plants. A spectacular pond shone like molten silver just outside the floor-to-ceiling windows. In the center of the room, a table had been set with an assortment of pastries and what I hoped was a carafe of coffee. I took off my coat, draped it across my arm and waited for the woman who had summoned me.

"Grace." My great-grandmother's voice was a verbal red carpet that rolled out to announce her arrival.

"Nana Grace," I choked out as I turned around to find a petite, ginger-brown woman whose small features did not echo mine. She was flat-out sharp in a designer suit the color of peach skins. A single string of pearls graced her neck like tiny petals on a small perfect flower. I began to feel shabby because, well, I was shabby. Her eyes lingered as if she was looking for something specific, something beyond how my clothing hung on my porky body or how my hair looked like it was hatching a plot to run away from my head.

"You look much like your father," she said as she took my jacket.

"Like my father?" I said the words aloud, framed in a question, because it had been a long time since I had matched my face up against the dim memories I had of him. Pictures of my father did not exist in my mother's house. After his death, she had sterilized the family photo albums.

"I'm sorry I don't remember much about my dad," I said. "I wish I did, but I ... I ..."

Nana Grace nodded as if the explanation was unnecessary. "You were only four when your father passed. You wouldn't remember very much, and what you did remember your mother made sure you forgot."

My head sagged to the side of one shoulder, as if the wonder of looking at a new observation about my life was just too much to bear standing up straight.

"Your father was a wonderful man. It was too bad he was murdered."

Murder. She had heaved that word up and out, knowing that my curiosity could do nothing but catch it.

"Suicide ..." I ventured to correct her. I thought that maybe because she was old, she had forgotten or hadn't come to terms with how her grandson had died. I was going to offer a further explanation, but her taut, bemused stare sucked the wet from my mouth, leaving my tongue stuck like a dying fish at the bottom of a dried-out riverbed.

"No," Nana Grace said softly, "everyone says suicide, but some know better."

She hung up my jacket, and then as if she were a geisha with a fan, elegantly gestured for me to sit down at the table. I felt like an ox getting ready to feed with a gazelle as I settled into a chair whose seat was only a fraction of an inch bigger than my butt.

"I'm sure you must be very hungry," said Nana Grace.

I was starving, but more than food, I wanted coffee, and Nana Grace made a ceremony of pouring it into thin-walled china cups. She didn't pretend to ask me if I wanted it black; even then, she didn't play like she couldn't read me. Without a word, she stiffened the darkness in my cup with sugar and dyed it dingy white with a long streamer of cream. I gulped; she sipped and asked, "you have a question?"

I had a million questions all wrestling with each other to be the first. After a few seconds, I let one win. "What do you have on my mother that she gave in like this?"

Nana Grace smiled. Then, with tiny hands that reminded me of delicate shells, she pushed a whole plate of lemon curd tarts and pink petit fours toward me. It took all the manners I had to select only two tarts. I forced myself to admire them as I waited for Nana Grace to speak.

"The truth," she crisply declared. "What I have on your mother is the truth. Grace, I'm sorry you don't know why you are here. There are many things you should have known before now, but it was your mother's wish that you not be exposed to them. Miriam gambled that I would die before you turned eighteen. She lost. Now you are of age to make your own decisions. Your mother brought you here because if she didn't, I would have come to your house. I gave your mother a chance to save what little face she has left. I let her have some pride."

Nana Grace's sense of satisfaction about this victory radiated across the table. She looked the same way we all look when revenge comes as sweet and cold as two flavors of Häagen-Dazs stuffed inside a waffle cone. I took another sip of coffee.

"You're grown, Rabbit, so now the truth is yours to accept or reject. Now you can choose to begin your journey or not."

The name "Rabbit" and the word "journey" pulled out the memory of a certain day in October.

"You do remember what Oba asked." It was a statement, not a question. As surprise pinched my lips into a small beak of flesh, I screwed my eyes deep into hers, trying to fathom how she knew about Oba.

"He exists, Grace," she smiled. "He wasn't a dream. He wasn't a figment of your imagination brought on by a bad batch of grits."

Finally, my jaw couldn't support the weight of my astonishment. My mouth gaped open. "I don't believe it. Nobody else saw him," I said.

Nana Grace shrugged like she were dismissing some normal and every day fact of life. "Nobody else was supposed to see him. His business with you was his business with you. And deep down Grace, you know that."

I picked up my cup and drank what was left of my coffee with deep gulps, as if there was a small fire in my stomach. Nana was asking for acceptance. She was waiting for me to formulate the question that would sever all manner of apron strings and cut new doors and windows into my universe. I closed my eyes and completely melted into my thoughts, pondering how raggedy and pitiful my past had been, and how my present was riding around in a car thinking that the only thing she owed me was food and a place to live. I desperately wanted better. I wanted to be a more authentic Grace. Oba had scared me, but with the fear had come a taste of glory and the promise of a new way to be in the world.

"So, who is Oba?" I asked.

"He is a teacher, a guide, an opener of the way. In ancient Greece, he was the god Hermes; in ancient Rome, he was the god Mercury. In Africa, he could be called Legbe, Ellegue, Elegbara or Eshu. You would know him best as the entity bluesman Robert Johnson met at the crossroads to bless his guitar. Now, in this time and place he calls himself Oba."

I opened my eyes and let my deepest needs control my mouth. "Exactly what was Oba's business with me?"

She waited until every part of my understanding was there to absorb the weight of her words.

"Oba's job was to prepare you for what I have to tell you. Let's just say he had to turn on some things, prime the pump, to use a cliché. You're young, Grace, so you haven't thought much about life, let alone about death. Now please don't be too concerned by my use of the word death. You are not going to die, at least not in the physical sense."

Shit, I thought, *what other sense was there?* Nana Grace smiled because the question was smeared all in my eyes and all over my mouth.

"There are many kinds of deaths, more than you can conceive of right now," she said. "But for now let's just talk about physical death."

"Okay."

"What I need for you to understand is that when people die, they become ancestors, and their spirits, living over in the Other World, remember clearly their lives here on earth. They remember the good they have done, but more importantly, they are shown and forced to come to terms with their great failures, their darkest sins. Many people die with so much left undone, unspoken and unreconciled that when they die and reflect on the mess they have left or the hurt they have caused, they hunger and thirst in the afterlife to make things right. They become eager to help those of us who are still on this breathing side of existence to heal ourselves so that the world will be a more dignified place to live. However, to be active in this world, the ancestors need to enlist cooperation and help from those who are sensitive enough to hear them and obedient enough to do their bidding." She paused to let me soak up the information she was giving me, as if she were warming up my brain with a little bit of knowledge before we leapt completely out of reality.

"You," she began again, "have been given the gift to hear and speak to the ancestors, and your work in this life will be to help them communicate with those of us in this world."

I heard every word that snaked out of her mouth, but I didn't really comprehend them. How could I? Information about yourself that is that bizarre, even if you instinctively know it is true, has to soak in drop by drop. Even then, you might not get it all. I began to think I should eat something because food would make me feel less funny. I picked up a fork and began to breach a wall of tart crust as Nana Grace continued.

"It is a serious and hard thing that has been laid on you, especially when you haven't been prepared, especially when all your knowledge has been shamed out of you. Because when you were little, Grace, you understood the world was full of spirits looking to you to speak for them."

She looked hard at me as if she expected some kind of response, but all I wanted to do was think about how the lemony goodness of the tart was like a patch of sun creeping up to conquer the darkness in my mouth. The smooth sweetness made me feel like I was far away, and at that moment I wanted to be on the moon.

"I have selected someone to help you come to terms with your sacred gift. You know Dr. Monroe. He lives next door to you." She stopped talking and waited patiently until Monroe's name hauled me back from my imaginary wilderness. I blinked a couple of times as my memory shuffled into the past and came back with pictures.

"The guy next door, the guy who was …"

Nana took the end of my words and knotted them. "Yes, the man who was speaking to Oba."

"I don't know him," I said, shaking my head.

Nana Grace's pearls shuddered as she shrugged her shoulders. "No matter, he will be able to fulfill the duties of a Habari gani menta."

"A Habri … who?"

"It is a Swahili phase for mentor. In English, it translates to the person who asks 'what is happening?' It is his or her duty to ask a young person assigned to them the important questions, and to listen carefully to the answers in order to help shape the young person's gifts."

I slid another tart under my fork and stuffed it into my mouth. *It did matter that I didn't know Monroe,* I thought. Except for a hello every now and then as he groomed his immaculate flower and vegetable garden, we had never talked. He appeared to be cold and distant. Not the kind of person who could help me give birth to anything, especially when I hadn't known I was spiritually pregnant.

"Why can't you be my questioner?" I asked.

For the first time since I had arrived, her eyes slid off my face and onto the pond outside the window. "I can't," she said softly. "I am scheduled to leave on a long trip in a few days."

"Why can't you stay?"

"I have no control over it, Grace."

Fine tremors of emotions began to shake my body. The fork in my hand swayed a bit and tumbled with a loud clatter onto the plate.

"I know you need time to think about all this."

"That's an understatement." I didn't even struggle to keep the sarcasm out of my voice, because sarcasm is one of the last refuges of the truly terrified. I reached with my hand for the tarts because all of sudden, it felt like my stomach wanted to come up and get the food all by itself.

I fell into eating, and Nana Grace watched with little reaction, as if my deep hunger was a normal part of the process of accepting who I was. When the tarts were all gone, I clumsily turned the plate and devoured the petit fours; first the pink, then the yellow ones, and when those were gone, I folded my napkin and got up to leave. Nana Grace rose with me and gently reached out with her hand to stop me before I bolted from the room.

"Grace, when I get where I'm going, I will contact you."

I was too numb and dumb to think about what she meant. I leaned in to offer a hug and to kiss her cheek. She smelled of a rich blending of very expensive perfume.

"I know this isn't what you expected, sweetheart," she said.

I put on my jacket and left.

"I hope you had a good visit. Please, please, have a wonderful day," the perky attendant called out as I rushed past. I wanted to tell her to shove it, but I realized as I was striding toward the door that it wasn't her fault my life was beginning to look like a comic book.

Mama was waiting, and I held my hand up to warn her to keep her mouth shut.

"I don't want to talk about anything with you," I shouted. "Leave me alone."

It was my turn to ride back angry. Mama had changed the radio station, and a young, slimmer Aretha was spelling out the meaning of respect for a man who hadn't understood the concept. I knew exactly how she felt. I slept again, but this time my sleep was full of dreams of oceans and the sounds of distant voices constantly calling me by my name.

"We can talk about this later," Mama said when we pulled into the driveway.

My eyes must have been lanterns of incredulity because she couldn't bring herself to look at me. "You're a couple of years too late," I informed her.

I can tell you now that all my anger that day was good fury wasted. Anger, even when it's justified, is a futile emotion unless you know how to use it. Anger, detached from constructive use, strikes your inner eye blind so you don't see what you really need to see. What I should have been worried about was what Nana Grace meant when she said she would be contacting me. Back then, my knowledge of how to travel and places you could go had been limited to real time and tangible space. Even then, I should have known better. I should have seen it coming. It was as obvious as Hip-hop songs would be if they were played as background music in a sushi restaurant. But I was so blinded by my anger with Mama that I didn't see the esoteric shit coming until it hit the spiritual fan.

5

THE NEXT MORNING, MAMA CALLED herself trying to talk to me. More than once, she asked in a sticky sweet tone, "come on, Grace. I think you need to tell me what Nana Grace said."

"Nothing," I kept saying over and over, until finally I blurted out, "she said that daddy didn't commit suicide, that he was murdered."

A look I now know was fear seasoned with unresolved grief thinned her lips into a taut frown. "What else did she say?"

Nothing else that Nana Grace had given me belonged to Mama, and I let the silence between us grow up tall, thick and thorny.

"You know, Nana Grace may be senile," she warned. "Perhaps, we can talk to Reverend Thornton about her sometime next week."

"No," I said to both statements. Even in my advanced state of mystical confusion I knew if Nana Grace was senile, then we should all wish to obtain some form of dementia. And I would have sooner taken spiritual advice from the man behind the curtain in the Wizard of Oz than from Reverend Thornton, because he was always telling people that money had to be tithed directly to him and his church in order to get into heaven.

After that, Mama and I didn't really speak to each other for days. What was there for us to say? I had been betrayed, yet I couldn't fully explain the full nature of the crime, because what had been stolen from me wasn't supposed to be possible. So I had no words for Mama. However, deep in the weeds of my awe and confusion, a forgotten lexis began to bloom like exotic African flowers and one night, with the thick tongue of a magic marker, I wrote down the petals of a proverb on notebook paper: *The truth lost in the morning comes home in the evening.* I posted this on my bedroom door with puddles of glue. I waited for Mama to come and try to tear if off, but she never touched it. I think she knew my missive was my garland of garlic, my set of stakes and crosses.

I fell into eating in a way that looked more greedy than spiritual. On this breathing side of eternity, devouring a whole pound cake is not considered an act of devotion, even if it is really good pound cake and you praise God for its existence in your life. What Mama thought about my appetite came out of Jamila's more than willing mouth. "You need to stop eating because you're disgusting," she would sneer. It did occur to me that maybe she was right, but my hunger had its own rules. My soul needed fattening, and my spirit was skin and bones needy.

My tastes in music also changed. No more jazz. I only wanted the blues. And I didn't want any of the new stuff played by the young bloods, the so-called up-and-coming. No, my ear had a taste for old school, the voices and sounds that spiraled out of our mouths and instruments when we black folks were more African than American. Most days I only listened to Robert Johnson, and most times I was only sampling his song, *Crossroad Blues.* It was like a prayer I sang to help chase away my growing fears of the unknown.

Two weeks crawled by like snails. I went to school and came home, always on edge, as I waited for Oba to come back or for Nana Grace to reveal more information. But nothing happened except that between homework assignments, poetry club and eating everything Mama tried to hide from me, I grew more curious about Dr. Monroe. Everything I actually knew about him I could have written on the back of fortune cookie paper. Even the usually rumor-rich sources of small town gossip were sparse. All people tended to say was that he was gay, but thankfully he was quiet about it. If he had a boyfriend, nobody had ever seen him. Folks found it funny that he taught religion at the university but didn't have a church home, at least not in Vigilant. Not that they seemed eager for him to come worship with them because he was a homosexual after all.

Family? There were whispers of a failed marriage before he had moved to our fair city of narrow minds and big mouths. People were content to leave him alone, but I couldn't, because for reasons I couldn't completely fathom he was now in charge of me. I even went behind Shanta's back to ask her father what he knew about my father's death and Dr. Monroe's life. I had gotten more sad silence than answers.

I became a nervous and jittery spy. I hid in the polyester mist of curtains and watched him as he went about his everyday business. There was Monroe with slim bags of groceries, or coming home from work with his arms full of books and papers. There wasn't anything mystical or magical about that, and my curiosity became frustrated.

"Who and what are you and Oba to me," I wanted to yell at him. But I knew that wouldn't get me anywhere, so I made knowing about Monroe like an assignment or a term paper that was due immediately. From the university website, I gleaned his academic pedigree: B.A., M.A., Ph.D in Comparative Religion, professor and author of the book, the *Mythological Wisdom of Africa. A book, okay, something more tangible*, I thought.

I went to the library, but the shelf was gap-toothed because the book had already been taken out. On a whim, I went to the desk to ask the librarian if another copy existed in a different area, or if I could get it by interlibrary loan.

The librarian was very tall, and her dark, gray cloud-colored eyes rained down a peevish look because this was something I should have been able to do myself. After a few seconds of typing, a jolt of surprise ran through her eyes, and she said with a smile, "oh, a Dr. Monroe put it on hold for you."

"Oh, how kind of him," I said, mimicking her cheerfulness in order to sound like this was an expected outcome instead of a strange event. Sometimes mysteries look like seven-foot men, but on other occasions they appear as a book given to you by a librarian who was made to prophesy, "this is some serious reading."

And it was serious, so serious that for the first time in my intellectual life, I had read something I couldn't even begin to understand, much less process. But what were myths to me then, except the exaggerated stories of strange humans, false gods and animals doing the impossible and improbable? What did I know about myths being metaphors for eternal truth, for the All and All behind the mysteries of birth and death? I knew more about physics than metaphysics, so I didn't understand that science couldn't explain my new role in life, only mythology could.

I had to talk to Monroe. When somebody gives you something that makes you itch intellectually, he or she should be the one who helps you scratch, especially in those high or deep places on your soul you are not yet strong or supple enough to reach.

So, one evening, I stood on the boundary of his property, where Mama's shaggy-dog lawn met his well-groomed one, and watched as he climbed out of his car. I readied myself to call out his name, but I was a couple of quarts low on bravery. My mouth moved, but nothing came out. At first, I thought he didn't see me standing there, but he stopped walking as he got to the head of the sidewalk that led up to his house. I wanted to run as he turned to face me, but curiosity suctioned my feet to the sidewalk. All I could think was, *how could a man look so much like a praying mantis and not be one?*

Monroe was just barely taller than I was, short for a man. He was all slender twigs of bone scantily covered with slight, but taut muscles, and the skin that covered this little bit of a man was the color of Belgian chocolate—the bittersweet kind. Nothing about his bearded features would beg you to notice him, but his eyes spoke clearly about the spiritual fuel that ran the machinery of his soul. You might forget his face, but if he ever swallowed you up in a stare, only total amnesia would allow you to forget his eyes.

"Good evening, Ms. Johnson," he said in a voice that was soft, but full of a kind of dignified authority that made me want to stand up straighter and square my shoulders.

For a long moment, I didn't know who he was talking to. I almost looked around for my mother. He waited patiently as I tried on the formality and found how good it felt. It was just a lick of power, but it was an important acknowledgement that I was grown in my own right.

"Hello, Dr. Monroe," I replied. "Thank you for the book?"

Monroe smiled slightly, like the question mark tacked on to the end was expected.

"Did you understand any of it?" he asked.

I was going to lie, just flat out not tell the truth, but something better in me made me say, "oh, hell no."

Monroe laughed, not in a mean way, but the way we all laugh when the truth is spoken in an honest way. "Concentrate your attention on the myth about the Hare and the Moon."

I nodded because I sort of remembered that part in the book.

"We will have dinner in about two weeks," he added. "Perhaps things will be a bit clearer then, Ms. Johnson."

He started to walk away, but just as he hit the stairs leading up to his house, he paused, and without looking back said, "please give my regards to your great-grandmother the next time you see her."

I shrugged. "Okay, but I don't know when that will be."

Monroe said nothing, but his silence was textured with metaphysical connotations. He was teasing me with the cosmic, but I wouldn't understand that until the next day.

6

"JAMILA AND I ARE GOING shopping. We thought you might like to come," Mama said as she leaned against the door jam of my room, a coffee cup snug in both hands. She sounded like she was in one of her rare good moods.

I instinctively settled my chest against the edge of my desk to obscure the open pages of Monroe's book when she began to wander around my room as if it were some place she had never visited before.

"No thanks," I mumbled, before turning my attention back to a detail I had just discovered on the dedication page: *To my son Evan, may wisdom and maturity draw us closer in the coming years.* Monroe had a son, and I wanted to spin that bit of information around in my mind and consider exactly what, if anything, that meant. But Mama had come for an answer to a question I had deflected with a shrug the night before.

"So, what were you talking to Dr. Monroe about last night?" she asked as she ran her fingers across the covers of my worn and well-used books of poetry, anthologies of quotations and African proverbs.

I sagged against the back of my chair and began to shed lies. "Financial aid. I was asking him if he knew about any scholarships."

She suspected, but couldn't straight out say that I was covering up something more important. Her small lips crept down to the shore of her cup to drink as she stood staring at the award I had won a month before for the best senior history project.

"You never talked to him before?" she asked.

"Never had any reason to."

She picked up the plaque and studied it. I wanted desperately to tell her to put it down because she didn't respect it.

"You know, it's a shame this is the only award you've won. Maybe if you had been active in a few more organizations ..."

"Mama, please."

We stared at each other, and suddenly, I felt like tussling for a scrap of my life. "You know what? I can't wait to go to Spelman." The level of smartass in my voice was almost high enough to earn me a smack upside the head with the face of a warm coffee cup.

"You watch that tone," Mama shot back. "You know I don't have to pay for you to go to school."

In another time, it would have been a real threat, but I sensed I had options. Without thinking, I blurted out, "doesn't matter, Nana Grace will pay for me."

I didn't know this, of course, but it sounded plausible, and plausible made the cup in Mama's hand shudder a little.

"Did she tell you that? You know she can't give you a damn thing without my permission."

I was about to jump off and call her a liar, when the phone rang. I lunged at it with the hope of the damned. I wanted it to be for Mama; instead, it was Shanta sounding peeved.

"Grace, what the hell been going on with you?"

"Um, hey Shanta. How you doing?" I answered, sweetening my words with enough artificial politeness so she wouldn't miss that I wasn't alone and didn't want to talk.

"I don't care if your mama is standing there, Grace."

"Well I do." I grinned like Aunt Jemima at Mama and prayed under my breath that she would take her foot off my neck and leave.

"Jamila and I are going shopping," Mama said as she left. "We'll talk about your attitude later."

I sighed. "Okay, Shanta, what are you mad about?"

"I'm not mad. I'm just wondering what you been hiding from me. My brother Oran said you came by the house the other day and asked Dad what he knew about how your father died. He also said you were asking some questions about your next-door neighbor."

Damn Oran. Shanta's baby brother was nothing but big ears and a mouth to match. He always had his nose stuck so far up in other people's business he could almost breathe for them.

"Yeah, I was there," I admitted.

"And?"

"And what?"

"Grace Anne, you know you can talk to me about anything."

The trouble was I didn't know that. How could I explain the un-explainable to someone who had professed not to believe in ghosts, spirits or what she called "hoodoo mess?" How to explain the exis-tence of Oba to someone who hadn't even noticed that he had used her body and her mouth to speak to me? I wanted to keep my best friend in the dark until the unreal and the impossible made more sense to me. I didn't have a lot of friends; I was afraid that Shanta would think I was crazy and not want to have anything more to do with me.

"Your father said he didn't want to talk about my father. He said even after all these years it hurt too much."

"So how come this is coming up now about your daddy?"

"It was some gossip I heard."

"From who?"

I sighed hard. "Shanta, I don't want to talk about this right now."

"Oh, hell no, Grace. If you talk to my daddy, you can talk to me. I'm coming over."

* * *

"You hungry?" I asked Shanta when she burst through the back door in the kitchen.

"No, I'm not hungry, Grace. I'm hurt that you don't trust me."

I nodded. I knew the shape of her hurt because mine would have looked similar if she had hidden information from me.

"Well, I'm starving, and I'm thinking about making spaghetti. Have you talked to Nikki lately?" I asked as I peered in the pantry, trying to locate a jar of tomato sauce. My back was to Shanta, so I barely heard her say, "Grace?"

The question mark grabbed my attention and shook it hard. I had to stop, but I didn't turn around because something felt different—was different—and I didn't want to confront the something whose quickening had cooled the air and made the room smell faintly of damp earth.

"What?" I asked reluctantly, hoping for normal but expecting weird.

"Between living and dying there is a third thing. Do you know what it is?"

Shock herded my breathing into a small space and made my teeth beach themselves on the shore of my bottom lip. Shanta had spoken, but her mouth had woven together the strands of some other entity's words.

I didn't say anything, couldn't say anything. I had no answer then. All I had were suspicions that needed to be confirmed. On feet leaden with dread and wonder, I slowly turned around. Shanta was smiling this big ribbon of a smile that didn't belong to her. I wanted to ask who she was, but all I could do was watch as she pointed toward the far wall of the kitchen.

My eyes followed the straight edge of her arm to a spot of light that hung like a glittery button on the refrigerator. I studied it, as a reedy whisper of uncommon sense told me not to look for an earthly source. I knew what the light was, and I understood I was supposed to accept its embrace, but fear made me straight-up stupid.

I stood there, my mouth open as the incandescent glow fattened itself with brighter and brighter layers of illumination. Then, snap! The darkness that had been pursuing me brought me down.

Panic, the thick creamy kind, smothered every rational emotion and pinned my airless lungs against the bone bars of my heaving chest. I fought against the dense silence until I heard Nana Grace's voice rise up into the deepening void.

"Let go, Grace," she said. It was a command, not a request, and I released my grip on this reality. I became, in that moment, a small brown shell of flesh spiraling out into the swift currents of an eternal sea. I could hear myself praying in the midst of all that unending dark, but not some prayer I had learned in church. No, this prayer was from a sacred place that until that moment was foreign to me. The flesh and blood of an ancient language resurrected itself in my mouth. I heard its cadence and rhythm, and then came the bone-deep translation of an Ethiopian text:

> *Through wisdom I have dived*
> *down into the great sea,*
> *and have seized in the place of her depths*
> *a pearl whereby I am rich.*

The chant came again and again. It was not the voice of the sea, but the acrid scent of a damp fall day that flicked on the light of a new consciousness. I became aware of my legs buried ankle deep in a carpet of red and yellow leaves that marked what appeared to be a sunlit clearing in the woods. Massive bodies of trees, whose shedding skirts of leaves I couldn't see, hemmed me into a pocket of light. I was disoriented and scared, but I knew where I was. I knew because bluesman Robert Johnson had, in the ink black of his voice, drawn me a musical map. I was standing at the crossroads. I was standing in the place that was the answer to the question the spirit in Shanta had made her ask.

Out of nowhere and everywhere, Nana Grace coalesced right in front of me. The words, "oh, okay," stuttered out my mouth because it was just easier than screaming incoherently.

She looked beautiful and serene in a wool suit that was the shade of greenish blue the sky always seemed to be wearing in pictures of Hawaii or the Caribbean. She smelled warm and alive, or at least the rich tones of the jasmine and ginger in her perfume gave me that impression. She offered me the bare minimum of a smile, and I thought

that a "hello," or "how are you?" would come after that. But what
came was admonishment.

"Fear is never an excuse for not doing what has been asked of
you, or what is right," she said.

I speak fluent spiritualism now, but back then Nana Grace could
have been speaking Greek or Latin or Swahili or any of the other
thousands of languages and dialects I don't understand. All I could
do was look at her, because my concerns were more immediate. I had
to deal with the state of my sanity.

"Am I dreaming?" I asked.

"You know you're not."

"Am I dead?"

"Of course not."

Nana Grace didn't wait for the question that sat frozen at the
back of my throat to thaw enough for me to ask it.

"Yes, I am," she confirmed. "It's been about an hour. My sister
Peaches will be calling your house in a little while with the news."

I found enough sense to ask, "why am I here?"

"Consider this the beginning of your initiation, Grace. A little
taste of things to come."

Her hand reached up to touch my cheek. I was surprised that her
fingers were still warm, and I thought for a desperate moment that
maybe this was just a dream, the kind of dream that feels very real
until your conscious tells your unconscious that it's time to wake up.

She shook her head and whispered, "no dream, sweetheart," and
with that, the darkness came for me again.

It was the violent rocking of my body that slapped me back into
breathing reality. An extremely panicky Shanta had strapped her fingers to the flesh of my arms and begun shaking me like an electronic
gadget that should work but didn't.

"Oh God, are you all right?" she whispered.

"Not really." I felt disoriented, like I was several beats behind in a
complicated dance.

"You just went out, Grace. Scared the hell out of me. I almost
called 911. What happened?"

I wanted to lie and say I had gotten too hungry, but the lying times were over. Shanta was more sister and blood than Jamila. Our love for each other demanded the truth, especially when the truth seemed to be using her mouth to tell itself to me.

"I had a vision."

Shanta sat down. "You mean like a religious vision?"

"Well, I didn't see God, and I didn't see angels. I think I was visited by my Nana Grace, and she told me that she was dead."

Shanta took several deep breaths, and she was about to ask me for more details when the phone rang. Shanta rose to answer it, but I waved her off, and I lifted myself up to grab the extension in the living room. Before I could say hello, a voice much like Nana Grace's, but higher and sweeter in tone, said my name without a question mark at the end, as if she knew before I picked up that it would be me.

"Yes?" I answered.

"I'm your great-aunt Peaches. We may have met once or twice when you were a little girl."

"I'm sorry ... I don't remember," I said.

"Of course, but I'm calling, family, because I'm afraid I have some bad news." She hesitated, as if waiting for me to offer her something she was very sure I was in possession of.

"I already know," I found myself confiding. "Nana Grace came and told me."

"Ah," Aunt Peaches said without any trace of surprise in her voice. "Then you are, my dear Grace, right on schedule."

There was nowhere to go but down on my knees. I held the phone straight out from my body like it was a dangerous animal. What came out my mouth was Shanta's name pitched in a one note song that was all about being scared out of my mind.

She came running and subdued the phone by taking it from my grasp. Then she looped her arm around me so tight it was like she was trying to keep me from floating away. "Shu, shu, shu," she whispered assuredly. "Tell me what happened, Grace. Tell me."

Sob-soaked gibberish was all I could talk at first, but soon my mind pulled in my runaway thoughts. What I started to tell Shanta was not what happened on the phone. No, I went back to the beginning of the story because nothing about my conversation with Aunt Peaches would have made sense unless she had the whole story. I told her the real deal about that day in the park. I even explained to her what had come out of her mouth from Oba. I told her about my visit with Nana Grace and Dr. Monroe. Then, in a voice worn down thin and fine by my fear of the unknown, I told her how only minutes before I had risen up out of my body into a nowhere that was decorated like some place, and how Nana Grace came out of that nowhere, smelling expensive and dressed like she was going to heaven. I gave her all the details about how Nana Grace had explained that she had just died, and that her visit to me was the beginning of my initiation, a taste of what was to come. When I finished with that part, I explained to Shanta what Aunt Peaches had said to me.

If girlfriend had gotten up and walked out, I wouldn't have thought less of her as a friend. If she had called later and told Mama that I needed help, I wouldn't have blamed her because what I was talking about could only be seen by most rational people as pure craziness. But Shanta pushed aside any doubts she had about my sanity to take care of my drama. Who else but Shanta, goddess of three-inch heels and strapless sandals, would try to make me bond with my reality by asking, "so, what kind of shoes was Nana Grace wearing? With that outfit she had to have on some serious shoes."

It was a raggedy-ass attempt to lend some humor to the surreal, but I smiled at the attempt. "I'm starving."

Shanta nodded knowingly, as if, of course, I would be hungry because I couldn't have experienced all I had and not be hungry enough to eat anything that wasn't bigger than my mouth and moving fast enough to avoid me.

She led me back into the kitchen and told me to sit down. She went looking for food and coffee. The freezer gave up some coffee. The refrigerator forked over some ham, good bread and expensive cheeses. I felt obligated to tell Shanta that this was all stuff I had orders not to touch, but she shrugged defiantly, "it's just food."

"Food is just another weapon Mama uses in the war against me," I reminded her. "If I eat this stuff, she'll just think that I'm trying to challenge her."

"Maybe you should be," Shanta sighed. "Maybe it needs to happen more often."

"Easy for you to say."

However, I didn't question the sandwiches she put down in front of me, and I didn't say a word when she started making the coffee because that was like a medicine I needed for my sanity to start healing. In a wordless ceremony that expressed the true nature of our sister-friendship, Shanta ground some beans down until they were as fine as salt. The smell that grew out of the pot snapped off the sharper edges of my anxiety. My lungs shook themselves out with a multitude of sighs that massaged my body from the inside out. What Shanta poured into a cup was as black as lost hope. It was serious coffee to go with serious thoughts of life and death and the meridian that ran between them.

"Grace, don't ever hide stuff like this from me ever again," Shanta said when she sat across from me with her own cup of coffee.

"But," I whispered, "I thought you didn't believe in things like this. You even told me once that you didn't believe in God anymore."

"Grace, I never said I didn't believe in God. I said sometimes I had my doubts, but as my daddy says, only God and crazy folks don't have doubts. All I can say is that you certainly got me praying again."

"I don't know what to do with all this."

Shanta laughed. "Gracie, I don't think you are going to have to wait much longer to find out."

Mama walked in as Shanta was putting away the food. Her eyes ran across the room as if she was seeing rat tracks on her clean kitchen floor that led to where I sat. She put on a smile for Shanta, but the upturned drape of her lips barely covered her anger.

"What are you girls doing?" Mama asked.

I looked down at the empty plate, and my shame told me to keep my greedy mouth shut.

"Oh, Ms. J," Shanta oozed, "something terrible has happened."

Shanta went on to tell Mama about Nana Grace's death, and how I was so rattled when I heard the news that she decided to help calm my nerves by fixing me some food. Mama just stood there, and then something small and indecent in her made her say, "good."

Shanta's face became unreadable, but I knew she wanted to call my mother out.

"How can you say that, Mama?" I asked.

Unrepentant, Mama looked at me, her face almost Vaseline-shiny with gloating. She was acting like an egotistical athlete who had won the big game. But there are no life events bigger than death except maybe your birth, and, as mortified as I was then, some soft voice of introspection and revelation told me that Mama hadn't won anything. What the ancestors want they claim. What Mama didn't know was that while she was out picking up stuff at the store, my great-grandmother had passed over and then come back from the dead to claim me.

7

ALL I FELT FOR TWO days after Nana Grace's passing was a hot molten mix of awe, generously laced with fear. I tried hard to keep those feelings hidden from the smug gaze of my mother, but fissures had opened up, and glowing plumes of emotions began to leap out. Mama caught me crying as I was getting ready for school.

She came from her room asking, "what are you crying about?"

I didn't know how to answer.

"What are you crying about?" she asked again, the edge in her voice sharp and angled like she wanted to scrape from my face all the emotions she hated. I would have given all I possessed, every crumb of my soul, years off my life for Mama to have laid her palms on my shoulders as a prelude to a hug or at least a sympathetic caress. Anything, I would have given anything. Instead, Mama grabbed my arm and her long fingers and nails contracted, sucking in a taunt fold of sweater-covered skin. I felt the tensing of her muscles, the familiar setting of the trap. Instinct told me to buck and wrench away, but a younger self, hidden in the deep shadows of nightmarish memories hissed, "stay still or it will hurt more." And I remembered and reminded myself that if I struggled, five acrylic talons would make new wounds to match old sets of scars.

"You know, Grace, I can give you something to cry about," Mama said. It was an old monstrous curse meant to reduce me to tears. My breath rattled in my lungs as time collapsed, and I fell back and back until I was eleven again and sprawled out on my bed, my body convulsing as Mama brought her beating strap down and down. She had demanded an apology for something I hadn't done, and was determined not to rest until she got it. My sister, scared out her mind, stood in a corner and prayed at the top of her lungs to Jesus to make it all stop. But I was bent on being mute because I wanted to be like the slave girl, Elizabeth, I had read about in a book. That girl, no older than me, had defied her mistress's ownership of her body and spirit by never uttering a sound during any of her beatings. In the book, Elizabeth had almost died for her disobedience, and in that hellish moment I had wanted to die too. I had kept my words and groans in my mouth until I vomited, and Mama, weakened by disgust, left me alone to howl into my soiled pillow.

"I'll give you something to cry about," my mother yelled again. The curse that had sent me into the past dragged me back.

I thought I didn't have enough breath or will in me to respond but some newborn energy made my mouth move. "Leave her alone."

I heard the word "her" and marveled at it. Calmness descended, bringing with it a small amount of courage. Mama heard it too and knew, even if she didn't believe, that my great-grandmother had died but was not gone. She let go of both my arm and spirit.

Fear of the unknown made her say, "you're crazy, Grace. Maybe you need to be hospitalized."

I wanted to say that if I were crazy, then the hospital would have to give us a family discount. Instead, as I backed away, the word "her" and its implication wrapped around me like a blanket, and I said, "I'm going to school Mama. I'll see you later."

* * *

I got to English on time, but I arrived feeling dazed, more out of this world than in it. As I walked into the room and stumbled down the row to my desk, Shanta looked up and her face became rumpled with concern.

"What happened?" she mouthed as I passed.

"Later," I said, and sank into my chair.

Up front, Mrs. Watanabe began trying her best to get us to explore the finer points of James Baldwin's *The Fire Next Time*. After twenty minutes, she realized she was looking at a whole neighborhood of folks whose lights were on, but who were not home. With a tiny smile that signaled her surrender, she closed her notebook. Then, for the sake of conversation, she asked what she already knew, "so, what is everybody planning to do after graduation?"

Now, we were her advanced placement class, her ever eager overachievers, so, yes, yes, yes we all had plans. The energy of the question connected our thoughts to our classmate's egos. Everybody put on their best dreams and flew out to party.

When I heard Shanta say, "Harvard," I got ready to say Spelman College. Except, that's not what happened. Somewhere in the time it took for me to take a breath to speak, Spelman was yanked out of my stream of thought and the words, "I don't know yet what I'll be doing," were inserted.

A dozen set of eyes turned on me, looking for the "just joking" clause, but I stood there fidgeting, trying to take the words back, trying to state the old truth, but my mouth was a verbal desert.

Shanta saved my ass by saying, "Grace is just kidding. She wants to go to Spelman."

I smiled and sort of did one of those "he-he" laughs like yes, I had been kidding. My peers shrugged hard like they were trying to shake off some of the weirdness I was emitting into the air. However, Mrs. Watanabe wasn't fooled. She may have been reincarnated several times, but she hadn't been born yesterday. She called on someone else to speak, but her huge, luminous eyes began to hang over me like dark moons, and her thin eyebrows seemed to become inflated with disappointment. She had written several letters of recommendation for me. I had told her even before I told Mama what colleges I wanted to attend. "I don't know," wasn't a detour she had expected on the road into my future. Ms. Watanabe would want and deserve an explanation, but at that moment I didn't have anything to give her. All I knew was that what I had said was true, but I couldn't have told her why it was true or what my new plans were.

She handed back test papers just before class let out. I flipped through the pages, scanning them for the delicate lines of her praise or criticism until I got to the back and uncovered her final analysis of my work, which was an A-. Now normally I would have taken my A with its tail and gone on home. Mrs. Watanabe handed out As the way she knew life would hand out commendations, so I should have been happy with my A-. But some vein of disappointment began to throb, and a sticky dissatisfaction glued me in my chair until everyone was gone. For a moment, Mrs. Watanabe thought I was there to discuss Spelman because she said, "Grace, what's the matter? I hope you're not thinking about not going ..."

I felt the smooth flutter of her gaze on my face trying to read me.

"This minus," I finally said. " I don't think ... it's fair."

She stood there. "Well, Grace, your work wasn't up to its usual quality ..." she started to say, and then something jelled. Some knowing that went far beyond the academic began to set up. She sat down next to me and turned the chair so that she could align her eyes with mine.

She smiled, but her lips were pulled tight and small by the weight of deep emotions. "I read in the newspaper that your great-grand-mother died. I'm so sorry to hear that. She sounded like a wonderful person. Do you want to talk, Grace?"

I began to shiver like I was wet and cold. "She was a wonderful person, but my mother told me she's glad my great-grandmother's dead."

"Your mother has always been a difficult person, but soon you'll be off to college. Your time is coming, Grace."

"I don't know if I can ever forgive my mother for all the things she's done," I blurted out.

Mrs. Watanabe leaned toward me, and in a whisper said, "Grace, there are few things in life that are unforgivable."

She then began to explain to me how her family had been among the Japanese Americans sent to prison camps during the start of WWII. She and her family—her mother, her father and her little brother not yet born—had been incarcerated at Santa Anita Race Track in a stall that had been too small to hold the lives of spirited and proud horses, let alone the complicated lives of proud people. Sorrow softened her voice the way water opens up the pores on skin, and she said, "the man my father was didn't survive the camps. He had been a successful businessman who loved America, and when America betrayed him, he came out of the camps as bitter as we were poor. My father struggled for a few years after we were released, but my mother called it joyless living and soulless survival. When I was your age, my father took his own life. What is so horrible is that my few good memories of him are tainted by the single one of finding him dead in all that blood ... all that blood."

She drifted off into silence, as if she had to find some higher ground within herself to stand on as her grief began to rise up as rivers of tears. I thought she wouldn't go on, but she continued to speak because she had to, because sometimes the only way out of the darkness in your soul is to keep moving toward the light, toward a morning that you know has to be out there.

"It has been a long journey across my bitterness and anger to find ways to forgive America for destroying my father's dreams. It has taken long hours of prayer to forgive my father for what I saw as his abandonment of my brother, mother and me. I had to come to terms with how my mother could forgive him so easily and then move on. I still have days when the anger creeps up on me and makes my heart hard and sharp so I still have to pray and pray. Forgiveness is a hard process, but you will find, Grace, that you either learn to do it, or you'll be destroyed by your unwillingness to do it."

We sat for a moment, walled off by her memories from the streams of voices swirling toward the future outside the classroom door.

"They say my father committed suicide," I offered.

"I know, Grace," she said. I felt that she wanted to elaborate but she knew I wouldn't have been able to handle an alternative version of my history. Not right then. Her hand reached out and took mine in hers, and she smiled at me the way my mother should smile at me but doesn't.

"Someday even your pain gonna be pretty," she said.

I looked up at her, and we both started laughing because it wasn't like her to truth-tell using words like that.

"You reminded me of a line from a poem by C. Tillary Banks that I was reading last night," she explained. "It just came to me. In the poem she says that suffering and disappointment are just invitations to grow spiritually. That adversity can be a profound teacher. Do you understand what I'm trying to say?"

I nodded yes, but it wasn't what I wanted to hear. Back in that day, I wanted the normal kind of life everybody else had, the kind of life that was filled more with ugly pleasures than beautiful pain.

"Go to college, Grace," she said. "You have too much talent not to."

I nodded and got up to leave, and I was almost out the door and back into the world of the young and happily clueless when Mrs. Watanabe's voice reached out to tap me on my consciousness. "Grace, please try always to do what is right, what is good."

All I could say was, "I'll try."

8

The week after Nana Grace's death, Mama pretended like there was nothing going on even after the obituary appeared in the paper with the dates and time for family hours and the memorial service.

"What are we supposed to say when people ask why we're not going?" Jamila had asked. Grief had erased some of the distance between us.

"Tell them to talk to Mama," I had replied. "It's not like it's our fault. We have to do what she tells us, you know."

"Yeah, I guess," Jamila had said.

Hunger haunted me the day before the service with a taste for something sweet. I went searching for a pound cake my aunt Aesha had brought by the house earlier that evening. She had also dropped off her opinion that Mama should be ashamed she hadn't at least let Jamila and me come to the family hour at the funeral home. Mama accepted the blessing of the cake before telling Aesha how far up her ass she could stick her opinion. Even though Mama was acting like the devil, Aesha was too Christian to snatch her cake back. She had left it on the table in its pretty homemade canister and I had gone upstairs to wash my hands before I dug in. By the time I got back, Mama had put the cake away, trying to hide it from me.

I was deep off into searching behind some old pots and pans in the pantry when the doorbell rang and rang and rang. My gut feelings pursed their lips to explain that the door was for me, but I didn't move right away.

Mama's feet expressed her impatience in quick, drum-like riffs on the stairs. She didn't bother to ask politely who was troubling her existence. I heard the door squall open, and in her best, Jehovah-Witness-go-away voice, mama yelled, "get the hell off my porch."

Not one, but two voices thinned by age asked to see me. I held my breath as the "no" my mother said came out like the hiss of cool rain on hot asphalt. There was a long moment of silence as old enemies drew out fresh words for weapons and began to stab each other. Mama yelled that they shouldn't be bringing their family's dirt up to her house. The two voices kept chanting in high tones that they were there to see me, not her, and that they weren't leaving until they did just that. Mama unsheathed a complaint about how all their root working had come to infect me.

One of the thin voices that I now know was Aunt Casmil's screwed itself down into a whisper. I heard my father's name, but the words after that seemed to run off from my hearing. Whatever was said was like spit in my mother's face because the last frayed strings of courtesy holding down her anger blew apart. Long years of hatred mushroomed, and tempers, superheated by vindictiveness, began to boil. She told them again to get the hell off her porch, but it was obvious by the way she kept raging that the ladies weren't moving.

The situation was mine to end, but I stood there listening until a male voice arched like a spear into the fray. He sounded familiar, but I couldn't put a name to the voice.

"Ladies, will you please just shut up," he yelled.

There was a moment of utter calm where I'm sure three sets of female eyes must have turned, and with long, furious stares told him what part of hell he could go to.

Mama ended the small ceasefire by saying, "as long as Grace lives in my house, she will abide by my rules."

Those words in Mama's acid tone woke me up and pressed me to rebel. I may be living in her house, but I still had rights. I crowned myself with an attitude and sauntered out like a broke-ass but still proud queen to start ruling my odd realm.

Mama's puffed-up shape was planted in front of the screen door. I couldn't see the origin of the female voices, but I could make out the burly form of my cousin Joe. His big frame was stuffed in a crispy new suit that was a size too small, so his shiny bald head seemed to pop out of his collar like a glob of brown oil paint balanced on the tip of its tube. I relaxed. With Joe there, I felt a little more protected. In another lifetime, before my mother had forced my father's sister Doris to choose sides, Joe and I had been more like siblings than cousins, a fact Doris always reminded me of on the rare occasion we saw each other when Mama wasn't around. "Don't forget your father took Joe in like he was his own son when my husband abandoned me," she would say. And I hadn't forgotten, even though it seemed like Joe sometimes went out of his way to avoid me at school.

"Mama," I said softly, trying to show some respect, even though I felt it was undeserved. "Is somebody here to see me? I keep hearing my name."

Mama grew rigid, as if her muscles were made of setting concrete.

"Go back to the kitchen, Grace," Mama demanded.

It was a direct order I disobeyed by standing there and waiting for an answer.

"Mama, are these people here to see me?" I repeated, adding a little assertiveness to my stubbornness.

"Grace ..." Mama warned.

I took a breath. "Hey, Joe," I asked, "who you got out there?"

Joe knew better than to answer back. He didn't like being a rat in a basket of snakes. At that point, Mama turned around, and I saw that mad was not an accurate description of her mounting fury. One of the worn voices snaked up and around Mama's body to tag itself with a name. "Grace, I'm your Aunt Peaches, and I'm here with your

Aunt Casmil. We're Nana Grace's sisters. Remember, I was the one who called. We're here because we didn't see you yesterday at family hour, and we need to talk to you."

If Mama had any shame about the fact that we hadn't paid our respect as a family, I didn't see it. I felt embarrassed because I should have had the courage to go by myself, but I had been thinking more like a girl than a woman.

"Mama," I said, "these women have lost their sister. We at least owe them our condolences."

Mama gave in, which is not the same as giving up. She peeled her eyes off me and left the room.

I unlocked and opened the screen door. The thin but firm voices belonged to two little doll-like women who I suddenly remembered were twins. They were the soul of sameness, from the shade of barely beige skin that laid almost wrinkleless across their birdlike features, to the pale butter yellow suits that had been tailored to fit their tiny frames, and they looked nothing like Nana Grace. But I could tell by the way they had fought Mama that they had their sister's iron fist and in-your-face attitude. Joe followed, looking around like a dog who expected at any moment to be yelled at again for doing nothing. I paused when I heard Mama's car pull out the driveway, then turned my attention to the sisters.

"I'm sorry my mother was so rude," I said.

They nodded and their eyes began to peck at my appearance as if they were trying to tear away the hull of a seed to get to the meat inside. Joe grunted as if there were no amount of sorry I could offer him as payment for his suffering. Probably at the beginning, when his mother had told him to chaperone the sisters, he had thought it was going to be easy work. How hard could it be to drive two bereaved little old ladies around? But then they had insisted on coming over here. Dirt had been thrown, and skeletons still dripping with the decayed flesh of long ago wrongs, had come jumping out of closets.

"Ladies," I said as I led them to the door of the living room, "why don't you have a seat. I want to say hi to Joe for a moment."

They accepted my offer with flatline smiles and what looked like knowing glances. I watched them arrange themselves on the couch before I asked, "your mother buy you that suit, Joe?"

Joe nodded with no hint of humor on his face. "Sure did. That's what I get for refusing to go with her to pick it out."

"So do you know why they're here?"

Joe's eyes narrowed as if he were trying to decide whether to give me a penny's worth of thoughts about our aunts. With a hand made beefy by football and lifting weights, he snatched up my forearm and pulled me across the foyer tiles until we were as far away from the living room door as we could get without going upstairs or out on the porch.

"I don't think they can hear us, Joe," I said.

Joe shook his head like he knew something I didn't. He twisted his lips into a tight little knot of flesh before they suddenly parted like an overtaxed spring.

"I know you are not supposed to speak ill of the dead or old folks," he said.

"But you're going to do both now, aren't you?"

Joe wasn't amused; his fingers tightened. If he saw me wince, he didn't appear to care. He wanted my full attention. "I've always known that Peaches and Casmil were kind of weird. But I didn't know how weird until now. Like today, I'm driving, you see. First, we went by the funeral home. Then they had me take them to the liquor store. I hear both of them talking. First, I think it is just between them, but then I realize that they are talking like their dead sister is right up there with them in the back seat."

I tried to cover my look of surprise with a tasteful collection of blasé emotions, but more of me would have been hidden if I were wearing a thong.

"My mama says that Peaches and Casmil are powerful conjurers because they can call on spirits to talk to them. She said Nana Grace was one, your father was one and she said you're probably one too."

I laughed a little too quick and loud. "Joe, Aunt Doris thinks that Hip-hop music is a form of devil worship. She also thinks the fifth

digit in the social security number is used to label black people so
that the government can keep track of us. So come on, Joe."

"Yeah, okay … I get your point."

Joe looked embarrassed, like he had hoped I had forgotten how
paranoid his mother could be, but nobody could forget because she
was so loud and proud about it. I did notice that the one suspicion
of hers I didn't pour out in my litany was the one Aunt Doris handed
out like it was her business card. She was always talking about how
a rich old white man in our town had been serial murdering black
folks since forever. She kept saying she had evidence, but she wouldn't
give out any more information because she was waiting for the right
person to handle her discovery. However, nobody, including me, believed Doris had proof of any crimes and everybody, including me,
had been sick of hearing her talk about it.

"Look, I'd better go," I said. "I'm sure they're wondering what the
hell we're doing."

I stepped back into the living room with my aunts. They were
huddled together like preening canaries, and as soon as I entered,
they snapped off their intense conversation. Both women smiled
up at me, but I noted that Casmil's lips formed a smaller bow of
friendliness than Peaches's, whose smile was all sun and full moon
radiant as if my arrival at that moment meant everything to her.

"I'm sorry I took so long," I apologized.

"Well, I'm sure Joseph felt he had a lot of our business to tell you,"
Casmil said.

"Yes," I murmured. My nerves began to manufacture a sticky sweat
from my unease, and I tried to remember if I'd put on deodorant.

"Can I offer you something? I know Mama has coffee and tea,
and I think we might have some orange juice." I smiled my best good
girl smile, but Casmil looked at me like I was on the verge of failing
an important final exam.

"You may bring three glasses," Casmil said as she glanced at her
smiling sister.

"Will there be anything else?"

"No, just that."

I walked into the kitchen and began looking for things. I finally found the cake tucked up in the cupboard's darkness behind boxes of things Mama thought I was less likely to devour. *Why not serve it,* I thought. My cousin Aesha's cake was considered a family treasure, and it was encased like the culinary jewel it was in a tin she had decorated with beads and glitter. The aroma of pure butter, perfumed with expensive vanilla and rose water, spilled out to herald the arrival of a tall pound cake wearing a lacy, sugar glaze veil complemented by an impressive crown of slivered almonds. It seemed almost a sin to cut it, but I placed slices of it on a tray along with silverware, cloth napkins and the glasses. I managed to put the stuff on the table in front of them without dropping anything. Then, not knowing what to do next, I watched as Casmil removed a pint of liquor from her purse, stood and poured enough of the bottle's content to form a puddle of dark alcohol in each glass.

"I don't drink," I said, licking at my lips.

Casmil looked at me as if she thought I must not have been using my better sense.

"Does that look like enough to drink? Besides you're not old enough to drink," she said sarcastically.

Peaches interrupted. "No, Grace, we are going to pour a libation with you in honor of our sister Grace."

"You do know what a libation is?" Casmil asked.

I had an answer, but she didn't wait for me to gather enough thoughts to say it. She began to explain that a libation was simply the pouring out of a small quantity of water to anyone in the spirit world for the purpose of encouraging peace and togetherness and to unite things that should be united.

"Usually it's water or gin," Peaches added, "but we decided to use scotch. Grace loved scotch."

The fact that the pouring of a libation wasn't exactly a Christian ritual began to bother me, but then I thought, *who was I to say anything since my butt hadn't kissed the face of a church pew in over a year?*

Peaches stood and looked dead at me, as if she was listening to my unspoken thoughts, and as Casmil positioned an empty plate on the tray, she said, "libations are part of many religions, Grace."

Surprised, I nodded in agreement.

Peaches handed out the glasses, and then her honeyed voice proclaimed, "to Grace, generations pass away and others stand in their place since the time of them that were old. Rejoice, and let thy heart forget that day when they shall lay thee to rest. Cast all sorrow behind thee, and bethink thee of joy until there comes that day of reaching port in the land that loveth silence."

Peaches's voice trailed off to dance with the silence in the room. Then, with tears skating slow curves down her face, she added, "that's from the Song of the Harper, an ancient Egyptian text from the twelfth dynasty. It was one of Grace's favorites."

"It's beautiful," I whispered.

Peaches poured her drop, followed by Casmil, and with a shaky hand, I poured mine. The drops worked themselves together, becoming a dark luminous pool on my mother's china plate. The ritual plunged deep into the sea of me and brought up tears created from something other than grief. In that moment, I knew I belonged, had always belonged, to these small women. We sat down, as family. I handed out the cake, and we ate in a fluid silence that allowed the words of the song from the Egyptian text to scatter themselves like seeds on the more barren parts of my soul.

"We did our best to keep in touch with you," Peaches said. Her voice seemed to swirl out of sadness into relief. "But your mother would always send back the letters and gifts we tried to give both you and Jamila. It got harder as you got older. We learned from other relatives that the more we tried to contact you, the more abusive your mother became, so our sister Grace told us to let it go because she had had a revelation that God and the ancestors would make things right."

Peaches paused and lay the slender feathering of her fingers on my shoulder. "Grace, we would like for you to be at the funeral tomorrow."

I knew what the answer should have been, but I just sat there. I wasn't thinking about how to get out of going, but how to bear the abuse that would come if I went. I was still my mother's daughter, and hell had no fury like a mother who thought her child was up-pity, ungrateful and disloyal. I would be repeatedly lashed in cruel and hidden ways by Mama's accusations, and guilt would be the salt rubbed in the wounds. The right thing to do was to say yes, but I had to go find some courage to put on first.

"Grace wants you there," Peaches said. I noted the odd use of present tense, but given what I had seen, what I had experienced, it didn't seem out of place.

"You're a grown woman now. You can make you own decisions," Casmil asserted, but her voice had a patina of understanding about my situation.

I was as grown as I could be without any money of my own and living in my mama's house. It wasn't going to be any different any time soon, at least until I went off to college. "All right," I said slowly. "I'll come."

* * *

I found Joe pinned up against the side of the sisters' gray Cadillac looking bored.

"They wish to be escorted by you," I said.

"You could have brought them out."

I shrugged my shoulders to form question marks. "I offered."

"So what did you talk about?" Joe asked as we entered the foyer.

I was trying to find an explanation I didn't owe him when Casmil's voice chewed through the air. "Joseph, what we talked about is none of your concern."

Big and bad had been confronted by small and badder, and Joe did what he was supposed to do, which was to open the door and offer his arms as perches for our aunts' hands.

"We will be by to pick you up tomorrow about nine. The funeral is at eleven," Casmil informed me as she passed by.

Peaches smiled and nodded her confirmation of the plan.

The stairs betrayed the sisters' aura of power by exposing the fragility of their bodies. Joe found they really did need to lean on him, and I watched him grow up into his manhood a bit as he told them patiently when and how to step.

The stillness they left me in hardened around all my senses, and for a moment I felt I would be shattered by it. Long breaths taken with my eyes closed became the string that held me together until I could bring myself to do the dishes. I began cleaning up as if I had done something wrong and had to wipe away all evidence of my crime. I ran the dishwater too hot and suds bloomed up around my hands like foam boils up around fatty meat. I tried to pray for acceptance of my so-called gift but why lie to God? He knew I still wanted him to make it all a dream. So, I prayed for something simpler and much more shallow. I prayed that I had something in my closet that I could wear to Nana Grace's funeral that didn't make me look too fat.

Mama came back much later, as a wolf dressed in mother's clothing, asking me all sugar nice about what had happened between the sisters and me. She was so sweet, and I was so desperate to be accepted by her even in a small, disfigured way that I almost told her everything. But some force greater than my lack of self-respect or esteem made me say, "we didn't talk about you." I took a breath. "I'm going to the funeral because it's the decent thing to do."

Decent. Mama didn't know how to fight that word. Decent is something even the devil knows how to be if it suits his purpose.

"I won't drive you," she said.

"You don't have to," I replied defiantly. "I have a ride."

9

THE DAY OF NANA GRACE'S funeral, I woke up to the sound of water smacking the shore of a beach. I was content to think the sound was part of a dream, so I lay there, letting my breathing dance in time to the sound of the waves and the slow backbeat of my heart. Just as warm currents of drowsiness were about to drag me back to sleep, I heard a man's voice clearly say, "Rabbit, get ready ... ready, ready ... ready ..."

I searched for tangible evidence of the unseen. I saved my sanity by lying to myself that I hadn't really heard anything. A lie was a better friend than the truth at that point. The lie let me think straight enough to shower, and then helped me push my round, peg body into the narrow hole of my suit skirt. The lie allowed me to walk, not slink past my Mother's room. The lie let me eat like a normal person. It sat with me as I drank one cup of coffee and ate, not devoured, two slices of toast demurely draped in butter and jelly. The lie, of course, would eventually fail me in front of a hundred or so people, but I needed the lie then, because I had no real vocabulary to explain the truth of what was happening to me.

* * *

"What did you women do, call each other to see how you were going to dress? They're in pink, too," Joe said when I opened the door. I shrugged because I figured he was poking fun at my clothes. The only dressy thing in my closet had been a cotton candy pink suit. I had never worn it, and I thought it made me look like a giant piece of bubble gum with a chocolate chip stuck on top. The suit was gaudy, but I looked respectful, so I had decided it would do.

Joe was one to talk; he was dressed in a baggy, but tailored suit the color of lemon pie filling. Yellow shoes, a few shades darker than the suit, stuck out like tailfeathers from beneath the cuffs of his pants. He was ghetto fabulous. Next to him, I looked like I was in a black dress and pearls.

"Joe, did your mama see you before you left the house in all that yellow?" I asked.

Joe laughed at my surprise. "The aunts said I could wear it. They wanted everybody in bright colors because they feel this is a celebration of Nana Grace's life."

"Well, you are certainly dressed for a party," I half-joked as he opened the door to let me walk out onto the porch. "Please tell me you don't have a hat to match."

Joe nodded. "It's in the car. Don't be hating on me, Grace, because I know I look good. Besides this isn't a normal funeral anyway. First off, they aren't having a minister preach the service. The aunts say they just want people to come up and share their thoughts, good or bad, about their sister. Also, they ain't having a choir, just a jazz band."

"Actually, Joe," I offered, "that doesn't sound so bad. Maybe that's why they're having it at the funeral home instead of a church."

"Yeah, well you tell your other relatives that. Most folks got their shorts, panties and thongs all tied in knots over one thing or the other. If they ain't mad about the fact that she was cremated, then they're pissed off because there's no minister and it's not being held in church. And if they ain't upset about any of that, then they're complaining cause they think it's a damn shame they're holding it at the white funeral home instead of the black one."

The choice of the funeral home had surprised me as well, given that our town tended toward being as segregated in death as it was in life. White folk knew they could be buried by the black funeral home, most just chose not to be. However, the fact that was unspoken, but well known, was that the Shaw brothers of Shaw Brothers and Sons Funeral Home preferred not to tend to the bereavement needs of the black community. Given their attitude, the selection of their funeral home had seemed a strange choice on the part of my aunts, but then who was I to talk about strange?

When Joe opened the car door, my aunts looked up and smiled. They were in pink, but their outfits were a paler color, as if milk or a tube of white paint had been added to the shade of cotton candy I had on.

"Thank you for coming," Peaches said. They looked smaller than they had the day before, like grief had soaked them down and they had shrunk a bit. As soon as I was comfortable, Peaches burrowed her hand deep into mine, and arranged her head on my shoulder. I was looking down into the silver halo of her hair, smelling the heavenly scent of her perfume when sobs that seemed a little bigger than the frame of her mouth began to spill out. I looked toward Casmil, desperate to know what else I could do to comfort her sister, but Casmil had aimed her attention at the front of the car as if the agenda for the day was posted on the headrest in front of her. Only the whispery rattle of her breathing betrayed the roiling pain of her fresh grief. Someone had to remain calm, and because she was the oldest by the slim margin of maybe five minutes, Casmil had decided it should be her.

"It's all right, Aunt Peaches," I whispered to her finally, and I told her what she already knew, what she had only days before confidently confirmed for me. "I saw Nana Grace. She's just fine. I know it's not the same as her being here, but still ..."

The sun glowed like a golden bead on the neckline of an expensive blue silk dress. *Heaven*, I thought, *had to be as stunning as that sky.* The afterlife I'd seen had been as beautiful as that sky.

"It's a wonderful day for a homegoing," I said.

Peaches fought to gather up some composure as she searched for tissues in her purse. "Yes, it certainly is."

This is what I know, what little bit I have come to understand. It may be a cliché when people say funerals are for the living, but honestly they are. The dead are honored, but for the most part they are otherwise engaged. Really, they have more complex agendas to attend to; they have newer, richer and more sacred dreams to dream. They really don't care where their remains come to rest.

Shaw Brothers and Sons Funeral Home seemed to rise up off the landscape like some great old European museum I had only seen in magazines. I began to wonder how my aunts had forced rich, powerful white men do their bidding.

"They owe us money," Casmil said as the car came to a stop at the top of an undulating driveway. "They owe us a lot of money. I told them they had to arrange our sister's funeral or all their loans would come due immediately. Sometimes you have to make people do right by you and others. Sometimes you can buy simple justice. It's not the same as real justice, but it will do."

I nodded. I didn't even bother to ask how she knew that particular question had been spinning around, looking for an answer in the back of my mind.

The senior Shaw, clad in a neatly pressed black suit and wearing a smile tighter than the control top panty hose I had on, came out to the car. Years of working with people at the worst times in their lives was the glue that held on the mask he wore to hide his disgust at having to cater to us. He was gracious to my aunts but only in the way that those with power are courteous to those with even more power. He nodded at Joe and me, and I shivered as if a needle full of poison had been shoved up my arm when I took the soft, well-scrubbed hand he felt forced to offer. He was all ready to dismiss us as unimportant, garishly dressed hangers-on, until Casmil's voice snapped like a set of fingers trying to catch a waiter's attention.

"This is Miss Grace Johnson and Mr. Joseph Greene, our departed sister's great-grand children," she said. "They are to be well taken care of."

His interest in our existence renewed, Mr. Shaw offered us seats in a small alcove off the main hall before he took the sisters to his office to check arrangements. On a leather couch as stiff as the bleachers in our high-school gym, Joe and I sat looking at a huge picture of Jesus and a table whose shiny surface held an accurate reflection of the floral arrangement sitting on it. Like lions in high grass, we were able to watch the world pass by without being seen.

Joe began naming the species of mourners. "Friends ... relatives ... nosey folks that loved her ... nosey folks that hated her ... nosey folks here just for the food ..."

I laughed; still, I was amazed at the number of people proceeding silently down the hall. It was a testament to a life well-lived, a life I was sorry I knew so little about.

"What was she like, Joe?" I asked.

"Who?" Joe replied.

"Nana Grace. What was she really like?"

Joe looked at me hard, as if he were trying to see if I was just asking to be asking or if I really wanted his answer. "Well, some say Nana Grace could be mean as hell—um, maybe the word isn't mean. Maybe what I'm trying to say is that Nana Grace didn't take stuff off of anybody, especially white folks. She could be nice, but she demanded that you act like you respected her and yourself. The aunts are the same way."

Joe cocked his head and offered me a thin wedge of a shy smile. "After we left yesterday, the sisters took me out to dinner and told me that you and I should have never been separated when we were little. They said that your daddy would have wanted me to look out for you and even Jamila like I was your brother. You know Grace, I always thought about you like a sister, even if I was too afraid of your crazy mama to act like it."

I looked at Joe like his mind had rolled out of his head and underneath the couch. He had gone deep on me, and I was startled because I hadn't realized that he had emotional oceans in him. In some small way, I thought the libation Casmil had poured had begun to work, the swirls of liquor tying back together a relationship that should have never been ripped apart.

"Thanks, Joseph," I said, and sank against him.

"No problem, Gracie," he offered, and curled his arm around my shoulder.

A young man, a Shaw son I suspected, gingerly poked his head in, and without looking at us said, "Ms. Johnson, Mr. Taylor, your aunts are ready."

I got up, but from the moment my feet hit the carpet, I felt disoriented, as if my body was no longer on speaking terms with certain parts of my mind. It took me a long moment to obey the command to walk. I stumbled once, twice, and when the floor tried to grab me again, Joe caught my arm and waited for me to steady myself.

"I guess I'm feeling this more than I thought," I muttered.

"It's all right, Gracie," Joe said. "I'm feeling it too."

I rode in the wake of Joe's assurance up to the room called Sanctuary of Hope. The sisters were waiting, standing in matching poses of arms clutching identical purses. All the smallness I had seen in them in the car was gone. It was as if they had stiffened and starched themselves with a steely variety of resolve that would allow them to get through everything tearlessly.

"You will sit with us," Casmil said.

We entered to the sound of a saxophonist and his band playing from Coltrane's "A Love Supreme." It was funeral music for the spiritually self-assured. The fact that I had the CD in my collection and played it almost every day connected me to my great-grandmother. I felt a little more powerful. My steps became steadier, and I didn't feel so self-conscious that row after row of family eyes, bright with tear-moistened curiosity, followed our passing like searchlights on prison towers.

I remember sitting down. I remember how the plush chair sighed just a little bit, politely complaining that I had plopped my butt on its face. I remember how Casmil rose to walk regally to the small podium. She asked that those who wanted to comment on her sister's life to please come forward. An older white woman with hair the color of sunlit sand brushed past as if she were being towed up the aisle by leashes full of dogs. The woman began to speak, but I didn't hear anything that sounded like words. What came out from between the vivid winking of her mauve-smeared lips was the loud breathing of the ocean. I closed my eyes to prolong the blink that I thought would stanch the booming clatter of waves, but all I wiped away was time. Slivers of seconds seemed to exchange themselves for a slice of an hour, because when I opened my eyes, the ocean noise faded and I heard Casmil say, "before we close, is there anyone else who feels moved to speak?"

I stood, or maybe I should say I was pulled up by something more powerful, more omnipresent. Unshackled from my reticence, my feet easily moved me forward until I stood beside my aunt. Casmil smiled and squeezed my trembling hand. I was surprised by the tenderness in her touch and the deep look of pride in her eyes, and I wondered what I had done to deserve such a sweet moment of softness from her. Now I know it wasn't what I did, but what she knew I would consent to do in the next moment, that had harvested her respect.

"Well done, Grace," she whispered before backing away.

I stood there hoping that some appropriate expression of sympathy would materialize in my mouth before my trembling ropes of legs snapped and dropped me. Words came, but not like I expected. I expected the spoken language of normal conversation or maybe even poetry. Hell, I would even have taken rap. Instead, I was compelled to sing, which would have been okay except that I couldn't carry a tune if it had handles.

"Wade in the water, Wade in the water, children. Wade in the water, God's a-gonna trouble the water," came pouring out my mouth like toxic waste polluting the pristine streams of people's artistic sensibilities. I saw people wince, and the mouths of some of the less than tactful and discreet folks fell open. I was mortified, but the part of me that wanted to run from the room had been disabled.

God had stirred an ocean in the universe, parting just for a moment the mortal veils of darkness that exist between the worlds of the living and those who are the ancestors. God troubled the waters, and souls rose up in me, dragging my arms high above my head, and once my shuddering hands were pinned on some crossroad's power line of communication, my body began to flap about. I heard myself moan, not in agony or pleasure, but a low, rumbling sound that went far beyond those simple emotions. What followed was another song in a powerful voice that was not mine.

I hit the first few notes of "Amazing Grace," and the band, knowing—feeling—that they were in the presence of something that needed the blessing of jazz was moved to follow. The somber bellow of the saxophonist underscored the melody, and the full meaning of the song's haunting plea for the richness of God's redemption. The whole room seemed to shudder as people discarded the barriers of decorum they had put around their souls and began to cry and wail like they were newborns. At that moment, my arms fell and I fainted. Joe says it was like I had run a marathon, and just as I reached the end, I fell out from sheer exhaustion.

10

I CAME UP OUT OF the spiritual sea to find myself on the couch of the funeral home office. I could feel my mouth winking like the gills of a water-starved fish. I opened my eyes to the blurry view of featureless heads floating in and out, until a flash of something big and yellow scattered them all aside. The couch jumped a bit as my cousin dropped to his knees and hunched over me as if people's curiosity were only studded with thorns of disapproval instead of genuine concern.

"Leave her alone," I heard Joe bark, and his big, damp hand curled up like an aggressive kitten along the side of my face. He was using his football field voice, but inside my head I could barely hear him.

"Maybe we should call her mother," a woman counseled.

I struggled to sit up, but I couldn't seem to find the reset buttons that would allow my arms and legs to work together. All I could manage was a soggy, "no, please, don't do that."

"See," the woman added, "she can barely talk. Maybe we need to call an ambulance."

Folks began to nod their heads and hum in agreement with the woman's view of my condition until Monroe's voice leapt out to dash their solidifying consensus.

"I think she's fine. I think we should give her a few moments alone with her cousin to compose herself," he said.

The stiff bristles of his authoritative manner swept people from the room. However, I knew once most of my relatives were out of my sight they would unsheathe their phones to call my mother and inform her that no matter how she felt about Nana Grace, she needed to bring herself down to the funeral home to look after me. They were wasting their breath and cell phone minutes. Given what had happened the day before, my mother wasn't going to lift a foot to come.

The silence that followed the closing of the door was medicinal, and I soaked in it a few moments until I felt firm enough to ask Joe to help me sit up.

"Whew," I whispered as the room began to bank and circle like a carnival Tilt -A-Whirl. Joe slid next to me and I clung to his shoulder as if it would keep me from being hauled back into the spiritual darkness I had just come from.

"Gracie," he whispered in a little voice I didn't know he owned, "are you really okay? I mean you aren't just saying you're fine, so people will leave you alone?"

"I'm fine Joe," I assured him, even though I wasn't sure. I didn't know what okay was supposed to feel like after what had occurred.

"You do know that what happened to you was God's doing?"

"I don't know, Joe. It feels more like I went crazy in public."

Joe's head wagged. "No, I've seen crazy in public plenty of times. Nope, this was different. It was like … like, you know, you opened the door between us and them."

"Them?" It came out as a question, but I knew exactly what he meant.

"You know ,those who have passed … dead people. I felt it. I think everybody else did too. It was all in the songs. Well, maybe not that first one, the first song was bad, but the second one, you tore "Amazing Grace" up. I didn't know you could sing like that."

"I can't, Joe," I said, and I waited for his curiosity to soften so that when I drove the point home it would go in straight and deep.

"It wasn't me singing."

He had to turn that statement over and over like it was a puzzle piece he wasn't sure belonged to the puzzle we were working on. "Oh, that's deep," he said when the piece finally settled into its odd-shaped hole.

"Yeah," I replied.

A light rap at the door was followed by the pinched face of the funeral director. He glanced at us, and his eyes skimmed the room to make sure we hadn't taken anything. "Your aunts would like to know if you are ready to join them," he finally asked.

"Tell them we'll be right out," Joe said.

When I stood, I was surprised that my legs held me up; my feet had swollen and were at war with the rigid cages of my shoes. I decided to live with the pain. If I took them off, I would never get them back on. Casmil and Peaches were waiting outside the door, along with the funeral director.

"It was a lovely service, wasn't it?" Casmil said to me as we slowly walked down the hall.

"I told her it was God's doing," Joe said proudly

Casmil eyes poked at the side of my face. "You do know Joe is right."

I nodded yes, but I still felt like a strand of hair that had fallen into people's spiritual food. I had lost control of my mind *and* my body, and been made to convey a message in a really embarrassing way. Acceptance was the least of what I felt. Confusion about what it all meant was a more accurate description.

"And thus, as Joe likes to tell us, 'it's all good'," Peaches giggled. It was a proper giggle, but a giggle nonetheless. I had to smile about how that piece of slang sounded so strange wrapped up in her perfect diction.

"You all are something else," I said.

"Yes, we certainly are," Peaches replied, smiling. "And so are you, Ms. Grace."

Nana Grace's friends from the Retirement Center made special efforts to tell me how much my great-grandmother had admired me, how she had always expected great things from me and how my singing had only proved that she had been right. "It's such a shame, that your mother didn't allow you to get to know your great-grandmother," said the woman who had gone up first during the ceremony.

After an hour, Casmil released me from my greeting duties to go feed at the buffet. Like a starving deer, I began to voraciously graze on pastures of hors d'ouerves. I remember now that a knot of relatives were discussing what they had heard about Nana Grace's will, and that eyes slightly sticky with envy glued themselves on me, but I didn't pay attention because the dessert table was calling me by my full given name. What was a rumored inheritance when there were wedges of red velvet cake and bread pudding encrusted with tiny jewels of currants? And what was the promise of monetary power next to slices of sweet potato pies cemented with a succulent mosaic of pecans and almonds? By my second helping of just about everything, I overheard people asking each other if I were hollow or something. Hollow was a good word to describe how I felt. My hunger was in the marrow of my bones and soul. A lot of energy had been demanded. Spirits had sung me dry.

I was deep off into artistically smearing a parker roll with butter when the Reverend Thornton, pastor of the church Mama belonged to, came up beside me. He was slightly out of breath and very much out of place. A late May chill still clung to the overcoat he had only partially unbuttoned when he had entered. I knew he hadn't known my great-grandmother, but he had been sent by my mother to come get me. He dropped his ice-cold hand down for me to shake. I wasn't eager to pick it up, and when he reached down to try to grasp my palm anyway, a swift jolt of attitude rammed my spine straight, forcing me to ignore the man's incredible good looks.

The Reverend is *fine, fine, fine*. When black folks say, "the blacker the berry, the sweeter the juice," he could be the picture beside the description. Pretty nose, pretty lips lined by a neat mustache, all of that highlighted by caramel-colored eyes. Standing there looking at all that manly beauty, it occurred to me, like a dirty joke, that the

Reverend had probably opened the noses of a lot of women before he found Jesus and Mrs. Thornton. I pulled back until the table prevented me from retreating any further.

"Hello, Reverend." My tone was all wary politeness, but he smiled as if he didn't care that I was uncomfortable in his presence.

"Grace," he said, "your mother said you were um, sick, so she asked me to come and get you."

I shook my head no very slowly. "I'm doing fine now, Reverend Thornton. I promised my aunts that I would attend my great-grandmother's funeral, and I want to stay with them until the end. Besides, if my mother had really wanted me to come home, she should have come herself."

The Reverend tipped his head like he thought I was a bit clueless. "Well, she felt she couldn't."

I shrugged and for some reason he took that as a sign to come closer. He leaned in. "Your mother believes that you are being unduly influenced by your aunts in ways that are not very Christian."

I could feel the look in my eyes growing harder, turning into a disrespectful stare. Trying to be grown, I said, "I don't think this is the time to talk about this."

"Your mother believes—"

"I really don't care what my mother believes."

"The Bible instructs us to honor our parents."

Anger pulled my hands up onto the shelf of my hips and cocked my lips. Harsh words, words I wouldn't have been able to easily take back were about to shoot out my mouth when a hand gripped my upper arm. Startled, I turned and found myself looking into Dr. Monroe's less than sympathetic face.

"Ms. Johnson," he said through tightly pinched lips.

I didn't answer because his eyes strongly suggested that I swallow every dark and sour word in my mouth. I sucked in a sharp breath and tried not to choke.

"Reverend, I believe Ms. Johnson explained to you that she wished to stay," Dr. Monroe said. He spoke in a voice that was soft, but full of hidden warnings. A tiny current of special knowledge running just below my full understanding of what was happening whispered that the tension between them was much, much older than me, that I was a new battle in a very old war. Their eyes locked, and Dr. Monroe allowed me to unhook myself. Breathless and panicky, I headed out into the hall. Behind me, my name swirled in a torrent of alarmed voices.

I wanted to fully honor my promise to my aunts, but embarrassment convinced me that I needed to leave. Soon enough, I would have to go back home to my crazy mother. I had defied her once, but I didn't know what she would do about twice, especially when the Reverend Thornton explained to her how I had acted. Without a coat and on aching feet, I obeyed the directive of an exit sign. I had left a mess at Nana Grace's funeral, but I was too pissed and scared to care.

11

IT WAS TOO COLD THAT day to have been wandering anywhere without a coat, but I was so preoccupied with my hurts and humiliations I didn't notice I was freezing until I was too far up town. It took me awhile to realize exactly where I had ended up. A rustic sign hewed out of logs announced that I was on the back side of a park I knew well by both its names—one official, the other more truthful. If you were white, the emerald island of ball fields and playgrounds was officially titled Bennett's Common. If you were black, you knew to call it Bigot's Park.

Now all of us in Vigilant were referring to the same long dead mayor. It was just that white folks chose to celebrate the good in the man while black folks chose to commemorate the color-coded hatred that had rendered all that good useless. Maybe if I had had a coat on, I would have been able to consider what the existences of two very different names for what was supposed to be shared common space said about Vigilant's history and memory. If I had thought about how the dark and light of people's attitudes toward those they consider "other" had come to shape landscapes and place, then I would have tasted the first sour warning of what was ahead. I would have known that beneath all that pretty, well-groomed grass was nothing but the figurative and real bones of unresolved racial contentions. However,

I was nothing but clueless back then, and all I could think about was where I could go to get warm, because I wasn't going back to face the Reverend, and I wasn't going home until I absolutely had to.

Bigot's Park was necklaced by thick strands of streets that swept like outstretched arms toward a line of old growth pines. Past the tips of the trees lay the gray skirt of Haven Lake and the quaint shops and restaurants that lined the hem of the boardwalk. It was deep into the afternoon, and I thought something had to be open. Once I found a phone, I could call Shanta and have one of her parents come pick me up. It wasn't much of a plan, but it was enough to keep me plowing ahead into a stiff breeze.

Some big-mouthed jays spoiled the quiet by arguing like drunks over spilled liquor. With beaks wide open and wings fanned out they dived at each other. I watched the gangster nature show until a small, black car pulled up beside me. I knew who it belonged to, and I wanted to run, but I couldn't make my feet obey. All I could do was stand there as the window slid down to reveal Dr. Monroe. I couldn't tell if the look on his face expressed anger, relief, disgust or a mixture of all three. He didn't offer a smile when he said, "Ms. Johnson, please get in."

I was too numb to demand that I wanted to be left alone. Shivering, I climbed in and gratefully settled into a heated leather seat.

After I closed the door, he handed me a loosely folded gray stadium blanket, which I struggled to wrap around me. Out of the corner of my eyes I studied him. He was dressed impeccably. His small, elegant body was covered with a very black, very expensive suit. His only concession to the sisters' desire for color at the funeral had been a smattering of yellow trefoils hovering in tight formation on the surface of a dull gray tie.

"Are you all right?" he finally asked.

My teeth rattled as I shrugged.

"Is that a yes or a no, Ms. Johnson?"

I felt a twinge of agitation, then some anxiety. "I'm fine," I stuttered. "Are you going to take me home now?"

He took his eyes off me and stared out the windshield. His slender fingers began tapping the edge of the steering wheel. "No, not yet. We need to talk."

"I guess I should thank you for saving me both times."

"That's one of the things we need to talk about."

"Oh." I sunk deeper beneath the blanket.

"I understand why you left the room. I wanted you to leave. However, you shouldn't have left the building. You caused a lot of worry and confusion."

"I just needed to get away from him," I offered.

Monroe sighed and leaned back in his seat. "You do know you were about to make a spectacle of yourself with the Reverend."

The way he said "spectacle" made it sound like it was a full sibling to the word stupid. I wanted to tell him that he wasn't my daddy. However, deeper instincts told me to keep that to myself. Monroe's air of authority reminded me of my encounter with Oba. I had to give him some respect, even if it was grudging because he and Oba had been thick as cold grits the day I had walked past them on the way to the concert.

"I need you to tell me why you were upset with the Reverend."

I didn't think. I just jumped at the question. "He was in my business."

"That's not an adequate answer, Ms. Johnson."

"Why do you care?"

Monroe smiled the kind of smile that was more in his eyes than on his lips. "In both life and death your great-grandmother has put a fine point on the fact that the ancestors have decided to work through you. What happened at the funeral home was a consecration of your new role and reality. She has entrusted your spiritual and physical well-being to me. More importantly, Oba has entrusted your spiritual development to me. You have been given a very powerful gift, and it is my job to teach you to be more mindful of the consequences of your actions. So, I pose the question again, Ms. Johnson, why were you upset with the Reverend?"

I sat there weighing and measuring the fear until I felt the need to confess. "It's like this," I said softly. "I was already embarrassed, and then Mama sent him to get me, even though she knows I don't like or trust him. If she loved me she would have come herself. If he was any kind of minister he would had told her that Jesus would want her to be there with me. Instead, he comes all full of himself, treating me like I'm stupid, telling me that I'm being led astray by my aunts."

I tried to keep my tears behind a solid fence of brave composure, but my emotions dug a hole underneath that fence and the tears escaped anyway. Sobs smacked my body around. Monroe said nothing. He just let me cry until he thought I was emotionally dry enough to comprehend what he had to say.

"One of my jobs, Grace, is to help you reconnect to the self that should have been but couldn't be until now."

I nodded, even though what he said felt like New Age mumbo jumbo, the kind of stuff you read on the sides of tea boxes or in those obnoxiously sentimental e-mails people forward and forward and forward because then they don't have to write anything real and honest.

"So, are you are like the Spirit of Christmas Future or something?" I asked. "I mean, first there was Oba, and then Nana Grace, and now you."

I couldn't really tell, but I think he smiled. I heard him go, "hmmm …," as if what I had said was an interesting take on our relationship. "I'm more like the 'or something,'" he said, and he sighed and closed his eyes like he was listening to music. "I need for you to consider something about your mother."

The word "need" connected to mother made me hold the blanket tighter. "Okay."

"I need for you to consider that while your mother's love is thin it does exist."

I didn't say anything, which I'm sure Monroe knew was my way of giving him the finger. I wanted to roll up my sleeves and offer him definitive flesh and blood proof that my mother's love was as formless as the emperor's new clothes. I was convinced that once he saw the new wounds, he would understand my mother had nothing to cover her nakedness.

"Sit with the idea, Ms. Johnson. Meditate on it."

I burrowed deeper into the silence and brought my truth out of hiding. "She treats me like crap you know."

"Yes, I do know."

"Then you understand ..."

"Yes, I know how hard this will be, but you must understand that you are now held to a higher—"

I didn't let him finish. "Like how high, Dr. Monroe? Because what you're asking me to do is like Mount Everest high. I'm not doing it. I don't have to do what you say."

Monroe opened his eyes and turned his head. The look on his face awakened rabbles of butterflies in my stomach. "I am the least of those whom you will have to answer to, Ms. Johnson."

I didn't ask what he meant because the childish side of me wanted to get back at him with what I thought were his own secrets. "What's going on between you and Reverend Thornton? Why are you angry with each other?"

I didn't expect an answer. I fully expected him to be one of those do as I say, not as I do kind of people, but there wasn't a small hiccup of hesitation in his voice when he began to speak.

"The Reverend and I are half-brothers. We are barely on speaking terms because our spiritual philosophies have set us on two very different paths. He chooses to believe there is no room for gay people in the Christian Church, and that Christianity is the one and only true religion. I disagree.

"On my part, there is the matter of how my brother chooses to run his church. I am of the opinion that the shepherd should guide his flock, not fleece them out of most of their spiritual and material possessions in the name of the Lord."

My jaw could have been a ball, because it was bouncing on my lap. Nowhere in all the discussions I had with other folks about Dr. Monroe had it come up that he was related to anyone in town, much less Reverend Thornton.

I finally found enough sense to confess the obvious. "I didn't know he was your brother."

Monroe shrugged. "Few people want to talk about situations that make them uncomfortable. In Vigilant, secrets are well-kept if people feel they need to be, and many people feel that who I am and what is between my brother and me qualifies as one of those kinds of secrets."

"I'm sorry," I mumbled. "I shouldn't have asked."

"No apology necessary," Monroe assured me. "You were honest with me, so I am required to be honest with you. That's how it works. You also needed to see if I could take as good as I've given. I understand that."

Monroe sat up suddenly and flicked over his wrist to look at his watch. He pressed his lips together into a deep frown as he double-checked what he'd seen with the dashboard clock. "I need to take you back to the funeral home. Your aunts are waiting to take you home. I wanted to go with you to talk to your mother, but my son is due to arrive from Atlanta and I'm running late."

Evan, I thought, and I remembered how the one line of the dedication page in Monroe's book had read: *To my son Evan, May wisdom and maturity draw us closer in the coming years.* I meant for it to stay a thought. But then I felt my lips pull involuntarily and my voice, full of someone else's desire, said, "years have passed, Monroe, and are you and your son any closer? Can you heal his pain?"

Wide-eyed and gaped mouth, I stuttered, "I'm sorry … I don't know why I said that."

For a long moment, Monroe's guard dropped and I saw a look of sadness so fierce I wanted to hug him, but then he swept that emotion up and put it away.

"It's all right," he said finally. "I know it wasn't you."

Then, who, I thought as he put the car in gear and began to drive. I wanted desperately to know who had used me, and the how, and the why, but I didn't have enough courage to try and break through the thick silence Monroe had wrapped around himself.

When we got back to the funeral home, Joe had the car waiting with our aunts tucked inside. They twisted and turned like nervous birds to look at me through the window.

"Think about what we discussed concerning your mother, Ms. Johnson," Monroe said as I slid into the back seat with Aunt Peaches. He nodded to Casmil, "she's fine."

He said fine as if nothing had happened, as if we had just had a simple conversation.

"We'll talk again in a few days," he added.

Home, bitter home. I didn't want to go back. Peaches reached for my hand and held it as Joe drove. I noticed he took the long way back to town so that the sisters and I would have more time to talk.

"It will be okay," Casmil offered.

I nodded, but I didn't believe her.

Joe didn't turn the engine off when we got to the front of the house. It was as if he understood that I needed the constant one note humming to modulate my attitude and realign my thoughts. I sat there trying to be poised, trying hard to find some way to tell the sisters goodbye without falling apart.

"We know," Peaches whispered. Her lips touched my cheek, leaving behind a mauve mark that branded me as theirs.

I took a stiff breath. "Okay, Joe, I'm ready."

Only then did he turn the car off, and he reminded me to sit there until he opened the door for me. The heat of a waning afternoon sun nibbled at the back of our necks as Joe and I, weighted down with reluctance, walked slowly up the sidewalk and onto the porch. The living room curtains flapped sharply, moved by the maternal hurricane that was gathering strength inside.

"Hum," Joe uttered. It was a hard, low sound, a protective growl.

"You go on," I said. "She isn't going to let you in. Besides this is my fight."

"Well, you know to give me a holler if you need me, but Peaches says you gonna be alright. She said that you don't know it yet, but you're packing serious spiritual heat."

I looked at him to see if he was smiling, because I thought he was kidding.

Joe grinned and shook his head. "Yeah, I know. Peaches is kind of different, isn't she?"

I was going to laugh. I really needed to laugh, but at that moment, the door swung open, and high irrational Mama winds reached out and snatched me off the porch.

12

IN MAMA'S STORM OF PROTEST, I was nothing except debris to be swept away or a small tree to be bent until I snapped and splintered. Her voice swung up and down in violent, high-pitched gale force scales as she said over and over, "Reverend Thornton said you were rude and belligerent to him. How could you embarrass me like this?" Of course, all the emphasis was on the word "me."

I decided to protect the vital organs of my ego by collapsing beneath my silence. For once, I didn't just willingly offer an arm and a leg of my self-esteem for her to pull off and maul. But the price of my unwillingness to proffer my usual emotional sacrifice was that she could accuse me of being a bitchy, uppity child, who had forgotten God's commandment and law about honoring parents.

"Who do you think you are?" she finally yelled.

Her words, their edges jagged, ripped through my newly thickened skin down to the bone, and I finally said what I meant, but didn't fully understand at the time, "you know who I am, Mama."

I expected to be slapped upside my head. I expected anything but the silence that followed. During the lull, this understanding came to me: Mama had always known. What was unfolding, blooming, bursting open in me, was no mystery to her. She knew after eighteen years, the paranormal chickens were coming home to roost despite the fact she had done her best to slaughter them.

"Ungrateful." It was all she could think to call me.

Some part of me that was still a daughter wanted to say, "I'm sorry." But I wasn't sorry. I was confused, but not sorry.

"Excuse me," came out of my mouth, slow and dignified. I backed out of the foyer, my eyes on Mama until I could take off up the stairs. I sat in the dimness of my room snatching breaths, listening the way small things do when they think something big might still come after them. The swift undertow of my breathing carried a frantic prayer, "please, God. Please, God. Please, please, please God," until I realized the prayer had been answered. Tranquilized by some reassurance that Mama was going to leave me alone, I unfurled my fingers from my palms and flicked on the radio. Josh Redman was playing and I soaked for a while in the hot licks coming off his horn, trying to think about nothing, but still thinking about everything that had happened that day.

My desk was an accurate reflection of my divided and scattered life. Term papers lay half-written, and a math book taunted me with an unfinished group of assignments. *Old life, old things*, I thought, and my mind ushered my attention to a piece of mail Mama or Jamila must have tossed there. I picked up the thin package. It was shaped like a children's picture book and wrapped up tight in a crisp sheet of brown paper. The handwriting was unfamiliar. While my name and address were efficiently carved on the front, there was no return address, an omission that felt deliberate. I ran my finger across the series of Malcolm X stamps and tried to read the cancellation mark, but it was smudged. I was happy I didn't need the nails I had chewed off days ago to break the tape along the back.

A copy of the book, *The Velveteen Rabbit* slid out into my hands, and I smiled as I realized it had once belonged to me. The book's faded cover was wrinkled and cracked and smelled of having lived in someone's closet for a long time. My fingers began to pet the familiar dog-eared pages. "Rabbit," I said, and the smile on my face grew fat and wide on rich recollections of happier times. My father had taken to calling me "Rabbit," because I had asked him every night to read the bunny book over and over until I fell off to sleep. After his death, after his so-called suicide, the book had disappeared, but I had been too deep in a four-year-old's nightmare of grief to notice. By the time I did remember, I knew enough not to ask my angry mother where it had gone.

I decided not to wonder where the book had been and who had sent it back to me. After a day of utter weirdness and a dose of my mother's bloodless love, the book gave me some solace. I told myself to just take in the sweetness of its existence. If I had ever needed the gift of my father's memory, I needed it then. I peeled back the cover and found, tucked against the title page, a small folded sheet of paper. My hand hovered over it; it felt hot, not in the physical sense, of course, but in that other, more metaphysical way. I wanted to leave it alone but I couldn't let it just sit there. My fingers carefully pinched open the corners of the note, and a different, more meticulous handwriting greeted me:

Good evening, Ms. Johnson,

Please take note of page 7.

Sincerely,
Dr. Monroe

At first I thought, "fuck him," because how could he even think my mother loved me. However, in that moment, like the moment at Nana Grace's funeral, there was little of me I controlled, and I began to read:

"*What is REAL?*" *asked the Rabbit one day ... "Does it mean having things that buzz inside you and a stick-out handle?"*

"*Real isn't how you are made,*" *said the Skin Horse. "It's a thing that happens to you. When a child loves you for a long time, not just to play with, but REALLY loves you, then you become real.*"

"*Does it hurt?*" *asked the Rabbit.*

"Sometimes," said the Skin Horse, for he was always truthful. "When you are REAL you don't mind being hurt."

"Does it happen all at once, like being wound up," he asked, "or bit by bit?"

"It doesn't happen all at once," said the Skin Horse. "You become. It takes a long time. That's why it doesn't often happen to people who break easily, or have sharp edges, or who have to be carefully kept. Generally, by the time you are Real, most of your hair has been loved off, and your eyes drop out and you get loose in the joints and very shabby. But these things don't matter at all, because once you are Real you can't be ugly except to people who don't understand."

I didn't exactly see myself as the rabbit then. I should have, probably was supposed to, but how often does the outer eye see the inner self clearly, especially when you're young?

But I was Rabbit back then. I was already shedding velveteen and leaking strands of stuffing through threadbare patches in my skin. I wouldn't want to believe my Skin Horse when he would say bluntly (because he was always truthful) that the price of being real was pain. Who in their right mind would want to know up front that becoming real meant bone deep suffering until you were blind and shabby? Truth be told, the bunny must have thought that his Skin Horse was delusional when he said that growing shabby wouldn't matter at all, because once you are real you couldn't be ugly, except to people who didn't understand. There are more folks out there that can't tolerate ugly than can understand real. The bunny knew this, and I knew it too.

13

I GOT SOME SLEEP, BUT not the good kind, not the kind that conferred alertness as a grand prize for having closed my eyes. I woke up in a panic crying for my father.

"Daddy, Daddy!" Those words exploded off my lips and bounded into the silence of my room. The panic in my voice pulled my body up bolt straight, and I sat in my bed wreathed in a sweaty tangle of sheets, shivering. It took me a few moments to realize I had been dreaming about being small and lost. I tried to call back the exact details of what had happened, but all I could remember was that the dream was about my father.

Suddenly, my room was suffused with the sickly, sweet odor of rotting apples. I wanted to call the smell imaginary, but I knew better. *This is augury*, I thought, and then the sunlit but empty corner of my room became full of the disembodied voice of a woman. "Go look in the closet," the voice said.

I knew it was Nana Grace speaking through an invisible slit in the veil between here and there. I also knew what closet she meant. It was a room in the back of the basement, sealed shut by a heavy, locked door and my Mama's barbed will. It was a place I had been beaten for going into when I was ten and still too innocent or ignorant to realize my survival depended on stealth. The little wounded girl inside me, the one who knew the acid kiss of mama's strap, twittered, *"careful, careful, careful,"* but I had orders to set sail into the unknown, and fear was not something I could use as an anchor.

I glanced at the clock as I dressed. It was after ten on Sunday, and Mama was off in church singing and praying that I would be changed. If I was lucky, the Reverend Thornton would preach one of his long, convoluted sermons, and I would have a couple of hours to look for what I was supposed to discover. On my way down to the kitchen, I searched for Jamila and was relieved to find that she had either gone to church or had snuck out to be with the horny, knuckle-headed boyfriend Mama didn't know about.

The basement door squealed when I opened it, and I froze. I waited for hidden trouble to come and find me, but nothing slithered out. Satisfied, I flicked on the wall switch and followed a flood of buttery colored light between boxes and other discarded items toward the back of the house. The door to the closet was as I remembered it, pale gray and featureless, built more to keep things out than in. I grabbed the knob, fully expecting a lock would dig in its heels. Instead, there was a soft pop, and the door swung open.

Cool air, scented with the smell of old clothes and the jasmine undercurrents of Nana Grace's perfume, rushed out. Ancient whispers guided my hands to the length of cord that controlled the light. With a jerk of my arm, I threw back the darkness to reveal a fabric-laden landscape of neatly hung men's suits and shirts.

"These are your father's possessions," Nana Grace whispered.

My breathing grew so shallow I almost fainted. With trembling fingers, I reached for the sleeve of a gray suit, one that seemed familiar. I pulled it off its hanger and put it on. I wanted to stay cradled for a few moments in something that had once held my father, but caution chased away the desire to linger. I had been sent for something else, something infinitely more important.

I was moved to plunge my hands past a line of shirts and pull from a hidden shelf a bulky shoebox. My arm grew thick crops of goose bumps as I pulled the lid off and extracted a large, cushioned manila envelope. Time had burned the edges of it sepia, but the ink used to sign the front was still bright. The envelope was addressed with my name and was etched with the disturbing line, "In the event of my death."

Nerves sucked my mouth desert dry and tried to unbolt my knees. More than anything, I wanted to collapse to the floor and examine the contents. But my new treasure could only be scrutinized later, when I was safe in my room.

I thought I was home free. I thought time and a bad sermon were on my side, but I was wrong. The ancestors had bestowed upon me their boon and then decided to see if I deserved the gift.

"What are you doing in here?" My mother's voice spun me around. She was standing smack in the middle of the doorway, hands on her hips and head cocked. In the dim light, I tried to read the temperature of her rage. She was hot, but I sensed her anger was mixed with other emotions because her bottom lip was trembling, and her eyes were wet with some kind of pain or sorrow.

"The door was locked, Grace. How did you get in here?"

I didn't answer because the truth was not something she would have accepted, and I was not in the mood to lie.

I slid the envelope under my father's coat and strapped my arms tight against my chest.

"What are you stealing?"

I could tell from the look on her face she knew exactly what I had found. "I believe my father intended for me to have this. I don't think it's considered stealing if it's addressed to you."

"You need to give that to me, Grace. We can talk about it later."

"I'll never see it again," I shouted. "You'll destroy it and pretend like it never existed."

"Grace, take off that coat, and give me that envelope."

"No."

Because she thought things were the same between us, she took a step forward, expecting me to surrender. But things weren't the same, because the day before, all my spiritual furniture had been moved and all the metaphysical locks changed. I stepped back, not out of

fear but to brace myself before I hurled my full weight toward the
door. Mama screamed as I hit her and charged past. My quick footfalls on the stairs mimicked the racing of my heart. I slammed the
basement door and flew outside. I couldn't keep what I had unless I
gave it away, so I ran over to Monroe's house and began to bang on
the door. Monroe didn't answer, but a young man did. I didn't have
time to fully consider who he was. All I thought was that if he was in
the house, then he probably knew Monroe.

"Is Dr. Monroe home?" I managed to wheeze.

The man's gaze took me in. I must have looked like something off
a bad TV show about teens, but his eyes didn't betray that he found
anything strange.

"No, he's not in," he finally said. "I'm his son."

"Evan," I said more to myself.

He smiled. "Yes, Evan. Do you need to come in?"

I considered the request and shook my head no. "Please, I need
for you to give him something. I think he'll know what to do with it.
And if my mother comes by, you haven't seen me, okay?"

"Okay," Evan said as he opened the door to take in my strange
offering. "Who are you?"

"My name is Grace," I yelled over my shoulder as I took off to go
hide out at Shanta's. "Your father knows who I am."

With a ton of trouble and all its consequences weighing me down,
I ran toward Shanta's house. The Mannings lived only a couple of
blocks away, but it seemed like an eternity before I reached their huge,
Queen Anne style home and the beautiful porch that necklaced it. In
a pond of shadows by the porch swing, I submerged myself and tried
to keep a breath down long enough to nourish my lungs. I wanted to
stay hidden at least until I could put enough words together to make
a coherent sentence. I realize now I was making so much noise that
the dead had no choice but to wake up and go tell someone living to
come help me.

Mrs. Manning came running out in a panic, looking for what
was suffering on her porch. She is what Joe would call a biscuit type
of woman, short, round, ginger-colored and soft enough in spirit to

help folks sop up their pain and sorrow. Her eyes pounced into the darkness and pulled it apart until she saw me.

"Grace, baby, what's the matter? Are you hurt?" She rushed up and flung her arms around me.

"I need to talk to Mr. Manning about my father."

"Ah, your dad," Mrs. Manning whispered. Her hand began to stroke the jacket I had on as she realized my request was part of the answer to her unspoken question about why I was dressed so strangely.

"Is he here?" I asked.

"Yes, baby, he is." She took my hand and led me into the house. "Do you want me to call Shanta? She's babysitting for the Grahams down the street."

"No, not yet."

Jazz was flowing from down a hall off the living room. Mrs. Manning had been painting, redecorating the house for Shanta's and my graduation party. I took in the changes she had made to the walls and the curtains.

"Looks nice," I commented as we walked toward the music.

"Thank you." Mrs. Manning surveyed her work with satisfaction before pushing open the door to the den.

Coltrane baptized us as we entered Mr. Manning's sanctuary of books and music. Neatness was not Charles Manning's forte, and in order to save her meticulous sanity, Mrs. Manning had swept him and his passions into one room. When he wasn't working, and it was rare when he wasn't at one of his three jobs, he was sequestered in his space, listening to music and dreaming about writing novels when he finally retired.

"Hey, Grace," he shouted when he saw me. The music descended into a soft whisper as he pressed the remote and got up out of his recliner to hug me. He was a tall man, as lean as his wife was round. Shanta had gotten his height, good looks and the powerful intellect that prowled ever hungry behind his almond-shaped eyes.

"Charles, she's here to talk about her father," Mrs. Manning explained. "And I think this time ..."

She didn't finish the sentence, because the look on his face told her she didn't need to.

The door snapped softly behind her, and Mr. Manning fell back into his recliner. Sadness watered down his smile. With a wave of his hand, he offered me the seat across from him.

"That your daddy's coat?" he asked.

"Yes, I found it this morning, along with something else."

"Thought so. He was always into gray."

For a long time, the only conversation between us was Coltrane's fussing until Mr. Manning cleared his throat. "You know, Grace, I'm so proud of both you girls. My baby's off to Harvard, and you're going to Spelman—although I do wish Shanta was heading South like you. You know how I feel: the blacker the college, the sweeter the knowledge."

I had to chuckle to myself. Mr. Manning was the only one I knew who wasn't all out happy about his daughter's fully paid trip to the Ivy League. Shanta's mother was another story. She was so high on proud, she would have had to point her toes for her feet to touch the ground. Mr. Manning had spent a great deal of time tying Shanta down to a more racial view of reality, and he was worried she would lose her blackness out in that elite white world.

"Shanta's too much like you," I assured him. "She'll come back different because you can't go anywhere really and not come back different, but she'll still be much the same."

He laughed in agreement. "You know your daddy would have been so proud of you."

I nodded. I didn't really know what to say. My father was a stick figure, a mere shadow that played with me in my four-year-old memory. He was a story here or there, a mummy of tiny remembrances wrapped up tight in Mama's refusal to talk about him or his life.

"He loved both his girls, but you, Grace, he was convinced you were going to be something else, something very special."

In that moment—that something—that so-called thing that was special, grabbed my tongue. "How did my father really die, Mr. Manning?"

The flow of time seemed to wither down to match the whisper of my breathing and the slowing clap of my heart. I closed my eyes and waited for what seemed like a long sip of eternity.

"You deserved an answer the last time you asked, Grace," Mr. Manning explained, "but you know how it is sometimes. You don't do what's right because it hurts too much. Your daddy was the best friend, maybe the only real friend I ever had." He sighed and ran his hand through his thinning Afro. He looked at me as if he still couldn't decide what to say or how to say it.

"I know this," he finally said. "Your father didn't commit suicide. Your dad was having problems with your mother. He was talking about divorcing her, but he wasn't suicidal. Lot's of folks, especially lots of black folks, believed it was a hate crime. But there wasn't any real proof, and the police didn't see any reason to investigate further. Your mother just accepted the report."

I held my breath and sat with that information setting off explosions inside me.

"So, Grace, are you going to tell me what happened to make you run up here? You mentioned that you found something else besides the coat."

I told Mr. Manning about the envelope and my confrontation with Mama, but I didn't reveal where I had hidden it.

"It was like Samuel to be prepared," he said.

"What I don't understand is why she destroyed all his pictures but kept his other stuff."

"Grief does strange things to people, Grace."

I shook my head in disbelief. "I don't think my mother is grieving. I've never seen her cry about my father. She won't even talk about him."

"That may be part of the problem."

"Grace," Mrs. Manning's head appeared in the door. "I'm sorry, but your mother is here."

I sighed. "Not as sorry as I am."

"I'll talk to her," Mr. Manning said.

"She won't listen."

"I think she will."

I was dubious and then some. As I got up, I removed the coat and laid it on the chair. If I didn't leave it with Mr. Manning, Mama would find some way to make it vanish.

"I'll take good care of it," he whispered.

Mama was waiting in the living room, trying to make small talk with Mrs. Manning. Mrs. Manning, who had never really liked my mother, was doing her best to pretend she was listening without rolling her eyes.

"I'm afraid I have an announcement to make," Mama began. "I'm going to have to punish Grace by not allowing her to have a graduation party. It seems she has stolen something from me."

There was a moment of stunned silence. I forced myself to study the rug. This, I suspected, was only the beginning of her revenge.

"You can't be serious. Grace has done so well in school," Mrs. Manning said.

"I won't be contributing to the party, I'm sorry. Now, if Grace were to give me back what she stole …" Mama's voice was all poison dipped in honey.

I looked up from the rug and stared at Mama. A stare meant to warn her that I was willing to suffer and fight for what I now knew belonged to me. "I'll die before I give you the envelope back."

Mrs. Manning gasped. "Grace, you don't mean that."

She thought I was being overly dramatic, pushed to the edge by hormones and my mother's unexpected announcement of my punishment. Mr. Manning, however, knew I meant it.

"Miriam," he said, "I think we need to step in the kitchen and talk."

"Nothing to talk about, Charles," Mama said.

Something broke inside him, and the truth tumbled out. "Samuel gave me the envelope to hold for Grace a few weeks before he died. He told me to make sure she got it when she was older. I gave it to you, Miriam, because I thought, who better than her mother to keep that kind of thing. Obviously, I was wrong. I owe Grace an apology for not following her father's directions. Grace hasn't stolen anything that wasn't hers to begin with. If anybody should be punished, you should be, but maybe what went around is coming back around. There will be a party, and Grace will be there. And I don't want your money. I'll do your share in memory of my friend."

Mama didn't say anything because there was nothing she could say. She had been caught in an old web of deceit made from hundreds of lies.

14

WHEN MAMA AND I GOT home, Mama went to her room and slammed the door. From the hall, I could hear her begin to quote scripture, but the meaning of the words escaped me, drowned in the undercurrents of her violent sobbing. I wanted to name her tears something simple, like embarrassment or humiliation, but the sound of raw grief echoed in her wailing. My mama stood in need of comfort. She stood in need of prayer but I couldn't find it in myself yet to do for her what she hadn't done for me. The only compassion I offered was to touch her door before I went and locked myself in my room.

I did the last of my homework, literally dotting the I's and crossing the T's on my childhood. Then I napped hard, like my past had been simple and my future was going to be even less complicated. I slept the sleep of the dead who are at peace. It was the last good sleep I would have for a long, long time.

What woke me was the high-pitched escalating whistle that follows in the wake of a heavy thing dropping from very far up in the sky. The bed shook like it had been hit, and I woke up expecting to find war, a catastrophe, or worse, my mother wrecking everything in my bedroom. Instead, the only thing I found was my scared self and the honking of an alarm clock. I was starving, and I followed the direct order of my stomach to get up and eat.

Jamila had the TV turned up loud, and curiosity about the volume drew me to hover between the dark of the foyer and the living room. She was propped up in a nest of couch pillows, watching a soap opera and painting her nails some exotic shade of red. For a long moment, I marveled at how she expertly laid down a shimmery layer of polish on nails that arched out like the petals of some rare, showy orchid. This was a body art I had never even tried to master, because polish on my nails would only highlight the damage done by the clinch and grind of my teeth.

"Hey, Jamila," I shouted over the voices of two actresses fitfully quarreling about how they were in love with the same man.

Her head jerked as if a spitball had hit her, but she didn't unhook her face from her nail work to acknowledge my presence. "Mama went to the evening prayer service, and she told me to tell you to keep your ass at home," she said.

"Jamila, I found some of daddy's—" The sound of the doorbell cut off my sentence.

Out on the porch was a dark-skinned man. He looked geek sharp in a black suit and white shirt with a stiff pink tie that hung down like it had been ordered to stand at attention. I looked at him askance, my whole face a sharp angled frown tersely asking: *Who the hell are you?* If I had been less wary, more alert I would have noticed that except for a more narrow face, kinder eyes and much taller frame, he was a beardless version of his father, Dr. Monroe.

"Grace." He tipped his head as if he believed a slanted profile of his features would render him more recognizable. "I'm Evan. Remember? From this morning?"

"Oh," I opened the screen and stuck my head out.

"I saw your mother leave, and I thought I would come over and check and see if you were all right."

I loved his voice; it was creamy, like a fresh cube of caramel. "I'm fine. I was a little freaked out when I saw you this morning. I'm sorry I disturbed you."

"Nothing to be sorry for. I gave the package to Dad as soon as he came home."

Hearing that the package was safe made me sigh hard and loud. It was an awkward sound, and I laughed to cover my embarrassment. "You just don't know ..."

"Glad I could help."

A mouthful of perfect white petals of teeth bloomed against his gingerbread dark skin, and desire began to spring up.

"Grace, who are you talking to?" My sister shouted from the living room. I glanced behind me, longing for privacy. *Retreat or advance*, I wondered.

"It's just a salesperson," I shouted before I slid free of the door and let it snap close behind me.

I looked like crap, but I assured myself that compared to that morning, I at least looked sane. Still, as I breathed in the grassy scent of his cologne, I wished that I had my sister's show orchid nails and long, bone-straight hair. I wished with all my heart that I were somewhere closer to being model-thin instead of heavy.

I shrugged. "My sister Jamila ..."

His smile disappeared. "Yes, we've met."

The ardor that usually swirled through men's voices when they mentioned my sister was missing from his tone. His tone had been cooled and tempered by some sort of revulsion.

"Really," I said, and meant to leave it at that, but curiosity had my tongue. "When did you meet her?"

Evan began rocking back and forth as if he were nervously sifting through his thoughts, trying to separate what he wanted to say from what he felt he could say.

"She came over in the yard the other day while I was reading, and we talked." He paused, I think to decide if I was close to Jamila. "Your sister's a piece of work," he finally commented.

What little family pride I had began to implode. Jamila must have said something really crass, because men usually didn't mind if she acted dense. Beauty in their eyes always seemed to trump intelligence.

"What did she say?"

"She asked me if my father was gay, did that mean I was too?"

"Oh, Jesus," I whispered. It was one of those Wicked Witch of the West moments in life when you wish somebody, anybody would come and pour water on you so you could melt away, leaving nothing behind but a bunch of clothes.

He laughed a bit. "It's okay, I told her it wasn't any of her business, but that I did give her some credit for asking what most people are thinking."

It didn't feel okay. I shook my head. "Look, don't cut my sister any slack. People are always letting things go with her because she's beautiful, so she thinks she can say whatever she wants to. People just ..." I stopped because at that point I thought my embarrassment was veering off into childish envy. "I'm sorry. If you can apologize for someone else, then I'm just so sorry."

"So people must cut you a lot of slack, Grace."

He was so subtle, and I was so completely wrapped up in being mortified that what he said went flying way up over my head, like the frilly skirts of dandelion seeds.

"None," I said.

He chuckled, and his smile became big and bright again. "No, what I mean is that you're beautiful, so people must cut you slack as well."

Warm embarrassment filled my cheeks and cascaded down my neck and into my stomach. I was too embarrassed to smile and he must have thought I didn't approve.

"Sorry if that sounded corny."

"No, don't apologize. I don't get corn that often."

We were standing there all warm and slightly intimate when suddenly my mood turned more cautious. Soon Jamila would assume her role as Mama's other mouth and eyes. Soon enough she would be all in my business, such as it was, turning a nice moment into something ugly.

"I better get going."

He nodded as if he understood why I was nervous. "We'll talk again soon."

"Yeah, well," I said, but what I was really thinking was fat chance, emphasis on fat, because he was just being nice. Men that looked like him didn't think twice about somebody that looked like me.

"I know my dad plans to have you over for dinner tomorrow. He asked me to cook so what do you like to eat?"

"Oh, I'll eat anything," I said. *Now he's just being nice to me,* I thought, because his father wanted him to be.

"How about Jambalaya? That's my specialty."

"That'll be fine."

"Cheese and jalapeno pepper cornbread?"

"Sure."

"Bread pudding for dessert?"

I started laughing. "Anything would be okay."

"Good, I finally made you laugh."

I said goodbye again and slipped back inside. Once I was out of sight, I scrambled to cling to the memory of his cologne and savor the caramelness of his voice. *Smitten,* I thought, when I got to my room. *Damn, I think I'm smitten.* It was such an old-fashioned word, the kind of word used by old folks in nursing homes, or at church when they were boring you to death by talking about how, back in the day, courting was really about love and not all about sex. It was a sweet word, a word that reminded me of Dinah Washington singing her signature song, "What a Difference a Day Makes" in a sultry, but iridescently happy voice.

*　*　*

I stayed up late reading a slender book of poetry by Lucille Clifton that Ms. Watanabe had given me as an early graduation gift.

"I'm going to miss you, Grace," she had told me as I unwrapped it.

"You were my North Star," I said, and we shared a long, teary hug in celebration of my escape to college and adulthood.

The phone rang, and I thought it had to be Shanta so I picked up without looking at the Caller ID.

I was astonished when Dr. Monroe's voice slid out. "I see you've been stealing fire from the gods, Ms. Johnson."

I thought about his comment and snapped back, "unlike Prometheus, I didn't steal anything that didn't already belong to me."

Dr. Monroe's laughter was more sonorous than his son's.

"Good one," he said, and I soaked up the water of his approval like the tiny seed I was then. "We need to meet and talk over some things."

"Yes, I saw your son this afternoon, and he said that you might be inviting me to dinner."

There was a long moment of silence full to its brim with dark disapproval. I sensed I had stirred up the beginning of a storm that was going to be all wind, lightening and no calm center.

"My son came over?" Monroe asked. But the question was rhetorical. He didn't need or want my answer. "Seven o'clock tomorrow." His words rode just above the whirling edge of his annoyance.

I was about to say, "I'll be there," but he had already hung up.

15

Even with all that had happened the day before, I still had to get up and go to school. Papers were due, and I had to attend graduation rehearsal or I wouldn't have been allowed to march. I got dressed and hoped the image in the mirror was lying about the fact that I looked like I had stains from coffee mugs around my eyes.

Jamila confirmed the mirror wasn't lying. "You look like hell," she said as I entered the living room to pick up my book bag before dragging myself into the kitchen.

I nodded, half in agreement, half to get her to leave me alone. She, of course, was goddess-from-some-other-planet-beautiful in a yolk yellow summer dress. Her smooth soft tongues of hair taunted my nappier ones about being drunk and disorderly. Mama sat at the kitchen table, hunched over a cup of coffee as if a night's worth of resentment was piled up on the back of her head. I was feeling bold enough to enter and found enough respect to move my lips.

"Good morning, Mama," I mouthed.

My mother waited until I turned my back to get down a cereal bowl, before brandishing her verbal knife.

"I can't believe you belong to me," she snapped.

I was supposed to take the cut and watch silently as my self-esteem ran warm and sticky as blood down the sides of my legs. I wanted desperately to shout back, "you know, I been wondering about that too." But as I looked into the belly of the bowl I was clutching, I realized that the night before, I'd discovered there were tender places on my mother-thickened soul. Places that I could attempt to stroke rather than stab.

"What was my father like?" I whispered.

A turbulent river of silence began to flow between us that grew higher and wider as the seconds crept by. Before the powerful currents of her wordless malice could sweep away my courage, I turned around to face her.

"Am I like him?" I demanded.

The question jerked Mama's head up. Her eyes were pinched into hooded slits. "You're like him ... too damn much like him," she snarled.

I wanted to throw the bowl against the wall and let the shower of shards speak for me, but why sink to her terrifying level of anger? I had asked and she had, to the best of her sorry-ass ability, answered. It wasn't the response I wanted or needed, but it was, I realized, the only one she could, at that moment, bring herself to give me. I sat the bowl down on the counter and looked at my watch. I needed to be up and gone because I was going to have to walk to school. Mama wasn't about to drive me, and besides, sane rabbits didn't kick wolves and then get into a small-enclosed space with them.

"Goodbye, Mama," I called out as I picked up my book bag. I didn't wait to see if she answered.

* * *

Two miles lay in front of me, and I had an hour before the start of first period. The sun was bringing up a full skirt of blue sky; the day was going to be pretty. I shifted my burden to hang on both shoulders and began walking. I was thinking so hard about hurrying I didn't notice a bright green car following me. Loud music, the kind that ordered young bodies to get on up and dance, dance, dance, finally caught my attention. I leaned down, expecting to see someone I didn't know in need of directions. Instead, I found a grinning, car-happy Shanta.

"Come on," she yelled over the joyous panting of her speakers.

I stood there all smiles, the tired draining out of my body because Shanta was happy.

"How you livin', Grace?" she asked. As I crawled into her new car, I turned down the music from a roar to a distant purr.

"Obviously not as well as you. This your new ride?"

Shanta laughed. "Yeah, my daddy surprised me with it yesterday. It's used …"

"Used is better than a bike or bus. Remember, the one-eyed woman is queen in the city of the blind," I said as I threw my book bag in the back seat.

"I was going to come by yesterday to show you, but I figured you were on lockdown."

"You guessed right," I grunted. It felt good to be able to finally let down my guard. I leaned back in the seat and relaxed. I expected Shanta to take off, but Shanta being Shanta needed to see if I was really all right so she pulled over to the curb and put the car in park.

"I also thought your Mama wouldn't be giving you a ride," she said.

"You're right again. Your parents tell you what happened yesterday?"

"Yeah. God, Grace, I don't even know what to say."

"Say my mother is fucking nuts, that's all you need to say." I sighed and told Shanta what had happened with Mama after I had gotten home, and how Monroe's son had come over later to see if I was fine.

"So what do you think is in the envelope?" Shanta asked.

"Don't know. I don't think Mama knew either. Maybe I'll find out tonight when I have dinner with Dr. Monroe. It will be nice to maybe see Evan again."

Shanta smiled. "So, is Evan cute?"

I laughed. "He doesn't have his father's praying mantis features so yeah, he's cute."

"You know, I keep thinking I've heard that name before."

Shanta began to repeat Evan's full name slowly, as if she was blowing dirt off each letter in order to uncover clues. When she was finished she began to pant, "oh, oh, oh," like she had finally discovered the treasure she had been looking for and it was better than she imagined.

"Grace, he's famous," she squealed.

I looked at Shanta to see if she was serious. It wasn't often Shanta squealed about anything, especially famous people.

"Oh come on, you're kidding, right?"

"No! Grace, he was a competitor on one of those reality cooking shows on the Food Network last year. My dad watches it all the time. He won. He got a boat load of money and a cookbook deal."

I shrugged because I was clueless. What did I know given that Mama hadn't purchased anything beyond basic cable. "Makes sense. He said Dr. Monroe had asked him to cook dinner. I just thought, you know, he was just being nice."

"Shoot, I'm not even going to say anything to my dad because he would be beating on Dr. Monroe's door tonight asking for samples and an autograph. Hell, I almost want to ask you to save me some scraps. You can stick stuff in your purse, pretend you have a dog or something."

I started to giggle, and we both fell out laughing until I reminded her of the time. We were about two blocks from school, stuck at the first set of long lights when I asked, "how was the prom last Saturday?"

Shanta shook her head. "Girl, you know, same old folks and fools, just better dressed. Calvin—that boy, and I do mean boy—went and got drunk. I ended up having to drive him home. Then he had the nerve to be pissed at me because I wouldn't give him none."

"Well, at least you have someone."

"Maybe you can date Evan."

"Yeah, right," I said. Smitten was one thing, reality was another. Especially when Evan was older and famous.

Shanta shrugged. "Well anyway, I'm beginning to think maybe my father is right. He keeps telling me that when it comes to men, not having one is better than dating some idiot. Dad never liked Calvin anyway."

"Speaking of idiots," I said, "did Ronald end up taking Nikki to the prom?"

"No," Shanta said slowly. "I guess you wouldn't have heard. Nikki just found out she's pregnant."

"You're kidding." My jaw dropped, and I reached to cover the long circle of my mouth with my hand.

"No, unfortunately I'm not. What's worse is Ronald's being an asshole about it. He keeps telling people it isn't his."

I hated hearing the news. I didn't particularly like Nikki but she didn't deserve what had happened.

"It's awful," Shanta continued. "I've heard Ronald's mama knows it's his and she's going to make sure Ronald takes care of her grandbaby, but she doesn't care too much for Nikki. Nikki's daddy's about to disown her because the closest he wants black folks to him is on the TV, not in his family. And her mother isn't too comfortable with the fact her grandchild is going to be some shade of mocha. All Nikki's going to be is Ronald's baby's mama which means she'll get a child support check ..."

"But not his love," I said, finishing her sentence, "and what she really wants is his love."

I struggled to keep my concerns for Nikki folded up and shoved deep in some emotional closet, but when tears began to plummet down the hills of Shanta's cheeks, everything I felt about the whole situation pushed against the door of my composure and tumbled out. We drove and cried, circling the parking lot outside the school like disoriented birds until Shanta found a student parking space. We pulled ourselves together with tissues and reassurances.

"It will be all right," Shanta whispered as we surged through a mass of chattering underclassmen.

I began to tremble. It was not a hard shaking, just a minor fluttering of my hands, as if my fingers were thin leaves and a brisk wind were licking them. Nobody else would have noticed, but Shanta did, and she leaned in so our arms smacked against each other as we walked.

"It's a soul tremor," she said softly, in a voice that was of her but not really from her. She then pulled off to go to her class, leaving it at that, as if I fully understood that a soul tremor was a sign of the big one, a sign that a magnitude nine spiritual awakening of the will of God and the ancestors was about to rumble across the fault line of my soul. I didn't fully understand back then. I thought the tremor was all about Nikki. I thought I was just feeling bad for her.

* * *

Graduation rehearsal was a long, dreary affair, more about how not to embarrass our parents than how to enjoy ourselves. I was drifting in jerky starts and stops toward a nap when I heard our ferret-faced principal say in his little ferret voice, "okay, ladies and gentlemen, you're free for the day. Graduation is on Thursday at six sharp. Please wear suitable attire underneath your gowns, and remember, naked is not considered suitable attire."

We laughed and swarmed out the auditorium doors like bees from a toppled hive. Shanta was valedictorian, so she had to stay after to practice her speech. I was on my own for another hour, and I was trying to decide if I should just walk home and take a nap when Joe came up beside me.

"Hey, Grace, what up?" he asked

I smiled, "Hey, Joseph, what up with you?"

"You okay?"

"Yeah, I'm fine."

We shared a moment of awkward quiet.

"What, you don't have a reputation to protect anymore?" I joked.

He looked away from me to some far off point down the hall because he already knew what I was going to accuse him of.

"Four years, Joe, and you never, ever really talked to me during school."

I was sort of kidding, just poking fun at the nature of the high school food chain. Joe had been one of the mighty whales, and I had been one of the fish the whales fed on. I expected Joe to laugh, but he didn't. His eyes came back to look at me saddled with regret. "I'm really sorry about that, Grace."

Sorry. I repeated the word like I had never heard it before. Joe had never expressed any type of sorry except maybe to say to his boys, "yeah, my cousin Grace, she's just sorry."

"It's okay," I said, trying to smooth down the surprise in my voice.

He shook his head slowly as if he were using it as an eraser to wipe a slate clean. "Shouldn't have treated you that way, but I'm gonna try to make it up to you."

As paper-shallow as I was back then, all I could think was dinner, maybe he would take me out to eat. However, my cousin had been diving for pearls of wisdom in the depths of his conscience. I watched as he reached into his pockets and removed a set of keys that he held up for me to admire like a piece of jewelry I had always wanted.

"Aunts say you don't know how to drive."

I grew uncomfortable as I wondered how this bitter nugget of information had come up in their conversation. I was ashamed that I couldn't drive. Mama had prevented me from learning, in part because driving would have fostered the development of independence, and independence would have taught me how to follow my internal north star out of her darkness and into a brighter, saner world.

"Our aunts say you need to learn," he said, offering me a crescent moon smile.

I still didn't move because I was afraid to trust my hopes.

"Come on," Joe said. "I see your girl Shanta got a car. I know you want that. Don't even lie and say you don't." He leaned down and pressed the keys into my needy palm, and my fingers swallowed the cluster of metal. Using two strides to match his one, I bounded down the hall after him.

The parking lot was full of graduates waiting for the future to begin. We had gathered in our traditional species' groups and were still acting like nothing would ever change. It hadn't occurred to us the mighty could fall and the nerdy could rise. The past would predict the future because what the hell did we know.

Joe's usual crew didn't let their surprise that he was hanging out with me simmer among themselves. They howled and hooted at him. As long as the whirls of insults were aimed at him, Joe didn't seem to care. He walked as if they weren't there, as if whatever score they were racking up with him would be settled later. It was when the conversational winds shifted and the verbal spit began to be about me, fat Grace, that he decided to become a knight and snap on some shining armor. When we reached his car, he opened the door and motioned with his head for me to get in. Anger had folded his face into narrowed eyes and a slit of lips.

I felt I had to say, "Joe, leave it alone. It's not worth it," because one wrong move on school property and he would be wearing Halloween orange jail clothes instead of his green and gold cap and gown for graduation.

"Get in, and you stay in, Grace. I mean it," he said, waving his finger like it was a wand with enough magic in it to hold me in place. Reluctantly, I climbed in to the warm silence of his car and let the heat seal me to the fake leather. He made the door clap hard like a tall stack of books falling. I winced and pressed my face against the glass like a dejected dog.

Joe crossed the parking lot like he had a ball under his arm and a Friday night crowd cheering him on. At first, I thought he was going to use his fists to say what was on his mind; the old Joe would have. The new Joe, the one I had just met in the hall, heaved himself up to his full height and stood there in front of his boys with a grown man's authority. It is a sign of true power when little has to be said for things to be done. Joe's mouth flapped wide a few times before his boys backed up and scattered. He came back to the car, bouncing on his feet like a warrior dancing after a successful hunt.

"Because you don't have a permit, we're going out in the country on some back roads. Then I'm gonna let you have the wheel," Joe said as he climbed into the car.

"You know you didn't have to defend my honor," I said, as I watched him check the mirrors and turn on the engine.

"What kind of man would I be, Grace, if I didn't? Like I said, I mean to make things up to you."

We rode along in the kind of fertile silence that nurtured my sense of being secure and protected.

"You know," Joe began, "the friends I have now, they ain't never going to be nothing. They're going to spend the rest of their lives smoking weed, drinking, and dreaming 'bout back in the day. I was on my way to being just like that until the aunts hired me to drive them around and do some of their errands and yard work, you know?"

I nodded, even though I hadn't known he had been doing all of that for Aunt Peaches and Aunt Casmil.

"Yesterday," Joe continued, "I was talking to them about getting a new car. I was just being selfish. I was thinking if I had to drive these women around, then the least they could do is get a new ride."

I offered Joe a look of incredulity, and he gave me a sheepish grin. "Yeah, I know, Grace, but like I said, I was just being selfish. Anyway, I thought they were going to say no right off, so I had my speech together. But Casmil looked at me hard, and she said, 'Joseph, you're right. We do need to get a new car.' Now I'm thinking, sweet, when do we go down to the dealership? But Peaches, she just smiled and laid this on me. She says, 'Joseph, we'll get a new car, but we don't want you getting used to driving us around because my sister and I think the future has better things in store for you.' I didn't know what they were thinking, so I asked, 'Like what?' Now Casmil gave me this look like maybe she had socks that were smarter than I am, but Peaches, she smiled and said, 'College, Joseph, we think you need to go to college.'"

Joe stopped talking then, as if he had to go inside and savor again the full sweet beauty of what the sisters thought of him. After a few moments, he said with a little awe, "nobody, Grace, not even my mother thought I could maybe go to college."

I didn't lie and say I did, because frankly like everyone else, I had whittled Joe down to just a job at the Pump and Go, if that. Smart had never seemed Joe's forte, but I thought nobody had ever really asked him to be smart. They had just asked him to run fast and tackle people on the football field. Nobody had ever had expectations for my cousin beyond what they thought his body could do, except for our aunts, whose inner eyes saw deep into souls and far into the future.

"They said I could go to a community college first, get my grades up and then transfer to a four year university later. What do you think about that, Grace?"

"I think that's a great idea, Joe," I agreed. "Maybe since I'm becoming a Spelman woman, you could become a Morehouse Man. We could be in college together."

* * *

Joe let me drive along empty roads that ran like neatly braided plaits of hair across the scalps of farmlands.

"Push the pedal harder, Gracie," he kept telling me. "It's just like learning to slow dance. After awhile, you'll be the one leading all the time."

I leadened my foot with a little more courage, until the car began to move faster. Joe laughed when I made my wobbly first left and right turns. When I almost took the car off the road and into a ditch and wanted to quit, he made me learn to back up. Only when I could aim the car and follow some of the simple lines of directions he had plotted out for the car did he let me stop.

"Good job," Joe said as we climbed out to exchange sides. I was exhausted, and for just a moment I draped myself against the passenger side door. I had closed my eyes and was letting the sun massage the taut lines of tension in my jaw when I heard a man call my name. It sounded far off, as if he were shouting from across a huge field or from the other end of a very long hall, but it was definitely my full birth name. I whipped around, but all I found were fields of very young corn on one side and a huddle of black and white cows on the other.

"What's the matter, Grace?" Joe asked over the roof, his eyes trying to follow where mine had gone.

"Nothing," I said tentatively. "I just thought I heard somebody calling me." I tried to play it off, but deep down I was rattled. Stuff was falling off my mental shelves, and cracks were forming along the ceilings and floors of my brain. Fine tremors flowed through my hands, and muscles quavered in my legs. Sweat began to mist my skin even though the back of my neck was slightly frosty, and a line of chills formed along my spine. Damp and cold, I opened the car door and dropped nervously into the seat.

Joe got in on the other side. "My mama said the old folk used to say you shouldn't turn around when you hear your name called unless you know someone is really there because it might be spirits coming after you." He paused and then glanced at me. "So are they?"

I wanted to tell Joe his mother was just full of her usual paranoid, government conspiratorial shit, but even as mystically ignorant as I was back then, I knew she and the old folks were right.

"I don't know. I don't think I'll know until tonight."

"Tonight. What's happening tonight?" Joe asked.

I told him about Monroe, and then I told him everything except how I felt about Evan. My budding crush was the kind of thing only a sister-friend would truly understand.

"Jesus, Grace," he said when I finished, because like Shanta he didn't know exactly what to say.

I had to smile when Joe reached and turned the radio to a jazz station he knew I liked to listen to. In ways both big and small he was trying to make things right with me. It felt nice, but I didn't want to be greedy, so as we hit the highway on the way back to the house I encouraged him to switch to one of his favorite stations. The upswing of an Ornette Coleman set gave way to the staccato word spitting of some musician who was much younger and more forceful. Joe began to bounce and sing. That song ended, and something that sounded to me like the same song began, only this time Joe didn't bother to shadow box with the rhythm.

"You know," he said, "this guy's stuff is not real. That's why his whole last CD wasn't any good."

I glanced at Joe. "Okay, so what?"

Joe was a connoisseur of his music the way I was about mine, but I didn't see the point in discussing Hip-hop's finer points because hell, I could barely understand what they were saying.

"The 'so what' Gracie," Joe said a bit indignantly, "is you have to see your reality for what it is, so you can walk your talk, you see. This boy here ain't rapping about anything he knows, so he's not real, and his music ain't either."

Joe began waving his finger as if he were scolding a child who was crouched and hidden behind the dashboard. "This boy doesn't really own his experiences, so his poetry is weak. It ain't about nothing at all. It's all bread, no meat." Joe laughed, and started to giggle.

"Ok, Joe, I'm feeling you."

The word "poetry," let alone the beginning line of a poem, was the last thing I had expected to come out of my cousin.

"Un huh, you like that, don't you, Gracie," he teased. "See, you're not the only one who can drop some knowledge."

"Never said I was, Joe."

Joe didn't consent to just let me off in front of Mama's house. He demanded I sit in the car until he chivalrously set me free.

"You don't have to do this," I grunted as I climbed out.

"You and me are going to have a talk about why you don't think you deserve to be treated like you're somebody," Joe said.

I shrugged, trying to toss the thought off, but Joe seemed to catch it and haul it back into view. "Maybe I don't need to be talking to you," he said bitterly. "Maybe I need to be talking to your messed up mama. Because, Gracie, it don't matter what she or anybody says, you're a beautiful lady both inside and out."

I began to walk away, but Joe wasn't going to let me wiggle out of the net of his compliment so easily.

"I mean it, Gracie," he called out after me. "You're real. There aren't too many folks that can say that about themselves."

I turned around and went back to throw my arms around him. Real. In the car, that word had been one flat, smooth, featureless description; an explanation I thought had nothing to do with me. But as I stood on the sidewalk soaking in the warmth of Joe's kindness, the word "real" grew a coat of fur and acquired the beginning of paws and a tail. Swallowing shallow breaths of the newborn summer, I thought about the book that had come to me out of my lost childhood, imagining the bunny asking in a slender, baby voice, "what is real?"

16

"I'M GOING TO MONROE'S HOUSE for dinner. He invited me," I announced to Mama as she sat watching TV in the living room. I waited for an answer even though I hadn't exactly hung a question mark on the end of my sentence.

"You're grown," she said in a low, taut voice.

"Don't wait up," I whispered.

I was surprised there hadn't been more resistance on Mama's part. In the past, a long, drawn-out battle would have ensued. I wondered if Monroe had called and talked to her. Despite my deep curiosity about my father's envelope, anxiety juggled my insides as I walked. Mama's welt of words had the feel of a warning that I was about to take another step too far. In the yawning shadows of the coming evening, I stopped to dance with a strong bout of indecision. One step forward into the unknown had suddenly made me nostalgic for the known, even if the known was full of Mama's craziness. But the world behind me was on fire with burning bridges, so I leadened my resolve with a couple of deep breaths and moved on up the sidewalk.

For some reason related to stupidity, I fully expected Evan to answer the door. When Monroe appeared instead, I had to rush to unravel the wrinkles of disappointment that sprung up suddenly around my mouth and eyes. The sly look of amusement on Monroe's face told me I hadn't been quick enough.

"Hello," I managed to mumble.

"Please come in, Ms. Johnson," he offered.

The interior of Monroe's house could have jumped up out of any of those fancy home magazines. I had to stop myself from gawking at his lavish furnishings. All the art on the walls, all the African masks and sculptures called out to me to stop sailing across the shiny hardwood floors and take in the full beauty of the living room's shorelines. Questions like how, and where, bubbled up out of my wonder, but Monroe seemed unconcerned with my curiosity. The sight of his back and his silence signaled I should follow him. Eventually, we reached the dining room where a table had been elegantly dressed, like a rich woman, in a long flowing lace tablecloth accessorized with china, crystal and silver jewels. It looked beautiful, but I was disappointed to see it was only set for two.

Monroe answered the unasked. "My son will not be joining us tonight, although he did insist on preparing dinner."

He pulled out a chair and motioned for me to have a seat.

"I'm sorry to hear that," I said.

I slid myself into place at the table and tried to convince myself that half a promise kept was better than nothing.

Monroe took the seat opposite me and sat back. "It seems my son is quite *smitten* with you."

He paused deliberately to let that particular word set up in my mind and sink in. He knew what he was doing. Everything, every new feeling I felt for Evan, seized up. "Smitten" was the cold shower. It was the string reminding the buoyant party balloon that no matter how high it flew, its navel was still attached to someone's hand. At that moment, I knew there would be no coincidences or accidents with Monroe. That word, that old-fashioned word, had not jumped up out of his vocabulary; it had come out of mine. The mystery was how had he come by it, how he'd known I'd said it to myself when I was nothing but alone. I opened my mouth to ask and then closed it because I really wasn't ready to know how much of me he could feel, see, and hear.

He leaned forward with a sigh. "I'm going to have to be blunt, Ms. Johnson. Your plate in life is about to become very full. You don't have time to be interested in anyone, especially not my son. The dead, whom I must teach you to serve, are demanding. Right now, they will not tolerate anything less then your full attention and loyalty. What you don't give them of your time and energy they will take in ways you can't even begin to fathom. My son doesn't understand this. In fact, I would go so far as to say he doesn't really believe in any of it. Evan is charming, but right now you don't need charming. Do we understand each other?"

For what must have been a long time, I studied the culinary galaxy of plates and glasses on the table. I suddenly felt confined and frightened. What kind of gift had I been given that I couldn't even have a crush?

"Do we understand each other, Ms. Johnson?" Monroe repeated.

I lifted my eyes up to study the look of deep concern on his face. "Yes, I understand."

He didn't look convinced but he didn't say anything. He stood, reached across the table, and poured me a glass of water I didn't asked for.

"So," he said. "How was your day?"

It seemed like a trivial question, especially given what had just transpired, until I realized that the "how was your day?" was the preface to what would be a long conversation. Answering his question was all about did I, or did I not, trust him. Not as a friend, because he wasn't supposed to be my friend, but as what my Nana Grace had called my Habari gani menta—the one who asked questions and helped me shape my fate from my answers. I decided I did trust him, because he had taken care of my envelope, and, more importantly, he had kept my confidence. With some timid effort, I pulled myself closer to the table so that I could plant one arm to be used as scaffolding for my head. My voice shuddered the way old rusty faucets do when new water spirals up their throats after years of non-use. "My friend Nikki is pregnant," I began, and those drops of words became a slow, halting trickle of facts laced with feelings and observations. I told him everything that happened, from the soul tremors to how I felt Joe was more a brother to me than Jamila could ever be a sister. I admitted that my hatred of my sister and mama had grown, and how I was scared and ashamed of that. I got down to the end, and then, as if all that had come before had been meant to clean out some eternal sediment, I finally added, "something strange happened when Joe took me out driving. Something that scared me. We were standing by the car and I heard somebody call my name loud and clear, but when I turned around, nobody was there. Does it mean anything?"

The news about the voice lifted the feathering of his eyebrows, and the set of his lips became as slender as a whip of licorice. I expected an answer. Something in the way his fingers stroked his forks told me he had one, but all he said after some thought was, "I think it's time for dinner."

Of course I was hungry, so I agreed with him. Monroe excused himself, and in a few moments dinner arrived at the table like floats in a Mardi Gras parade. First, there was a salad of field greens, whose creased and feathery leaves had been laid out as a nest for small green figs that had been split open to hold smooth pebbles of soft cheese and slivers of sugar crusted almonds. The salad was a bright introduction to a steaming mound of jambalaya that was a treasure trove of pearly rice strewn with gems of moist chicken, thick smoky lips of ham and shrimp the size of a big baby's fists. At first I ate like a normal person, nibbling at the salad like I had seen strap-thin models do on TV. But the jambalaya set off something deep in me. It took all my company manners and some fear of looking greedy in a deranged sort of way, to not open my mouth like a growing sinkhole and shovel the food in.

Baby bites, baby bites, I kept reminding myself, until Monroe broke the fast of our non-conversation by saying, "tomorrow at three, you have an appointment with your great-grandmother's attorney concerning her will. You probably know him or have heard of him.

His name is Cedric Blair. He's located on Main Street. I can write it down if you wish."

I shook my head no. I knew where Mr. Blair's office was located. He was the only African-American attorney in town, and anyone black knew where his office was.

"You are to go alone," Monroe continued. "If your mother insists that it is her responsibility to accompany you, inform her she is to call me. That should end the conversation."

I couldn't imagine my mother would give a good damn about what he had to say about anything, but I nodded as a powerful but hidden tide of recollection began to wash up memories of the envy laced gossip I had heard at the funeral about Nana Grace's will.

"So the rumors are true about my inheriting money from my Nana Grace?" I asked.

"Yes. You stand to inherit the bulk of your great-grandmother's estate." Monroe took a sip of water as he studied me for my reaction.

I shifted, letting my fork hover between my mouth and the plate as if to underline my growing sense of mystical confusion.

"She's not dead to me," I confessed in a small voice. "I mean ..."

"Yes," Monroe murmured. "That's because life after death to you is no longer a matter of conjecture or speculation. It is fact."

"Like it is to you, because you knew she was going to die and you knew she would come back to see me the day we met."

"Things did go as planned." Monroe laughed, but I didn't laugh with him.

"How about dessert?" he offered.

Evan had made bread pudding veiled in a pecan bourbon sauce. What was beneath the veil was not the usual cheap quilt of white bread glued together with a spit of eggs and sugar. No, he had designed a thick, fluffy sweet pillow from bread that spoke French and had been allowed to luxuriate in a butter-laden milk bath heavily scented with nutmeg and cinnamon.

"My God, this is so good," I said as thin-skinned raisins fattening on Cointreau burst open on my tongue. I ate until I was delirious with gratification and satisfaction. I felt the warm quiver of a sugar-high crashing. Tiredness was calling sleep, and sleep was coming at a dead run.

I yawned. "So can I see my envelope now?"

I expected Monroe would get up and secure it from its hiding place. Instead, he looked at me and said without any hesitation, "no. Not yet, not tonight."

"Why?" Agitation cut through my composure. I had waited for what was mine, and now he was saying I had to wait some more.

Monroe ignored the question.

"I gave you an assignment the night we met, and I need your assessment of the myth I had you read in my book."

"I want my envelope, Dr. Monroe."

"I want my story, Ms. Johnson."

"You mean the story about the hare and the moon? I read it, but I don't really remember what it was about."

Monroe sipped his water. "You found nothing instructive, nothing meaningful in the story?"

I shook my head because I was angry.

"Then I want you to stand up, and to the best of your meager ability, tell me the story," he ordered.

"I'm not giving you some dumb story," I had the nerve to say, like I wasn't supposed to be scared of him. "I want my envelope."

Monroe smiled the way cats must smile when mice lose their little minds and think that they can jump bad.

"Oba controls the envelope. He now decides when you deserve to get it."

My mouth fell open, and I wondered if Monroe was telling the truth. I decided it had to be the truth because lying about Oba seemed to me almost as bad as lying about God.

"Why do I need to tell you this story?" I asked.

"Because we are from a powerful storytelling tradition," he growled. "So stories are important. I didn't give you this myth for your entertainment. I didn't give it to you so you could lie to me that you didn't remember it. This story owns you and will direct you. It will be your escort into the future. Without full knowledge of what it means, you will be ineffective. So get up and tell me the story."

I stood up and leaned against the table to keep from shaking. I closed my eyes to conjure up the story from Khoi tradition, and it came rising up, fragrant with all its deep meaning.

"The moon," I began, "decided it wanted to tell people what death was like. She chose a tick to carry the message. 'Tick,' she said, 'Go tell people that just as I die and rise again, so they will die and live again.'

"Tick started out with the message, but met up with a Hare who wanted to know where he was going. 'The Moon,' Tick explained, 'told me to go tell people that just as she dies and rises again, so they will die and live again.'

'That's an important message that people need right away,' Hare said. 'I'm faster, why don't you let me deliver it?'

"Tick reluctantly agreed and the Hare ran off with the message, but when he reached people, he announced, 'I'm sent by the moon herself to tell you that just as she dies and doesn't rise again, so you will die and never live again.'

"When the moon found out what Hare had said, she was furious. 'How dare you tell people something I didn't say?'

"She hit the Hare on the nose, and ever since that day the Hare's nose has been split, and people still believe the wrong message."

"So what does this say to you?" Monroe asked.

I dwelled in the dark behind my eyes, playing hide and seek with a thought that seemed so trivial I didn't want to reveal it. But it was all I could come up with and Monroe was waiting.

I said, "I don't understand why the Moon was so pissed off. I mean, it wasn't like the Rabbit deliberately disobeyed her. He just messed up the message. It's like playing that stupid game of Telephone. I mean, we all mess up things we hear and then try to pass on, right?"

"Do you know what the word obey actually means?" he asked softly. He knew I would have to open my eyes to discern if I heard him correctly. I found he was not looking at me, but just beyond my slumped shoulders, as if something new had been put up on the wall and he was considering whether the new thing belonged there. I was tempted to look behind me, but I thought if nothing was actually back there then I would look stupid. I had more than reached my quota of idiocies for that night.

"No," I said in answer to his question. "I don't know, or you wouldn't be asking me."

"Yes. Well the basic meaning of the word obey is 'to hear, to listen', but not just passive listening. The Greeks and Hebrews viewed the word 'obedience' as an active response. One hears, one grasps what is communicated and then one acts on it. So you see, the Hare actually did disobey. He didn't get it right, and the result is a failed message about how the Moon found its immortality through its mortality. How, just as the moon throws off the dark to be reborn in the fullness of the sun's light, so too can we throw off death to find a consciousness which transcends death."

"But in your book you said it wasn't a failed message because the Hare is really a trickster figure. He serves as a lure to the spiritual quest because the challenge to people is to learn to ignore the Hare and to discover what the Moon really said."

Monroe smiled, not the cat smile, but the large gift smile that tells me I have finally learned precisely what he feels I need to know. "So, you did understand."

I didn't smile back. The myth had done its job; it had made me hungry for understanding. It made me ask, "okay, you said it was mine, so what does it mean to me? What happens now?"

Monroe didn't respond immediately. The look on his face became enigmatic. I thought maybe the discussion was over and done for the night but he leaned back in his chair. "Do you really want to know who's been calling you?" he asked.

It was a simple and thin question, but one whose metaphysical mass and spiritual weight sank me back into my chair. I sat there thinking about shedding, about how in my other mysterious gift book, another rabbit, one no less magical than his African brother, had desperately wanted to shed his toyness in order to be flesh and blood real. What was "real" going to mean to me, and how much was

I going to suffer to become this "real?" I said "yes" before "no" had a chance to sprint past it on the way out my mouth.

Monroe's gaze scanned my face, checking my determination for flaws and weaknesses. When he seemed to find none, he said, "all right, Ms. Johnson, let's begin."

17

I THOUGHT THAT THINGS WOULD start with a whimper, the erudite whisper of an explanation from Monroe, maybe the reverent utterance of some prayer. What I got was the bang of actions speaking louder than words.

The well-lit reality of the room began to crumble from the outside in, the way loose dirt whooshes down the sides of a freshly dug hole. A hard prickling sensation flexed my fingers into fists, and leapt like electrical current up my arms, short-circuiting my desire to run from a darkness reeking of the presence of things I felt but didn't understand.

This journey out of my body felt different. With Oba and Nana Grace, I had been flung into the light of a place that was of some other time, but still decorated like a reality I understood. Oba's and Nana Grace's visitations had been more like dreams. In Monroe's dining room, I became intangible and I was terrified. I began to demand, as if I had the power to do so, that I become concrete again. I wanted the scaffolding of my bones back. I wanted the thick and thin stratums of my muscles and tissues to inflate beneath my bag of skin. I hungered to feel my lungs snatching in and then extruding a breath. I missed the subtle footfalls of my heart herding my blood down trails of veins.

A desperate prayer of "oh, God, please" was answered with the loud roar of an ocean unfurling sheets of waves with loud, hard snaps.

"This is the opening of the way, Ms. Johnson. One of the nexuses of the crossroad," Monroe said. His voice was all up in my thoughts as if he had seamlessly wired himself into the frantic babble of my inner dialogue.

"The spirit that called you this afternoon is here," he continued. "You will not see him. You will not need to. You are to listen, listen only. This is an order, not a suggestion. What is required of you now is an act of faith."

I had too many doubts right then about God's sanity to have even the required mustard seed of stuff needed to do what was being asked. I knew I was to surrender all my worldly reasoning, I understood I was supposed to be still and believe, but I struggled the way all young things struggle until they realize that they aren't being trapped, but cradled. Faith required that I stop flailing, and when I did, new systems of understanding unfurled and installed themselves. The unseen ocean stopped roaring, and I felt my terror melt away into the depth of its stilled waters. I began to listen. I began to obey.

He who was ancestor circled about, his fluid movement creating a breeze that dragged against my skin like a long silk scarf. The scent of smoke, thick and acrid, slid up my nose. I shuddered, but I held my place and my tongue. He was sizing me up, measuring what I had against what he required. After a moment, he spoke.

"Yes, you are the one I need. You do not know me, but we are related. I am the father of Grace, Casmil, and Peaches. I am your Great, Great Grandfather. Where to begin now that you are here, dear Grace? Outrage. My story is about outrage! What they did not burn that July night in 1919, they painted with our blood. Like demons unleashed from the bottom of hell, the so-called moral white men of Vigilant descended on the homes and businesses of their Negro neighbors and torched them. The said cause of this riot was that a Negro man disrespected a white woman, but it was really about white folks' fear of black advancement.

"In those days, I had endeavored to become a carpenter and was apprenticed to a Mr. Reynolds, who owned the largest colored shop in the town. I worked along with my best friend, John Boyd. John was engaged to my sister, Amanda. They were to be married a week before that Christmas, but fate had other troubled visions for their futures.

"That July night, Boyd and I were busy sweeping up, when stones and bricks shattered the windows. Outside, we heard men shouting, 'kill all the damned niggers!' Mr. Reynolds ran out with an old shotgun, hoping to make the mob fall back. He was the first to die. Like demons will, the mob set the shop on fire. Flames as tall as trees pushed men and women screaming out into the street, where we were set upon with fists and clubs, bricks and guns. John and I were separated in the melee. From a grove of trees, I watched as they caught him. Someone split open his head with an axe, and as he writhed in agony, they doused him with kerosene and set him on fire.

"I escaped with my life by being a coward. I, who had been a proud soldier in the Great War, ran like a frightened deer. I, who had been awarded the French government's highest military honor for bravery in battle, hid behind the skirts of barrels outside a farmer's barn. Snakes in the crowd found me and started to beat me senseless. Only the cries of a white woman to have mercy on me saved my life. God was good, and I was grateful, but like my friend Boyd, I should have died. I was spared only to suffer greater tragedy and do infamous harm.

"That night my sister had gone to a friend's home, to plan events for the NAACP. I had trust in God that she was safe. But this God who made humans free allowed those insane with hate to exercise it that night. My sister was on her way home when a man named Abraham Gilmore assaulted and raped her in front of his cheering friends. How much hate must be in you to take from a woman that which is sacred and should be given of her own will?

"She had to grieve Boyd's death even as she struggled with her indignities. Later, when she found that she was with child, such was the nature of my sister that though her baby was conceived in evil, she felt her mother's love could redeem it. She moved away to live with our aunt in Detroit, away from the prying eyes that either pitied or despised her condition. But her son was stillborn, and his death, so soon after Boyd's, destroyed all that was left of Amanda's soul.

"Amanda never spoke of the outrage, but witnesses pulled my ear with the man's identity that I might defend her honor. I made the mistake of telling my sister what I was going to do. Horrified, she made me promise I would not take revenge. She reminded me that colored men had no rights whites had to respect, and that colored women had even fewer. Justice would come at the end of a hangman's noose, and my life was too full of promise. In her last, lucid and sane moments, she begged me to go to college and to work hard to improve the lives of our people. Three weeks after the funeral of her son, she found my small gun and walked deep into the countryside. Dressed in her wedding gown, she took her life.

"I moved away to keep my word. Ten years crept by, but I did not forget, nor did I forgive. All my prayers to Jesus could not stanch the flow of my grief at losing Amanda and John. In 1929, fate, in one of her crueler moments, led me back to our hometown on family business. I learned from an old friend that Abraham Gilmore still lived there and had done well. Revenge made my heart small and hard. I went back to my room to get my gun. Angels whispered that I had a good wife and three fine daughters. Angels whispered that vengeance belonged to the Lord. But Vengeance told me that she was sweeter, and that I would not be satisfied until I dined on her.

"Mr. Abraham Gilmore was not hard to find. His habits were well-known. Grin like a fool and white people will give a Negro man all manners of personal information. He was at his favorite bar, and he had his youngest boy with him. He raised not a brow when I shuffled like I was meek and mild into his presence. He was eating what he did not know was his last meal: beef, boiled potatoes and peas. His boy noticed me and did not smile. He was all of ten, maybe younger.

"I said to his father, 'you do not know me, but do you remember that night in the summer of 1919 when you met my sister?'

"His confusion lasted for a long moment as he searched through his cluttered memory for that day. Then he smiled the small snide smile of men who have done great evil and remember it fondly. How much does it take to kill a man? Not much. In the Great War, I had killed men I did not know, men who had done me no wrong. How much hate does it take to kill a man in front of his young child? More, much more, and I had more than enough. I pulled out my gun and shot him. With joy, I watched the life flee from his eyes as his boy, covered in a damp shroud of his father's blood, screamed and screamed.

"I remembered nothing for hours after that. My life was done. I let the police come and take me. I was guilty. Oh, but I did desire a trial, but not to save my life. I wanted people to know how my good sister struggled to take back the decency that had been stolen from her. I wanted people to understand what would make a good and decent man enslave himself to his rage. But a mob stole me from justice's frail grasp. I was dragged from the nightmare of the jail, hung up like a pig and slaughtered.

"Eye for an eye. I paid the devil's price for my revenge. Still, my sin has stained each generation. My hatred poisoned the young Gilmore boy. How could it not? I dipped him small and helpless in his father's blood and brains. So as a man, he has dragged this wretched trauma about, sowing the seed of bigotry and hate, sowing the seeds of other murders. Even in his old age, he is still waging secret wars against us. Enough. Enough."

He stopped because I could not go on. The exertion of listening had siphoned all my energy, and the hollowness felt like it would swallow me. I began to shudder hard, my body flailing my limbs as if it wanted to cast them off.

"Easy, Ms. Johnson, easy," Monroe whispered. Then his voice became more distant, like he had gone across a huge room to have a conversation with someone else. "She has done very well," I heard him say, "but she is tired, very tired, Please let her go."

18

THE NEXT THING I REMEMBERED was Mama yelling, "don't you mouth off to me, Grace. You're getting your hair done. I won't have you embarrassing me at graduation."

Her voice sounded muffled, as if she was talking to me from behind a door. Unfortunately, it was just an illusion. Through a veil of confusion and exhaustion, I watched my mother stalk around the living room, looking for her purse. She was full of anger, the kind of swirling fury that in the past had led to things like books and punches being thrown.

"You're not listening to me," she yelled.

I didn't bother to answer her. Mama was the devil I knew, and I had to deal with a devil I didn't know and couldn't name. I had lost some time, hours and hours of it. The space between the moment Monroe had asked the spirit to release me and the moment I was aware that Mama was ranting about my hair was nothing but snowy static. Panic constricted my breathing, and I ran the plump heels of my palms up and down my arms to keep the chill of fear off me.

"What time is it?" I asked softly.

I wanted to hear something like 9:15 or 10:30, anything but, "what's the matter with you? Are you hung over? Did that man get you drunk?"

That man rang hard in my ears. Not using his name was Mama's attempt to strip Monroe of the power she sensed he was handing down to me.

"I had dinner with Dr. Monroe," I said. "I told you I was going. You said it was okay."

"I said you were grown. You know that's not the same as permission."

I refused to concede the point and gave Mama a sly smile. "I assumed that was your way of telling me I could go. Dr. Monroe and I had dinner. There was no drinking, so I'm not hung over."

Hung over would be easier, I thought. Hung over had a cause. Hung over had a cure.

"So what did you discuss with him?" Again, no name.

I handed her the part of the truth she would have to deal with. "He's the executor of Nana Grace's will. I have an appointment with Attorney Blair at 3:00. I'll walk to his office from the hairdressers."

Money seemed to make me a better daughter because Mama smiled. "Do you need me to go with you?" she asked

I shook my head. "No, Dr. Monroe told me I'm to go by myself. He said if you had any questions or objections, you could call him."

That news smeared all the happy off her face. "Maybe I'll do that," she retorted.

I knew she wouldn't. Mama understood if she pushed Monroe he would shove back and she wasn't used to dealing with people who not only had my best interests at heart but knew how to protect them.

"What time is it?" I asked again.

"Ten. Our appointments are at 11:00. We'll be leaving here in about fifteen minutes."

"I'll wait outside," I said.

I slid out the door into a day that was all peacock blue sky and melted butter sunshine. I glanced over at Monroe's house hoping that maybe, just maybe, the sight of it would bring to mind what had happened after the story had ended but nothing came to mind.

"Ms. Johnson."

Startled, I looked down the porch stairs to find Monroe looking up at me.

"Good morning." He accented his greeting with a small nod and a slender crescent of upturned lips I assumed was a smile.

"Morning," I mumbled, and then I went looking for words other than "what the fuck happened to me?" to express myself. My search was fruitless, and after a few moments of silence Monroe ushered out an explanation, "What you're feeling is normal. Sometimes the first real sessions are too much and your mind shuts down."

Erased was a more appropriate word choice. It was more like my mind had rubbed out everything I was desperate to know.

"Hours, Dr. Monroe, I've lost hours. I don't remember walking home or going to sleep. I don't remember getting up, or getting dressed or eating ..." Bewildered, I threw out my arms as if Monroe was going to toss a gift of real revelation up to me.

"It was a very intense session, and the information was deeply personal."

My memory of the story made me fold my arms back up across my chest.

"The man in my vision said he was my great-great-grandfather. He said he was Nana Grace's, Peach's and Casmil's father. Nobody in my family has ever talked about what he told me. I never heard about it in school. I can't believe nobody ever said anything about something this important."

Monroe looked at me as if he wished he could be as innocent as I was then. "History is what a community chooses to remember." He paused for a moment. "And silence is one of the most effective ways to conceal terrible acts of violence."

We were interrupted by the front door swinging open as Mama and Jamila came out on to the porch. Their laughter-filled conversation dissolved when they saw Monroe.

He nodded at both of them. "Good morning, Miriam. Good morning, Jamila."

Mama said nothing. She unsheathed a stare that was meant to cut him down, but Monroe couldn't be moved by something that small.

Polar bears and penguins could have lived in the icy silence.

Finally, Mama turned on me. "Grace, get in the car."

I wasn't in the mood for obeying. I desperately needed to finish my conversation with Monroe, so I stood there trying to frame my question, and Mama lost it.

"Get your black ass in the car, Grace."

Anxiety fueled by fear drove me down the porch stairs. I stopped in front of Monroe and anchored my eyes on his face. I was Rabbit looking for advice from my Skin Horse. I was the Hare consulting her Moon.

"I don't understand any of this. What am I supposed to do?"

Monroe's head tipped a bit, and I watched in amazement as the stern look on his face collapsed into soft layers and folds of concern. He reached up and put a hand on my shoulder as if he were trying to prevent me from falling forward. Only when the sea of my quivering body was stilled did I realize I had been trembling. Eyes closed, I lapped up all the compassion concealed in his touch.

"It will be all right, Grace," he whispered. "After you've seen Mr. Blair, we will sit down and talk again."

I nodded and smiled. "You finally called me Grace," I said.

"You earned it. You did well last night. Now go and get in the car. I need to talk to your mother."

Without looking back, I walked away. In the backseat, I let the sauna-like heat strip out my fear. I expected I would be reamed up and down by Mama once Monroe was gone. But nothing happened. Neither Jamila nor Mama said a word to me when they got in the car. It was like I didn't exist during the time it took to drive to the hairdresser, and for one of the first times in my life I felt safe and free.

* * *

I didn't go willingly to Mrs. Minna's Glory Be to God Hair and Nail Emporium. Usually, I saved Mama the money by doing my own hair, but the choke chain of Mama's expectation about how I should look for graduation was too tight around my neck to make resistance practical.

Mama didn't give a crap that I hated how Mrs. Minna did my hair. She didn't care if I was a victim of the woman's old school philosophy that all hair of African descent with the nerve to be kinky should be subdued into straightness, if not by the smoking teeth of a hot comb, then by the fire of a chemical relaxer. There was no room in Mrs. Minna's hair rhetoric for locs, a mane full of braids or even the conservative and neatly manicured cap of a 'fro. Because Mama agreed with her, I got what Mama would pay for, which was a hairstyle that looked like I had on a cheap wig from the dollar store.

When we arrived, Mrs. Minna's was full of women getting their hair done for the next day's graduation and the parties following the ceremony. Old school rhythm and blues accompanied the gossip being dished out. Signifying laughter swirled up and through the thin threads of smoke wafting off banks of hot combs and curling irons. CP time was being fully observed, so even though we had arrived early, I could rely on the fact there would be another hour or so wait before Mrs. Minna would see me.

I didn't even want to pretend I was part of a functional family by sitting cozy with Mama and Jamila, so I headed toward a single chair against the back wall. Tucked between two women partially hidden by hairdryer hoods, I picked up an ancient copy of *Ebony* and pretended like I cared about the state of fashion in black America. Every now and then, I peered over the tops of the well-worn pages, surveying the intimate dance between groomers and those being groomed. Most of Mrs. Minna's employees were extremely busy, dividing their attention and skills between two or three clients. The only person who wasn't occupied was the new man Mrs. Minna had just hired. He was still establishing his clientele, so his chair sat empty off and on. I watched him helping others by handing them supplies or gracefully sweeping up swatches of cut hair. Dark-skinned and thin, he stood out like a sparrow in the midst of parakeets, not only because he was an older man in the midst of younger, flightier women, but also because he was quiet. Unlike the others, he kept a hold on his tongue, speaking only when spoken to, choosing not to join in the cacophony of snaps and the dishing out of dirt. He looked disinterested, but he was reading the world around him in intricate detail and taking all kinds of mental notes.

"His name is Izzo," the woman next to me said over the roar of her dryer. She was an older lady, someone I didn't know. Miss Lady had gotten bored with her magazine and decided to make me her business. "But if you're interested, he's taken," she continued.

"I'm not interested," I said.

I tried not to a glance at her because I knew even a small taste of interest would inspire her to serve up a full banquet of her opinions. It didn't work.

"Yeah, he's got a wife and six kids back home in Jamaica. He's working hard to get them all over here with him. He used to work at GM, but when they closed down his plant and laid him off, he went back to school to learn to do hair. He's nice-looking though. A little old for you, but even if you're interested, he's taken."

I was almost glad when Mrs. Minna yelled out my name.

Mrs. Minna was a big woman, not big as in belly over the top of your panties fat, but big as in tall, broad and muscular. In another life she would have been a draft horse with a long showy mane, although I think the horse would have been smarter. All that body mass had a set of huge, well-harnessed breasts to match it, and it was with those breasts that she stanchioned my head as she assessed its condition. Her hoofish fingers pulled my hair as if she were untangling cheap yarn. She kept digging and looking at Mama like I was a cause so lost she shouldn't even bother. Then she said out loud like I had no feeling or even an identity she had to respect, "why'd you let your hair get this bad? It looks like crap."

Everybody in the salon heard her and, depending on where they were in the spiritual evolution of their soul, they either laughed or looked away from the emotional carnage. Nobody spoke up in my defense at first. Mama and Jamila just nodded like it was a terrible truth they had always known about me.

All I tasted for a long, terrible moment was the tartness of my fury as it rose out of my wounded heart. I was pissed, and it was this pissiness that pulled hard on the lines of muscles in my legs. I flew up out of Mrs. Minna's chair, and, with balled fists fastened tightly to my side, walked over, sat in Izzo's chair and waited to see if he was the man I thought he was. I half-expected him to deny me service. After all, I was putting him on the spot by trying to make him show up his boss. But Izzo said nothing. He didn't even look around the room to take the temperature of popular opinion. From a cabinet he took out a cape, wrapped it around my neck and began a gentle, nonjudgmental assessment of my hair.

Mrs. Minna just stood there, her mouth working up and down, but with no words coming out.

"Grace, you get back over there," Mama yelled like she had forgotten that less than an hour ago that tactic hadn't worked.

I didn't move out of Izzo's chair.

"She had no right to insult me," I yelled back at Mama. "It's my hair, I'll do what I want with it."

"Amen," somebody said. That broke the moral ice. Other people began to murmur that Mrs. Minna was wrong, and it hadn't been very Christian of her to insult a paying customer. All Mama and Mrs. Minna could do was sit on the shore and seethe.

"Bunch of old cows," Izzo said under his breath. I had to smile because Mama was included in the description.

"Let's say," he began thoughtfully in a voice that spoke of white beaches and sunnier climate, "let's say, we just cut all the old straight stuff off and leave you with a little Afro for now. Then maybe later you can decide to dread if you want."

I nodded. It sounded good. It sounded like a new start.

"You know, miss, there's not a thing wrong with your hair. You got what my mama use to call a warrior's crown, because each strand of hair stands up for itself, pointing up and up to God in a beautiful, full and powerful way. You know our ancestors used to believe that hair is the closest thing to the Divine. Communications from the gods and spirits pass through it to get to the soul." Izzo paused, and then in a low voice meant only for my ears he whispered, "your hair is no simple thing, sister. I can feel it. Lots of people trying to talk to your soul, so your hair got to be right."

I just closed my eyes and let him wash and cut it down. When I opened my eyes, the mirror revealed not the old me, but a glimpse of the person I was becoming.

I looked at Izzo with gratitude and some shame. "I don't think my Mama's going to cover this. I can't pay you for this right now, but I will pay you."

Izzo shook his head, "Consider this a gift. This has been more than a blessing for me, sister."

"No," I said. "I owe you more than you know."

Mama moaned out loud that I looked like a damn ground hog, but she was almost nothing to me right then. I glanced at the clock. It was close to three. I didn't bother to say goodbye to Mama. I didn't even glance her way as I walked, head held high, out the door.

19

I SHOULD HAVE BEEN IN a hurry to get to my appointment with Attorney Blair, but store windows kept offering their reflection, and I kept stopping to shyly sample my new image. By the time I reached the plate glass of the law office, I was a true believer.

"Are you Grace Johnson?" A receptionist asked in a low voice as I stumbled in out of breath and barely able to speak. She was an older, blond-haired woman with muddy green eyes the color of frog skin. When I nodded my head, she twisted her lips into a glossy mauve knot and put a check mark in a huge black appointment book. Without looking back up at me, she said, "Please have a seat. Attorney Blair will be with you in a moment."

I sank into the large mouth of a leather chair and marveled at how a place that had looked like an ordinary storefront on the outside could be something so totally different on the inside. The reception area was small, but money had been spent on lush carpeting and expensive tables and bookcases. Across the room, saltwater fish, as vivid as swatches of African fabric, swirled in the depth of a huge corner aquarium. Watching the sinuous movements of fins and tails rounded the edges off my nerves. I was almost calm when a door beside the desk swung open. The small reception area grew even smaller as the ex-linebacker bulk of Attorney J. Cedric Blair entered.

Large and in charge was the only cliché I could think of as my eye followed the dark gray line of his suit up to a pinecone brown face holding broad, flat features. Attorney Blair was eggshell bald, but he had the kind of visage that baldness left looking distinguished and formidable.

I struggled to get out of the chair, rising and then dropping like a newborn calf until, with a shove from both arms, I was finally able to totter to my feet. Attorney Blair stuck out his large hand and offered not a greeting but an observation.

"You cut your hair," he said.

I stood there looking at him. I didn't know what to do with that slice of the weirdly personal. My mouth went dry as I shook his waiting hand.

He nodded. "Please, come this way."

I followed him down the short hall, still chewing on the oddness of his greeting, wondering how he knew, or better yet, why he cared what I looked like.

Finally I blurted out, "so, you didn't say if you liked my hair or not."

I didn't expect a reaction, much less an answer, but as he opened the door to his office and stepped aside to allow me to enter first, I saw he was smiling. Not the rubber band tight smile that masked irritation, but a loose ribbon of a grin that revealed he saw something in me he admired.

"Your hair is quite lovely, Ms. Johnson," he replied as he offered me a seat in front of a brass ornamented cherry wood desk. "It makes you look like the grown woman you are now. I'm sorry if I was rude."

"Grown," I said more to myself. "I don't feel too grown."

"Well, few of us do at your age," he said as he lowered his bulk into his chair. "As you know my name is J. Cedric Blair. We can talk more about me in a minute, but first things first."

Part of his bulk disappeared as he reached down to open a drawer. At first I thought he was unearthing some papers, but what he brought up was a plain silver tin and two cloth napkins.

"Your great-grandmother and I used to have a drink of Scotch when she came for an appointment, but as we got older, we switched to these." He pulled off the silver top to reveal thick disks of chocolate covered cookies. The smell of food woke my lightly dozing appetite.

I forced myself to select one cookie. "What are they?" I asked

"Double stuffed Oreo cookies dipped in Godiva Chocolate," he said with mock awe.

I busted out laughing, because like Nana Grace, I could appreciate gilding an already well-endowed baked good with a thick coat of expensive chocolate. I beat back a rabid urge to stick a whole cookie in my mouth.

"So how long were you Nana Grace's attorney?" I asked.

"Forty years," he said around a bite of cookie. "She plucked me right out of law school. It was a good match, better than some marriages. You sounded like her with that line about the hair."

With womanly daintiness, he wiped his thick fingers on a napkin before opening a desk drawer and removing a manila folder. "I have to tell you, Ms. Johnson, I read your great grandmother's will with both a sense of honor and sadness. Grace was not only a client but a deeply cherished friend. She was intelligent and charming, but what I most admired was her fierce dedication to making the world a better and more just place. She was convinced you would be up to managing her legacy. I hope you are worthy of the faith she had in you."

From the inside pocket of his suit he took out reading glasses and began to read the last will and testament of my great-grandmother. When he was through elucidating all the treasures and sums with numerous zeros after them, all he could say was, "when you turn nineteen next year, you'll be a very wealthy woman, Ms. Johnson."

I knew better than to celebrate. I had won the lotto, but with all kinds of strings and ropes and wires attached. Swirling in the pit of my stomach with all the other emotions from the night before was the realization that Nana Grace's money probably came with grueling expectations.

"If you wish," Attorney Blair continued, "I will remain your attorney, but if you choose to select someone younger, there are many other attorneys who can provide you with excellent advice and counsel. You will need to find a good financial advisor and accountant because your tax concerns have gone from zero to a bitch. I can help you with that choice if you like. Try to keep quiet about this, even though most people in town already know. Soon enough, everybody's going to want to be your friend, and every long lost relative you didn't know you had is going to come with his or her hands out. Your great-grandmother has done you a favor by not releasing anything to you until next year. You have some time to plan.

"If you need money in the near future, you can relay your request through Dr. Monroe. Later, we will work on how to handle charities and other, let's just say, less polished requests. And just as a warning, money makes romantic love ... well, complicated. As a father of adult daughters, all I can stress is that when you select someone to date, use your head, not your heart, or other places."

Embarrassment warmed my cheeks, and I choked on some cookie.

"Questions?"

"Yes," I said. "How did my great-grandmother earn all this money?"

"Investment in the stock market, real estate. Your great-grandfather died young but left her well off. He was also a man who didn't believe women, especially black women, should be subservient to anyone except God. So he encouraged her to start her own insurance business and was happy when she succeeded. Grace was ambitious. She had many reasons to be ambitious."

He grew silent and let the word ambitious hang there waving like a crooked finger, inviting me to dive deeper into the subject.

I accepted the invitation. "Why do you say that she had reasons to be ambitious?"

"What do you know about what happened to her father?"

I sensed Attorney Blair was fully aware of what had transpired the night before. Monroe, I suspect, had told him I had excelled in the task that had been given to me.

I leaned forward, took two cookies and sat back. "I have been given everything, except what transpired after my great-great-grandfather was lynched."

He peered over a peak of his laced fingers, smiled and nodded. "Given" was enough of a conjuring word. It was the sign and symbol I understood that something infinitely more important than money was being handed down to me.

"This is what happened. Vigilant was racially cleansed. Whites confronted blacks and told them they had less than 24 hours to get out of town. Black people's houses, farms and other property were illegally confiscated and sold for little or nothing. Grace was ten when her father died, but she vowed she would get justice for those who had suffered because of what her father had done. When she finally had the money, she hired white members of the NAACP to go undercover and buy as much of the property back as she could with her money. She then donated the deeds back to the families of the true owners. Black people moved back in and stood their ground despite death threats. As you can imagine, Grace made a lot of enemies. So she moved to Indiana and stayed there."

Frozen by incredulity, I sat motionless. "I don't understand why nobody wants to talk about this. I just don't."

Attorney Blair shrugged. "There is an old African saying that goes 'shame has many watchmen.' White people have kept silent because they were ashamed or don't care what happened. Black people, especially black men, have kept silent because they were ashamed they weren't able to protect their families during the riots in 1919 or the expulsion. Everybody has kept silent even though a terrible price has been paid for that silence."

"What do you know about the Gilmore family?" I asked.

Attorney Blair looked as if he knew the question was coming. "On the outside they appear to be a well-off, fairly respectable family, but if you scratch the rind deep enough, what oozes out is a long, violent tradition of involvement in the Klan."

Suddenly the memory of that strange day of jazz and Oba fully resurrected itself and I shivered. "I've met Jonathan Gilmore." I began to confess. "I ran into him last October at a store on the other side of town. He called me a … a … nigger bitch. I was too scared to say anything because I felt I was in danger. Talk about shame."

Attorney Blair leaned back in his chair and stared for a moment at the ceiling. "Your gut instincts were correct, Ms. Johnson. Recently, Jonathan was arrested for passing out hate literature. Last year, he and some of his *friends* were considered suspects in the burning of black homes in Detroit and the savage beating of a gay man in Lansing. A lot of money and a couple high-powered lawyers got him out of that. You didn't need to be messing with him. At least not right then."

"I'm supposed to do something about the Gilmores, but I don't know what or how."

"In time, it will be given to you," Attorney Blair asserted.

Given. I weighed the meaning of that word, but I still wasn't sure about anything.

"I suppose I should deal with what I do know," I said softly. "I don't want another attorney. I trust you. I like the cookies ritual. Can we still do the cookies in honor of Nana Grace?"

Attorney Blair began to laugh. It was deep-throated and warm. The sound of it made me wish I had known him when I was young and Nana Grace was still alive.

"My door and my tin are always open to you, Grace," he said as he picked out a cookie.

"I hope I can live up to Nana Grace's legacy."

Attorney Blair looked at me and smiled. "I got a feeling Ms. Johnson," he said, "that's not going to be a problem."

20

IT DIDN'T OCCUR TO ME Mama might try to pick me up from the lawyer's office until I was standing out on the sidewalk and spied her car on the other side of Main Street. Jamila saw me first, and with a Judas-like flick of her hand, pointed me out to Mama.

"Damn," I whispered as I pretended I hadn't seen them by looking up the street. Providence produced a slow moving truck, and when its huge lumbering gray body obstructed Mama's view, I took off toward the next intersection, skirting around a corner.

"Grace," Mama's voice chased after me, and I had half a mind to turn around and go back to confront her. My legs, however, decided to obey common sense. I ducked down the narrow throat of an alley that flanked the back of the main street's stores.

Why? I wondered as I hid in the smelly shadow of a set of dumpsters, had Mama even bothered? It wasn't like she wouldn't have had an opportunity to attack me later in the privacy of the house. Why try to do her dirty work out on the street? A string of breaths finally brought up the reason from the depth of my memory. Mama's older brother George and his wife were arriving from St. Louis to attend graduation. For her older brother, Mama would put on a cheap mask of civility and play sane.

Fifteen minutes passed, then twenty and there was no sign Mama had come looking for me. My rising appetite gored me into almost frantic pacing. When I remembered I had some graduation money, and it was samples day at the grocery store, my mood grew less edgy and more luminous.

Mid Town Grocery was crowded, so the only carts left were the lame ones, the ones whose useless wheels made loud "ack-ack" noises as you pushed them down the isle. I ack-acked up to a platter of coffee cake samples. I meant to just taste. I had every intention of laying just a sliver of buttery crust on my tongue and letting it melt down layer by crispy layer until all its veiled flavors of cinnamon, nutmeg, and vanilla were revealed. But my appetite was acting thuggish. It made me think, *why buy the cow when the whole pail of milk was sitting in front of me?* Shame should have rescued me from myself, but it just stood there in the midst of all my other mortified emotions acting like it didn't know my name as I began to stuff garlands of pastry into my constantly chewing mouth.

Most people didn't seem to care that I was committing criminal gluttony. Some folks rolled up their eyes like yo-yos beneath arched curtains of eyebrows, but for the most part, nobody said a word as they hurried by to hunt and gather dinner.

Finally, a husky male voice reached out to warn me, "you know, we ain't trying to feed you a meal."

I stopped in mid-chew. Without even turning around to confront who was behind me, I threw two packages of the coffee cake into my basket and ack-acked off toward canned goods. Doughnuts followed on the heels of chips and dip, which begot a big jar of crunchy peanut butter that desperately wanted to be with some crackers. All the while I shopped, I was trying to hold and sort out in my mind everything that had happened to me. *I was like a new puzzle*, I thought. All kinds of pieces poured out on some dark table, but there's no picture on the box. I don't know how I was supposed to put this all together.

"Who am I now, really?" I thought I was just addressing the crowd of messed up thoughts and emotions inside my head, but in a moment I realized that my anxiety had made my mouth a damn speak-

erphone. People who shared the aisle with me stared, trying to assess whether I was crazy, and if I was crazy, was I dangerous. I wanted to leave my basket and slink out of the store, but hunger wouldn't let me make that polite decision. I lowered my head and bravely tried to move on, but the cart hit a pair of honey-brown pants legs. I sighed and looked up to say, excuse me, only to find the person I had to ask forgiveness from was Evan. He smiled a perfect smile of invitation, but I didn't know what to say. So he took the initiative and said what he knew I needed to hear: "I like your hair, Grace."

Say thank you, you moron, my inner voice yelled. My lips, however, weren't listening, and something like, "okay," limped out of my mouth.

His eyes slid off me to study the dietary chaos in my basket. I wanted to say "you know this stuff isn't all for me," because I thought he had to be making some ugly judgments about who I was based on what I was going to eat. Instead, I uttered a lie that at least had a house in the same neighborhood of the truth. "I'm not going to eat all of this today. I was going to save some for tomorrow."

Evan looked at me with compassion.

"I counted nine items, so let's use the express lane," he said. Then he bent down and healed the lame wheel on the cart by turning it to face the same way as the others.

"Store security's been following you for a while," he said in a low voice as he began pushing the now silent cart into the produce department.

Embarrassment set fire to my cheeks. "Well, I was kinda acting a little strange."

"Small minds ..." he said and stopped suddenly in front of a bin of tomatoes. He eyed the pinkish fruits as if they were lesser creations of God because they had been spawned in a hot house. After a few moments of indecision, he placed two in a clear plastic bag and knotted the top. "I told them you were diabetic, and that you were waiting for me, and it was my fault I was late. It seemed to mollify them."

I exhaled an "oh," and then stupidity got my tongue. "They believed that shit?"

My hand crept up to cover my mouth. "I am so sorry. I shouldn't have said that."

He laughed, and holding up the bag with the tomatoes said, "did you know, Grace, that tomatoes were once called love apples, Pomme d'Amour?"

I did know, but I didn't respond because I couldn't make up my mind if I had heard him correctly. I stood there wondering if my brain was playing some type of weird scrabble with my perception of words and their meanings.

He smiled as if my befuddlement was a charming aspect of my personality. "Let's go check out," he said.

The woman running the register knew my mother from church, so I said hello just to be polite as I placed things on the counter to be scanned. She didn't say a word to me. Her batting eyes and big mouth smile were offered only to Evan as she tried to figure out who he was and why he insisted on paying for my food even though I was holding out money.

"Evan Monroe, huh?" she said as she handed his credit card back to him. Evan didn't return her smile. He just chose paper instead of plastic and started to pack up the food.

"So, Grace," she asked, "will we be seeing you and Mr. Evan in church on Sunday?"

I wanted to say, "bitch, you know I haven't been in church in over a year. What makes you think I'm going to show up now?" but I just shook my head and followed Evan out of the store.

"Of course, I'll pay you back," I offered as we walked across the parking lot.

Evan shook off my words. "How about you pay me back by going to get some coffee at Alamode down on Fourth Ave?"

I looked at his car and then back at him weighing one against the other. He drove a cavernous Cadillac with all kinds of silver trim. It was the kind of car someone older, careful, and conservative drove, the kind of car that belonged to someone who didn't date people like me.

"Really?" I asked as I watched him fumble for his keys. The trunk sighed as soft as a baby when he popped it open to put in the groceries.

"Yeah, let's get something good to eat." He opened the passenger door and held it and held it until the sheer weight of his patience stuffed me into the silken palm of a leather seat.

"I saw you going in the store, and I thought I would catch up with you and ask you how you were," he commented as he started to drive.

"Well, thank you," I said.

I expected the rest of the short ride to the strip mall on the outskirts of Vigilant to be filled with awkward silences. But what was born between us was more like an elegant pause between steps in a dance.

Alamode was quiet. The lunch crowd had gone, and the dinner crowd was just beginning to filter in. I was happy nobody I knew was in the place. We sat in a back booth and looked at menus loaded with the pie, cobblers, and cakes the restaurant was famous for. I was going to order what I always ordered so I would have some time to make up something to say.

"So how was dinner with my father?" he asked.

I looked up with a start and smiled. "It was fine. Thanks for cooking dinner. The food was wonderful."

"I'm glad you liked it." He paused and cocked his head. "So, did Dad regale you with tales of the mystical and magical, or did you get one of his lectures about the unfathomable way of God and the Ancestors?"

The undertones of sarcasm made me squirm. I pretended to read the menu.

"I think it was more the unfathomable ways of God and the ancestors," I answered, my truth neatly told, but not fully revealed.

"Yeah, the one about how the ancestors and spirits speak to us from the grave to help us change our lives. He's convinced he can do it."

"Well, maybe he can."

"He's a professor of religion. He shouldn't be acting like he's a TV psychic."

Right then, I wanted him to take me and my spirit-talking self home. There had been nothing fake about the night before, and if he could think this about his father, what would he think about me? I started to get up, but before I could stand, a voice distant, feminine and desperate surfaced. "No–please give me time."

Shallow waves of shivers shuffled through my body. I looked behind me to make sure I hadn't dipped into a conversation at another table. Nothing. There was nothing in the booth behind me, but the palpable sensation of some other entity's needs and longings.

I looked back to find Evan staring at me. "Are you all right?" he asked, his face sweet with concern.

I shook my head. "I'm fine."

"I have to warn you about Dad. He can be difficult, pedantic."

"That's funny," I pushed back. "He also warned me about you."

Evan's self-satisfied expression dimmed. "Yeah ... I bet he did. So do you believe in all that spiritual stuff?"

"Yeah," I said. "I found talking to your father fascinating. I think it helps to be open-minded about spiritual things."

"Maybe so."

I decided to change the subject. "My friend Shanta told me you're famous. We don't have cable so I didn't get to see you on the cooking show."

Evan laughed. "I was on television. That's different from being famous. People think it's the same, but it's really not."

"Well, it must have been wonderful to win." I said.

The waitress arrived, and Evan ordered coffee and cherry cobbler. Like an idiot, I said, "I'll take the Better than Sex Cake."

Better than Sex Cake was what I always had when I came to Alamode. As I had confessed to Shanta and Nikki, the cake was probably the closest I would get to the real thing any time soon. It didn't occur to me that given who I was with, I might want to order something different until Evan asked, "so is it?"

"Is it what?" I asked, innocently.

"The cake ... Is it better than sex?"

I wanted to go live with the crumbs on the floor, but I choked back my embarrassment, smiled, and answered honestly, "I wouldn't know."

I expected a lecherous grin, the kind the boys in school would have given if they had heard my confession about my virginity. Evan's expression though, immediately became thoughtful.

"So," I said, resisting the urge to cloudy the dark sky of my coffee with all ten of the little tubs of cream the waitress had slid onto the table, "how long are you in town for?"

"Oh, I don't know. I came to visit Dad because I needed to get away for a while after the show to rethink what I want to do with my life. Also, Dad and I haven't been exactly on speaking terms. My fault, his fault, you know how that goes with parents sometimes ..."

Yeah, I thought, I did know how it went. Only with my mother, it had always been my fault, my fault.

"So is that why I've never seen you over there?" I asked. "I mean, we've lived next door to Dr. Monroe for over ten years and I didn't even know he had any children. But then again, it's not like I had any real conversations with him until a couple of months ago."

Evan hesitated. "Sometimes I wondered if he remembers he had any children. When my mother divorced him after he figured out he was gay, he didn't get custody. Frankly, I'm not even sure he asked for it. He just drifted out of my sister's and my lives."

The surge of loathing in his voice snapped and crackled with the kind of bitterness only unhealed hurt could produce. I took note of it, folded it up, and put it away in the thickening file of my impressions of him. I thought he was going to leave it at that, but he decided to plunge me deeper into his life.

"I'm 25. I'm the executive chef of my mother's restaurant in Atlanta. We do excellent New Orleans style food at fairly reasonable prices, so we're busy and successful. I thought I was everything I wanted to be. Then things just started to fall apart even after I won on the show. I couldn't get it together. I've always loved cooking, but it just didn't seem worth the hours from hell and all the work that went with it. One night, I was sitting with one of my chefs—Roland, the man who should have gotten the job my mother gave me. Anyway, we were just talking, and I told him how I was feeling about things. He just sat there, smoking this big black cigar and when I was finished, he looked up at me through all the smoke and my crap and he said, 'you know, boy, things aren't never gonna be okay with you 'til you get right with God and your daddy.'

"I told Roland it was easier to talk to God than my father. But Roland was convinced, and anybody that can cook a gumbo as good as his couldn't be too far wrong. So about a month ago, I told my mother I was putting Roland in charge and taking a leave of absence that might become permanent. I drove up here from Atlanta."

I sat there with his story, hefting it up and down. It felt way too light, like oranges after they had been juiced. The rinds of details were there but the pulp and juice of truths had been squeezed out. Roland, I mused, must have said infinitely more because it felt like infinitely more was wrong.

"Vigilant is like coming from someplace to nowhere," I commented. "Well, maybe not nowhere, but damn near close to it."

Evan laughed. "Well, Vigilant is different, small, and quiet. I've been able to get some sleep for the first time in a long time. So what about you, Ms. Grace? Where are you in your plans?"

"I'm supposed to go to Spelman in the fall," I said.

"Yes," Evan nodded. "Beautiful campus, full of women who are as intelligent as they are beautiful. You'll fit right in."

I crumpled up my face with doubt as the waitress delivered our food. My slice of mocha chocolate cake slathered with buttery caramel, topped with cumulus mounds of whipped cream, penny-sized flakes of toasted coconut and huge twigs of chocolate shavings tasted wonderful. I decided when I had finished the last spoonful that it had been well worth my embarrassment.

Evan asked me about what I like to read and what kind of music I listened to. As I answered his questions, I watched with almost rapt fascination as he ate his cobbler. I envied the shiny cherries that rode like burgundy balloons into the deep sweet darkness of his mouth.

"Would you like to try some?" he asked.

"Oh, yeah," I said, but when I realized Evan knew I wasn't exactly talking about cobbler, I got flustered. My hand accidentally smacked the porcelain cheek of my half empty coffee cup. Mortified, I watched the cup spin, spewing coffee in an artful, but messy arch before crashing and breaking on the floor.

I struggled to gather up buns of napkins to help wipe up the mess.

"It's all right, Grace," Evan told me as he helped the waitress pick up the shards. It didn't feel all right. I felt dumb and clumsy.

"It's been a long day," I sighed.

"Then I'd better get you home so you can rest."

I nodded and thought that when I got home, I wouldn't so much sleep as hide under my bed.

In the car, I could barely look at him. How stupid and grace-less and totally transparent could I be? I might as well have plastered "what I was thinking" on a billboard beside the highway. I noted with relief the line of cars outside my house that signaled that the St. Louis wing of Mama's family had arrived for my graduation. Mama would still be mad at me, but she wouldn't show out in front of her brother and his wife. She would ask questions, but they wouldn't be as pointed.

"Can I see you again tomorrow?" Evan asked as he stopped the car.

My mouth flapped open and closed. In a rush of flighty words, I explained how graduation was the next day, so, no, I couldn't go out with him. Then the girlish part of me that believed in romance told my common sense to shut the hell up and invited him to my graduation party.

"I'll see you tomorrow then," he said as he helped me carry my groceries up on the porch. I didn't believe him. Why would I believe a twenty–something man, a man with a career, a person that had been on TV, even if he didn't think that made him famous, would want to show up at some overweight, eighteen-year–old girl's party?

I waved as he drove off, knowing that it would be forever and then some before I would see him again.

* * *

Laughter, hugs, and congratulations from Mama's older brother George, and his willowy wife Jean, greeted me as I walked in. Mama stood, glaring from a seat in the corner of the living room. Her eyes tried to pinch open the skin of my conscience and make it bleed guilt.

"Gracie girl," my Uncle George cried. He was as big and nice as his sister was little and mean.

He tipped his head back and forth as he inspected me. "I don't know if I like your hair," he said. "You know the Bible says long hair is a woman's glory. It's supposed to be her crown."

I laughed as I thought about how my snap of hair now spoke a different gospel truth, about how God in all of His or Her feminine incarnations wanted women to be free to be who they were.

"I'm not bald, Uncle George," I said. "I still got a crown. It's just an African one."

Everybody busted out laughing except Mama. Her face was a frozen wasteland, hiding fault lines of troubled emotions.

"Jamila and I waited for you for two hours," Mama said finally. Her brother looked at her hard. The expression on his face sternly told her to back off.

"I didn't ask you to pick me up," I replied calmly and then I decided to just tell the truth. "Besides, Evan, Dr. Monroe's son, asked me out for dessert and coffee and I went. I invited him to my party tomorrow."

Aunt Jean oh'd and ah'd a bit, like normal women do when we hear that somebody may have found new love or even some lukewarm leftover love. "Is he nice looking?" she asked.

I nodded. Aunt Jean stuck out her tongue and giggled, and I wanted to giggle with her.

"Well, I do mind," Mama hissed. "And I've told you you're not having a party."

There would have been no antidote for the venom I was about to spew. But before I could say anything, big brother turned on his little sister.

"You leave her alone, Miriam," Uncle George said in a voice that filled the room. "I think what your daughter here is just trying to tell you in a nice way, is that she's grown."

21

CAPPED, GOWNED, AND HELD CAPTIVE by seventy-five years of Vigilant High School commencement tradition, I sat listening as Shanta gave her valedictorian speech. I hadn't heard it until then, because even though I had asked, Shanta had refused to show it to me. Of course, it wasn't your usual sweet and creamy confection of hope and dreams of the future. Shanta was too much like her revolutionary-talking daddy to hold back on her views that all people should be fighting and, if need be, dying for social change and justice around the world. Grown folks squirmed as their consciences were roughed up by her accusation of indifference and procrastination. We, her peers, had heard this fire and brimstone appeal from Shanta before, and so we just settled into our seats pretending to listen.

I was staring out across the auditorium when Shanta said, "we must assume responsibility for the world, or at least the part of the world we live in. So I leave you, and especially my best friend, Grace Johnson, who will be fighting evil in this world, with these words: Learn to listen, for listening is not passive. It always demands action. Listen and learn and then be prepared, fully prepared to use your gifts and talent to make our world a better place. Thank you."

Polite applause followed. I was clapping in time with everyone else when some guy named Justin, who hadn't talked to me since seventh grade, leaned over and in a loud, smartass voice asked, "you some kind of superhero, Grace? What's up with Shanta talking about you fighting evil?"

He was only asking what other people were wondering. All the eyes from my class had turned when Shanta mentioned my name to see if they had somehow missed something in all the years they had known me. I wanted to melt into a puddle and drain off into a dark corner to be mopped up by the janitor after everyone had gone.

"I don't have a clue what Shanta is talking about, Justin," I said finally. The long fangs of my stare sucked the smugness off his face, and he scrambled to get out of my way as we assembled to march out.

Shanta knew I was upset when she pulled me aside into a less crowded part of the auditorium lobby.

"Did I embarrass you?" she asked joyously, as if to mock my feelings of mortification. On her face was this fierce smile, a ridged bow of lips that should have told me that even though I was looking at Shanta's body, somebody else was at home.

"Evil, Shanta?" I asked as I looked out through a row of picture windows toward a gown-clad sea of familiar faces getting ready to head off into separate forevers. A brackish smell scented the hall, unsettling my stomach. I heard Shanta's gown rustle loud as she pushed up close, close enough so that what was in her could jump off on to me, close enough so I could feel as well as hear the undulating hum of the other world in her voice. "The story, Grace. You know I'm talking about your great-great grandfather's story."

The who or what that was in Shanta gave me too much credit. That the story from my ancestor Freeman would, of course, involve my fighting evil had not come to mind. Back in that day, the story was still unreal, and evil to me was something cartoonish. It was all about the coyote trying to hurt the roadrunner or the mad scientist in B movies trying to take over the world. Evil was what you became if you got too hungry or you were PMSing and you were irritable. Unless you were a character in a cartoon or comic book, you didn't go around saying, "you know, I think I'm going to go out and fight evil today."

Shanta's mouth moved. "All I did was spiritually out you. Simple as that, no mystery. Today for you is less about graduation than initiation. Graduation is easy. Initiation is harder because it's about the events that cause some power or gift to erupt. It's all about becoming real."

"Who are you? Are you Oba?" I found enough courage to ask because it occurred to me that Oba didn't have to be seven feet tall and dark as tar at night. He could be the skinny white boy Justin Dupree asking me a dumb, but significant question. He could be Shanta, smiling like she was crazy and then some.

"What does it matter, Grace?" Shanta's mouth answered. "The truth is the truth no matter who's telling it. Gotta go, and so do you in more ways than one."

Shanta reached up and with an elegant swipe of her fingers turned my tassel. She walked off leaving me with a naked body of truth I had to somehow learn to clothe. I had graduated but to what? My future seemed full of circumstances an eternity beyond my control.

It was a Vigilant High tradition for graduates and their families to assemble in the parking lot under an ugly crepe paper flower arch for a last spree of photos before the caps and gowns had to be returned. I shook off the effects of the mystical and rode out on the coattails of other graduates' jubilation. It was hot out, and I was not looking forward to meeting up with Mama on a shimmering asphalt lake of heat even if she was going to be surrounded by other happier relatives.

Earlier that day, Mama had called me to her bedroom, and I had gone because I had wanted that day, my day of days, to be nice, even if I had to feign belly-up submissiveness in front of her. Depression shadowed me as I watched Mama cup her hands to catch splashes of her long dark locks. She was dressed in a slip; the turquoise blue suit she had bought for the occasion was laid out neatly on the bed. Mama knew I was standing there but didn't bother to look at me.

"After the ceremony," she had said, "I'll fix a nice dinner, and we'll eat with George and Jean and Jamila."

I folded my top lip up under my teeth. She knew damn well that after graduation I was supposed to be at the party Shanta's parents were still kindly allowing me to share. Dinner, even a nice dinner, was no kind of reward for my achievements. Not for the grade point I had maintained. Not for the college I had worked so hard to get into. Mama had once told Jamila and me that our only job was to do well in school. *If that was the case,* I had thought, *then like a good employee, I deserved to be paid. I wanted my party.*

I'd tried to craft some kind of compromise. "Mama, I'm going to Shanta's house first, and then I'll be home."

Mama had sighed loud and hard. "No, you had your chance to do what I asked to get your party, and you didn't do it."

"No, you had a choice to do what my father wanted, and you cheated me," I'd shouted.

Her lipstick hand had shuddered to a stop, and for a long moment, Mama was silent as she kneaded her mouth, transferring color from a darker lip to the paler one. "Don't try to make your father into some kind of hero, Grace," she had said, but her voice was quavering so her words had fluttered loud then soft. "You don't understand. He left us. He left me alone to raise you. I got you to this day, not him."

Madness, nothing but madness. I couldn't believe she considered his death something as simple as abandonment. "He didn't leave, Mama," I had shouted at her. "People say he was abducted and murdered—lynched. Everyone believes that but ..." I couldn't get the "you" out; it hurt too much. It represented everything that was still wounded and bleeding between us.

"Suicide. I was his wife, I should know."

Indignation and the truth made me draw myself up off my belly. Something in me broke, rearranged itself, and then grew stronger. "Nobody that knew Daddy believes that." She threw down the lipstick case or maybe it just fell from her trembling hands.

"Who the fuck told you that?" she'd yelled

"Doesn't matter. All I know is it feels true." I'd walked away, leaving her with a rattled expression on her face as vivid as her mouth.

Fragments of that rattled look still haunted her eyes when I found her in the parking lot standing next to Uncle George, Aunt Jean and Jamila. I gave her a limp hug, one she barely returned.

"So, you off to your party now?" Uncle George asked as he embraced me and then whipped out his camera to take pictures. He looked hard at his sister and then looked soft at me. Something in his look told me he had heard the argument that morning and had come down firmly on my side.

"Yeah," I said. "I'm off to my party."

He nodded. "Good. Good. Maybe tomorrow we can have that family dinner and hang out together."

He glanced again at Mama. Mama said nothing.

I smiled to celebrate my victory. "Yeah, Uncle George, I would like that."

* * *

It was Shanta's house, so we had Shanta's music. Our party was literally jumping because the bass line of whatever Hip-hop songs she had told her brother to spin seemed to grasp the floorboards and shake them. Invitations to the neighbors left no one at home to complain that the music was loud enough to knock birds out of the air. I collected myself enough to meet and greet, doing this weird pantomime of pretending I could actually hear the messages of congratulations and good luck roaring out of people's mouths. The room was packed with folks I knew, some since childhood, but the argument with Mama had left me feeling isolated, as if all my senses were shrink-wrapped. So I did what any good woman would do. I ate for comfort.

First, I laid into some ribs. The boomerang of gray bones were wrapped up with thick ribbons of flesh, dripping a sauce whose molasses sweetness made my tongue beg to be whipped some more by the electric surge of habanero peppers. A pint of potato salad accompanied a quart of greens with icebergs of salt pork bobbing in a sea of vinegary pot liquor. I followed a rumor of red velvet cake to a dessert table and ate a cream cheese frosted mountain of that before filling another plate with Seven Up cake. I snuck up the stairs to go sit with Shanta on a balcony her father had added to look out over their huge yard. From lawn chair thrones we two African princesses watched our subjects dance to undulating rhythm in celebration of our coronation.

"How are you feeling?" I asked Shanta, who looked serene, dressed in a gauzy skirt and halter top.

"I'm fine," she said, "just fine."

I shook my head slowly. "We had another one of those moments back there in the auditorium." Nothing else had to be explained. Spirits speaking through Shanta was now just part of the complicated symmetry of our friendship.

"Mmm ... I know," Shanta said easily. "This time I even remember what they told me to say to you. You know, Grace, I like it when they come. There's this rush of pure power, and then when they leave, I feel so blissful. But then I'm only asked to host; I'm not being asked to do. For you, I expect things are very different."

"Infinitely more terrifying," I said. I hadn't told her about what had happened in the last two days because I was still wrestling with the details myself. But Shanta had known something powerful was going on because of my hair. When she had first seen me that morning, she had reached up, touched my tender carpet of naps and said, "change is a coming, huh Gracie?"

"Blissful?" I asked.

Shanta began to giggle. "Gracie, I'm so hurt I had to hear you were going out with Dr. Monroe's famous son from some folks I only halfway know at my job."

I rolled my eyes. "What have you heard? God, you can't even piss in private in this town," I lamented. "Don't be hurt, nothing actually happened. All I did was go out and make a fool of myself. I'm sure you heard all about that."

"Didn't hear anything about that, but I did hear something about some tomatoes."

I couldn't imagine who had overheard us in the produce department, but then I had been acting so strange, someone might have been trying to eavesdrop. I smiled as I thought about those tomatoes. I had sat them on the desk in my room like they were flowers in a vase.

"God, you know salad will never be the same again."

Shanta busted out laughing. "Tell me you at least tried to invite him to our party," she pleaded.

"I invited him, but he's not coming. Why would he?"

"He'll come because why wouldn't he? The man made a pass at you with tomatoes. I mean, he made tomatoes romantic."

I laughed and for a blessed moment, Shanta and I were as we had been before October and Oba, half-grown kids talking half-grown kid business. Like who really shouldn't be wearing this or that, and did Ms. Thing over in the corner of the yard really think people would believe she didn't have a weave when she had gone from a snap of hair on her head to tresses flowing around her butt, almost overnight.

It was a nice interlude before my mama invited ugly and stupid to join the party. My body sensed that all hell was bouncing up against the fence of my reality, trying to break loose. Tension snapped me up out my chair, and I stood there, head-cocked and fingers flexing.

"Gracie, what's the matter?" Shanta asked, jumping up to join me.

Before I could say, "I don't know," I knew. Joe's voice, fueled by panic, rocketed up the stairs. "Grace, Grace, you got to go home. Your mama lost her damn mind, and she throwing all your stuff out on the street."

22

I TUMBLED DOWN THE STAIRS and landed in a room full of guests who had stopped dancing, eating, and talking to stare at Joe and then me. I wanted to cling to a slim-to-none hope that maybe I had misheard my cousin or maybe this was the climax of a nightmare and in a moment I would wake up scared, but still sane. But the stricken look on Joe's face told me no, that what he had said and what I was feeling was all too damn real. Pure panic made me bolt toward the door, but Joe's thick straps of arms snared and encased me. I flailed about until Shanta threw herself into the clunky whirling of my forearms and legs. Her love and Joe's strength exceeded the potency of my adrenalin, and I stopped struggling. All I had left was my voice, which I balled up into a scream and began swinging. "Let me go Joe! Let me go! Let me go see!"

Joe tightened his grip. "No, Gracie, No, Gracie. You can't ... go by yourself," he grunted. "People have to go with you."

"Listen to him, Grace," Shanta whispered. "Whatever has happened, we'll get through it."

"How?" I wailed. "How?" Sobs chopped down my voice. Exhausted, I sagged deep against Joe.

Knots of frantically gossiping people untied themselves when Mr. Manning bounded in the living room. "What the hell is happening?" he yelled.

Joe strained to keep the emotion out his voice as he explained how he had been riding by my mother's house and had watched her dumping and scattering things, my things, out on the lawn.

"God Damn, Miriam," Mr. Manning uttered, and then he fell silent for a moment as he tried to figure out what to do next.

"Grace, you come with me," he finally said. Because he knew Shanta and Joe wouldn't stay, even if he ordered them to, he signaled for them to follow. He looked around the room. "Please everybody, remain here until we find out what happened."

"Ain't nobody heard that," Joe said as he and Shanta each took an elbow and urged me to start walking toward the door.

"Yeah, I know," Shanta's daddy replied, "but it's hard to keep flies off fresh shit, and there's a ton of it out there."

We got in his car and sat with the motor running, as if we were lost and needed directions.

"Grace, baby," Mr. Manning said, turning around so he could see me in the backseat. "I'm not going to lie and tell you I know what to do about this. If it gets too much for you to handle, let Shanta or Joe take you back to the car or you all walk back to the house." He paused and gave me a weak smile full of sadness and sympathy. "No matter what, Grace, you'll be staying with us."

I nodded. It was a slender plan, but it had enough buoyancy to keep me from being pulled under and drowned by Mama's rising madness.

What was usually a short drive seemed to take forever. The world floating by the window felt distant and foreign.

"I hope somebody didn't call the police," Joe said as we approached the corner.

I knew better. Our neighbors were nice, but nobody wanted to see full-blown craziness going on right outside their doors. As we made the turn, we were greeted by the sight of white cars haloed with slowly revolving wreaths of red and blue lights.

"Jesus," Joe moaned.

Mr. Manning laughed dryly. "Maybe it's a good thing they're here. It'll keep me from trying to kill her."

I closed my eyes, as we got closer. "Is it bad?" I asked Shanta when the car slid to a stop.

Her fingers curled tight around mine. "Yeah, Grace, it's bad."

I opened my eyes to find all my stuff sprawled like wreckage after a storm across the front lawn and the sidewalks leading up to the house. The presence of the police kept the small, but growing crowd at a polite distance, but it was humiliating to watch people visually picking through my things. A police officer was up on the porch, talking to Mama, arms folded across his chest as he listened to the rant that must have accompanied her rapid, jerky, gesticulations.

"You and Shanta stay in the car," Mr. Manning said, "until I can get a police officer to come over and talk to you."

I mouthed an okay and watched as he and Joe crossed the street toward two cops standing next to a car watching the crowd.

"Do you see Jamila or my Uncle George?" I asked. I found myself wishing it was winter instead of summer so that a pitch black blanket of evening dark would have covered everything in front of me.

Shanta pressed her face against the pane. "No. Maybe your uncle and aunt have Jamila in the house or maybe they took her over to one of your cousins until this mess blows over. God, let's hope so."

I nodded, because even though Jamila and I didn't like each other, I still couldn't help but worry that maybe she'd been hurt.

A uniformed woman with darkish blond hair and green eyes peered in and motioned for Shanta to open the door. I trembled slightly when the quiet of the car became suffused with the chattering of the crowd and the humid heat of the day. Almost instantly, I wanted to go back into the leathery cocoon of Mr. Manning's car and seal myself back in. But Shanta tugged at my hand, and I stepped out and stood next to her.

"Hello, ladies, my name is Officer Cash. Which one of you is Grace?" The officer's eyes darted from my face to Shanta's, until I nodded.

"I understand you weren't expecting this?" Officer Cash glanced behind her for emphasis.

My lips began to tremble as I shook my head no.

"I think we need to sit down and have a talk away from your mother and from all this. Your next door neighbor, Dr. Monroe, said we could use his place. Do you know Dr. Monroe?"

I nodded.

"Are you okay with doing that?"

"Yes," I whispered. "I'm okay with doing that."

Humiliation chilled my courage as my eyes snapped on to the faces I recognized in the crowd. Officer Cash moved her body and her authority between me and the stares.

"Close your eyes and just move with me," Shanta murmured as she collared my waist with her arm.

Sodden with exhaustion, my lids fell easily and my head followed, sealing my chin to my chest.

"Go," Shanta whispered, and with that I fell into the urgent swing of her walk.

The dark behind my eyes could only save me from so much. I could still hear the soft sizzle of "ahs" and the muffled pop, pop of "there she is ... there she is."

I bunched up some resolve and used it to snuff out an eruption of sobs. A few more steps, I convinced myself, and I could cry with people who wouldn't see my tears as a part of my mother's sad show.

"We're here at the porch," Shanta announced after several feet.

I opened my eyes to take the steps on my own. Monroe stood waiting in a smear of light, arms folded, his head cocked to the side. He was the Skin Horse assessing the condition of his now suffering and threadbare rabbit. *Did hate make you as real as love?* I wanted to ask him

"Hello, Grace," he said softly, but he knew not to ask me how I was.

"Let's go inside," he said to Officer Cash.

Monroe's huge living room seemed to shrink as I dragged myself and all my drama into it. He offered Officer Cash a chair, then the phone rang, and with a nod of his head he excused himself to go answer it.

I sank into the mouth of a big leather couch with Shanta. Silence followed, and it was the silence that finally broke me down. Tears began painting my cheeks with all my pain, and hurt hissed and crackled in my breathing like seeds in a shaking rattle. Shanta abandoned her mask of fearlessness and began to cry with me. My friend, my sister, planted her face in my hair and held on to me as if she knew she was the only thing holding down my sanity. As if she knew that if she let go, I would willingly descend to the darker side of crazy with my mother.

"You can't let your mother win," Office Cash said. Her strong voice easily pierced the dense fog of my pain. There was a "been there, done that" tone in it that made me look up. She smiled a sad smile of recognition and commiseration. "Yeah, my mother was a bitch. She threw my brother and me out of the house when I turned fifteen and my brother was ten."

"Can't you arrest her mother for what she did?" Shanta asked.

Officer Cash shook her head, the heavy swing of her blond ponytail emphasizing her assessment of the situation. "No, legally she's done nothing wrong. All the destruction is on her property. I assume you are eighteen. She doesn't have to take you back in. All we, the police, can do is provide you with some time to pick up your stuff."

Stuff. I thought about all my things lying as wreckage out on the lawn. My things were no longer just clothes or CDs or paper. They were the instruments my mother had used to humiliate me.

"I don't want any of it back," I blurted out.

Officer Cash looked at Shanta, and I knew in that instant they had decided to gather up my things just in case I was stubborn.

"You don't know what you'll want later," Officer Cash said gently. "Besides you want to be the one to control how your things are handled. You don't want to give your mother any power. You also don't want strangers taking your stuff. There's nothing worse than realizing people are wearing your clothes, or they're selling your things on eBay."

"Yeah, Grace," Shanta chimed in. "Some folks are bold enough to do that crap."

I sat there, my silence saying I was leaning much more toward no than yes.

Office Cash persevered. "Some ladies across the street brought over some boxes and bags. I don't want you out there picking things up. Your mother is still ... well not rational, but why don't you let your friend and your cousin start?"

I shook my head. "No."

"Grace." Doctor Monroe voice reached out with authority from the doorway. "Let people help you. Besides, we need to talk."

I knew then I would have to give in.

* * *

"I have some tea ready for you," Monroe said after Shanta and Officer Cash left.

I shrugged and followed him down a short span of carpeted hall and into his small and starkly modern kitchen. Everything from the cabinet to the stove was either silver or black, which sharply contrasted with the red walls and white ceiling. He pointed to a seat at the table, and I took it. Through dull eyes, I watched as he poured something hot and bitter smelling into a black functional mug.

"This is medicinal," he said as he pressed it into my quivering hands.

The first steaming, sour taste flared my nostrils, and I poked out my tongue.

"You'll feel more settled in a moment," he offered in response to my look.

"I guess you were all out of the cherry flavor," I joked.

Monroe smiled. He took out some crackers and spread them artfully on a plate before he sat down across from me.

"All right, Grace, this is what I know," he began. "I got a call from Mr. Manning. Jamila is with your uncle at a hotel out by Haven Lake. He got in a fight with your mother about her treatment of you. He and your aunt left with your sister once Miriam started trashing your room. He'll be by the Mannings tomorrow to talk about what you want to do. Where you may want to stay for the summer."

I nodded. "Mama has ruined everything."

"No, not everything," he said. "You've done well, Grace, considering."

The tea began clearing out the rubble of thoughts and feeling so I could begin to tumble out of sadness into the more purifying clarity of anger. "So, do you still think my mother loves me?"

He sat with the weight of my question for a long moment. "I stand by my original answer. Her love is thin, but it exists."

"I don't see how you can say that."

"My answer is my answer."

Agitated, I sat back in my chair and looked at him. "This morning, some spirit came and told me today was less about graduation and more about initiation. So is this part of my initiation? My mother throwing me out of her house? I don't think it's supposed to happen like this."

He gave me a sly smile. "Congratulations. You know the difference between your imagination and a visitation. Initiations take different forms, but it's usually an event that goes along with some power or gift erupting from your deepest self.

"So am I allowed to ask, why me?"

I expected the time-honored but not very soul satisfying answer of "why not you?" But Skin Horses are always truthful.

"Some things," Monroe said, "are just yours to suffer and do for the greater good, for the sake of justice. And sometimes they are yours to do, even if it costs you everything you love, even if it costs you your life. That is why, Grace, becoming real doesn't happen to everybody. It doesn't happen to people who break easily or who have sharp edges or who have to be carefully kept."

I shook my head slowly in weary disagreement. I had been my mother's child for too long. She had filled me so full of doubts that I was scared of damned near close to everything that was mine to understand and do. Malevolent and crazy, my mama had rendered me all but naked of the glorious ways and meaning of my shamanic heritage. I had been delivered to Monroe spiritually deaf, mute and blind. "What," he must have thought, "am I to do with this child?"

Then, in a strange, unreal little moment, he reached out and touched my hand. I felt the pulse of a deep and powerful connection.

"Do I get a cape with this?" I asked.

Monroe laughed. I was quick, but he was quicker. "What do you need a cape for, Grace?" he asked. "You already know how to fly."

23

IT WAS DEEP INTO THE night before I fell asleep in the Manning's guest room. Shanta and I had talked until my thoughts were too thick to shape into words. Exhaustion pressed me down on the small bed and wouldn't let me back up until almost noon the next day. I lay there wrapped in covers and a thin veneer of sunlight, groggily thinking about what would come next. I was happy about my freedom, but terrified of the homelessness.

The door to the room opened, and Ms. Manning's voice floated in through the crack. "Grace, baby, you up?"

"Yeah, I'm up," I called out. With some effort, I flipped over and sat up on the edge of the bed. A glimpse of my half-naked body in the mirror convinced me to make a cape out of the sheets.

"How you feeling?"

I threw out my hands and shrugged, because I couldn't exactly describe the texture of the numbness I had erected to protect my sanity.

Mrs. Manning's head bobbed. "Yes, yes, I suppose you don't want to talk about that yet. Are you hungry?"

I nodded. The one thing my numbness hadn't dulled was my appetite.

Mrs. Manning's lips cracked open into a wide smile. "That's a good sign. Now, your Uncle George called, and he'll be over in about an hour. I washed some of your clothes. They're on the top of the dresser. Okay?"

I glanced at the pile of jeans, T-shirt and underclothes and marveled at the thoughtfulness. Even in the midst of all the chaos, she had done for me what my own mother wouldn't have bothered to do.

"Mrs. Manning, I'm so sorry ... about all this." I closed my eyes to keep the tears in. The bed sank and settled with her weight, and I leaned into the waiting cradle of her soft thick arms. She smelled of bacon, flowers and all the security I was seeking.

"This is not your fault, young lady," she whispered. "You're not responsible for your mother's actions."

I still felt the burden. It should have occurred to me my mother was capable of all kinds of ugliness. If I had been a better friend, I would have just given in and stayed home. Then at least Shanta would have had the kind of graduation party and memories she deserved.

"You're not responsible," Mrs. Manning repeated, as if she knew what I was thinking, "Now get dressed."

"Is Shanta awake?" I asked, even though I suspected she wasn't.

"No, Shanta's not here, honey. She got called into work. Charles dropped her off on his way to the plant. I told her not to go, but you know how your friend is about money. She's probably still got her first dollar hidden somewhere in her room."

Money, I thought, I needed to think about money, especially since I had to make my own way in the world. Stuff wasn't cheap or free, and the cost of trouble had to be tallied up and paid for.

"Mrs. Manning," I began as I got up off the bed to gather up my clean clothes, "I don't have anything right now, but when I call Attorney Blair to tell him what happened and where I'm going to be living, I can ask for a check to pay you for letting me stay here."

Mrs. Manning laughed. "My husband and I wouldn't take anything from you, Grace. We've already talked about it."

"But ... I have money."

"I know, Grace," she said over her shoulder as she headed out the door. "I know you have money, but we won't take any. Now get dressed."

* * *

Lunch was a pale, gold avalanche of scrambled eggs festooned with rubies of crisp red bell pepper and golden veins of sharp cheddar cheese. I was smacking on cords of bacon and chorizo sausage when Mrs. Manning ushered my uncle into the kitchen.

"Are you hungry, George?" Mrs. Manning asked as she cleared plates from the table and pulled out another chair.

My uncle shook his head. "No. Thanks."

"Well then, I'll leave you two alone to talk."

Uncle George looked as weary as a drought stricken tree. Worry and regret had wilted his confidence and dried up his usual ready smile. I got up to hug him and he flinched. Horrified, I traced the current of pain to its black and blue source on his right arm.

"My mother hit you, didn't she?" I asked, shaking my head with disbelief.

Uncle George smiled sadly and sat down at the table. "Nope, she threw something at me, and I didn't move fast enough."

"I hope you hit her back."

"Grace, I've never hit a woman in my life, and even though your mother may deserve to have her ass beat, I'm not going to start now."

I collapsed back in my chair and stared at my empty breakfast plate. "Are Aunt Jean and Jamila all right?"

A grunt rattled out of my uncle's throat. "I had to put my wife on a plane this morning. She was about to take your mother on. Bad enough my sister's acting the fool; I don't need my wife in on it. Jamila is doing okay. Shaken up but ..."

"But she wants to go back to Mama, right?" I already knew Jamila would go back, because the burden of Mama's anger had never been hers to shoulder and haul. Suffering had been my role in the family.

"Yeah, Jamila made all kinds of excuses for Miriam. All kinds. Finally, I had to stop her by telling her there were no excuses for what Miriam did to you. None. Parents don't act like that. Jamila just shut down then and wouldn't talk. Jean said it was almost like she's been brainwashed. Maybe so. I don't know. All I know is this: I haven't done right by either of you girls. I should have known ..."

"How would you? I never said anything."

"And I didn't ask either ... but I should have known."

His eyes lifted off from me to stare out the kitchen window, as if his regrets were becoming real out on the Manning's lawn. Silence followed more silence. Then I realized that in a convoluted way, he had opened a door to the past and was standing there waiting to see if I wanted to step in and ask the one question whose answer I both deeply desired and feared.

"Uncle George," I asked, "why doesn't my mother love me?"

The kitchen grew smaller, and the air thicker with the fetid scent of a shared history that, like a festering wound, needed to be scraped out and cleaned. My uncle's eyes returned to me. I thought he was going to give me some of the same "thin love" crap that Monroe kept handing to me.

"Our mother used to tell people that your mother was born a difficult baby and never grew out of it. She was smart, but she was always up for an argument and could change moods like they were dresses or shoes. What your daddy saw in her, except that she was beautiful, hell, I don't know. Maybe he thought he could fix her, and maybe for a while he did. They were happy for a year or two, but Miriam was Miriam, and after a couple years, your daddy wanted out."

My uncle paused as if he needed to breathe more deeply to begin the laborious task of raising the damaged hulk of the truth out of a sea of lies.

"Like too many folks, they thought having children would sweeten a souring marriage. You were born, and you came right out the box looking like him, acting like him. Like all daughters, you had your daddy wrapped around every little finger and toe. He carried you everywhere, bragged on you to anybody. Most women would have been proud to have a man take care of his child like your daddy took care of you. Not my sister. She fought him on everything he tried to do with you. I think she was jealous. Things didn't get any better when they had Jamila. In fact, things seemed to get worse. One night your father called to tell me he was going to get a divorce and ask for full custody. He said he was calling because he respected me and that he didn't want our side of the family to think that he would ever take you and Jamila from us. That was the last I heard, until maybe two weeks later when your mother called to tell me that your father was missing."

The word missing seemed to make my uncle hurt. He breathed in a deep, ragged breath, as if the news and the pain were only hours fresh instead of years old.

"Anybody ever talked to you about that time?" he asked. His voice was muffled, like he had wrapped it up tightly to prevent a torrent of terrifying grief from leaping from it.

I shook my head. "No, not really. All I ever heard from Mama was that he committed suicide."

"Do you believe he committed suicide?"

"I never knew anything different until Nana Grace told me it wasn't true. Mr. Manning told me that he and a lot of black folks thought it was a hate crime. Mr. Manning also told me Mama just accepted the report."

"Yes," my uncle said. "That sounds about right. This is what I have put together from what little your mother offered, and what the police report said and didn't say. It was October, fifteen years ago. Your father went for a walk with his dog and was never seen alive again. He went out because he had told your mother he wanted a divorce, and, of course, there was an argument. It took your mother a full two weeks to report that he was missing. Maybe she thought he would cool down and come back, maybe she was just pissed off about his decision to leave her, but she didn't report him gone until his job kept calling to say he better come in or he'd be fired. Valuable time lost. Only your mother didn't seem to care. She just kept saying, 'well, he was going to leave me anyway.' Lot of folk told her she was being childish. But it seemed to be all about her and her pride."

I shook my head, trying to loosen up the silt of my memory. I tried to conjure up how a four-year-old might have felt about the ending of her world, but my mind had erected castle walls of denial and forgetfulness around my sanity.

"The police are bad now about dealing with black folks' concerns in this town," my uncle continued, "but back then they were even worse. It took those jokers days to mount a search. They even had the nerve to tell us that given the circumstances, your father was probably off drinking. They had this, 'that's what you black folk do' kind of attitude. Relatives and friends did most of the looking. We hung up posters. We searched the woods. Weeks passed and we didn't have any leads. Then we had a prayer vigil down at the big AME Zion church on Luther Avenue. When the prayers were finished and the minister asked if there was anyone who needed to speak, you stood up with your four-year-old self and said that people thin as paper had come to you during the night and whispered that your daddy was down in the apple orchard by the lake."

Uncle George went quiet for a long time.

"Next day," he finally said, "a farmer found your father's remains hanging from a tree in an orchard down by Haven Lake. Coroner ruled it a suicide because of the circumstances surrounding his disappearance. Everybody told your mama it just didn't seem right your father would kill himself. But your mother wasn't having it. She just wanted it over and done with. She wanted to go on with her life."

Some long dormant emotions began turning, arching up toward rebirth.

"Paper people," I whispered.

My uncle gave me a small knowing smile. "Yes, the paper people. Nana Grace had to explain to me that you were talking about spirits. That's the thing that threw your mother deep into crazy, because the paper people didn't just stop with that prediction."

My uncle's open palm began to tap the table as if he needed to make sure I was awake and listening, not just with my ears, but with my very soul. "They kept coming back after the funeral, night after night, using your mouth to confront Miriam, demanding she seek justice. She would call me over and over again, screaming that you were possessed and evil. Here you were her own child, exposing the depths of her selfishness over and over again. There was no forgiving you in my sister's hard and crazy heart for that kind of pain. She beat your gift out of you like it was a bad habit. Made sure you couldn't— wouldn't—use it. Except gifts like that don't have expiration dates, and they don't die. According to Dr. Monroe, the paper people are back."

"With a vengeance," I whispered. For some reason, my words smoothed over the rougher edges of my uncle's agitation. He sat back in his chair, satisfied that his point had been fully made.

"How do you know my father's death wasn't a suicide?" I asked.

"More than anything for me, it was the dog. Police report said your daddy strangled the dog before he hung himself. But your daddy loved that dog. He wouldn't have harmed Little Jack. No, Grace it was a lynching. Somebody killed him."

"Do you know who did it?" I asked.

He looked at me, his eyes filling with a resolve that both frightened and fascinated me. "I think, Grace, that's something you're supposed to look into and settle. Which is why Dr. Monroe and I think that it would be better if you went to live with Aunt Casmil and Peaches. They know more about what you need to be looking into, they know more about your gift. Besides your mother's not going to let the Mannings alone. She's been calling over here all morning. Mrs. Manning said they had to turn off the phone."

Deep down inside, I knew it was true. Mama wouldn't leave me alone if I remained in town. She wasn't scared of the Mannings, not in the ways that mattered. Sticks and stones and Personal Protection Orders wouldn't even faze her. My mama needed the fear of God and the ancestors put into her, and the only people I knew who could do that were my Aunts Peaches and Casmil, and my not-so-dead-great-grandmother, Nana Grace.

24

MY DECISION TO LEAVE THE next day struck Shanta as too damn swift and soon. She wanted me to stay, to plant my feet, square my shoulders and wear my mother down with my defiance. My leaving, she explained, both to her parents and me, was too much like cowardice, like I was giving up and running away. That I was running away to save her family from the stench of my mother's madness didn't seem to matter to Shanta or her parents. They were willing to live with the smell of turmoil. But, out of love, out of respect, I just couldn't allow that to happen.

"My aunts only live twenty miles away over in Carsonville," I whispered to Shanta as we sat on her bed like inverted parentheses. Backs snug and locked against each other, souls meshed like finely strung nets of roots. In the sun speckled quiet of her bedroom, Shanta's clock, the clock we had found together at the tackiest garage sale in the world, loudly ticked down to the moment when my uncle and Joe would arrive to go out to my aunt's house, my new home.

"Come on, Gracie, stay."

"Twenty miles," I repeated, as if this simple logic were medicine enough to cure her desperation.

"Soon it will be more than that," Shanta blurted out. "Soon it will be hundreds of miles."

My finger crept up to cover my mouth. I was only seeing dimly what Shanta had already brought fully into focus. Within two months she would be in her new world of Harvard. That we could be together one last time was the best reason to stay with the Mannings, but I shook off the temptation.

"Do you think we'll always be close?" Shanta asked in a tear-dampened whisper.

I bit my lip to pinch off my liquid sorrow and offered what I knew to be true. "Always. Not even death ..." I didn't have to finish the sentence. If anyone knew, Shanta knew this was a promise I could literally keep.

"Twenty miles isn't bad," she finally conceded.

"You could come with me today and help me move in."

Shanta shook her head. "My mother said you needed to be alone with your aunts so they can get used to you and you to them."

I shrugged and laughed. "I get the feeling it'll be more me getting used to them. According to Uncle George they've been waiting for this to happen since forever. They were hoping to get their hands on Jamila too, but you know ..."

"Well, when you get settled, we can go out shopping for our dorm rooms."

"Yeah," I said, and I was happy for a few seconds, then every thing in me shifted from bright to dark as if the moon had suddenly swallowed the sun. A nest of premonitions hatched, leaving in their scurrying wake entrails full of dread. I couldn't suppress the shiver.

Shanta stiffened. "Grace, what's the matter?"

"Nothing," the ancestors made me whisper.

If ever I needed Shanta to become a vessel for spirits, I needed her then. I wanted the other world to name its festering work, to tell me in full what kind of darkness it was pouring the foundation for. But Shanta couldn't give me any more milk of understanding. They were weaning me off her.

"Really, Grace, what's the matter?"

"Nothing."

It was a lie, and Shanta knew it, but she didn't ask me again. She knew enough to leave it alone.

"Grace, your uncle and Joe are here." Mrs. Manning's voice floated into the room seconds before she appeared in the doorway. She looked as cheery as the red T-shirt she was wearing.

Shanta and I trundled off the bed, pausing to hug. No tears, just a semi-brave whisper. "It will be all right," I promised her.

"You know you will always have a home with us," Mrs. Manning said as we walked slowly through the living room.

I nodded and tried to remember if I had forgotten anything. "Yes, I know. Thank you so much for everything."

"You have a visitor. He said he wanted to surprise you, but I thought that might be a little much."

I reached the front door and turned around to look back at her and Shanta. "Who?"

"Evan," Mrs. Manning eased out the two syllables of his name as if she knew it would make me skittish.

"Oh crap," I whispered under my breath, just out of reach of her hearing. I glanced at what I had on and sure enough, I looked as rumpled as I felt in my one-size-doesn't-quite fit-all pants and my favorite, but faded "Got Cake?" T-shirt. *Why*, I wondered, *had he come given what he must have seen the other night?*

"I don't even know what to say," I admitted.

Shanta laughed. "How about, hello Mr. Gorgeous-brother-who knows-how-to-cook?"

Mrs. Manning rolled her eyes and shook her head. She knew what I was thinking, what I couldn't help but think.

"Shanta, please. How about you just say hello. He understands that what happened the other night wasn't your fault. Besides you might want to go rescue him from our men folk. When I left, Charles was talking nonstop about recipes, and Joe and your uncle were interrogating him."

"Oh Lord," I said as I swung open the door and stepped out into a pretty, but broiling hot day. In a dense patch of porch shade, I stood for a moment looking down at the knot of manhood talking and laughing beside the SUV that Uncle George had rented. Evan was dressed casually and looked at ease. When he finally glanced up and saw me, he waved, then he gestured toward my Uncle George who reached into the open car door and handed him something.

A huge smile hung on the end of his hello when he reached the porch. It was all I could do to say, "hi," without pinning my eyes on my shoes.

In his long arms, he was cradling a bouquet of salmon colored roses wrapped up to their glossy bright heads in white paper. I found myself admiring them, but when he said, "these are for you," and extended the cone towards me, I acted like I had no clue what they were.

"They're beautiful, aren't they, Grace?" Shanta coached from behind my back.

"It's hot, so let's get them in some water," Shanta's mother added.

I reached up for their fragrant fullness and then reluctantly handed them over to Shanta and her mother who oh'd and ah'd over them as they disappeared into the house.

"I guess you figured out nobody's ever given me flowers," I admitted.

"I consider it an honor to be the first."

Pity flowers, I thought. What else could they be but pity flowers?

"Look, I don't know what to say," I blurted out. "I'm ashamed of everything that happened."

Sadness crept up and garbled the rest of my words. I crossed my arms to protect myself from his sympathy.

"You're not responsible for who your mother is or what she does," Evan said. "But I'm sure it doesn't hurt any less."

I shrugged because I didn't quite believe him. It's one thing to say you're okay with crazy, but it was a whole other thing to see it live and performing in person at a theater in your life.

"Thank you for the flowers," I said, and I was about to suggest I should probably get ready to leave when he took a few careful steps forward.

"Can I give you a hug?" he asked.

"Yes," budded on my lips and he gathered me in. He smelled faintly of fresh ginger and the watermelony scent of newly mowed grass. I marveled at the lullaby of his breathing. How the simple rising and falling of his chest drained away some of my awkwardness, replacing it with a little trust and comfort.

"I'm sorry I wasn't here to help," he whispered. "I was in Lansing visiting a friend overnight."

"That's okay." I sighed, relieved he'd only heard about my mother's craziness, not actually seen it.

"Hey, Grace, time to go." Joe's voice flew up from the bottom of the porch stairs and tackled the moment. I did my best to ignore him, but Evan knew he had to give in.

"I'll give you a call later," he murmured as he released me.

Evan nodded and smiled at Joe when he passed him. Joe didn't exactly smile back.

"Who sent you up here?" I asked, trying and not succeeding in acting like I wasn't mortified.

"Both of them," Joe grinned. "They wanted me to catch you before you started swapping spit."

"Joe," I moaned, "I don't think Mr. Manning or Uncle George said that."

Joe's eyes got bright, and his grin cracked open into a deep laugh. "Yeah, you're right, but Mr. Manning and Uncle G thought that Evan might be getting a little too friendly, a little too quick, and I agreed."

"He was just being nice."

"Well, what you call nice, Gracie girl, other folks call macking."

"Oh please," I shouted as I grabbed the door and tumbled back into the Manning's house.

"So soon?" Shanta asked, as I walked back into the kitchen. She was drinking iced tea and nibbling on a molasses cookie that was almost as round and wide as a saucer. She held the sugar-encrusted hem toward me, and I shook my head no even as my appetite suddenly sprinted from normal greediness toward ravenous.

"Yeah, Joe got all big brother on me and kind of chased him off."

"Joe shouldn't be in your business," Shanta said.

Mrs. Manning looked lost in thought as she lifted out my precious bundle from the sink. In the time I had been gone, she had rubber banded a small plastic bag half full of water around the stems and rewrapped them.

"Have your aunts find you a vase as soon as you get there," she said as she handed them to me. "It was so thoughtful of Evan to bring these to you."

I nodded and ran a finger over the petal's curves, imagining them as the tender slope of his lips.

"Grace." Mrs. Manning's voice spilled like ice water into the lap of my romantic reverie. "Don't be too hard on Joe. He's like a brother. He just wants to protect you. It's nice to have sisters, but you need brothers too. You let him sniff Mr. Evan out and see if he's really all right. After all, men know men. Do you understand what I'm saying?"

I heard her, but I wanted to think Joe didn't have to sniff around. I wanted to think that everything I needed to know about Evan had been in that embrace on the porch.

I nodded my head slowly and half-lied to Mrs. Manning. "Yes, I think I do understand."

* * *

"You ever been to your aunts' house?" my uncle asked as the van leapt into a high-speed sprint. Some of the boxes in the back rattled as they slid back then tumbled forward.

"No," I said.

My uncle laughed, and when he glanced at me, his eyes were as shiny as his smile. "Well, you are in for a treat. Let's just say your aunts live different."

"Yeah, you sure can call it different," Joe agreed.

I shrugged. I didn't care because it was better to be wanted by the eccentric than hated by the so-called sane. I felt relieved. Each mile

unraveled more of the cocoon I had been entombed in. Safe and secure from my maternal predator, I was being reborn.

"Evan looks like a nice young man," Uncle George said after a few
more miles.

I smiled. "Yeah, he does seem nice."

"Charles was elbowing me and whispering that he's some kind of
famous cook off of one of those reality TV shows."

"That's what I heard. We don't know each other that well."

"Well, he was acting like he was your man." Joe stuck his opinion
over the front seat like a sheet of paper with childish writing on it.

"Don't mind Joe. He's just concerned like I'm concerned," Uncle
George said.

"Concerned about Evan? Why?"

"We saw how he was holding you," Joe interrupted.

"He asked me if I wanted a hug, and I said yes."

"He needs to be worthy of you, Grace," my uncle announced.

It took every bit of my manners not to ask him if he and Joe and
Mr. Manning had been smoking something while they were waiting for me. To me, the issue was not if Evan was worthy of me, but
whether I was worthy of him. A hug was one thing, but in reality,
I couldn't see it going beyond that. What could I be to Evan in any
version of the future except trouble in mind and spirit? I would be
baggage he would have to explain and make excuses for. I was human
okra; normal looking until I got bumped, and then I started to ooze
strange voices, strange actions, and strange energies he didn't even
believe in.

"Look, Grace, I haven't been the best uncle. I should have done
more to help you with your mother, but I care, and I don't want a man
to mess over you."

"Look, nothing's going to happen," I offered. "If it's any consola-
tion to you two, Evan's father's not going to let it happen anyway."

Uncle George got indignant. "What? His father doesn't think
you're good enough for his son?"

I wanted to open the door and roll out.

"No it's more like, Dr. Monroe doesn't think Evan is good enough for me. Actually it's a little more complicated than that."

"He's right. He's not." Joe grunted.

"Lord, can we talk about something else?"

From my lips to the ancestor's ears, the climate in the car seemed to change from present to past, and the conversational winds shifted and surged with it.

"You know all this land?" Uncle George asked, lifting and waving his arm as if to underline the bright fields and dark naps of forest along side the highway. "All of it used to belong to black farmers before—"

"Before my great-great-grandfather murdered that white man Abraham Gilmore," I finished.

My uncle snatched his eyes off the highway for a moment and looked at me. "I wasn't going to say it like that. We were never allowed to say it like that. Who told you?"

"I just remember hearing one of the relatives whispering about it," I said solemnly.

Of course, my explanation was a shadow of the truth because I couldn't see what my uncle would have done with the mystical reality of how I had come by the information.

"Not too many young folks know about that night, I guess, because not too many old folks want to talk about it or remember," Uncle George continued. "But that incident messed up whole generations of black folks—white folks too—except they don't realize they're messed up. Even now, people are still suffering."

"Well, I knew about it because my mother never stopped talking about it," Joe said.

Uncle George laughed. "Maybe because your mama sees a conspiracy in everything. I'll never forget when she told me about how the government could track black folk by the fifth digit of their social security number. She got mad when I told her that I didn't think it was true."

"How do you know it's not true?" Joe teased. "Lots of things you can't see or feel are true. Right, Gracie?"

I didn't turn around to look at my cousin, and I didn't answer his question. I just sat there, wondering how much of Joe was in that statement, and how much some intangible, spiritual other.

The highway took us to the edge of a small hamlet named Carsonville. I had only seen it in passing when Mama had dragged Jamila and me up to Lansing to go shopping. I had known that my aunts had lived out that way, but never had the courage to go looking.

"Here we are," my uncle announced as he made a left turn down the wide mouth of a dirt road.

"I don't believe this," was all I could say as my aunts' house rose up on the slope of a hill like something straight out of a cartoon. 1524 Over Ridge Road was a quaint two story farm house plain in style and form, except the sisters had painted its clapboard skin a shade of blue I had only seen in Kool-Aid and kid's candy.

"Do they just like blue?" I asked, looking over my shoulder at Joe.

Joe shook his head. "You got me. Last time I said something about the color they told me blue was sacred. I thought Casmil was going to beat my ass when I told her I didn't think God would have been offended if they had just painted a room or some furniture blue."

Uncle George sighed. "Yeah, Joe, you were lucky. I'm a grown man and Casmil's an old woman, and I wouldn't want to be on the wrong side of a fight with her. You know, these women take their religion seriously. I don't know why you said something like that."

"How many acres do they have?" My eyes took in the woods that ran up one side of the road.

"About ten acres, maybe a little more," Uncle George said as he pulled up in the front yard. "Your great-grandmother was able to purchase some of the land that was lost during the riot to give back to people. She only kept a few acres for herself, and she gave those to her sisters."

Before I was fully up their porch steps, Casmil and Peaches spilled out to gather me up and in like I was a long awaited harvest. They were dressed in identical gray suits, as if my coming were some classy event to which I had been invited but had forgotten the invitation read formal. I was the dirty, rumpled sock in a pile of clean, pressed and folded laundry, but for once I didn't feel like it mattered.

"Welcome home!" they said, almost in unison.

"Your room is this way," Peaches offered. As soon as I crossed the threshold of the door, her tiny arms locked with mine and we were off and up a huge staircase.

"Your uncle and I will be up in a minute after I put the flowers in a vase," Casmil called after us.

I took note, as Peaches and I climbed, that the frantic blue outside appeared to be only skin-deep. Inside, the sisters had leaned on the serenity of beige walls and carpet to support and contrast their selections of furnishings and paintings.

"Here we are." She opened a door and stepped aside to allow me to fully take in the beauty of the room. Words broke apart, scattered and dissolved on my tongue in a series of "ohs" and "ahs." I timidly walked around the room, touching things to make sure that what was in front of me was not made of desperate dreams. My fingers caressed the smooth cherry wood of a canopy bed that had been set sailing, like a tall ship, on ocean-blue carpet. I picked up decorative bottles on a matching cherry dresser and studied them like they were the artifacts of someone else's happy life. I turned on and off a small television before sampling swatches of music from the radio of an expensive sound system. I was too shocked to cry. I had expected less, would have been happy with less.

"Aunt Peaches, I don't know what to say," I finally confessed. "Thank you."

"Nothing to say, baby," Peaches said. "It was, and is, our pleasure. I told Joe to put your boxes in another room just down the hall. You can go through them when you've had some rest and feel up to it."

Our pleasure. I said those words to myself, framed them on my tongue so that I could remember them.

When my uncle saw the room, he gave a low little whistle of delight. "I'm going to come live with you," he joked, but then he got serious. "Gracie, I got to be getting on the road, so I'm going to take

Joe back home. I gave your aunts my phone number so you keep in touch. Don't let my sister back into your life. I don't care what she tries."

"Thank you for everything, Uncle George," I whispered in his ear as I hugged him.

"I wish I had a different truth, Grace," he said, "but what is *is* and must be dealt with."

"Yes," I admitted, "but I don't know how to begin."

"It will come," he whispered somberly. "It will come."

I was about to cry because I didn't want my uncle to leave now that he had helped rescue me, but Casmil said in a firm voice, "you will need to get washed up and dressed for dinner."

I was tired. All I wanted to do was lie in the center of my new bed and look between the covers for a nap.

"We invited Monroe over to have dinner with us," Peaches explained.

I wanted to say I would have been happier if we were dining with his son but I didn't.

"He is bringing over your father's envelope." I turned around to find Peaches and Casmil looking at me the way they had during Nana Grace's funeral. Sonorous intuition told me there would be food on the table, but that dinner wasn't going to be about eating, it was going to be about ceremony.

Monroe could not just give me my package, he had to have Oba's blessing. Even then, I knew Oba didn't give anything without a firm expectation of payment. Oba's demands of me, I vaguely suspected, were going to be less about spiritual joy and more about duty, sacrifice and obedience.

25

AFTER MY AUNTS LEFT ME alone to dress, I stood for a moment and savored the sweet newness of my circumstances. My battered hopes slinked out of the depths of their hiding places to graze on happiness. I put on Ella and she sang about blue sky being over her and me. *What to wear now that I was free in both body and mind?* I mused. Staccato grunts accompanied my efforts to lift a borrowed suitcase filled with some of my worldly clothes on to the bed. I fingered the zipper key warily. Unpacking was going to be like cracking open spoiled Easter eggs. After all, detergent could only do so much to remove the stench and stains of homemade emotional shit.

I was relieved to find that Mrs. Manning had organized the cotton and polyester wreckage of my life in such a way that I didn't really have to think about what to wear. She had paired and pinned certain things together so that if I was too muddled or depressed to make a decision for the first couple of days, all I had to do was pick up a package of stuff and put them on. As if the best had to be saved for last, she had placed my father's coat at the bottom of the suitcase. I hugged it, wishing that I could gather more memories of my father from its itchy touch. No memories came, but the rough swirl of wool against my cheek brought comfort.

I slid into a pair of black pants and a blouse, confident that if nothing else, I matched. Then mid-breath, as if someone had shouted, "take five," Ella stopped singing. Something like the dulled edge of a frozen knife slid across the back of my neck, sucking my breath away.

Hold ... hold, hold, I told myself as I waited for other cosmic shoes to drop.

The roar of waves from an unseen ocean rolled up the silence in the room and put it away. From a corner beside the bed, the ripe smell of fresh turned earth saturated the air. Queasiness snuck up on me as the interior of the room bled out into whiteness, and the door behind me yawned open. At first I sensed Aunt Peaches' presence only as hard prickling along the length of my spine, but then she spoke, "Rabbit real, rabbit real, are you ready, ready, ready? Are you ready?" Her disembodied voice was tinny and strained, as if it could hardly bear the weight of the words Oba had first spoken to me.

Fear, the size of a peach pit, rose in my throat and I forced myself to swallow it back down. "Yes, Aunt Peaches, I'm ready," I said.

"Good." The tug of her fingers on my sleeve hushed the ocean and brought Ella back on stage to bebop about blue birds and gray skies now gone.

* * *

The dining room was set for a meal I was suddenly desperate to devour. Hunger winds fueled by changes in my spiritual temperature began to howl against the wall of my stomach. The growling was loud, incessant, embarrassing. From behind me, Peaches's voice stroked at my awkwardness. "All is understood here. What is happening is too powerful for your body not to react to it. Now, let's get you fed."

As soon as we entered, Monroe broke off an intense conversation with Casmil. He smiled, stood and pulled out a chair for me to sit down.

"Grace," he said.

"Hello, Dr. Monroe ... Aunt Casmil."

My greeting to my aunt fell into a black hole of sullen attitude. She nodded but that was about all.

I couldn't figure out why she was pissed, so I gushed, "what a beautiful table."

And it was. Delicate, thin-lipped china dishes and napkins floated like water lilies atop a lapis colored tablecloth. I could almost imagine the silverware as bright fingerling of fish.

Her, "thank you" was frosty, and I looked at Monroe to see if he would provide some explanation. He offered a look that said, not now, later.

Peaches motioned to her sister. "Casmil, please come help me in the kitchen."

Casmil rose. "Your flowers are in the living room," she said, each word sounding like she was snapping pencils in half.

"I don't think Aunt Casmil likes me very much," I whispered as they disappeared into the kitchen.

Monroe rested his chin on the back of one of his hands and looked beyond me. "Casmil is more like Nana Grace than Peaches. She values honor, discipline and respect of oneself and others. Words should be followed by deeds. Promises are sacred and have to be kept. You may find you will come to appreciate that about her."

I shrugged. "Maybe."

After Mama, I felt I didn't need a Casmil. I liked the fact that with Aunt Peaches, I would be loved unconditionally. I was her baby, would always be her baby, because in her world I was her child and I needed to be cared for.

Monroe grew quiet and I knew he was looking for a way to broach a subject I didn't want to talk about. "My son said he came by to visit you at your friend's home earlier today."

I tried not to grin, but I couldn't keep my tiny smile from inflating. "I know, I know, you don't approve," I said.

"I only bring it up so that you may keep in mind my warning about getting involved with him."

But, I thought, as I stared at the table, *I didn't care.* I wanted the hug Evan had given me to become a kiss, and for the kiss to become infinitely more. "He just came by to give me some flowers, okay? There was nothing romantic about it."

My dark beige lie, my half-ass attempt at denial made Monroe sit fully forward, as if he needed his forearms planted on the table to support the weight of what I assumed was his growing impatience. Except what came out of his mouth sounded more desolate and despondent.

"My son's attempt at comfort can't cover the pain of what your mother did to you. It's a loss, and you need time to recover and reconcile with it. Without breaking any confidences, I can tell you that my son has his own personal problems he needs to tend to. Then there is the matter of your father's envelope."

I panicked a little and snapped, "it was just flowers."

"Grace, I warned you before that with this gift came great responsibilities, and once you open you father's envelope—"

"You know what's in it?"

"No, but I can promise you this: once you open it there will seem to be no end to what the world will demand of you. Upstairs you gave your sacred word that you were ready, but are you really? Peaches is willing to accept that you are. Casmil, however, thinks that you're still too immature and undisciplined, that you're a girl being sent to do a woman's job."

"That's what you were arguing about, wasn't it?"

"Discussing, yes."

I felt a little shame-faced and small at being called a girl, at being accused of not accepting responsibility. Still, I wanted what my hormones were telling me I needed.

"I'm sorry, but you know, I want …" I started to confess.

"Yes, I do know. You want the comfort of a relationship. But you must understand that any relationship you enter will be difficult. There will always be secrets you will not be able to share completely with him. You will have to do things you may not be able to fully explain. Whoever you are with is going to need all the understanding he thinks he has and more to comprehend whom you have been called by and the purpose you now must serve."

"So are you with someone? Does he understand?"

Monroe smiled. I knew he didn't want to give up this detail of his life, but the deal was he had to. "Yes, and sometimes."

"Will I get to meet him?"

Monroe smiled again. "Someday."

"I'm sorry," I said, "I didn't mean to get in your business."

"I understand, Grace. You just want to know what your future may look like."

As if she believed enough was enough, Aunt Casmil appeared in the door. Aunt Peaches stood behind her, looking up at the ceiling like she was trying to keep her opinion from coming up like bad food. She didn't look happy. There had been, I suspected, an argument in the kitchen, and Peaches had come out on the losing end of the metaphysical smack down.

"Let's open things now, before dinner," Casmil said.

As hungry as I was, I knew better than to object or to even offer a compromise.

I expected only my father's envelope, but Casmil went back into the kitchen and reappeared with a wood chest a little bigger than a shoebox. She placed it on the table and edged it toward me. The top was intricately carved with figures of open mouth dolphins leaping over embossed ocean waves. My fingers began to caress the dark, polished surface. Without asking, I knew it was my father's work. I looked from my aunts' expectant faces to Monroe's more serious expression and wondered: *Did some prayer have to be said, or some chanting verbally decanted?* I couldn't think. I was too eager. I wrestled a bit with the carved top, and when it popped off, I found some cowries shells, each as big as a cat's paw, nestled in red velvet.

I fingered the cloth. *Red,* I thought, or was made to think, by those who are eternal, the color of the ancient god Shango, whose symbol, the double-headed axe, represented swift and balanced justice. Red, the color of the headdresses enslaved women wore when they wanted to state that they were children of a God they knew would vanquish their white masters and mistresses.

The room began to cool. I smelled the ocean and heard once again its distant, constant breathing. I knew to touch the shells. I was told in small whispers to stroke them. As I ran my fingers across their glossy, mottled surfaces, words unfurled from my lips like ribbons caught on the tips of strong breezes. "As strong as your houses I will be," I began to chant, "to the seas of eternity I will go, and from those seas I will return."

I realized then that the ocean had a different meaning for me, and that Casmil and Peaches had been sent to invoke it in my father's name. The shells were a sign of a more powerful and symbolic reality. They were the tools of a new way of life and living. Although back then, at that moment, I couldn't have told you what the shells were for, I comprehended their power. I understood their spiritual connection to a more African view of eternity.

I felt faint. The room began to rise and fall as if I were being pushed on a swing. Up blended into down, and then into darkness. Somewhere in my memory, tucked away, is the sensation of picking the envelope up, bursting open the seal and watching flakes of congealed glue flutter bit by bit onto the table, like plaster falling from aging walls. But I couldn't tell you where in my mind that sensation and picture would be. I came back out of the nothingness that had swallowed me to find the husk of paper on the table, and my cupped hand full of a simple red cloth bag cinched at the top by a wrinkled length of black satin cord.

I looked at my aunts and Monroe through swirls of wooziness.

"Please open it, Grace," Monroe instructed.

I stuck my finger into the bag's navel and pulled. What tumbled out when the cord gave way was a small pewter rabbit figurine and a folded up square of paper burned brown around its edges with age. Like magpies and babies, I went for the pretty stuff. The rabbit was cute, arched as if it were leaping across the moon of the myth Monroe had given me. I fingered it, ignoring the paper, ignoring what I thought was ordinary for what I believed was more important.

Monroe sucked in a breath infused with both eagerness and impatience. "Rabbit, could you please look at the paper."

The sound of my basket name, the name my father had given my spirit, startled me out of my reverie. I nodded and picked up the wad.

It took some effort to unwrap it down to where I could lay out the full page. The paper was thick as cotton cloth and smelled like green tea. With an extended finger, I followed the dark lines of the gray-blue ink. The center of the page was covered with what looked like a drawing of tinker toy parts: an oval bisected by a horizontal and vertical spoke. Around all four sides my full name was written in a tight, formal script. I pushed it toward Monroe and my aunts so that they could take a closer look. An expression of recognition rippled across Monroe's face, and then that knowledge seemed to push him back into his chair. I watched as tears tiptoed into the corners of Peaches's eyes.

"What is it?" I asked.

Monroe closed his eyes. "What you have is your father's elegant attempt to protect and guide you."

"Elegant," Aunt Peaches murmured. "I like that choice of words."

"Your father was a very powerful conjurer, diviner and healer. I'm sure your mother never told you that," Casmil said.

"No, she never really told me anything about my father."

Casmil grunted in disgust. "Well, no matter. Past is past. The bag is called a mojo hand. It's a power object. All the things that we will teach you to gather and put in it will imbue it with what is called Ashe or the living powers of the wilderness. It has a soul called a mooyo, and it will protect you."

I must have looked stunned because she paused and summoned up some kindness and reached over to touch my hand. "Do you understand what I have said so far?"

I nodded.

"The bag is not as important as what your father drew on the paper. It is a yowa cross from the Kongo Cosmology. It can be interpreted as a type of crossroad. The vertical line can be viewed as a path, and the horizontal line as a watery boundary separating the world of the living from the world of the dead or the ancestors. Each quadrant represents the passage of souls from birth, life, death and rebirth."

Casmil paused to touch each quadrant, then allowed her finger to hover reverently above the point where the lines crossed. "This is the center of the four winds. The place where the land of the living is linked to the land of the ancestors. It is considered sacred ground. When a person takes an oath here to become a healer, diviner or spiritual warrior, they are saying they are endowed with enough knowledge and insight from both worlds to move confidently between them."

She stopped and allowed me to take a breath and think, and then some small revelation came, and I looked at Monroe. "All of you know what's going to happen, don't you?"

The truth moved like vivid shadows behind the curtains of their stern expressions.

"Yes," Monroe finally said.

"Tell me what you know?" I asked.

Monroe hesitated. "It doesn't work like that. We're not allowed."

"Why can't you tell me?"

"Because the decision to take the journey must be yours alone. So things must unfold on a timetable that is not necessarily ours."

I sat there shaking my head, both in wonder and in fear. "Is it Oba that says that it has to be done like this?"

"Yes, and others even more powerful than him," Casmil added.

Peaches was all sweetness when she assured me it would be all right. "If your father didn't believe you could handle it, you wouldn't have received his things."

Casmil was all about duty and the dare. "There are no bloodless births, Rabbit," she said. "And much is expected from whom much has been given."

26

NO REST FOR THE WEARY or, for that matter, the wicked. I got two days to press my roses and my unrequited longing between the pages of a book of Gwendolyn Brooks's poetry. I got a little bit of time to shed old skins of worry before I had to put on new ones. The second of those days Shanta came over, and we went out to explore my new hometown.

The sun was wearing a beautiful scarf of summer sky, and to beat off her divaish shine, we decided to get ice cream. Balancing huge wands of cones, we took a long walk on short streets and marveled at what a difference a body of water made in shaping a town. Carsonville was a dowdy bridesmaid standing next to Vigilant, with its showy veils of beaches and huge diamond ring of a lake. It was Carsonville's lot in life to provide the gas stations and bait shops tourists stopped at to get directions to the real entertainment.

"Boring as all this is," I told Shanta, "I'm glad to be here."

Shanta laughed. "Yeah, in your case boring is better."

But the pit of my stomach roared at me that boring wouldn't last, couldn't last. That this day was the best of a little bit of time before something awoke and, like Yeats's rough beast, slouched into my life to be born.

The next morning, there were no more roses to press, and the sun was enshrouded in clouds, hidden like a pearl in the gray mantel of an oyster.

"So why is the house blue?" I asked my aunts as I opened a box. They had come into my room in matching pink sweat suits, looking like they wanted to talk, but when they saw I was cleaning up and re-organizing my room, they'd settled like exotic birds on the rumpled sheets and covers of my unmade bed. For five wordless minutes, they watched me alphabetize my CDs on a small shelf.

"Blue repels evil. It's the color of healing," Casmil said. The word "evil" poked me erect, although I didn't turn around to read their faces.

"Yes, it's an African belief brought to America," Peaches added.

I picked up a CD and looked down to find the unsmiling visage of Robert Johnson staring up at me from the jewel case. Across the top in blue letters was the title, *Crossroads*. I thought of Oba and felt the air in the room become slightly more still. No coincidence this, some distant part of myself reflected.

"So," I said as I made a space for Robert on the shelf, "all this blue is protection. Sort of like an architectural Mojo or hand."

I felt their eyes leave my back to look at each other.

"An accurate and beautiful description, Grace," Peaches said.

"We also put up a grove of bottle trees at the back of the property," said Casmil.

"Bottle trees?" That turned me around to see if they were kidding, but the calm expressions on their faces told me that kidding lived in a whole different universe of thought.

"You know what a bottle tree is," Casmil asserted.

She was right. I had seen pictures of the trees from the 1930s in a book. Their upward growing limbs were stripped of leaves, and each branch ended in an empty blue or green bottle. These trees were thought to protect a person's home, the gleam of the glass captur-ing and disempowering evil forces and troubled spirits. When out of curiosity I had checked out bottle trees on the Internet, I found that most people used artificial versions of them only as yard art. I had never seen bottle trees erected as a "visual prayer for protection."

"Ok, what are you protecting yourselves from?" I put the question out like bread and waited for the meat that would make it a meaningful sandwich.

"You," Peaches corrected. "We're protecting you."

My nerves misted my neck with sweat. "All right, what are you protecting me from?"

"Joe's mother will be here in a minute to talk to you about that," Casmil said.

It was not the answer I expected. *Joe's mother,* I thought, with a whole bunch of exclamation points after it. Crazy Doris? Conspiracy Doris? The woman who thought that the government was out to get everybody in general and black folks in particular by any means necessary? I couldn't figure out how she fit into our conversation. But then I remembered the tale of conspiracy that was her calling card.

"That doesn't exactly answer my question," I said.

"Yes, well ... Doris has the answer, and she wishes to be the one to convey it to you," Peaches said.

"That's still not an answer."

My aunt said, "in a minute," and meant it. Before I could take a breath, Doris was out on the porch, yelling loud enough for us to hear her upstairs and making the doorbell sing like a hysterical bird.

Doris was a woman shaped like a bee and as fast as one. She flew in, all dime-shiny in a silky silver blouse, carrying a grocery bag in one hand and a man's briefcase in the other.

"You all live too far out," she complained as she darted deeper into the coolness of the air-conditioned living room. She spun around, looking at things, and then her eyes landed on me.

"Hey, Doris." I tried not to stare at her, but it was a hard thing not to do. Doris had always been a connoisseur of very different looks, but that day she had arrived with her hair cut down to almost nonexistent, and what little was left, she had dyed red. Not the auburn shade of cherry wood or Irish Setters, which would have looked okay with her butterscotch-colored skin, but the red-red of clown noses and Valentines, the brassy kind of red that confirmed people's suspicions that she was a spokesperson for "crazy."

I didn't push my thoughts about her hair into the closet fast enough.

"What? You don't like my new do?" Doris challenged.

I shrugged and smiled. "I'm not going to lie. I kind of liked it better when it was brown."

She laughed. "Girl, that was so long ago. Besides, that's boring."

Casmil cleared her throat. "You and Grace can go out to the sun porch. I made some cake and coffee."

"That's okay, I brought some real food. What Grace and I have to talk about ain't no cake and coffee kind of conversation. Actually, it's a get-tore-up-on-liquor kind of conversation, but she's too young, and I'm too old to be drinking that hard."

"All right then," Peaches said.

Concern had plowed deep furrows across the foreheads of both sisters. They were unusually quiet as they led Doris and me down through a section of the house I hadn't yet explored. Peaches smiled sadly before she and Casmil left us alone.

The sunroom was small and constructed mostly of windows like a greenhouse. It was like a beautiful crystal broach clipped on to the breast of a huge flower garden.

"It's pretty out here," I said to make conversation.

"Yeah, I guess so," Doris replied as she reset the table with her own plates and silverware. From the bag, she produced a covered casserole dish and a basket of homemade rolls whose folded lips had been carefully smeared with the golden gloss of real butter. The smell of something chickeny drew me away from the banks of windows to the table.

"What are we having?" I asked.

"Chicken and dumplings—the strip kind, not that fluffy cotton ball stuff." Doris spooned out narrow, glistening ribbons of dough and pieces of chicken backstroking in gravy so thick and smooth it reminded me of heavy cream.

I seated myself at the table. "Looks good."

My eyes searched for the briefcase and found it propped on the couch. Curiosity and some unnamed dread made me keep looking at it, tracing its worn shape and wondering what it held, but Doris didn't seem ready to talk about it, so I turned my attention back to stuffing my face with dumplings.

"I had to make a whole pot just for Joe," she said as she finally sank into a chair across from me.

"Yeah, I don't doubt it." I laughed, imagining Joe's big baby self standing by the stove and making sure he got his proper share.

"He wanted to come today. He's worried about you, but I told him maybe you would need him more later."

I couldn't help but take note of the word "need." I squirmed a bit. "Yeah, he's like a regular brother now, overprotective."

"He told me you have a boyfriend."

I tried to stop my smile from flopping open into a grin. "No, not really. What's Joe's problem? He doesn't like Evan?"

"Joe likes him ok. I'm just being nosy now. So what's this Mr. Evan like?"

I told her everything I knew, which didn't take long.

She nodded. "He sounds nice to me, Gracie."

"Yeah, well I hope I'll be seeing him again."

After that, we ate in silence until something about the briefcase, the way it just sat there like the proverbial elephant in the room, made me ask, "so why are you really here, Doris? Why are Peaches and Casmil acting so nervous and secretive?"

Doris didn't answer right away. She took her time gathering up her thoughts as she chewed on the nub of a chicken wing. Finally, she looked at me. "Do you think I'm crazy?" she asked, dragging the conversation from cozy to butt-naked frankness in less time than it had taken for me to lick the last bit of gravy off my fork.

I couldn't lie, but I tried to humor-coat the truth. "I don't think that as a pot, I should be calling you black."

Doris smiled without humor. "Nice try, Grace, but I raised six kids, and I know when I'm being snowed. Answer the question."

"Well," I began tentatively, "I don't think you're crazy. I think you're paranoid, which is kind of different ... I mean, come on. Some of the things you come up with are a little far-fetched."

Doris sat back to think, tilting her head back and forth as if to sift and resift memories of her actions.

"Yeah, maybe so," she agreed. "Sometimes I do go over the top, but that's just the red hair and big jewelry part of me. I'm not crazy, and I have every right and reason to be paranoid. I got enemies, real enemies, and so do you. You just haven't known about them ..."

I nervously finished her sentence. "Until now."

"Yeah, until now."

27

DORIS GOT THE BRIEFCASE AND bounced it up on to the table between the dishes. The latches grunted high and short like old men exerting themselves to get out of low chairs. The acrid incense of decomposing paper filtered into the space between us as she lifted out a leather-bound book. Embossed on the front in florid gold lettering was the name, Edmond Gilmore.

"I stole this," Doris confessed as she flipped open the book to the first page. "About a year ago, I got hired to do some work for a woman named Susan Gilmore. Maybe you remember the family from all the hubbub about her son Jonathan getting the mayor's sixteen-year-old daughter pregnant?"

"Yeah, I heard something about it," I admitted.

"Well anyway, she wanted me to clean up her father Edmond's place, because the old man was going into the hospital and the house where he stayed was a mess. Social Services said he couldn't go back there until it was taken care of. It was good money, so at first I didn't really care that I knew the old man was nothing but a Klu Kluxer. It didn't even bother me that he had all kinds of racist stuff sitting around. Believe me, I took nothing but pleasure in throwing that shit out. But one day I was sifting through Edmond's so-called library, and I found this nice-looking book. I was just gonna pass it by—you know put it back on the shelf—but something told me to flip it open.

So I opened it up to the first page, and there was this short little list of seven names, and each name had a date and the word death next to them. I still didn't think anything of it. I flipped through the rest of the pages, and they were empty. But then it was like God put a foot on the back of my neck and pressed down hard. I was forced to look—really look—and what I noticed was that the first name on the list was Freeman Johnson, the name of Peaches's, Casmil's, and Grace's father, and the last name on the list was your daddy's.

"In between were the names of people who had the last names of black families who had lived around here like forever. I couldn't make any sense of it. Back then I didn't know anything about how Freeman died, and it was still a rumor about your father. It didn't make any sense, but I knew it was important."

As if God was still whispering orders in her ear, Doris allowed the book to break open to a page she had marked with an envelope. My eyes swept the firm handwriting, but I couldn't bring myself to fully concentrate on the words.

"So I stole the book," Doris continued, "and I told that Susan woman I wouldn't be coming back to work for them. I did a little detective work. I contacted some of the oldsters in the community about the other names. It turned out all of them were the names of children who had disappeared, just come up missing one day. It went as far back as the 1930s ... never was anything about any of them in the newspapers though. I took time to check that out at the library."

She stopped there for a moment, waiting for me to connect all the big bloody dots to get the full horrible picture.

The last innocent part of me whispered, "what you're saying is that you think this Edmond Gilmore person killed all these people, including my father?"

"Him and maybe some others. According to the sisters, a mob killed Freeman after he shot Edmond Gilmore's father, but they wouldn't say anymore than that to me."

"Did you show the list to the police?" I asked.

Doris laughed. "Show them what, Grace? I stole a book from a rich white man's house, and if that weren't enough, I'm going to accuse him of several kidnappings and murders based on just a list of missing black children? Anyway, up until now it hasn't been a problem."

Doris removed the small manila envelope and handed it to me. *Another fate-filled envelope*, I thought. My emotional pressure dipped, signaling the beginning of paranormal hurricanes.

"I've had this book for a year now, Grace, and I've never heard from the old bastard. But the other day, I get this letter from him demanding that I give him his 'legacy' back, or else he'll come get me and mine. And to make sure I understood he knew who my people were, he sent along this print of a postcard." Doris hesitated. "I don't want to give this to you, Grace. If it were up to me ... well, you know I would go on up there and take care of it myself, but Casmil and Peaches say it's important that this be handled correctly. They say you need to handle it for things to be right."

The old me didn't want the envelope, but the new self, the one who had become Rabbit, was eager. In that moment, I became less mortal and more spirit. In that moment, my fingers became instruments that could tear open the doors of graves. The envelope gave up a postcard neatly labeled, "Freeman Johnson's lynching."

A yellowish darkness began to spread into the room like tea steeping in hot water. Hot breezes, pungent with the scent of tobacco and decaying leaves, licked at my cheeks, and Freeman's voice hummed like an irritated hornet in my ears: "They lynched me. They trussed me up like a hog and hung me."

All I could do was nod because the postcard confirmed this brutal truth. The camera had been an unbiased witness to the depravity of my great-great-grandfather Freeman's body dangling like a macabre piñata in front of a huge crowd of jubilant white men, women and children, all dressed in suits and dresses as if they were going to church or a party.

"They stole from me," Freeman's voice continued, as if what had been taken had been some simple thing like clothing, but it was nothing as simple as that. He sighed and began to calculate his incalculable losses. "Bones distributed as souvenirs. They chopped off each finger and gave them away as prizes. Ears, both taken. Some teeth. Hanks of hair. Skin flayed off to make watch fobs."

Queasiness coated my mouth, slick and bitter. I wanted to look away, but my eyes were pinched off from my will. I was made to concentrate on the image of a small white boy, his mouth bent up into a misshapen grin of satisfaction.

"The boy is Edmond Gilmore," Freeman said. "They brought that poor child fresh from his father's funeral to watch me hang for his murder. Because I killed his father, he became a monster. He is still alive, old now, but before he leaves this existence, I need for you to tell him I am sorry for killing his father. If he were now to confess all his crimes and to offer his victims some remorse, he would still receive the gift of God's grace and redemption."

At that point, I stopped obeying; I didn't want to hear what he was proposing. In light of what had been taken from others and me, how the fuck could we even be talking about sorry and God's grace?

I looked at that postcard, really looked at all those happy people celebrating the slaughter of a human being, a human being who had been a relative of mine. All I understood was how justice had been mobbed by those who had decided to take their "eye and a tooth" before a jury trial could happen. In that moment of blood lust, they had become worse than the man they had lynched and just as evil as the man who had set the madness loose to prey on all of us in the first place. Any sympathy I might have had was deadened by the look of cold satisfaction in all their sets of eyes. It was a look that said this rougher form of righteousness was reserved only for those of color, for those who looked like me.

Anguish filled my throat, forcing in the breath that made me all too human again. My whole body shuddered as Freeman disconnected from me and passed back over. Left alone with all that huge madness floating around the sea of my soul like a lost and doomed ship, I began to sob.

"Warriors don't cry," some distant voice intoned, but I was not yet a true warrior. I began to pray the prayer of the desperate and the inconsolable. "Oh God, oh God, oh God," I cried out, rocking back and forth. Then came the whirling confusion. Rage began to shorten the long muscles of my body until I was like a snake coiled to the point of striking at what it most feared. Doris, sensing my mood was white hot, tried to hold me, but what strength she had was not enough. My fury crested and I pushed her so hard, she let out a soft yelp of surprise and pain. I began to move through the house past the dark, old eyes of my aunts, who knew the trajectory I was on but not how I would land.

* * *

How deep is the dark when your consciousness wanders off into oblivion and takes its own sweet-ass time getting back to you? I surfaced, pulled up by the cartoonish sound of my voice messing up the words, "too much, this is too fucking much." It took me several raggedy breaths to realize I had taken flight, only to land, flat on my back, on a couch. As soon as the living room stopped feeling like it was fishtailing, I opened my eyes and sat up. My aunts stood in front of me, their beige skin flushed reddish by anxiety and concern. I appreciated that they didn't ask how I was doing because I didn't know. One minute I felt sweetened by euphoria. The next moment, my emotional tongue was gagging on the bitter taste of rage.

"Doris," I whispered, "is she all right?" The last thing I remembered was that I had flailed at her like she was a swarm of angry bees.

"Yes, baby," Peaches, answered. "A little frightened. We explained to her that you would be fine and sent her home. "

"Ohhh ... how long have I been out?"

"You mean gone," Casmil corrected. "Three hours."

"Jesus."

I requested coffee, hoped for food, but Peaches brought lukewarm chamomile tea instead. I sat there, the small brittle teacup clattering like teeth in its saucer, as I tried to line up what I had experienced with logic and reality.

"So, do you think you can do what has been asked of you?" Casmil asked, pulling an armchair closer to the couch.

I wanted to ask how she knew, but then I realized how stupid that was. Of course they knew. They had been in on the plan. They also knew I was angry. How could I not be? No one could absorb that much evil and not be sliced to the quick of their soul.

"I don't know." I said each word slowly, trying to keep calm, trying hard to modulate the escalating frequencies of my resentment and bitterness. "Your father wants me to go and offer his apology to a racist white man. A man who killed my father, several children, and who knows how many other black people he didn't feel the need to write down."

"What you think, Grace, is not important. He has explained what he needs, what is required of him by God and the ancestors to receive some measure of peace. You must be courageous enough to obey. I thought Monroe explained that to you."

Peaches was quiet, her head bent down as if she were trying to balance on her neck the weight of her father's request with my legitimate right to be angry. "Please," she said, "it's not just about us. Others need to know how their loved ones died, and if Gilmore doesn't confess …"

I opened my mouth to yell at them, but some better self snatched my inner ear and ordered me to suture my rage, to become, until further notice, mute. I leapt up from the couch and ran up the stairs, condensing my world to the breath and depth of my new room.

I wanted to scream a banshee wail of pain. Instead, I put on Etta James, and at the top of my stereo's lungs she sang about my pain for me. "I rather go blind," she confessed to some man, but I twisted her lyrics, hammered down its heartbreak meaning to a razor's edge, because at that moment I would have cut out my own eyes rather than do what was being asked of me. I wasn't thinking about Freeman's need to alleviate his guilt over Edmond Gilmore's feelings when he was a boy. I didn't even understand why he felt guilty, given all that had gone down. Hadn't he merely stood up for himself and our family? His sister had been raped, his best friend Boyd, Amanda's fiancée, had been murdered by marauding white men. Later, the whole black community of Vigilant had been punished for what he, one man, had done justifiably. Black homes had been burned down, and black businesses taken. In the end, nobody white had been punished, and no compensation had been paid for damages done to person, property, or pride. Even if a million years had passed before my great-great-grandfather had seen the man who had raped his sister, it seemed to me that he had had a right to take matters into his own hands, especially in a world where justice was often unattainable for black people.

"But the moral question," my better self, God's advocate, asked, "is whether one round of the unspeakable killing somehow justifies the next round, conducted in the opposite direction."

"But," I whispered into a thickening internal darkness that was hardening my empathy and soiling my decency, "the murder of my father, the furtive, horrific stealing and then killing of black children and my father had not been round for round. Edmond Gilmore had not killed justifiably. He had killed because he could. He understood that because he was rich and white he would never be suspected, and that if anyone in town knew, they would, out of loyalty, keep his secrets."

Cultivating rage is hard work. My better nature said, "why don't you sleep on this?" So I climbed into bed. I slept on and on for days, rising only to devour the meals my aunts selected to leave outside my door. They accepted my cloistered silence, confident that eventually I would thaw the hell I had frozen over and do what needed to be done. Until then, they had decided to watch over me from a distance. I felt their maternal presence as I slept, even in the deepest and roughest seas of my disquieted slumber. I heard and was comforted by the fervent chanting of their ancient and eloquent prayers.

After a week, sleep wouldn't come at night, so I took to walking for hours and hours around my aunt's property and out to the shiny plot of bottle trees they had created to protect me. Then one night, that ancestral world of fields and trees didn't feel like a big enough womb, and I slipped as quick and quiet as any rabbit from the yard out onto the road leading toward town.

28

I WAS A MORSEL OF souring flesh, swallowed whole by the dark mouth of the night. Down the empty throats of dirt roads I floated, stopping only to savor the tea-like scent of rain brewing in the black cups of clouds. Compassless, I seemed to be following an internal map, that, for reasons I couldn't fully fathom, led back to the ice-cream parlor Shanta and I had visited. When I hit the asphalted lip of Main Street, the sound of a car's engine sliced open the silence. At first I was too numb to be concerned that somebody might want to hurt me, and I kept walking past the dark, lifeless bodies of shops. Only after the car had followed me for more time than seemed sensible, did I turn around. Sensing the change in my movement, the rusty white Escort paused and pulled to the curb. After a short spurt of mechanical wheezing, the engine died. I watched as a dark-skinned, older black woman, dressed in an Easter purple housedress, hatched from the passenger side door. For a long moment we stood in a dim spot of a streetlight, our curiosities circling one another.

"Are you Grace Johnson?" she finally asked. In the somberness of her voice was the full kick of desperation.

I didn't break the shell of my vow of silence with yes or no because some sudden flare of knowledge told me that she already knew who I was because she had been sent to find me. The sky above us moaned thunder and parted its dark skirt to flash a skinny leg of lightning. She pushed off from the side of the car and moved in closer. She looked old, old, old, but I sensed that nothing as simple as age had made her that way. Her eyes were sunken wells whose rims had been painted black with worry. Worry had also cracked her lips and made her cheeks look like the rumpled sheets of collapsed parachutes.

"He," she began, "I mean, Dr. Monroe, said I would find you out here by the park." She pushed her arm up slowly, pointing across the street toward a dark somewhere. I couldn't see anything, yet the hidden landscape of swings and picnic tables seemed to resonate.

"I used to bring my daughter here to get ice cream and play."

I had to nod, as déjà vu blossomed into a revelation. My wanderings had not been aimless.

The woman took a breath to feed her extremely skinny courage. "Dr. Monroe said you probably wouldn't talk, but he said you needed to listen to my story. He said maybe we could help each other."

I nodded again, and she gave me a shy look of gratitude.

"My name is Lawanda Parson," she said as she offered her hand. Her fingers felt like bony twigs covered in old rubber, but there was something powerful and significant in the strength and duration of her grasp. Before the flesh of our hands separated, I felt an almost electrical pop of connection, and my mouth suddenly became saturated with the tangy flavor of canned peaches. Not the antiseptic, slimy taste of those yolk-yellow, store-bought crescents, but the briny-sweet and sumptuous essence of sun-fattened globes of real fruit packed in mason jars and bejeweled with the black stars of cloves and the long velvety brown scepters of cinnamon sticks. Startled and awed, I rushed to think it imaginary, even as the warm damp air around me became suffused with the fragrance of vinegar and spices, even as my lips had to curl up to seal in a brimming pool of drool. The sky moaned again, accompanied by the heavy breathing of the wind and spittle-like drops of rain. Lawanda looked up. "Let's sit in the car," she offered.

I slid into the worn, but immaculate car. She turned on the interior light and fastened her eyes on me as if she were hoping, beyond what little sense of hope she had left, that I could offer an answer to a horrifying question.

"You look more than tired," she said. "You look like you've been wrestling with the devil. Believe me, I know the look."

She reached for her purse, and from the depth of a small universe of keys, candy wrappers and shopping lists, she pulled out an aging picture whose surface had been worn down to grimy dullness by the caresses of fingers and kisses. She leaned over to present me with the snapshot of a beaming, little fawn brown girl with a perky rack of beaded braids.

"Her name was Annika," Lawanda said in a reverent whisper.

I looked at Lawanda and then down again at her daughter's picture. The name pummeled my awareness and then shortened the strokes of my breathing. I knew who she was, even though I had only glanced at Gilmore's list. My mind had seized all the children's names and permanently installed them in my memory. I would forget who I was before I would forget them.

Feeding off the milk of my horror, Annika decided to enter this world again. All childish desire and no adult restraint, she flew into me. I felt the slight, involuntary jerking of my body as she pushed aside my will and climbed up the scaffolding of my soul. She curled up tight behind my eyes and watched her mother's vivid grief through me.

"She was kidnapped thirty years ago," Lawanda began. "I put my four-year-old baby girl down for a nap, went out to hang up some clothes, came back to find the window open and her gone. As gone as if she never existed. The police didn't look for children then like they do now. They especially didn't look for black children. They blamed me of course. 'Should have watched her,' they'd said, 'should have been more careful. Shouldn't have been a single mother ...'" Her voice trailed off, and we, the living, on both sides of existence, sat listening to the roar of the rain.

"You never get over it. Oh, you go on because people say you have to, because it would be doing the devil's work to commit suicide, but you never get over it ... never ... never. Not a day goes by that I don't wonder what she would have grown up to be. What would my grandchildren look like? What I want, Miss Johnson is to know what happened, that's all. I want to know who took my baby and why. I don't expect to find her alive, but if I could find her body and lay it to rest, if I could have a grave to visit ... Dr. Monroe said you may be able to help, but you would be reluctant to become involved. But if you know something, can find out anything, I beg of you, give me some peace, Miss Johnson."

I started to tell her to please, call me Grace, but it was not my voice that found its way. My lips moved, quivering open, and a small, small voice tumbled out.

"Habari Gani, Mommy. Habari Gani." That was all, but it was enough. As quickly as she had come, Annika was gone. The void she left dropped me into darkness, and I lost a little bit of time. I came back after a minute to Lawanda just staring at me, her expression flashing furiously between belief and disbelief. I could almost hear her asking God in a panic if I was real or, a fake psychic TV. She wanted, with all her heart and soul and sanity, for me to be real.

"Spiced peaches," I offered, as all things mysteriously came together in my mind. "It was the last thing you fed her before she was kidnapped."

Lawanda nodded and began to cry. Her sobbing pushed and pulled at her thin body so hard I thought she might disintegrate in the swirling undertow of her pain. Finally, between ragged breaths, she was able to get out, "her uncle taught her a little bit of Swahili when he decided to celebrate Kwanza at his house and she loved it. Wouldn't stop saying, 'Habari Gani Mommy. What's the news, Mommy?"

As best I could, I gathered Lawanda into my arms. "I promise you, I will do what I can," I whispered, and that seemed enough of a promise to calm her sorrow.

* * *

By the time Lawanda dropped me by the house, the rain had stopped, and the pink of a new morning foamed up like frothy cream between the trees lining the eastern part of my aunts' property. I looked up toward the rain-slick façade of my new home and was grateful for its Kool-Aid blue offering of physical and spiritual protection. I should have been through with my anger. I should have been thinking about the numinous wonder of how it felt to speak for Annika, but my anger wasn't through with me yet. It's heaving mass still writhed, stiffening my neck and snapping my jaw tight. I decided I needed to pray for the power to find some peace, but all I could summon from out of my pain was a fiercer version of Psalms 109.

"God, do not ignore me," I said, "for Edmond Gilmore's wicked and deceitful mouth is open against us, speaking against us with a lying tongue. He has surrounded us with hatefulness; he has attacked us for no reason. He has repaid kindness with accusations; even as I make this prayer for him, he repays good with evil. He has given us hatefulness in exchange for love."

"Pray a different prayer," spirit voices cried out.

I did not obey; I went on.

"Appoint a wicked man against him. Let an accuser bring him to trial. When he is tried, let him be found guilty. Let his prayer be counted as sin. May his days be few. May others seize all his possessions. May he be driven from his home. Let no one—no one— be kind to him. Remember forever every sin his father's fathers committed. Let his mother's sins of ignorance and moral blindness never be blotted out."

"Pray a different prayer!" The whirlwind of their demands buffeted my body.

I was supposed to give up; I was supposed to give in, but by then I was no longer whispering to God. By then, I was ranting loud enough to wake the living. "Damn him, God. Damn him, for he has persecuted the poor and needy to their destruction and pushed the broken hearted to their deaths. He loves cursing—let it come back on him. He hates blessing—let it be millions of miles away. Give this as a reward to my accuser. He who demeans my soul for no good reason."

Finally I had to stop. Out of breath, spiritually spent, I stood there shaking. I was too distraught to hear Monroe approach from behind, but I knew when I felt the grip of small fingers on my rocking shoulder that it was him pulling me back from the edge of madness. He walked me to the porch and we sat on a bench. He instructed me to breathe until, like buckets dipping into a well, each breath brought up needed tears. Exhausted, I laid my head on his shoulder.

"Let us continue, Grace," he whispered, and then in his professor's voice he picked up the threads of words where I had left off with my Psalm. "Oh Eternal One, deal with Grace out of your better side. Kind as you are, save her, for she has a wounded heart. Help her. He will know that you have done it. He will see it is the work of your hand. Let him curse. You will bless. When Edmond Gilmore rises up in his arrogance, pull him down with shame. Let him be clothed in dishonor. If you do this, Oh Eternal One, Grace will compose thanksgiving songs and will travel far and wide singing them."

"How am I to handle this, Monroe?" I asked. "I want to kill him."

Monroe was silent for a long moment as if he knew he had to give some respect to all my hurt. "Vengeance is God's alone," he said finally. "You and Edmond Gilmore are involved in this tragedy because your great-great-grandfather could not wait on God."

I wanted to sit up straight and look at Monroe to argue more effectively, but I was too tired to move much more than my lips. "So I'm not supposed to be angry?"

"Grace, you have every right to be furious, but there is such a thing as righteous anger. A task has been charged to you, and you must learn to use your anger to serve this purpose."

"What if I do as I'm told, and he doesn't confess or apologize or ask for forgiveness? Am I supposed to just walk away? Am I supposed to just let it go?"

"God and the ancestors are asking you to be merciful, Grace, not weak or stupid. You are to trust there will be justice."

"I don't know if I believe in justice anymore."

"Justice always prevails over injustice and oppression. It's just that sometimes you have to fight long and hard for it. Let's go in and put your aunts' minds at ease. We can talk more about this tomorrow."

My aunts embraced me like the mothers they had become. They clutched at me as if I had been away for a long time in a distant place. I didn't think I deserved their welcome, but in their minds I was a prodigal daughter who had finally come home.

29

EXHAUSTED, I CURLED UP BENEATH a cave of quilts with my bag and its soul. The rust red husk of fabric, with its center of silver and paper, crackled softly beneath my moving fingers, offering some solace for my pain. Sleep came, but it was wreathed in a vision masquerading as a dream.

There was a slow fade into the brilliant illumination of frost white sunlight. The transition was so gradual I didn't feel any real anxiety. It felt two dimensional and fuzzy, like a sleep dream, until I found myself standing next to a woman I didn't know on a tiny island of sugar white sand. I looked down at my bare feet and then up and out. All around the patch of land, gray water ran smooth as a sheet of foil to the horizon. Above us in the vault of blue sky, a yellow sun hovered like an egg yolk suspended in its albumen. It was hot—Africa hot—but, of course, I was the only one sweating like a spent thoroughbred in the red dresses we both were wearing.

I held out my arm and tried to catch a non-existent breeze.

"Do you know where we are?" I asked. My voice buzzed and hummed as if I were trying to talk through a blanket of static.

She didn't answer; she just turned to look at me. Something in the way her body unfolded into that small movement told me I wasn't in anything like a dream. No, she and I were perched on another version of the crossroads. I studied my new partner, taking down that she was young and extremely beautiful. Beautiful in the way Jamila is considered beautiful: thin waisted, balloon-breasted, abundantly hipped. She had big hazel eyes that shimmered bright with intelligence against her coppery brown skin. *Was I, I wondered, supposed to recognize her from the way her long raven hair swirled in deep currents around her shoulders? Was the almond shape of her face, with its delicate assembly of features, supposed to remind me of a name?*

"Do we know each other?" I asked.

The woman's eyes took me in as if my presence had finally registered with her. She ignored my question, raised her arm, and pointed toward the firmament. "My name is Kadija Lyons. Can you tell me if the sun is rising or setting?"

I concentrated less on the question, which at that point didn't make any kind of sense, and listened more to the sway and rhythm of the words she had spoken. Her voice was chirpy, scented with southerness, and I recognized it. Memories began to fall quick and fast like lines of dominos, back and back to that day in Alamode eating pie and Better Than Sex Cake with Evan. She had been the ethereal voice in my ear, pleading for me to give her time. Awe made me want to back away, but out of the whirling of my surprise came the realization she had come to me in search of metaphysical comfort. She was desperate to finish with this life in order to begin the next.

I remembered Casmil's explanation of the cosmograph my father had drawn for me: the four-armed Tinker Toy with its knobs representing the swirling of all earthly souls from birth to life to death and then back.

"Your sun is setting," I whispered, "into the water, into the realm of the ancestors."

She stood there for a long moment, contemplating my directions, taking my word as permission to reset her eternal compass. Then, the slender, copper pink rails of her lips parted to reveal teeth as bright as beading on a wedding dress. She leaned in toward me. "Thank you, and would you please tell Evan I love him, and that I don't blame him for what happened."

The white light took me back faster than it had brought me. Before I could cry out for answers to the sudden explosions of questions in my mouth, I was back beneath the quilts on my bed. Wide-eyed and even wider-awake, I shivered as if the dead woman had infected me with some strange fever.

I fell back into the kind of sleep where even visions couldn't flourish. The cool wetness of the previous night's rain would ripen into midday heat before I would wake up to the sound of the phone ringing. I didn't bother to answer it. I wasn't expecting a call from Shanta, and who else would be calling me?

"Grace, baby, are you awake?" Peaches's voice made me turn over and open my eyes.

"How're you doing, Aunt Peaches?" I asked as I sat up. Drowsiness hung on my body like a sopping wet towel. From a hunched over position, I turned my head and tried to bring the room into full focus. I found Aunt Peaches standing in a slat of sun by the window, her hand screwed down over the mouthpiece of the cordless phone as if she were trying to keep something smelly from flowing onto the floor.

"It's Evan," she said.

I closed my eyes and sighed. No coincidence this.

A hard frown rumpled my aunt's lips. "I can tell him to call back later or not at all."

Inwardly, I had to smile at her thinly veiled attempt to prevent our conversation.

I shook my head. "No, I think I need to speak to him." I paused for a moment to mix in the numinous. "Aunt Peaches, he's been sent to me."

Peaches molded the word "ah" when the complexity of my reply resonated with her.

With a respectful nod, she handed me the phone and left.

I tried to sound upbeat and failed. "Hello," crawled out like it needed to be on vitamins.

Silence. Then I heard, "hey, Gracie, how are you?"

My name was nothing but brown sugar in Evan's mouth, and hearing it made me almost smack my lips. *How to answer,* I wondered. What had Monroe told him? Nothing, I finally decided. Monroe wouldn't have confided in him, and maybe, I mused, it was best I didn't either.

"I'm a little tired," I answered.

"I've been thinking about you, wondering how you are. Do you think you're up to going out?"

"Um ..." was the only sound I could bring up at first. Then, I did what needed to be done. "Maybe you can come over and we could have coffee and talk?"

"Wonderful. I'll see you in about two hours." He hung up quickly, leaving no time for me to back out of my decision.

I sat with the phone in my lap, looking at it, stroking its plastic edges.

Peaches, who I suspected had been lurking in the hall pretending not to listen, looked in on me. "Is he coming over?" she asked, even though she knew the answer.

"Yes, he'll be over in a little while. But I don't know ..."

Peaches sat down beside me on the bed, and I allowed myself to lean against her.

"What don't you know, Grace?"

Slowly, in a voice so soft I almost thought she couldn't possibly have heard me, I told her about my vision. "Why do I feel like I've been fooled?" I asked after I was finished. "It's not like Evan and I are even seeing each other."

Aunt Peaches nodded her head, a been-there-done-that kind of nod. "Evan made romantic overtures. You haven't misread any signals, Grace. How would you know there was unfinished business with another relationship?"

"I should have listened to Dr. Monroe. He warned me about getting too close to him."

"I suspect Dr. Monroe warned you off for many reasons other than that. Kadija came to you because you can do for her what she can no longer do for herself. She came, in part, as a warning to you that Evan has things to work out emotionally concerning her death and has not done so yet."

Tears wanted to come, and I struggled hard to keep them down. "Why now? Why couldn't she wait until later? I don't know what I'm supposed do about ... about ..."

About, I thought, *the avalanche of pain, sorrow and insane madness threatening to bury my sanity so far down in hell, the devil wouldn't even know where to find it, let alone God.*

Peaches's arms closed around me, pulling in the edges of my spirit that were crumbling. "What's yours to do is yours to do," she consoled.

"What if he doesn't believe me?"

"The message is sacred and must be delivered. His response is not your concern. Although you'll have the measure of the man and his maturity by how he responds. Now why don't you get ready?"

"You mean spiritually ready, don't you," I asked, although, I didn't know what "spiritually ready" looked like.

Aunt Peaches nodded. "Yes, baby, spiritually ready is exactly what I mean."

* * *

My music was as close as I could get to the poetry of a spoken prayer for a God I now feared was insane. I showered to the Sonny Rollins track, "Why Was I Born," and dried myself off to the fierceness of Nina Simone's "Strange Fruit." My aunts took it upon themselves to help me select some clothes when they realized I was trying not to make a decision. From the slim pickings of my dressy wardrobe, they pulled out a dark green summer dress. *Great, I look like an avocado,* I thought, as I pulled it down over my hips.

"Baby, I would have killed for your behind when I was your age," Peaches said. "Besides, avocados don't have faces."

I didn't even bother to ask how she knew what I had been thinking. I just laughed and marveled at how even in the face of the darkest kind of sorrow, I had found a way to be self conscious about my size.

"You need a little makeup," Peaches insisted as she tugged and straightened an errant fold of my dress.

I couldn't see Casmil behind me, but I knew she must have rolled her eyes. "It's not a date."

Peaches ignored her and began to study my face. "You wouldn't need much, just enough to let Mr. Evan understand that you take yourself and your gift seriously. Sometimes wearing lipstick is like highlighting an important passage in a book."

"No," Casmil cracked. "Most times lipstick is just paint in a tube."

Peaches eyes swept off of me and on to her sister. For a long moment, there was the sparking of sibling tension in the silence. A boundary had been violated, and the universe of their relationship had to be realigned. In a measured voice, pitched softer and sweeter because I was present, Peaches spoke a few words in a language I didn't understand. The snarky look on Casmil's face drained off suddenly, and she left the room.

"What language were you speaking?" I wasn't brave enough to ask what had been said.

Peaches laughed and under her breath said, "Twin."

"Oh."

"Sometimes Casmil doesn't understand the subtler arts of communication. There's a time to be blunt and a time to be more nuanced. You must learn ..."

Before she could finish speaking, Casmil came back into the room, holding several brown and silver wands of lipstick. If she was upset or angry, I couldn't tell as she handed them to her sister. Peaches shuffled through the limited selection slowly as if she were studying something deep and serious. A faint smile appeared when she reached a decision. "Sit down at the dresser."

As if it were a knife, Peaches unsheathed a reddish-brown blade of solid gloss and began to butter my lips with long strokes.

"What color is it?" I asked when she finally finished.

"Mystical Mocha. Don't you think that's apropos?" She answered as if stuff like that wasn't supposed to leave me feeling disquieted. "Casmil, she looks beautiful, don't you think?"

Casmil smiled and nodded, despite her sister's admonishment. I knew she was looking for something in me more substantive. I gazed at myself in the mirror. Beautiful? No. A little more sophisticated, maybe, and then I realized that Peaches was right. I did feel a little more confident in myself.

* * *

"Wow, you look wonderful," Evan commented when I opened the front door to let him in. He had on a pair of gray pants and a black shirt that contrasted nicely with a halo of Black-eyed Susans in his arms. Despite everything I knew, I couldn't help but grin. I liked the attention, even though I knew it was probably a cheery mask he was constructing to hide grief and pain.

"I'll take those lovely flowers," Peaches said. "Why don't you and Evan go sit in the living room, and I'll bring some coffee."

We settled on the couch, and I tried to sit close, but not too close.

"You know we could go for a drive," Evan said.

I was tempted, but I shook my head. "No, I'm a little too tired. It's been a hard couple of days."

"Dad said you were still having a hard time, but he wouldn't tell me anything else except, of course, he would appreciate it if I would stay away from you."

I laughed nervously. "Yeah, he told me that as well."

"Well, how do you feel about it?"

"I want to see you …" stuttered out my mouth, and then what I wanted, but didn't need to happen, happened.

He scooted over and slid my hand into his, making sure our fingers intertwined. I looked up at him, and all I could imagine was how, if everything in my life were different, our first kiss would have begun with that touch. How, like tendrils of breezes his fingers would have gently stroked my arms, and the smile on his face would tell me he knew he had me; like the fox in *The Little Prince*, I was willing to be tamed. Greedy with need, my heart yearned for the dance of lips, hands, and tongues that would leave me breathless and happy, my whole body tingling with desire.

Damn, I wish you were mine, I thought. But I knew in the deepest way, a way Evan wasn't even cognizant of yet, that he still belonged to Kadija.

I slid my hand out of his and tried not to look at the confusion on his face.

"I'm sorry." I sat back and searched for a place to begin. "This is how it is …" And at first I thought I was just going to tell him about the last couple of days, but no, I knew I had to start the story at its proper beginning. He had to know where I had been before he could even fathom where I had to take him. I went back to that warm day in October when Oba first appeared. I talked nonstop for almost an hour, never daring to look at him because I might see disapproval or disgust, and I would lose my courage before I got to the truly terrifying part of the conversation, the part that included his life.

As if she knew wits had to be gathered and second breaths taken, Peaches brought in a tray of coffee, mugs and a serving plate laden with a pyramid of sugar cookies.

With a small, fanlike sweep of her hand, she gestured toward her offering. "Evan?"

"Thank you, but no," he said with a tentative shake of his head.

I watched him lean over, rest his arms on his legs and knit his fingers together. *Not a good sign*, I thought, that he was suddenly so uncomfortable. Peaches went ahead and poured some coffee for me.

"You okay, baby?" she whispered as she pressed the mug into my hands.

"I'm fine." But I desperately wanted to follow her as she left the room.

"So," I said, attempting to break the thickening silence before it got too hard for logic to penetrate.

Evan cleared his throat. "So ... do you know what you're going to do?"

"I'm waiting for a sign." Those words came out in my voice, but I hadn't formed them. I was barely through with taking one step and the spirits were informing me when I would have to take the next one. I suppressed a shiver by reaching for a cookie. It was still warm, buttery soft, small enough to inhale in one bite.

"Sign? What kind of sign?"

"I don't know yet. Anyway, look, I only told you this because I needed you to understand what's been going on with me, so that what I have to tell you will make some kind of sense."

"What?"

"Last night a woman named Kadija appeared to me in a vision. She told me to tell you that she still loves you and that she forgives you for what happened."

Panic and disbelief tugged the ends of his mouth taunt, and his eyelids fluttered. *Please, don't lie. Please, don't deny her existence or say that she never meant anything to you,* I prayed.

"How do you know about ... Kadija?" he asked.

Everything, every little thing he thought he had hidden from the world about their relationship—love, shame, guilt—was in that small pause he had to take before he could bring himself to say her name. I wanted to ask him how she had died. I wanted to ask him when. How long had they been together, and what had he done that she felt he needed her forgiveness? She had stayed behind out of love. Contacted me out of love even when she must have sensed he was moving on to replace her. She wanted her life, her feelings to be recognized by him. I realized it was my responsibility to make sure they were. I took a long sip of coffee before I responded.

"As I said, she came to me in a vision."

Incredulous, he shook his head in long slow arcs of nos. "My father told you about this, didn't he?"

"No."

"I told him not to tell anyone. He should have kept my confidence."

I meant to glide the mug in my hand to a soft landing on the glass top of my aunts' coffee table, but irritation flexed my arm, and the mug dropped like a hammer. The noise was an abrupt, coffee-drenched pop. The cookies swayed, and then toppled, spewing sparks of crumbs on to the carpet. I resisted the urge to run to the kitchen to get something to clean up the mess.

"You're your father's son!" I yelled. "You know how visions work even if you say you don't believe. You know he didn't have to tell me anything."

Evan got up, his eyes still and huge, as if right then he was seeing more than he had ever seen in his life and didn't know what to do with all the newness. I understood I was supposed to be a conduit for Kadija's love and forgiveness, but she was dead and could afford to be merciful. I was alive and being seriously messed with by a man who obviously didn't want to deal with any kind of reality.

"Maybe you want to blame your daddy," I continued yelling, my voice thick with new authority. "Because then you don't have to take responsibility for whatever happened to Kadija. I don't know what you did, but I do know this: you're trying to use me like a bandage on a knife wound. I've got enough on my plate; I don't want to clean up your mess. Whatever you need to do, Evan, to make it right, do it. If you have to grieve, grieve."

All the anger holding in my tears crumbled and I began to cry. Exhaustion dropped me to my knees, and I tried to gather up the remains of cookies from the rug.

Evan made no effort to move. It was as if all my shouting had stuck a pole up his spine and nailed him to the floor. "I'm sorry," he finally stuttered.

I didn't look up. I felt too embarrassed for me and too disappointed in him. All I could bring myself to do was whisper, "please, just go home."

30

FOR HOURS AFTER EVAN LEFT, I slowly paced the heat-saturated shadow of the veranda, folding up my thoughts about him like damp laundry and trying to put them away. Beyond the castle keep of bottle trees, beyond the mystic blue skin of the house, battles for justice had to be fought. Whether I liked it or not, I was a warrior and Edmond Gilmore had to be confronted.

The gait of my pacing became faster; the frantic drumming of my feet on porch planks cut slits into the eternal firmament, loosening up ancient Zulu praise songs I could conjure with. My lips began to carve the air. I didn't care if I was loud. I only stopped chanting when I realized there was a postal carrier standing there with an Express Mail package in his hand, looking at me like maybe he needed to call the police because a crime of craziness was in process. He was older, white, his bulk wrapped up in a uniform that was a scant inch away from being too tight. If he could have thrown his portable signature device at me and run back to his truck, I got the feeling he would have. Instead, he stood as far away as he could before he handed his machine to me.

"How are you doing?" I said as I scrawled my name in the little tab of space.

"Fine," he answered, then paused to look at my signature as if to make sure he had it memorized so that when he related stories of the strange behaviors of black folks to his buddies, he would have my name right.

The package was from my Uncle George and marked, "Photo." At first I thought it was just a graduation memory, but what slid out was an eight by twelve picture. The image, I didn't immediately recognize: a tall, smiling, dark-skinned man sat holding a small, scraggly dog on a park bench. Pressed up close to him was a young girl with a snatch of braided hair shaped like a fish hook with a yellow ribbon fly on its tip. The girl was wearing a big smile full of teeth and happiness, and in her arms was a stuffed rabbit. Next to her was a bigheaded boy with next to no hair on his head. He had his arms crossed over his puffed out chest as if he were trying to show he was grown.

I recognized the boy first; Joe then, was like Joe now, and with that moment of revelation came the thought that I was the little girl, and the man holding the ugly little bit of dog was my father. A small note, written on the back, confirmed my guess: *Samuel Oliver Johnson, Grace, age four, Joe, age four.* I had never seen the photo, and I laughed sarcastically as an antidote for the rush of pain. The truth was I had never seen a picture of myself as a little girl. If Mama possessed any photos, she sure as hell never revealed them to me. I had accepted that then. Couldn't do anything but accept it if I wanted to be sane. But the truth set my mind free. Standing there, I knew Mama's grief had been suffused with more craziness and anger than sorrow.

"What are you looking at, Grace?" Casmil asked as she opened the screen door and came to stand with me on the porch. She didn't ask me how I was, or about Evan, and I was grateful.

"Uncle George sent me this." I lowered the picture so she could see it.

"Ah," she said, but the slender smile accompanying the moment of recognition was woven tight with sorrow. Her small hand came up to touch it, fingers curled as if she were calling for the distant past to come out of the shadows to be stroked and petted.

"This was the year before ..." The soft strand of her voice snagged like wool thread being dragged across splintery wood on the word "before." She looked at me to see if she had to explain, but I knew what "before" meant.

She continued. "This was your father with his dog, Little Jack. Your daddy loved that dog even though it was mean and looked like something a cat threw up. This is you with the rabbit you named Velvet. Your daddy had given you that toy at Easter, and you dragged it around like it was sewn to your hand. And Joe, Joe loved your father because his own father had walked off, and Samuel treated him like he was his own. You and Joe spent a lot of time together when you were very young. Truth be told, Grace, even though he was young when your father died, I don't think Joe ever got over it. Your mother didn't exactly want him around after the funeral and I think, even though he had other brothers and sisters, in a very deep way, he missed being with you."

"I don't remember."

"You had to forget to survive in your mother's house. No shame in that, Grace."

No shame, but all different species of regret. What earthly court could I take my mother to for the theft of experiences and time? Where could I go to appeal for the recompense of dreams and relationships? Could I sue her big time for stunting the growth not only of my, but other folks' self-esteem? My soul began to riot, and the cacophony of bitter discontent rose and rose until I heard my aunt say, "leave your mother to God, Grace. You have other things to do." The fever about my mother broke then, because she and all her hateful ways were really small petty things compared to the evils I had been ordered to embrace. Business, I had to get down to business.

"Does Joe know how my father really died?"

"Yes," Casmil said, leaning in a bit as if the porch were full of people we needed to keep secrets from.

"Does he know about the others who were murdered?" It felt strange and disconcerting to say the word "murder" because then, it was no longer just a word. The word now had faces attached, including one that looked much like my own.

Casmil nodded. "He demanded to know what was what with you. He wouldn't leave his mother alone until she told him. He wishes you'd talk to him about it, Grace. He wants to be the one to go with you when you decide to confront Mr. Gilmore."

I nodded. The picture was the sign of what to do next and, of course, Joe wanted to be the one to go with me. The boy in the picture was now a man who wanted to protect his family. He was my brother, had always been my brother, if not by the shallower designation of blood, than by the deeper ties of spirit.

"It feels right he should go," I agreed. "I'd better go call him."

31

SO YOU READY TO DO this?" Joe asked as he came around the side of his car to open the door for me.

"Yeah." I paused to look back over my shoulder toward the house. My aunts were still standing on the porch, glued shoulder-to-shoulder by the sap of their worry and prayer. That morning, when I had announced I was going to confront Edmond Gilmore, they had become as still and silent as birds before a storm.

"Maybe ... she doesn't have to do this," Peaches had offered. Casmil's stare, boney and bare of sentiment, had made her take it back. Faith, a harder currency than love, had to be put where their mouths had been. Talk had been talked, so the walk had to be walked.

"Take care of Joe," Peaches had whispered after she placed on my cheek the plum-colored talisman of her small lips on my cheek.

"She will," Casmil had asserted under her breath.

Of course, Joe didn't feel like he needed to be cared for.

"So do you know where this bastard lives?" he asked.

I cocked my head and looked at him as I settled in. "You already know where he lives. If your mother didn't tell you, then you looked it up."

Joe grinned. "So we're going to 535 Rich Racist White Man Lane."

"Joe," I sighed.

"It's true, Gracie girl. Tell me it's not," he said, and then his mood shifted from teasing to dead serious. "You should have told me yourself about this, Gracie. I didn't need to learn about it from my mother. I didn't need her telling me I had to stay out of it because it was yours to do."

I couldn't argue with him; it was true it should have come out my horse's mouth. "Like you would have taken it any better from me that you shouldn't do anything," I offered.

"True, but at least it would have come from the source." Joe pushed on the accelerator. "And you know my mama was right."

"About the important stuff, yes," I admitted. We hit the highway and hurtled toward the outer racial frontier of Vigilant. "But I'm not going to let her have all the glory because some of the other stuff she's paranoid about is just craziness."

"Wish the hell she was wrong on this though, you know."

"Yeah Joe, I do."

I was getting nervous, but Joe's anxiety opened him up. Words gushed out of his mouth the way water did out of a busted fire hydrant. He didn't realize my concentration had been hauled out from under the spray of his sentences. Bearing witness to truth and tragedies is a complicated, textured business, and I was being readied. Joe's mouth was moving, but I couldn't hear what he was saying. My breathing sizzled and crackled in my ears as if my lungs were frying each breath to a brittle crisp. Darkness bled in, and someone played a distant backbeat. Nina Simone began singing hard and loud the lyrics to *Sinnerman*, and when she hit the chorus, a surge of power seemed to come down in a suck of breath that shook me back into this living world just in time to hear Joe rapping lines from Martha and the Vandellas's *Nowhere to Run*.

My eyes flickered open fully, and I stared at Joe.

"What …?"

"What were you singing?" I asked.

"That's off some real old school, I think. It just came to me."

Or it was given to you, I thought, because there was old school and then there was *old school*.

"Got meaning for you, Gracie?" he asked.

"Yeah."

"Something eerie?" he teased.

I laughed a bit. "When is anything not with me?"

"I hear that, Gracie girl, but it's all good."

We stopped talking as the landscape changed, going from narrow streets crowded with small homes to wide lanes of black top leading up behind Haven Lake. Bed and Breakfasts and summer cabins grew into monster mansions nestled on acres of lawn and privacy fencing.

"Here." Joe's voice snapped off the cap of silence. His arm arched up to point at a home that sat so far from the mouth of its driveway, it looked like a dollhouse on a green ledge up against the blue wall of a room.

"You scared?" Joe asked, turning onto a narrow pipe of gravel road. We were two odd Jonahs slipping deeper into the belly of an unseen white whale.

I shook my head no. I wasn't afraid for me, but Joe was another story.

"Joe," I said as we coasted into the large loop of the driveway turnaround. "I'm going to need for you to stay in the car." I looked at him to make sure he understood that I really meant it.

"I don't think so," Joe said as he turned the engine off. "I need to have your back."

"My back's got." I reached out to touch his massive arm. Beneath his moist skin, his determination to protect me was setting hair triggers on the long coils of his muscles. "Look, I need to do this alone." I took a breath made from frantic prayer. "Promise me on Daddy's grave that you won't try to come rescue me."

Joe wagged his head. "No, he wouldn't ask that of me. All I'm giving you is fifteen minutes, Gracie. Then if you're not out, I'm coming after you."

I nodded. It was the best deal I was going to get out of him. In a way he was right. Anything more than a few minutes was too long and too deep into dangerous.

"I'll be careful," I assured him, but I saw nothing but a brother's deep worry in his eyes.

What had been a very warm day had cooled considerably. Clouds were being pushed across the sky by the tines of a hard breeze that was musty with the scent of rain. My hand shook a little as I knocked on the massive oak door. I waited, anticipating I would eventually have to ring the bell, but the door cracked open slowly, and a tall, white woman with gray eyes and a horsy mane of salt and pepper hair appeared. She looked at me for a long moment as if she thought I couldn't possibly be real. When she realized I was tangible, I saw her jaw tighten.

"Yes?" came out, arid and cold, stripped of even a normal graciousness.

"I am here to see Mr. Edmond Gilmore."

Surprise arched her badly drawn eyebrows almost up to the coarse edge of her hairline. "Are you selling something, because if you are, we're not buying."

"No, I'm not selling anything. I am here to see Mr. Gilmore on some business …"

I hesitated a bit, and then something made me add, "please tell him Grace Johnson—Samuel Johnson's daughter, is here to see him."

"He won't see—"

"Please," I interrupted. "Just inform him that I'm here."

My voice jabbed at the soft belly of her emotions like a spear. Unease erased the color from her cheeks. She puckered her lips up into a rumpled button of chapped skin. *Okay,* I thought, *she's not going to willingly let me in,* but something in her was praying about the past. Something in her saw me as a light at the end of a long and bloody tunnel. That "something" in her made her reach out to test my mettle.

She leaned forward out of the door a little. "He doesn't like *you people*," she warned.

I felt the swift kick of "you people," but I didn't flinch. "Yes, I'm aware of that."

She stared at me, and I expected the door to come at me like a hammer seeking to drive a nail down and away, but something decent in her wanted what was indecent in her life to be over. She may have suspected she was living with a monster, had some suspicions about what the monster had been consuming all these years, had maybe even wanted to destroy the monster but just couldn't figure out how to do it without destroying everything else she loved. But now here I was, a true victim of the monster's crimes, ready and maybe even able to take on the monster, and her soul knew it had to save what was left of itself by letting me into her brightly lit, well-furnished living room.

"I'll tell him that you're here," she murmured. She went off down a hallway walking slowly as if she were adjusting the burden she was carrying in order to take on more. A man's voice rose and fell. The harshness in it drifted down the hall like a sour smell. The woman came back with the look of someone who had been whipped and beaten by words. I knew the look; I had worn it many, many times myself. Tears begged to be released, but she kept them behind her pride. "He's down the hall and to your left. You did you say your name was Grace?"

"Yes," I nodded.

"Grace," she repeated.

Her gray eyes searched the pockets of mine for some bit of understanding, "You know," she confessed, "I don't like what he's been teaching my son Jonathan."

She walked off, leaving me to tend to my growing nervousness alone.

"Yea, though I walk through the valley of the shadow of death," I chanted as I followed the carpet down to a stark white, curtainless room where the evil I had prayed not to fear existed in electronic luxury. Edmond Gilmore sat in a big black leather lounger looking at a television that was almost as big as the wall in the room. Propped up in that chair, he appeared harmless enough. If I had met him at any other time and had no history, he would have been just a little old man with dark hair he was too vain to allow to get gray. But I knew who he was and what he had done.

"Grace Johnson, huh," he said, looking at me as if I were proof black folk were inferior. His dark eyes slithered down me, trying to find the saltiness of fresh emotional wounds or the tender scabs of civility he knew must barely cover my anger. The small sharp teeth of his malevolent knowing nibbled goose bumps into my skin. He licked and licked until he found the soft exposed heel of my history. "I met your father once."

It was a demon's tease. Each word was smeared with the memory of my father's blood. Anger caught my resolve in its teeth and began to drag it toward hell.

Words, I need words, I prayed, as I took a breath to brace myself and begin to pull myself back from the abyss. Anger wouldn't get me anything but life in prison and worse, spiritual failure.

Words came. "I have been sent to offer you my great-great-grand-father Freeman Johnson's apology for killing your father."

The past made Edmond Gilmore struggle to sit up. "What kind of shit is this?" he asked.

"I have also been sent to tell you that all your crimes are fully known."

"Crimes …?" Incredulity was all in his voice, but he smiled the way snakes must smile when a rabbit has been dropped into an aquarium with them.

"I have your book."

The smile vanished. "Then, girl, you know that all you have is a list of names."

"I have been sent in the names of those you slaughtered to offer you a chance at redemption. Their spirits request you do what is right and confess to their murders."

"I want my book back."

Evil loves its evil things, I thought. "No," I said.

"It's just a list of names, girl. Not proof of anything."

"I know you killed my father. I know you killed all those children."

My naked defiance made him get up out of the lounger. Old, but whip thin and snake fast, he edged close to me. He expected me to step back; it enraged him when I didn't. There I was, this black woman he despised, all up in his face telling him that I knew all his filthy, bloody business, offering him some damned redemption for the price of his reputation and the rest of his life on this earth in some prison. He raised his arm, cocked it like a fang to slap at me, but snakes don't realize that sometimes rabbits know how to fight back. My body shuddered hard as something large and powerful surged up into existence. I stared at Edmond Gilmore, and what or who he saw in my eyes made him put his arm down and back away.

"Get out of here," he yelled, his voice bucking with panic and the threat of violence.

Even if I had wanted my legs to move, they would not have obeyed the order. My lips quivered and then opened to allow the thunderous voice of something ancient and unyielding to roar out. "Trust not that time will forget you. For judgment regards a lifetime like an hour. A man's reputation remains after death, when his deeds will be heaped up around him. Judgment is eternal, only a fool ignores it."

The drain of energy was almost too much. My knees buckled, and I struggled to keep from falling. The room dimmed almost to dark, but then the sound of Old Gilmore yelling that I was possessed by the devil seemed to snap the lights back on. Another time, another place, maybe if it were on TV, that kind of accusation would have been almost funny.

Aware that at any moment Joe would be like the cavalry riding in armed with adrenaline and righteous fury, I turned to leave, only to find the door blocked. Jonathan Gilmore stood looking at me, his expression creased razor-sharp, the look in his grey eyes revealing he was ready to dig for my blood.

The monster he called grandfather was babbling, "kill her. She's the devil ... devil ... devil ... devil."

"I've seen you before, nigger..." Jonathan said, and took a step forward.

"Yeah," I said, "but I'm not the same person you met then."

Young snake slid forward again, but this time the ancient ones had no more patience or poetry. "Move!" I shouted, and whether out of volcanic fear or spiritual confusion Jonathan moved aside.

I left them there hollering at each other. The old man accused Jonathan of being a coward. Jonathan shouted back that he wasn't afraid; however, there were no sounds of his footsteps behind me. The woman I had met earlier came flying down the hall to break up the fight. For a moment, I thought she didn't notice me even though our shoulders brushed hard as she ran past. But as she got farther down, I heard her yell back, "you take care, Grace. You better take good care."

32

I LEFT THE GILMORE HOUSE starving in that extreme spiritual way, where a roasted chicken is a better blessing than prayers.

"I need to eat," I said as I climbed into the car, trying not to sound desperate. Joe said nothing. He didn't ask what I wanted or how much. He didn't even ask what had happened. He just found a burger place and bought a lot of them. I ate until I was out of stomach and breath. It took all the energy I had left to say, "thank you."

Joe handed me some napkins so I could wipe my mouth and hands. "No problem, Gracie."

I sat for a while, trying to steady my thoughts enough to land them back in reality. I looked at Joe because I wanted to talk, but all I had were tears, and the kind of loud sobbing that sounded like children pounding their fists on the windows of the car. Joe gathered my bucking body in, trying with all his physical might to bandage my emotions, but it was all too much. So, he shouldered some of the pain by crying with and for me.

"I wouldn't tell anybody," I said after I stopped shaking.

"No shame in crying about stuff that needs to be cried about," he said. "You got some heavy stuff on you, Gracie. If you weren't crying, there would be something wrong with you, and if I weren't crying with you, there would be something wrong with me."

When we got back to the house, my family gathered around the living room table. Joe, my aunts and Monroe nursed cups of coffee as they waited for me to hand out the details of what had happened.

"It doesn't seem like enough," I said when I finished. "It feels like he's going to get away with it."

Monroe sipped his coffee and gave me a long, deep look, "Reverend King once said, 'The arc of the moral universe is long, but it bends toward justice.'"

But what if this arc didn't bend? I knew from the crime shows on TV that many crimes went unsolved. I wanted to say as much, but I took my cues from my aunts, whose faces were like shut windows and closed doors.

I was almost too drained to climb the stairs to my bedroom and almost too tired to call Shanta, but I picked up the phone and dialed. Before I could get beyond hello, Mrs. Manning said, "hey, Grace baby, Shanta's already on her way over. She said she felt something was wrong with you and flew out the door about half an hour ago. You okay?"

"Just a little lonely for company," I half-lied.

Mrs. Manning weighed my voice, sifting for the truth and found most of it. "Well, it sounds like more than just that, but Shanta should be there in a moment."

And in a moment, Shanta did tumble into my room with a box of chocolates and shoulders to cry on.

"Jesus, Grace," she whispered, sinking her elbows deep into her knees as the weight of my experiences bent her over. A thick curtain of braids covered what I knew were deep currents of concern on her face.

"I don't know what next," I said. "I think it's just waiting until I get the next sign."

"Too bad about Evan."

Even as I said, "Dr. Monroe was right. My plate's too full to be concerned about him," I found myself wondering how he was doing. Was he still in town or had he gone back to Atlanta? "How's my mama?"

Shanta didn't even try to sprinkle sugar on the shit. "Your mama's been telling everybody that you needed to be out of her house because you didn't know how to act."

"And do people believe her?"

"Actually, no. I think most folks are coming around to believe what she did to you was crazy."

"Jamila …"

"She's all right Grace, but she doesn't exactly miss you. They don't miss you, and maybe you should try not to miss them."

"Yeah, I guess." However, something in the confrontation with my father's murderer had allowed me to miss them both, especially Jamila. "They lost daddy too, you know."

Shanta shook off my sense of the situation with all her body as if she were shaking off water after a swim. "Yeah, Miss Softy Heart, but they're not at the point of recognizing or considering that yet. All they're thinking about right now is how to go about putting you down. You understand?"

"Guess so."

I sensed it was more complicated. Maybe the substance of our grief had rendered us incapable of truly feeling anything but a multitude of shadows.

"So when do I get to see your father's gifts?"

"Now, I guess." From under my bed I pulled out the ornate wooden box containing the seashells and my mojo bag.

"Tools of the trade," Shanta said under her breath as she studied the profusion of cowries and the pewter rabbit with its carefully folded picture of the cosmography.

I began to flex my fingers. "What did you say?"

Shanta laughed. "I didn't say anything."

I knew better. Shanta's voice had leaped from its usual melodic tones into that greasy sizzling sound that told me her body was about to be used as a microphone.

"What do you know about the others who died?" Shanta-who-wasn't-Shanta asked as her long fingers danced along the backs of the laughing dolphins on the box.

I started to say I didn't know anything except what Doris had told me, but the essence of small voices, like crescents of waves from very distant seas, rolled onto the shores of my reality, and then came the blood-soaked whispers of truth:

"Annika Parson, four-years-old, stolen while sleeping; strangled. Dymond Clayton, five, assaulted as she walked to school; strangled. Effie Maria Williams, six, died on her birthday, taken as she walked home from a party at her grandmother's house; strangled. Malcolm Branch, one month old, snatched when his mother left the room to get a bottle; smothered and disemboweled. Perry Washington, seven, caught one Sunday evening while fishing; strangled. Macy Henry, seven, snatched on her way to church; strangled. Belinda Atkinson, twelve, taken as she left to go to the store for her mother; strangled."

When I finished, I was too sick with sorrow to get dressed in pajamas to go to bed. I remember Shanta helping me crawl under the covers with all my clothes and shoes on, and that was all until I woke up around midnight.

I turned on the lamp and padded down to the bathroom and back. I should have sensed the change of atmosphere before I got to my bedroom door. The pungent smell of rotting apples and the crisp cold of a long ago fall day had permeated my room, but those senses didn't kick in until I saw the dog perched like a nasty blonde wig on my bed. I recognized the dog, knew who it once belonged to, and re-membered its name. That the dog was my father's beloved, but dead Little Jack was beyond strange, even for me. But there he was on my bed, growling, as mean in death as he had been in life. Some wiser part of me told me to speak to it:

"*And in the gardens of my heart,*
Daddy, I hear you calling me.
Now I am fully here.
I will take you to the blue world under.
Now, Daddy, I'll take you home."

Fed, Little Jack stopped growling, and I watched as he leaped into the air and landed with a very mortal sounding thump. With legs spinning like whirligigs, he scurried out of the door, and I was made to follow.

Stop, stop, I thought to myself as one foot after the other pulled me down the stairs into the living room. But I didn't belong to me; I was a bystander to the flight of my own body. Other forces with richer purposes manipulated my fingers to unlock the front door, and I tumbled into the muggy night as if a giant had slung me out into the yard.

33

DARKNESS SWALLOWED THE VISION OF the fleeing dog, but I kept running. Land and houses flew by in a black ribbon blur of trees, windows and doors until I ran out of mortal breath. The world spun into a wild orbit, and the air thickened into the waters of a dark, turbulent ocean. Muscles and tendons unthreaded themselves, and my arms, like scissors, rose and fell, rose and fell against the grains of stiff waves. I swam until I felt the burn of exhaustion, and I wanted to succumb to the cresting and heaving of currents, to the trashing jaws of death itself. But the dog that had come out of my father's eternity brought the gate of its teeth down on the meaty part of my palm. Pain exploded, and I wailed a wail that seemed to multiply until it grew into the high-pitched call of a police siren.

"Don't move!" a voice ordered.

I opened my eyes to the realization that, like Dorothy, I had landed in Oz, only I was in the African-American version where the winged monkeys were white policemen in dark uniforms with guns. In a few panicky seconds, I absorbed the fact that I was standing upright and it was now day. My clothes were caked with a grimy, gritty skin of dirt. My hands and feet looked like the muddy faces of garden spades. I eyed the monkeys warily, watching with fascination and dread the Cyclops eyes of their guns.

"Put your hands up where we can see them," a voice yelled.

It took me a few moments to connect the dots of words with lines of action, but eventually I stuck my arms up as high as my tired muscles would allow.

"What's your name?" one cop barked as his partner frisked me.

"Grace Johnson," I answered. Then I knew enough to keep my mouth shut even as they kept asking me what I was doing out there. When I didn't answer, they roughly pulled my arms behind my back and snapped handcuffs on my wrists. My rights were read to me as if the police officer reciting them hated the fact Mr. Miranda ever existed. I knew how to keep silent, but I couldn't decide who I would call to contact my attorney. *Or maybe*, I considered after a little more thought, *everything had been set up already*.

Where was here, I wondered? I looked up to see the back of a small, slumping bungalow whose owner didn't seemed to care that the grass wasn't cut and filled with hanks of weeds. Better-kept homes rose up on each side, and their white owners were standing at the fences, looking to see what a black girl, who didn't belong in their neighborhood, had done to disturb their Sunday morning.

"What the hell is that?" asked a woman dressed in a fuzzy pink robe that matched the curlers in her pasta-colored hair. She pointed toward a corner of yard about ten feet away from where the police-men and I stood. I turned and looked. The grass toward the back of the property had been pulled out and trampled down. In the mouth of the clearing it looked like someone had gouged out an oblong hole and strewn the ground with cowry shells. I looked at them, and then I looked down at my now filthy outfit with matching filthy hands, and knew "the someone" who had done all that had been me.

"It's nothing," a cop yelled over to the lady. She shot him back a look that said she didn't believe him.

"This is freaking weird," one cop said to another as they led me across the yard toward a sagging fence gate. Out on the street three or four police cars sat, their sirens doing mute waltzes as other officers erected webs of yellow tape.

"Why are we waiting to take her down to the station?"

"Chief radioed he wanted in on this one, and considering whose property this is, and considering there's been skeletal remains found, I can understand why."

"Yeah, heard he's kind of got a soft spot for black folks."

"Oh God," I whispered as I shook my head to try to loosen some memories. Questions with nothing but horrible answers began to assault my attention, so I barely noticed when a white man in a dark suit approached and said my name. *He's one of the monkeys,* I thought, although the suit told me he was the dominant one in the group. I gave him a vacant stare and went back to meditating on my questions.

"Ms. Johnson," he said again, "I'm Chief Atkinson, and I'm going to be riding with you down to the station."

Some soft concern in his voice caught my attention, and I tipped my head and glanced up at him. Atkinson was a tall thin man with angular features that looked like they had been roughened and wrinkled by hard living. A healthy mop of heavily salted-and-peppered hair accented blue eyes that reminded me of toilet-bowl water.

He smiled a bit at my interest and turned to one of the policemen. "Let's get her out of those handcuffs once we get out of sight of the crowd. And see if you can get her something to wipe her hands with."

The cop he had spoken to started to protest the release of his prize, then thought better of it. I followed Atkinson to a waiting car. When I was freed and seated, I wiped at my sore hands with a pack of moist paper towels. Beneath the dirt, my palms glowed reddish, and the skin around my nails was slightly shredded and torn. Considering that I must have been digging all night with a nasty, mean, intangible dog, they looked pretty good. Atkinson climbed in beside me, and I sat looking in my lap as we waited for another police officer, one I hadn't seen before, to get in to drive. I noticed he was black and had to take another look because the city of Vigilant was not known for hiring anyone who was much darker than slightly scorched vanilla pudding. Atkinson caught a whiff of my interest and laughed.

"New recruit since I came in last year. I thought the Vigilant police department needed to at least enter the 1960s. Mr. Cooper here is hopefully the first of more to come. "

Officer Cooper nodded at me, then said to his boss, "long or short way back to the station, Chief?"

"Long," Atkinson answered. "Ms. Johnson and I need to talk. And Officer Cooper, nothing said here leaves this car."

The officer nodded again. "Yes, sir."

We sat for a while listening to the humming of the car and breathing the rising stink off my body.

"I'm going to make the assumption," Chief Atkinson finally said, "that you don't know where you are or how you got here."

He was right. I didn't have a clue. Everything looked familiar, but I didn't really recognize anything.

"You are just within the city line of Vigilant. Your aunts reported you missing this morning about the same time one of the neighbors next door to where you were found reported hearing a disturbance. The property belongs to a Mr. Edmond Gilmore, and you're being arrested for trespassing. Also, of course, there is the matter of the grave you seemed to have found."

I nodded that I understood, but I kept my eyes deposited in my lap examining my hand for more damage until he said, "shells" in this slightly awed voice, as if he were holding an actual one up for me to look at because he had never seen one before. "I haven't seen shells used like that since I visited my mother's people down in South Carolina. Down there, the older black folks would scatter them around the edge of a grave. They said it was a way to show concern and respect for those who had died because shells represented the promise of eternal life. They said it was an African belief."

I shrugged to keep from shivering. I was nothing but tired, and every muscle seemed to be whimpering about its pain. Atkinson kept looking at me, his blue, blue eyes tracing and retracing the side of my head. "I have a story, Ms. Johnson, that I think is connected to what I believe is going on here. I used to live in Vigilant a long time ago, probably before you were born. I left like a lot of folks to find my future in the big city. I was a cop in Detroit for years, but I got tired of all that. So when the job of police chief opened up here, I came home."

He paused to let those words sink in and then continued. "I was raised here by a black couple—the Atkinsons, maybe you heard of them? They took me in when I was about five after my biological mother decided she didn't want a kid complicating her drug addiction.

"She dropped me off at Madie May's and Carl's house before she left town. Only thing she ever did for me that made any kind of sense. The Atkinsons became my parents, ended up adopting me. One of the best things I got out of the whole deal were some sisters and brothers. They didn't care if I was white and would beat the asses of anyone who did. I had three brothers and three sisters ... there were four sisters, but when I was sixteen, my baby sister Belinda disappeared one day and was never found. I never got over that; I became a cop because of that."

Surprised, I turned my head, and I looked at Atkinson really hard. There was no trace of lies in his story, so the connection between us went from puddle shallow to ocean deep in the time it had taken for him to say her name.

"I know about her," I said simply.

Atkinson nodded. "I had a long talk with your aunts this morning. They said you might have some proof about several murders and kidnappings committed by Edmond Gilmore."

I took a breath. "He's not going to confess to any of it," I said.

The chief smiled. "Oh, I think either his pride or his anger or just plain ordinary police work might be old Edmond's undoing. There's a body on some land he owns. He can't just ignore our questions."

"Maybe."

"Well, Ms. Johnson, it's like my mother says. We need to wait and see what God will do."

"So are you going to ask me how I know about this?" I asked, because I was trying to fathom what was coming next.

Chief Atkinson was quiet for a long moment. Then, in a soft voice that was still strong enough to carry the burden of serious secrets, he said, "I don't care how you came to know it, Ms. Johnson. I just care that it's been done."

34

THE CARDBOARD BEIGE WALLS OF the interrogation room made me feel like a mouse in the bottom of a shoebox. At a grimy wooden table I burrowed my behind into a chair, hunched over and wondered just how bad I looked from the other side of the two-way window. Help was coming, but the box didn't have a clock, so minutes were worth the same as hours.

"Baby, don't say anything until Attorney Blair gets there," Peaches had counseled when I was allowed to call. She had tried to cover up her worry with her usual bright scarves of optimism and had failed.

"I'm okay, Aunt Peaches," I had tried to reassure her. "I won't say anything."

It was a promise easily kept because the police were content to leave me alone.

Finally, the lock smacked, the door opened, and the gray-suited brawn of my lawyer filled the room. I frosted a small hello with a weak smile.

He settled into a chair across the table from me. "How are you doing?"

I shrugged. What was there to say?

"I understand you were found on one of Edmond Gilmore's properties last night, and while you were there, you uncovered some remains."

I moistened what felt like an inch of ash on my lips and nodded.

He grunted thoughtfully as he ran his hand across his face. "What kind of questions did the chief ask you on the way in?"

In a dry whisper, I told him about my ride. "His sister's black and she was murdered by Gilmore," I said at the end of my explanation.

"How do you know?"

I leaned close and told him about Aunt Doris and the book.

Attorney Blair's expression went blank. "The police aren't going to charge you for trespassing," he finally said, "but the chief would like to ask you a few more questions."

Nerves rolled my stomach. I wanted to get up and walk, but my back had hardened into a Gordian mass of muscle. How to explain the unexplainable?

"What happened last night is more metaphysical than logical," I warned. "Besides, he said he didn't care how I came to know anything."

Attorney Blair smiled. "There is a time for logic and a time for the mystical," he offered. "The man that is a brother and son in Chief Atkinson doesn't care. However, the legal system on which earthly justice is built demands the logic of evidence and probable cause. So there are things he needs to know and understand in order to do what needs to be done."

I nodded my head that I understood. "Okay, I'll talk to him."

Chief Atkinson arrived with an offering of coffee and two sausage and egg biscuit sandwiches.

"Sorry, this is all we could get," he apologized as he placed the food in front of me. Hunger made me ignore the fact that my breakfast was more grease than meat, and that the coffee was so sweet it could have been used for syrup on pancakes.

"The media is already howling at the door," Atkinson said. "I'm going to try and sneak both of you out a side door so you don't have to deal with them right now. I know you're tired, Ms. Johnson, but just a few questions?"

I swabbed the grease off my fingers with a thin napkin. "Okay," I said.

"Susan Gilmore said you were at their house yesterday to see Edmond Gilmore."

The gray-eyed lady from the day before now had a name. *Did she now have a thousand second thoughts about letting me in,* I wondered.

"Yes," I said as I took a bite of the next sandwich and chewed slowly.

"Why did you go to see him?"

I took another mouthful of food and kept chewing until my anger found its sharpest tongue. "I went there to confront him, because I wanted him to know I knew he was a murderer. I wanted him to know that I knew he had killed my father and other people."

Atkinson drank in my fierceness, but his expression didn't reflect how it tasted to him. "What did he say?"

"He didn't admit to anything. It wasn't what he said. It was how he reacted."

Atkinson twisted down his pen to write a sentence on a narrow spiral bound notebook. It was like he had found an unexpected puzzle piece and was trying to see how it fit in with the rest of the chaotic picture.

"How do you know Edmond Gilmore killed your father and the others?"

"You want the spiritual explanation or the logical one?"

Atkinson looked up from his notebook. He understood the difference. Any man who knew the African meaning of the cowries I had scattered on the grave understood and appreciated the difference.

"Give me the logical explanation for right now."

"My father's name was on a list in a book that belonged to Edmond Gilmore. Your sister's name was on the list. And another name of a young girl named Annika Parsons. Her mother had told me the story of how she had gone missing."

"It was just a list of names?"

"Yes, nothing else."

"How did you come by this book?"

I shook my head slowly. I knew I couldn't tell him Aunt Doris had stolen the book, at least not until I had spoken to her.

Attorney Blair shifted his hand on the table so that his fingertips came together. "She can't reveal that right now. If you need to see it perhaps we can arrange to bring it in."

Atkinson looked at Attorney Blair, and in that split-second of silent counsel, a decision was made to let the book stay in my possession, to pretend for a while that they knew nothing about it.

"I think I can do without it for now," Atkinson replied, "but do you remember the rest of the names on the list?"

There was, of course, no forgetting them. However, it took me a moment to gather up enough strength to bear them out of my memory. In a singsong voice moist with grief, I said their names aloud as if I were speaking the lyrics of a sad, yet transcendent blues song.

"My God," Attorney Blair said under his breath when I had finished. "I knew some of those young people's parents back in the day."

Chief Atkinson sighed. "Yeah, some black folk always thought there was something going on, especially after Grace's father was found, but there was never any real evidence of anything. It looks like Gilmore may have spread things out. He knew he could depend on people not caring much about black children coming up missing." The chief paused and looked at me struggling with my pain, trying not to cry. "He knew he could depend on the police to call a lynching a suicide because it was just easier to believe. Who knows, there may have been others involved."

What was left of the rest of my sandwich was nothing but grease on rigid cups of bread, but I took a bite anyway.

"But even if there had been evidence," Attorney Blair added, "who was going to go after him in court? You and I both know the rich and powerful can buy a different kind of jury and justice. Nobody black ever had any hope of getting even simple justice in this town, and we might not get it now."

"Unless he confesses, I know." Atkinson said. "My sense is Ms. Johnson rattled him, hurt his pride. He might get cocky, make a mistake. Or maybe someone in his family will reveal something. Susan

Gilmore was freaked out by the whole incident when I talked to her on the phone."

"So what happens next?" I asked.

"I'll send someone out to question Gilmore," Atkinson said.

"No, no." I whispered. "I mean the body?"

Atkinson paused sharply and in that moment he became more of a son and brother than a cop. "Yes, of course." he said. "We're going to send the remains to the state forensic lab and hope for identification. The names on the list will give us a place to start gathering information and DNA samples from the families." Atkinson glanced at the ceiling. "You know, for my mother's sake I hope it's my sister's body. My mother has never forgiven herself for sending her to the store that day. Even now, twenty something years later, she still thinks, what if."

"And for your sake too," I said.

I knew how vast the universe of my pain was because it seemed to run forever into the past and up to the evolving edge of my present. But I could only imagine how it was to be a cop and not be able to solve the one crime that mattered the most to him and his family.

"Yes, Ms. Johnson," he admitted, "for my sake as well."

35

THE NEXT MORNING WAS A dull gray day, the color of dryer lint. Low riding clouds, their bellies full of heat and moisture, had yet to spawn their rains. Outside the living room window, bright swarms of birds were having a smackdown at the feeder as I remembered how the day before, my aunts had made a ceremony of undressing me when Attorney Blair dropped me off.

"This is grave dirt, so it is no simple thing," Casmil had informed me after I had peeled off my clothes and showered. Then I watched as she took out a small pearl handled penknife and, from a sleeve, scraped crumbs of mud onto a bright yellow square of cloth.

"Pull the ends together," Peaches had instructed, handing me a long length of rough twine. "Tie a knot for each name on the list, and as you do, we will pray for courage and healing."

I heard her instructions, but all I could bring myself to think as my fingers fumbled to bend the string was, *Why had a supposedly merciful God allowed any of this to happen?*

"Doubt is normal," Peaches had whispered when she helped me place the sunny bright bundle into my red bag. I had been too tired to cry then, and I was still too tired to weep as the lint skies shuddered and huge drops tap danced down the window.

Like the birds in the yard, my stomach tried to scatter when the phone rang. The aunts picked up and I heard small sad cries of "yes, we understand," followed by the low murmur of subdued conversation.

Aunt Peaches's voice flew out from behind me as both of them huddled in the doorway, "Baby, it's Mr. Atkinson"

I picked up the receiver. "Hello, Chief Atkinson."

Atkinson cleared his throat. "Ms. Johnson, Edmond Gilmore confessed to all the murderers."

"All! He confessed to all of the murders?" My voice was soft, but it registered the magnitude of my shock. I had thought it would be eternity, or at least forever with a couple of days tacked on, before Gilmore would confess to anything beyond being rich, old and white. "All ... how?"

"Almost a deathbed confession," Atkinson responded. "He suffered a massive heart attack yesterday afternoon. Last night, his pastor called the station saying that Edmond Gilmore wanted to confess to a serious crime so he wouldn't die with his sins on him. We get up to the hospital room and his family's there with his lawyer. The pastor offers prayer and old Edmond confesses not to just one crime but everything. He gave dates, names, and places. Irony is that his doctors say he might actually live."

Atkinson sighed deep and long, as if his grief had caught up with him and he had to spend some time to push it away.

"So what happens next?" I asked

"We haven't charged him yet, so I can't release too many details, and you may not want them now anyway. There will be a short press conference at three this afternoon. You can come, but I have to warn you that once it's out in the national media that these were hate crimes, Vigilant's going to be crawling. People already know from this morning paper that you were the one who found the remains. The media was thick where you used to live. I sent someone out to keep them off your mother's house. It will only be a matter of time before someone tells them where you are. Watch it on TV maybe.

As soon as I've contacted most of the next of kin, I'll hold a private, families-only meeting to answer questions and deal with concerns."

"Ok," I said. "So how are you doing?"

The chief was silent for a moment as he fumbled to find the personal voice behind the mask of the professional. "Don't really know yet. In some ways it was better when I suspected but didn't know. My family is all tore up, and I'm concerned about how black and white folks in Vigilant are going to react. A lot of old racial wounds are probably going to be torn open by this. Could be as one of my buddies from Texas used to say, 'All tornadoes, no Oz' around here for the next few weeks. Well, I got some more calls to make. We'll talk privately real soon—and Grace?" He paused to make sure I was listening.

"Yes?"

"Thank you."

I mumbled goodbye and hung up. A wet kind of numbness began to creep through my body. My knees softened, and I reached for the edge of the couch to steady myself.

"Baby." Peaches's hand began to rub my back, trying to corral my gathering hurt.

"Why don't I feel happy about this?" I asked. "We won, didn't we?"

"Dr. Monroe's on his way over."

"I don't want to talk to him."

I knew Monroe would ask me to think, to process the nature of my feelings, and right then, I was feeling nothing but the kind of pain that felt too vast to label.

"Now more than ever you will need Monroe's help. This is only just the beginning of the grieving all of us will have to do," Casmil said.

* * *

When Monroe arrived, we sat side by side at the table in the dining room. My throbbing head bowed over a cup of mint tea. I had wanted coffee.

"You need to drink something that'll relax you," Peaches said when she saw my disappointment.

"Stop being childish," Monroe uttered under his breath. "She's right. And you need to remember your aunts' burden of pain is as great, if not greater, than yours."

I ran a finger around the cup's edge. "I'm sorry, Aunt Peaches. This is fine."

"It will be all right baby, because you have made it all right," she said as she went back to the living room to sit with her sister.

Monroe leaned back and looked at me for a long time. His strange eyes burrowed and sifted deep to the throbbing roots of my despair. "What are you thinking, Rabbit?" he finally asked.

"I don't know."

"Make something up then."

I laid my thoughts out in front of Monroe like I was snapping cards off a deck. Why did God let this happen? Why did the good and innocent have to suffer? Tears, and more tears until I was out of questions and just proclaimed, "I think God has abandoned us."

Silence followed as Monroe picked up and sorted the hand I had dealt him, then he replied, "it's a mistake to think we are entitled to an explanation. There is no understanding evil, Rabbit."

"God doesn't care," I asserted.

"What you did, the execution of your gift, is evidence enough that God is still working in the world."

I felt like a piss-poor instrument of the will of the divine. God had picked better folks in the past. Job, King, Rosa Parks, Gandhi, Ann Frank, Spiderman. My faith in God hardly measured up. I was damn near close to not believing in Him. I wanted answers, answers I felt Monroe hadn't given me. Propelled by frustration, I jumped up. My chair squirted out from under me, falling with a loud thump. The noise brought both aunts running.

"I'm going outside to sit in the garden." I backed away toward the door as if any comfort my aunts had to offer was now poisonous.

Peaches reached out, hands cupped as if waiting for me to pour myself into them. "It's raining."

Casmil caught her sister's sleeve and gently reined her in. "She won't melt."

"Let her go," Monroe agreed. "What she wants will find her."

It was pouring the kind of viscous warm rain that clings like glue to everything it touches. After the night before, I didn't relished being soaked, but still I headed out past the manicured plots of gardens, deep into the veins of tree shadows and underbrush. On the canopies of leaves rain rattled like seeds inside small gourds, keeping time to the ponderous thumping of my feet. I ran until, out of breath and almost out of mind, I tumbled into the circular clearing of bottled trees my aunts had erected as my protection against evil.

I stared up into the kaleidoscope of glistening orbs, into the narrow pupils of ancestral eyes and began to scream, "I want ... I want..."

Only, I didn't know what I wanted, except that like any wounded animal I just wanted the pain to go away. I closed my eyes and raked in bushels of small breaths. Moments piled up high and wide until the distant barking of a small dog dragged my attention back into this world. I saw Little Jack running, like he was high and crazy, along the broken hem of tree trunks just before I saw the image of a young black man dressed in jeans and a purple shirt standing neat and very dry several yards in front of me. *Was he a vision or just fractured desperation?* I thought

We stared at each other until some omnipotent voice hidden in the silence informed me that we were father and daughter visiting across the boundary of an invoked crossroad.

"Hey, Rabbit." My father's voice was as smooth and vibrant as jazz played on a saxophone. I smiled, but words like father, daddy and dad withered in my mouth.

My father smiled and nodded. "It's hard being real, isn't it, but you have done well by all your names."

It was the best of praise, but there was no solace in it. Standing there, I wanted to yell that I was angry because his death and all the other deaths had been senseless. I wanted to cry out that the years without him had been horrible and that his death had left me an orphan because my mother hadn't really wanted me. I wanted to beg to go with him because nothing made sense, because God was working in mysterious ways that scared the shit out of me. I didn't want my earth any more; I wanted his heaven. I was fighting to crack open my mouth so I could pour out my heart, when I heard Evan calling to me, "Grace ... Grace."

I couldn't imagine how he had followed me. How he had known to look for me there? I was shocked, but I didn't turn to answer him. I knew if I looked away, the connection would be broken, and I would lose my father to an eternity he might not return from.

"If you knew the ending Grace, the beginning would not trouble you," my father said, his voice soft, fading. I didn't understand what he meant, but there was some comfort in his words.

"Grace," Evan's voice reached out frantically, like hands searching to save someone who might be drowning.

My father cocked his head. "Answer him, Rabbit. I am nothing but the past to you. He's the present and maybe the future if he gets his act together. Besides, he's baked you some brownies."

A girlish giggle burst through the hard crust of my hurt and blossomed as large and as full as my aunts' heirloom dahlias. On the breathy notes of my joy, my father faded away.

When I looked up again, Evan was standing there, soaked and breathing hard, looking and wondering if grief and turmoil had rubbed me down to raw, throbbing silliness.

"I had to see you," he began, "and I thought ... well, I thought... My father says I have to leave if you want me to, Grace."

"No, don't go."

"Are you all right?"

"I'm fine." I let him gather me up into an embrace meant to heal my hurt. "Where are my brownies?" I asked, because I wanted the sweetness of my father's humor to linger a bit before the world turned hard and sour again.

He looked at me. "How did you know I had brownies?"

For Kadija's sake and mine I didn't lie.

"My father just told me that you baked some for me. That's why I was laughing."

There was that perfect moment of understanding between us, when I knew everything I had said was accepted as truth, as fact, and that nothing further had to be explained.

* * *

We all decided to watch the news conference because I thought maybe it would be the first step toward closure, a dim spark of hope at the end of a long tunnel of madness. I sat next to Evan on the couch, not boyfriend and girlfriend close, but near enough so our hands touched.

At exactly 3:00 p.m., Chief Atkinson punched through a set of glass doors, followed by the mayor and a couple of city councilmen. He approached the bank of microphones and stood there waiting for some semblance of quiet. Though I had met the man only once, I could read in the stiffness of his stance that something had gone terribly wrong, some aspect of the tragedy had metastasized. I sat up suddenly, bracing for the news of uncontrolled events. Monroe, who must have known something was coming, leaned back deep in the chair he was sitting in.

Atkinson began to speak. "On July 15, at approximately 9:00 a.m., Edmond Gilmore confessed to the murders of seven people over a period of thirty years. Although he was in frail health due to advanced age, he was arrested and was being held pending arraignment." Atkinson paused as if he was trying to balance something wide and heavy on something thin and narrow, then he continued. "Unfortunately, Edmond Gilmore passed away at one twenty p.m."

On television, the conference room went silent for a second as fuses of thoughts sizzled, and then came an explosion of "who, what, where, how?"

Atkinson called for quiet and waited for the boil of voices to turn themselves down to a simmer before he continued. "Of course, we

will continue to investigate these murders to see if others were involved."

There was an air of defeat in Atkinson's manner as he dispatched
questions with a stiff "yes," "no," or "no comment." Edmond Gilmore's
death was not the revenge of victims' dreams. It felt to me like fate
had given us a dollar's worth of justice and then proceeded to snatch
ninety-eight cents of that back.

I was trying to remain calm, trying not to talk to the television
about what was fair when a woman asked the mayor if he had any
comments. Fool that he was, it didn't occur to him to decline, to wait
for a more appropriate time. No, the evil of ignorance made him
get up and say, "perhaps this was for the best. The murders he was
accused of were committed a long time ago. Now that he's dead, the
city of Vigilant can move on."

He smiled like he had said something profound, but as the
cameras panned in, they caught the cracks in the dam of Atkinson's
reserve. His anger and hurt glimmered wet in his eyes, and he abruptly
walked out of the press conference. My heart and spirit followed him
out. Tornados were coming, and Oz might as well have been three
million miles away.

36

THE MAYOR'S WORDS AND IGNORANCE seeded the storms of discontent that brewed around the news of the murders. The why and how of the victim's deaths, the whispers that the Gilmore family had probably known about the crimes for years and was now showing very little remorse snatched the scabs off black people's sensibilities. As outsiders began to pull back the blood-soaked curtains to reveal the full horror of the crimes to the world, black folks decided we didn't want to be spectators in our lives anymore. We began to talk about the stuff in Vigilant that was separate and all the things that were unequal.

A lot of white folks, especially those in power, didn't know what to make of black discontent. Yes, the mayor was an idiot. Yes, what he had said sounded callous, but wasn't the essence of what he had said true? Edmond Gilmore had been caught. Edmond Gilmore was now dead, so now couldn't everything go back to normal? Why were black folks suddenly complaining about everything and nothing? Why were we suddenly putting Vigilant's history of lynching and racial cleansing out on the street like trash that needed to be picked up?

Black community leaders were having a hell of a time convincing some the murders didn't cry out to be met with whirlwinds of vengeance. They desperately tried to quell the anger by exhorting everyone to remember that Dr. King had said that violence did nothing but intensify the existence of evil in the universe. But who was King to some of us, especially the younger us, except a historical character who hadn't lived by the sword, but who had certainly died by it? What to do to reap a positive harvest from blood-soaked soil? A hastily formed ministers' alliance decided to call for a racial reconciliation rally in Bigot's Park.

A few days before the rally, Shanta called. "Did you hear the latest rumor?" she asked.

On the phone, her voice had sounded wormy with anxiety. I left a plate of eggs to get up and go pour myself a cup of coffee. "Which rumor?" I asked. "There's been so many of them."

"They say a couple hundred Klansmen are camping in the woods up behind Haven Lake."

I contemplated the narrow pond of blackness in my mug. "Shanta, that's the kind of strangeness Aunt Doris usually hands out." I wanted to laugh but I knew there would be no joke in it. It was one thing for Doris to speak fluent paranoia, quite another for Shanta the rational queen of math and science, to talk in the dialect of conspiracy theories. "Maybe there's a couple of racist assholes holed up somewhere, but I think by now the police would have noticed if that many crazy white folks were in town."

"It's not just Doris saying it. Besides she doesn't look so crazy anymore."

"Oh, come on, Shanta."

Shanta sighed a mother's kind of sigh, and then as if to prove her point said, "you still getting threatening phone calls?"

I sipped some coffee and savored the bitterness. "Wish I hadn't told you about those."

"Well, are you?"

"Nothing the aunts can't take care of. I swear Aunt Casmil could teach a course on creative ways to say, go fuck yourself."

"You tell your aunts my daddy says they need to change their phone number."

"I don't think—"

"Aren't you scared?"

"Yeah, sometimes."

Shanta paused. "I hope you're not thinking about going to the rally. I know several ministers have been asking you to come and speak, but there are just too many variables. Too many people have agendas that don't have anything to do with protesting for justice or honoring the dead. Fights have been breaking out. Most white people have put up no trespassing signs everywhere, not that reporters are paying any attention. Everybody's afraid there's going to be violence."

"I'm not going, honestly. I just wanted to grieve in peace," I assured her.

And I hadn't planned on going to the rally except Joe came by that day all hyped up, saying, "hey, Gracie girl, we got to stand up and be counted because your daddy was the kind of man who would have wanted us to."

I still didn't want to go but I said, "okay."

Vigilant looked nothing like a sleepy tourist town. Street after street was congested with huge coach buses and link after link of cars. License plates told the story of rides made from all over the United States.

"I don't think we can find anywhere closer than this," Joe said as he selected a parking spot I estimated was a good half a mile away from where the podium for the speeches was supposed to be set up. I nodded in agreement, and we began to walk. I was relieved to find that since there were so many strangers in town nobody recognized me.

By the time Joe and I had arrived at the outskirts of the park, all we could see was a solid mass of black people carrying signs and lustily shouting, " No Justice, No Peace." It was an amazing sight, one that made me proud, yet I could feel there was some tension in the air.

A few whites had joined the parade, but most stood on the edges of the snaking crowd, watching as if we were nothing but cattle going to slaughter. Every now and then voices boomed out, "why don't you all just go home!" It didn't help people's nerves that the temperature had rocketed upward into the nineties. It also didn't help that the leaders of the march were running late, so no one was there to direct the crowd's arcing currents of both positive and negative energy.

Although I had dressed for the heat, it seemed to make me sick as Joe and I joined a stream of chattering students wearing Michigan State University T-shirts. Images and voices began to swirl like chunks of brightly colored food being smoothed down in a blender.

"Joe, I think I need some water," I said as I stumbled toward a park bench and began to sizzle on the baking slats.

Joe touched my arm. "Maybe we need to go home."

"No, I just need a drink. I think I saw somebody selling some water a little ways back."

Joe went off, and I closed my eyes to keep the world from spinning. I felt Oba's arrival out of the ether of the all and all before I saw him. The air suddenly cooled a bit, like the park bench had been shifted into the shade of a large tree. The spiritual temperature changed as well. All the frantic outside noises were stripped away, leaving only the slow breathing of ocean waves. I opened my eyes and looked up and up at all that tall omnipresent blackness until I met Oba's intense gaze. I didn't know what to think. I didn't understand why he was here. Hadn't I done what had been asked of me?

"Hello, Rabbit," he said as he turned his palms up and spread them apart as if he were creating an opening for me to go through. "It is said, 'There is no greater love than this, that a person lay down his life for a friend.' Here's the question, Rabbit: could you lay your life down for an enemy? Could you do it for Jonathan Gilmore? You will have a chance to save him from physical death."

I looked at Oba and thought a multitude of unspiritual things like, *Okay, now I know God is crazy. Why in the hell would I want to save a man who probably knew his grandfather had killed children and my father?*

I almost said the blasphemous, "what the fuck?" when some deep understanding sprang up: If evil dies unjustly, it mutates into something more deadly. Who knew what might have been, if my great-great-grandfather had thought about the life of the child

Edmond before killing his father? I also considered the gray-eyed lady in the monster's home. "If I do it, do I survive?" I asked, and then I knew to add, "on this breathing side of existence?"

"Some things only God knows, and God has not chosen to reveal that outcome," Oba said.

I sat there numb, not knowing exactly what to think, wondering and maybe hoping the heat was the final straw, and that I was now officially insane.

"Do you understand what is being asked of you?"

I gave a tentative nod. "Even knowing what I know, I'm scared of dying."

"Perfect love casts out all fear," Oba said, as if "perfect love" was something I was carrying on me, and I just had to remember what pocket I had put it in. "The decision, of course, is yours to make, Rabbit."

It was a trickster god type of question in all its convoluted glory. Oba turned and walked off into the crowd. I watched his back until he disappeared, not into the perspective of distance, but into the mist of the sacred and eternal.

I sat shaking as a rough mix of voices began to boil up around me. I heard somebody yell, "here they come."

I set off in a run. The crowd pushed, pulled, and then parted. I saw a small line of white men marching and shouting about white power.

I knew the variety of rage in Jonathan would demand he be first in line. People in the crowd were in the mood to confront the evil before them, and they surged towards the group. Even as my feet found space to push myself through a whirling maze of bodies, I was trying to come to a decision by pulling petals off a metaphysical daisy: "do I ... don't I ... do I ... don't I ... do I ... don't I ..."

I saw the gun but the not the person holding it. It waved like a wand, reducing everything to something like a chaotic dream. I ran in front of Jonathan Gilmore, hoping beyond hope that just knocking him down would be enough.

Then I felt two swift punches below my ribcage.

The sensation forced my head down, and my mouth contorted into a circle of lips and teeth as buds of red bloomed in fast forward across my shirt. Quakes of pain and terror rattled my feet from under me, and I fell, fell, fell onto a sun-drenched patch of grass. I screamed, prompting others to join with me in my panic-stricken wail for help. I felt hands flip me over. I heard crescendos of prayers before the unconsciousness my brain had ordered arrived and I slipped away.

37

I HAVE THIS MEMORY LEFT over from the hospital I feel I should share. I'm not even sure if it is real because it has the texture of fever and drugs. I believe I was coming out of unconsciousness after surgery, and I felt myself trying to shove aside the darkness the way you push away dirt to get out of a hole. Eventually I saw a circle of light with Monroe's face stamped on it, and stopped digging.

"Exactly why did I save him?" I shouted up to Monroe.

"Love," Monroe shouted back, "but not the kind of love one has for God or friends or lovers, but Agape, the love of redemptive good will for all people. It's the kind of love that makes it possible to save an enemy."

"Like when Jesus said love your enemy."

"Yes," Monroe replied, then he chuckled, "Dr. King once said we should be happy Jesus didn't say, 'Like your enemies,' because like is such a sentimental and affectionate word. King's view was that it was hard, perhaps impossible, to be affectionate toward a person whose avowed aim is to crush you. Agape love allows us to get past the hate. It allows us to recognize that all life is interrelated, all humanity involved in a single process. You did what one human sister should do for a brother."

"I'm tired of being so damn magnanimous."

"I know, Rabbit," he told me, "but it's important that you are."

Love, I am beginning to learn, is stronger than death and an even greater mystery than life.

38

THERE WERE MOMENTS IN THE hospital when I wished with all my heart and scarred stomach that I hadn't saved Gilmore. Especially when my pain was all claws and no mercy, especially when I knew he wasn't the least bit grateful. Smug and grinning, Jonathan Gilmore told television reporters he'd wished I hadn't bothered. "Death," he'd explained, "would have been better than the humiliation of being saved by some fat nigger."

My mother did an excellent job of pretending she was enraged that the blood of one of her babies had been spilled to save a devil like Mr. Gilmore. She even had the nerve to blame God and Jesus for what happened. But most people in town knew my mother's indignation had the texture of something shoddy. They knew my mama was lying about Jesus, because it was not him she was pissed at, it was me. Out loud, my mother felt she had to say I was heroic, but my act had uncovered emotions and history she wasn't ready to face, much less deal with.

"Why" questions began to surface the way old ruins and dinosaur bones are sometimes revealed after the catastrophe of earthquakes or floods. I knew I wasn't supposed to have doubts and misgivings, and yet, as I stared down the barrel of all the consequences of my actions, I still wasn't above asking myself: *what the fuck was I thinking?*

Affirmation came in the shape of a missive from Mrs. Watanabe. Since it wasn't written in crayon or crafted from letters cut out of magazines, the hospital allowed me to read it without opening it first. Mrs. Watanabe had taken the time to write to me from her summer home in Japan, so I took the time to savor the act of opening it. The paper seemed to emit the perfume of her kindness, and her desire for the well-being of my spirit was incised in the smooth strokes of her handwriting. There was a certain efficiency in how she had sealed the envelope so that even my stubby fingernails were enough to open it. On stiff stationery, the color of the crust on a good loaf of white bread, she had written two quotes from Dr. Martin Luther King.

The first quote, "Injustice anywhere is a threat to justice everywhere," came up bland in that blah, blah, blah sort of way we usually hear famous people's words. However, Ms. Watanabe was using the first quote to sterilize and anesthetize the skin of my thinking before she used her pen to do some real surgery. The second quote had a scalpel's edge, and the emotional blood that leapt from the incision, like the physical blood that had bolted out of my bullet holes, forced me think hard about what I had done and why I had done it.

If a man hasn't discovered something that he will die for, he isn't fit to live.

"To a true warrior for peace," she had written at the bottom. Then she had signed her name in English and in Japanese because she knew I could appreciate how this symbolized her view of herself as a product of both those cultures. I decided then I had to hold tight to what Mrs. Watanabe was telling me. The ancestors would, of course, give me a final exam later that day.

* * *

Officer George Johnson, who is a distant twig of DNA on my mother's family tree, was the last person I had expected to come visit me. George lived two towns away and we hadn't really talked in years.

We knew enough to wave, "hey," to each other at family events, but that was all. He had called early yesterday, saying he wanted to talk to me about the shooting.

He arrived looking majestic in his uniform, and as soon as he walked in, the rank odor of unresolved anger soiled the atmosphere in the room.

"How you doing, Grace?" he asked. Lines of weariness ran like cracked earth under his gray-brown eyes, and his lips seemed to be trying to find a smile but couldn't quite uncover one.

"Seen better days," I responded.

"Yeah, I bet."

"Have a seat, George," I offered. "You look worse than I do."

As he sat down, he began to explain that he had just pulled some long hours of overtime patrolling the weeklong country music festival.

"So how was it to work a country music concert?" I asked, just to make small talk.

He laughed a bit, almost to himself really. "The only difference," he reported, "between arresting drunk black folks and drunk white folks at concerts around here is that the music is different and the white folks have on cowboy hats. Other than that, they all fight about stuff that doesn't matter, they all think they can sing, and they all throw up in the car."

He waited a few moments as I gave an obligatory laugh, then he leaned back in the chair. To the tune of a small hard sigh, he removed two folded envelopes from the breast pocket of his uniform. He handed them to me as if they weren't clean. "I had heard you been getting death threats. These came to my mother's house. I guess they thought she would make sure they got to you. They about gave her a heart attack when she read them."

I smiled weakly and didn't ask the obvious question of why his mother René had taken it upon herself to open mail addressed to me.

"Well, please tell René I'm sorry about this. I mean, it's not like people don't know where to find me."

Like dangerous snakes and lethal spiders, the two letters had arrived brimming with venom. The first letter was from a "sistah" who had reached out from her world of hate to tell me she wished I had died because I wasn't nothing but a sorry Uncle Tom who didn't care nothing about our people. Then, as if to emphasize her point and her ignorance, she wrote around the edge of the paper, "I wish you dead, I pray for your death."

The second letter, from some guy named Martin, was just as pointed. Even though Martin lived under a different rock than the "sistah" and they didn't know each other, Martin was still willing to help make her dreams of my demise come true. He wrote that I had prevented Jonathan Gilmore from becoming a true white patriot, and for the price of one bullet or even several he was willing to finish the job. Mr. Martin also kindly noted that I must be one stupid nigger to help protect a man who hated my people so much. Then he wrote cheerfully, "but that's how you people are."

"I don't know these folks," I said. "Actually, these are pretty tame. I have been called worse things on better grades of paper. I especially like the ones done in crayon. Nothing says hatred like 'Nigger Bitch' done up in cornflower blue."

I laughed, but I knew my cousin resented my rose-colored attitude.

"You know there are protesters. They're saying you don't really care about black people. That you're not really black."

I nodded. I had seen and heard them talking like the loudest drunk and bitter uncle at Thanksgiving. They were all over the television asserting that I was either ignorant or a race traitor who desperately wanted to be loved by white people. Even some older black people who had lived enough history to know better had the nerve to announce that I obviously didn't understand how justice was supposed to work.

"So what? It's not like they can take my black person's card away. I'm black whether they want me to be or not."

"This is some serious mess, Grace, and you don't even act like you really care if the person who did this is caught." His voice was filled with the unspoken accusation that the shooting wouldn't have happened if I had just stayed out of it. If I had just gotten out the way, he was thinking, then I wouldn't be in the hospital, and he wouldn't have to be reading the type of racial hate mail that pushed all his buttons as a black man.

"You don't understand," I said, because suddenly I did understand that it wasn't a matter of caring about who had done it. It was a matter of learning to accept that God could know but didn't have to tell. That the shooter had come and gone brilliantly costumed in anonymity did not really surprise me. That the police still had no clues to the shooter's identity stood as evidence the ancestors perceived the act, not as a horrible crime, but as a necessary catalyst to some larger and greater good.

"No. No ... What I don't understand is why you did it ..." He started and then stopped.

I let my mood darken a bit. "Go ahead; say what you're really thinking."

For a moment, he just looked at me. "It's my duty to protect people like Jonathan Gilmore."

"And since I'm not a cop and it's not my duty, why did I?"

"How many black folks do you know who would have, Grace?"

"I don't know. I don't think anyone knows what they will do until they're up against it."

"And you were up against it."

I stared straight at the tornados of contempt brewing in his eyes. "It was my obligation," I said. "He had rights worth protecting. He's a child of God too. He is somebody's son."

My cousin left upset and still confused. He left still thinking I was crazy, even though I had told the truth.

Dr. Monroe was right when he said my so-called gift would always be more infinitely bitter than sweet, because sometimes to obtain justice for others, I would have to sacrifice myself. In the end, when all is said and done and reverently meditated on, I suppose I could do nothing else but save, Gilmore.

39

"CAN ANYTHING BE DONE?" I asked my doctor as he made his last examination before I was released. My stomach looked like a road map to some corner of hell nobody should have to visit. I had been told that the incisions made to save my life might generate excessive scar tissue. However, I wasn't mentally prepared for the fleshy sculptures that were erected in memory of the violent journey the bullets took through my body,

Dr. Wilson, who looked like a fat, jowly lizard baking in a brilliant spot of artificial aquarium sunlight, remained silent as he scanned my chart.

"So ... can anything be done?" I asked again.

"Keloids," he said, his voice sterilized of anything I could perceive as true empathy. "It happens to African-American skin sometimes. You could have plastic surgery, but more than likely that wouldn't correct the problem and might even make it worse."

Strands of a misshapen combover shifted and fell like damp, loose straw across his forehead as he covered me back up in a perfunctory manner. He started to walk away because he thought his job was done.

"So my bikini days are over," I tossed out. Not because there were bikini days before. I was real about that, but because now all hope for bikini days in the future were gone even if I got skinny. In midstride he stopped as if he had come up hard against the end of the connection that held him in my life. He had daughters my age, so he knew what I was really talking about was not some stupid bikini but the terrifying reality of being disfigured. I could sense him turning my sarcasm over and over until finally he understood the depth of my concern and turned around.

"Be grateful to God because it's a miracle you survived," he said. "And it's been nothing but miraculous how quickly you healed." He paused for a long moment. "And I want you to know, I think you were very brave."

"Are you sure you don't mean crazy? My sister and a lot of other folks have been handing that word out like Halloween candy."

He laughed soft and sad. "Yeah, unfortunately I've heard a few people say something like that. I wish I had a cure for stupidity, ignorance and indifference."

"Even if you did, most people wouldn't take the medicine."

"Yeah, that's the truth. It's hard to bear witness. Most of us don't want the burden. Anyone ever tell you that old joke about who contributes more to a good breakfast of bacon and eggs, the pig or the chicken?"

I shook my head no. Jokes had never been my thing. Half the time, I'd never understood the punch lines.

He smiled. "Well, the answer is the pig because the chicken merely donates, but the pig is committed. Anybody who's had the nerve to criticize you is merely donating his or her opinions about what you should have done. None of them would have had enough courage to shed blood for something they believed in. "

"Thank you," I said.

"No, Grace. Thank you."

As the doctor left, Attorney Blair and two white FBI men walked in. Suddenly, my hospital room felt stuffed to the corners with their thick bodies and Attorney Blair's hovering bulk. Stiff with black-suit authority, the agents angled their eyes to look for crumbs of lies around my mouth as they asked the same question dressed up several different ways: Did I know who shot Mr. Gilmore? Of course, Attorney Blair and I noticed their questions were wrapped up tight in their belief that I was involved in some conspiracy. Because in their black and white view of the world, a normal lamb doesn't lie down with a lion, let alone save the lion's life, unless the lamb was up to something. I don't care how they make it look on TV, real interrogation is not entertaining. I think with the police, everybody (especially dark-skinned everybodys) is guilty until proven innocent, so they framed their questions to circle around like hawks looking in high grass for prey.

"If I had wanted him dead," I said finally, "it would have just made more sense not to bother to save him."

"You say that like you knew you had a choice," the taller agent said.

"We all have a choice to do or not do what's right," I offered. "Besides, I am going to try to work on forgiving the Gilmore family."

I knew the two agents wanted to look at each other; instead, they glanced at Attorney Blair who shrugged as if to say, "are we done now?"

"Good luck with that," one agent said under his breath.

"Yeah," I replied, "tell me about it." There's nothing like trying to do the impossible for the ungrateful.

"If we have any more questions, we'll contact you again, Ms. Johnson," one agent said.

"Gentlemen, you shouldn't have anymore questions." Attorney Blair's booming voice underlined the assertion. The agents nodded at him and left.

Attorney Blair took a moment to relax and wipe the seriousness off his face before pushing the button to call the nurse to the room. "Your aunts are waiting out in the car with Dr. Monroe. The press is wall-to-wall outside."

"Oh ... great. I was hoping this was going to be a non-event," I said.

I sighed as I thought about how all the excitement and activity would ruin my first chance to think more about living than dying.

"It'll be all right." Attorney Blair grinned as if he looked forward to the challenge. "I'm going to push people aside, and Joe will follow with you. Just like in the days when we played football."

40

SOMETIME DURING THE FIRST FEW days following the shooting, I'm sure the people who run Vigilant tried to estimate how long I would be a tragic black celebrity. They expected that after a couple of weeks, even folks with gluttonous curiosities about bad news would be sated and turn the channel on the TV or put the newspaper with my picture down on the floor for their dogs to piss on. One month tops, I'm sure they thought, and I would be a urine-stained memory. One month tops, and life and the tourist season would go on as planned. They miscalculated; the national media continued to press for information because really, who can resist gawking at a story featuring riots, racial cleansing, murders, crazy white folks, equally crazy black ones, and no kind of earthly justice for the guilty?

Yet, even knowing this, I was still stunned by the number of people beyond the hospital lobby window whirling about like pigeons after breadcrumbs.

"Do you want to say anything?" Joe asked as he positioned himself behind my wheelchair. He squeezed my shoulder to inject some reassurance that between him and Attorney Blair, we would make it past the hoard of news beggars.

At first I thought I didn't want to say anything, but then it occurred to me that I had to start driving my own story or other people would commandeer it and take it places I didn't want or need for it to go. "Yeah, I think I should say something."

"Make it short," Attorney Blair said as the automatic doors slid open.

A woman reporter I recognized from one of the national news shows was the first to stick a microphone in my face. "So, Grace, what do you think people should learn from your actions, and how do you really feel about Jonathan Gilmore and his family?"

I looked into her bright, greedy eyes and then into the camera beside her. "Well, I think all I want to say for now is things would be much better in this town and in the world, if we all learned, as the Bible tells us, to love our neighbors as we love ourselves."

Phony concern and authentic disbelief shaped her lips into a pout. "That's it? I don't understand? Aren't you angry?"

"Fuck, lady, ain't that enough?" Joe said as he steadied the wheelchair and pushed me away, forcing the eavesdropping crowd to scatter. "We wouldn't even be here if everybody understood that," he shouted over his shoulder.

Behind us, Attorney Blair took a stand to gather in and answer the rest of the questions.

"You know what's going to be in the paper tomorrow," I teased. "Big, menacing black man, protecting a crazy-savior-wanna-be black woman. Juicy story complete with all the popular stereotypes of us as either angry or magical."

"I don't care what the fuck they put in the paper," Joe said, "as long as they put in what you said about love."

* * *

I hadn't even settled in when the mayor of Vigilant, the less-than-honorable Joseph Tyson, came by the house, hat in hand, and holding behind his back a bright but poisonous bouquet of assumptions. If he had had a pinch of brains and a smidgen less self-importance and arrogance, he would never have darkened (or maybe the word is whitened) my aunts' door with what he came to offer me. However, the smug unknowingness that often afflicts politicians made him stand there and push the doorbell.

"Look who's here to see you." Aunt Casmil led him into the living room where I sat looking through a stack of welcome home cards from my friends. The sarcasm in her voice was as prickly as cactus. For a long, disappointment-filled moment, I looked at the man everybody, even his wife, called Turtle. People called him Turtle because he looked like his mother had had an interspecies affair with a snapper. He was short, bowlegged, and his head was too small to go with the barrel-roundness of his torso. It also didn't help matters that he seemed compelled by demons of bad taste to wear various shades of green almost exclusively. The saucers of sweat laid out on the underarms of a lime colored polo shirt announced he was hot and nervous. He became even more uneasy when I gave him a lackluster, "hello."

"I'll be nearby if you need me," Aunt Casmil said before she added with a hint of mock concern, "be nice, Gracie."

Manners made me accept his damp hand. It was a weak hand-shake, full of evidence of character flaws, and it left me with the childish desire to yell "cooties" and wipe my palm off on the side of my pants.

"Please have a seat," I said as I kept trying not to think about the fact that I had better things to do, like take a nap.

"I'm glad to see you're doing well," he offered as he sat down in an arm chair across from me.

"What can I do for you, mayor?" I asked.

"Well, it came to our attention at the last town council meeting that we hadn't properly rewarded you for your act of heroism. I mean, considering ..."

"No reward is necessary," I said.

"No, no," he continued. "We need to make up for the error on our part. A week from today, we want you to come down to the court-house for a ceremony and reception."

I must have looked at him like he had just invited me to sleep with him because splotches of pink began to stain his cheeks. "I really don't want anything. I'm sure you're aware the man I saved is not the least bit grateful, or for that matter, happy I saved his life. In fact, I would say the only people happy I saved his life are his parents. Most black folks think I've lost my damn mind, and white folks just wish I would move my heroic ass to some other town so that things could get back to normal."

"No, that's not true. The community is grateful."

The politician in him almost sounded sincere. I almost wanted to buy into his illusions, but illusions were a big part of the problem. Illusions were what had allowed evil in all its dark majesty to flourish unchecked.

I allowed the curvy, fake smile I had pasted on my face to flatten. "Mayor, let's just get this all out on the table. This isn't about gratitude. This is about you and whole lot of other people in this town trying to smooth over what happened. You believe giving me an award will somehow stop the outside press from poking around and asking how a racist serial murderer lived for years and years in the small town mist of Vigilant without people in authority asking any real questions about missing and murdered black people."

The mayor's face turned salmon, and his beakish mouth began to flap. "I'm sorry you feel this way. Frankly, I don't understand why you blacks felt we could have done anything."

I sighed because I knew he wasn't going to get it. "It isn't just about being any kind of sorry," I continued, "because none of us are clean, none of us can take an honest look in the mirror, and not see something of Gilmore lurking there. Let's face it, sometimes we are just God's big version of cockroaches. Maybe most times the roaches are better. But we can't transcend our history until all of us in this town honestly look at it and try to grapple with what it meant, what it can mean. I don't want your award because that's your way of trying to shove everything back under the rug. If you want to honor me, then start acting like you're the mayor of all of Vigilant and not just the white parts. Do you even understand that it was your dismissive statements at the press conference that caused the Racial Justice Rally to be held? If you had just treated the murders of the black citizens of this city seriously, from the get go, none of this probably would have happened."

At that moment, Mayor Tyson understood completely that he should have never, ever, come to see me. If he had a shell, he would have tucked himself down into it.

"I'm sorry you feel the way you do. I'm sorry we even offered," the mayor said as he stood up and rushed out in a most unturtle-like manner.

He left all hard-hearted because here I was telling him that he was ignorant. If he had stayed a little longer, I would have told him it was nothing to be ashamed of, because more often than we would like to admit, we all have our ignorant moments.

41

I HAD ABANDONED THE IDEA of meeting Mr. Gilmore until Chief Atkinson called me to come down to the station because he had been arrested after a fight in a bar and was now howling that he wanted to talk to me.

"I want to come in," Joe said as he pulled into a parking space near the door of the station. A frown of concern unmasked what I thought was just too much brotherly fierceness. *I don't need the drama*, I had thought.

I shook my head. "I'm just here to listen, Joe. I don't need you coming after him when he says something you don't like."

Joe went silent, squaring his shoulders away from the steering wheel as if I had slapped him. His frown grew thin as dark wire.

"I've been with you through everything, Grace," he finally said, his voice swirling with a yin and yang, sweet and bitter mixture of anger and love. "I still have clothes stained with your blood. I deserve a little more respect."

I nodded, could do nothing but nod. The sea of my memory of that day had finally begun to give up its wreckage of details. In the whirlwind of chaos that had followed the bullets, Joe had somehow been the first to find me. Above the din of screaming and the riot of footsteps carrying people away, he had covered me screaming and begging, "please God, don't let her die."

"I'm as grown as you, Grace."

"Maybe more than me," I murmured. "Maybe more ..."

I turned, laid my hand on his shoulder and waited for him to look at me. "I'm sorry. I forget sometimes I'm not the only one who needs some kind of closure."

* * *

"He's been down here yelling to speak to you since we picked him up on a drunk and disorderly this morning," Chief Atkinson informed me as we stood outside the jail room. "His wife refuses to bail him out."

"Did he say why he wants to talk now?" Joe asked. "I mean I saw him on television talking about how he would rather have died."

Atkinson's looked bemused. "He just keeps saying you ruined his life. Well anyway, he's still half in the bag, and he smells about as bad as he looks, but I thought maybe you might want to hear what he has to say—if anything. I know my staff would appreciate it if you could talk to him so he'd shut up. He's in one of our holding cells, and I'll be standing right behind you."

Anticipation jolted my heart into a quick sprint as Chief Atkinson opened a thick door that went toward a brightly lit back room that held four cells, all of them empty except for the one holding Gilmore. He was seated on a lumpy, sheetless bed, looking for all the world like somebody had tried to do plastic surgery on his face with a fist. The skin around his eyes and lips was the color of fruit punch and cigar ashes. His dark greasy hair was doing some kind of wild, interpretive dance on the top of his head in honor of his rough night outside some bar. The smells of stale sweat, festering loneliness, rotting pride, and vomit competed with the heavy musk of Eau de pine cleaner.

"Wake up, Gilmore," Atkinson called out. Blurry gray eyes that were too much like his mother's focused on me and then refocused as if he couldn't quite believe his wish had been granted by the police fairies.

"Hello, Mr. Gilmore," I said as I tried to keep down a feeling of pity. He didn't deserve pity, but I couldn't help but feel for him because he had fallen so far from grace he couldn't even begin to figure out how to get up.

We stood there in silence for a long while, until he staggered up to the door and thrust his arms through the bar. I noticed how his hands hung limp, like damp, dirty rags.

"You ruined everything," he said. "My wife's divorcing me."

Behind me, Atkinson and Joe hovered closer.

Gilmore didn't seem to notice them. "My boy, who's all of ten, told me I was a dumb asshole."

"Hmm," I uttered. I was surprised his young son knew what he had for a daddy. It wasn't often fruit fell a mile from its tree.

Gilmore adjusted himself more upright. "I had to hit him, because he was being disrespectful. I hit him so hard it should have knocked him out. But my boy can take a punch. He stood there like he was more man than me. Got up in my face saying, 'where does all that hate in you come from? You don't just hate black people, you don't love Mama, and you don't love me.' The boy thinks soft like his mother." Gilmore shook his head like he was trying to shake off loose bits of fallen plaster from his crazy-looking hair. And then, what I think is the last thing in this world I would ever hear him say, came out wet and full of despair. "The boy thinks I don't love him. Why would he think that?"

I had felt that hurt, had known that kind of pain all my life, and despite all my anger, the reach of my compassion exceeded the grasp of my hate. I reached out and touched his hand just for a moment, surprising myself. Joe took in a breath so deep I thought he would burst. "Grace, what the..." he blurted out.

I held up my hand, demanding silence and space.

"It's okay, Joe," Atkinson whispered.

Gilmore's eyes didn't move off me; he was startled and disconcerted. Some meanness sprang back up in his gaze and tried to push me out of the room, out of his life. But my touch was in his memory, and I could not be moved.

He gave me a drunk's wide-mouth sneer. "If you're expecting me to be thankful for what you did, I ain't got nothing for you."

I shook my head. "I don't need your thanks. I used to think I wanted it, but now I know I don't need it. I only did what was right." I turned around toward the door. "Take advantage of your second chance, Mr. Gilmore. Maybe in time you can earn your son's respect back."

"You want to wash your hands to get the ick off?" Chief Atkinson joked as we stood in the hall decompressing and shaking off the willies.

"Yeah," Joe said. "Maybe we can go and get you some rabies shots."

I laughed and shook my head, then Chief Atkinson got quiet and those blue eyes tried to read the depth of me.

"So really, why did you do it, Grace? Why did you save him?"

"I meant what I said," I replied. "Besides, if he had died this madness would have just started another cycle of revenge and retaliations. The ancestors say, if evil dies unjustly, it mutates into something more deadly."

"Maybe," Atkinson said. He sounded unconvinced. "You know, we're no closer to finding the shooter."

"Yes, I know."

"Those ghosts you speak to wouldn't happen to have a clue?" The policeman in him made him ask.

"No, they aren't telling," I said, because of course, it was not a matter of if they knew, but what they chose to reveal.

"They aren't concerned with justice?" Chief Atkinson asked.

"They don't have to be concerned with earthly justice," Joe said.

With a knowing smile, I complimented my brother's wisdom and reached to change the subject. "Will I see you at the memorial service, Chief Atkinson?"

"Oh yes, my mother and all my brothers and sisters will be there. Yesterday, some kids from one of the elementary school brought some boats by the house. My mama was really touched; she thinks it a wonderful idea."

It had been Shanta's idea to hold a memorial service for the victims down by the shores of Haven Lake. "God lives in the sky, but the ancestors dwell for eternity in the water," she had told me. It had also been her idea that those who came to commemorate the lives of the victims would set sail paper boats folded and decorated by school children. Love for a man who was as much his daddy as he was mine inspired Joe to suggest placing votive candles in their small bellies. "They'll shine like the stars," he said, "you know, to remind us that life is eternal."

I left the station, believing everything was finished, that all the redemptive I's were dotted and all the T's in the truth were crossed. But nothing is done until the ancestors say it is done.

42

JOE WAS QUIET AS WE drove home. Quiet enough for me to know he was trying to keep his opinion about what had happened at the jail to himself. Why, I knew he was wondering, had my anger cracked and failed like a broken limb? Why the hell had I fed even a crumb of compassion to an unrepentant white man? Joe's body went stiff with agitation, triggering his fingers to clutch the steering wheel, setting off his leg to plunge the accelerator deeper. Released from the cage of normal highway speed, the car eagerly leapt forward, and the view outside the windows began to blur like thick smears of paint on wet paper.

"It wasn't about him," I said when my concern about his driving began to taste more like fear.

Joe tossed me a look and pulled over to the side of the road. The engine purred along with Herbie Hancock on the radio. I smiled. Herbie, master of fusion and funk, so badass, some said he could turn shit into gold. I could have used some of his magic right then. We listened for a while, letting the unspoken settle down into the music before we tried to deal with it. I really didn't feel like talking. I was as confused as Joe about whether I had blessed evil instead of condemning it.

"It wasn't about him. It was about me," I said softly. "I think I want to begin to forgive now and move on. I want to transcend the hurt, and reaching out was a way to ..."

Joe wasn't having it. "Grace, you took bullets for that asshole, and he couldn't even say—"

"Like I said, it's not about his gratitude ..." I groped for words, cresting one hill of thought about the nature of forgiveness before moving on to the next thought, deeper and deeper into the uncharted wilderness of my emotions. "Touching him was like giving him the first word in a long conversation about good and evil that he can either have or not have with himself."

"He's evil, Gracie, and he ain't gonna have that conversation."

"It's not just about good and evil. It doesn't even matter if he begins the conversation."

"I still don't get how you see it."

I hesitated, finally grasping a shadow of the truth. "Hope. I think it's all about hope."

Joe smiled big, his anger spent. "Sometimes hope's a sucker's bet, Grace. Mike Dodson the poet said, 'I'm gonna scream before I hope again.'"

I shrugged and chuckled. "Phillis Wheatley said, 'with tow'ring hopes, and growing grace, arise.'"

We sat again, still not completely agreeing but happier.

"I see you been reading books again, Mr. Joe," I teased.

Joe gave me a polite nod of his big head. "Bad habit I picked up from you, Ms. Grace."

I laughed, and then the music on the radio became suffused with static and Joe's voice slid out wrapped as someone else. "So now what of yourself will you extend to your mother?"

I took a breath and held it as Herbie played on, his complex melodies barely audible above the rising one note hissing of the spiritual. I hadn't wanted to deal with my mother, at least not in this lifetime. I didn't think I owed her anything, certainly not forgiveness. In fact, I thought it was almost easier to forgive the Gilmores. It hadn't been their job to love me. My mother should have loved me unconditionally and hadn't, even the thin love Monroe had talked about didn't seem to exist.

I looked at Joe, ready to blurt out, "not a damn thing," but my cousin's face was plastered with a fierce cartoon of a smile. The same smile Shanta had worn when the ancestors had her tongue. I bit down on those words and swallowed them. I knew eventually I would have to deal with the question. Sooner, rather than later, I understood, I would have to answer to those omnipotent others who expected my sense of mercy to be equal to their own.

I closed my eyes and the static dimmed, leaving behind a smooth caress of piano jazz. "I'm so tired," I whispered more to the invisible others than to Joe.

"Damn straight, Gracie," Joe grunted after a moment "You got a right to be."

When we pulled up to the house and I saw Monroe's car, a sense of unease uncoiled itself and slithered through my body.

Joe opened the car door for me and offered the ledge of his arm for me to grasp. "Were you expecting him?" he asked.

I stood and grimaced as tendrils of pain climbed my half healed scar. "No, he didn't mention he was coming over to visit."

We entered the house to the sound of laughter, the bright burst and flares of joy that usually follows the telling of a joke. The scent of happiness led to the sun porch where Peaches, Casmil and Monroe were seated at the table. A pitcher of ice tea and tall thin glasses were perspiring next to Mt. Everest size slices of red velvet cake.

"Cake," Joe shouted and charged in. I leaned against the door-jamb because I knew better than to just enter. The electricity of the sacred was in the air, invoking Monroe's unspoken rules for my obedience. I waited for his invitation to take a seat.

"Hey, baby," Peaches said. Her smile was welcoming and took the edge off of Monroe's now somber presence.

"Hey, Aunt Peaches. How are you?"

"Fine. You look a little tired. "

"Yeah, I am a little."

Peaches glanced at Monroe, her eyes silently pleading my case for a chair. Monroe creased his lips thinner and ignored her.

"Grace." Casmil accented her clipped greeting with a curt nod. She didn't look at Monroe; as usual she wasn't going to cut me even a thin slice of slack.

"Aunt Casmil," I asked. "What were you all laughing about?"

"Oh, just old times," Peaches said.

I watched her hand Joe a piece of cake big enough for a room full of folks. As if performing magic, Joe waved his fork, smacked his lips and made half of the moist crimson layers disappear. He grinned at me and held his plate close to his chest, as if he had to protect it. "I bet you want some of this, Gracie," he teased. "Well, I ain't giving you any."

I laughed, couldn't help but laugh at Joe's attempt to peel off some of the seriousness from the atmosphere in the room. Monroe smiled, but I sensed his impatience.

"Joseph," Casmil interrupted. "Why don't we go to the living room? Dr. Monroe needs to talk to Grace about her mother."

The mention of Mama made me stand up straight and cross my arms across my chest as if that would prevent a jumble of hostile emotions from pouring onto my face. On the way out, Joe the kid, who was now Joseph the man, touched my shoulder in a way that said that whatever it was, he was going to be there for me.

"Have a seat, Rabbit," Monroe finally offered.

I lowered myself gingerly into the chair and tried not to look him in the eyes.

"Would you like some tea?" He lifted the pitcher and invited me to drown my thirst.

I nodded, and he poured the dark brew into my glass.

"So, Rabbit, how was your day?" He asked the question that had marked the beginning of our relationship and would, I knew, bind us together far into the future—deep into eternity.

The tea was honey sweet and deliciously cold. I drank half of it before I began to tell the story of what happened at the jail. I

drained the other half as I edged up to the memory of how I had been
challenged by the ancestors to do for my mama what I had done for
Mr. Gilmore.

"And what are you willing to do?" Monroe asked, sitting back in
his chair so that he could observe my reaction.

Now I knew what I was supposed to do. Learn from the first
event and smoothly connect it to the next. The moral linkages were
clear and obvious, but I wasn't feeling it.

"I don't want to do a damn thing for her," I said. "My Uncle
George said not to let her back into to my life."

Monroe stared at me. "Sometimes, Rabbit, when there is a murder
in the family, the one who dies isn't the only victim. You know that.
Your mother has suffered."

"A lot of people suffered, but they didn't take it out on me or
other people. They didn't use their grief as a reason to abuse and
abandon their children. If anything they used it to protect."

"Everybody doesn't come out of tragedy stronger or sane."

"Monroe ..."

"Give as you would like to receive, Rabbit. There will come a time
as it does for all of us when you will need from someone a kind of
mercy and forgiveness you may well not deserve."

"Monroe, I still don't want—"

"This is not about what you want."

"That's obvious. Why don't you tell me something I don't know?"

Damn it. It was a figure of speech I didn't expect him to take me
up on it. I thought I was going to get the backhand smack of a lecture;
instead I got something deeper, a rare glimpse of the man behind his
iron mask of myths and rules.

"Every Monday, for more years than I care to count," he began, "I
pray for my brother. Then I call and leave a message on his voicemail
at his church. Nothing more than I would like talk to him sometime."

"Does he ever call back?"

"No, but it doesn't matter. When and if he's ready, the door is ajar.
He will just need to walk in. Do you get my point, Rabbit?"

I gave up but not necessarily in. "Yeah, okay," I said, although I still couldn't see how I was ever going to let my mama anywhere near me.

"Give your mother a call," Monroe said. "Offer her a little mercy."

* * *

I waited until later that night to call Mama. I planted myself at my desk and pulled my bag from its special place at the bottom of a drawer. I thought about the rabbit as I picked up a pen and began to draw a picture of the cosmograph, remembering how ending should become beginnings, how death should give way to the newness of life. I put on Miles with his mean, psychotic, but utterly brilliant self, to accompany me on my journey back into the past. "Bitches Brew" was playing when I picked up the receiver and dialed my old number as if it belonged to a stranger.

"Hello." Mama's voice sounded tight.

"Hey, Mama, this is Grace."

I tried to interpret the whir of silence that followed. Was it pissed annoyance or the kind of relief that came from the unexpected but welcomed offer of a second chance?

"Well, I didn't think I'd ever hear from you again," she said

I absorbed the punch of her dismissive tone and countered with a respectful but sarcastic truth. "Yeah, well Mama, God works in mysterious ways ...so how are you doing?"

"Fine."

"How's Jamila?"

"Fine."

Miles's horn seemed to scream out a cacophony of, "I told you she was going to be a bitch about this. Yeah, I told you so."

I prayed that I could squeeze out a softer attitude from my hardening heart. I prayed for a sign of new beginnings, for a sign of Monroe's rumored thin love. "So are you coming to the ceremony of remembrance? I think Daddy would want us all to be there." I said.

I expected the abrupt "fuck you" click of the receiver. Instead, silence became more silence.

"Did you and Jamila get the paper boats the children made for you? " I asked.

Silence, and then I heard the soft rattle of a sob. The unexpected eruption of Mama's unresolved grief made my own body began to sway and shake, unearthing my own hidden sorrows, and for a moment Mama and I were mourning together a man we had both loved and violently lost.

"Well Mama ... if you can," I said, my voice quaking.

I heard my mama whisper, "maybe," just before the dial tone began to sing.

43

A LETTER CAME IN THE mail, full of spirits whispering about moral ambiguities. In ink as faint as wisps of smoke, a frail hand had traced my name and address in downhill lines across the envelope. As my fingers drew out a slip of raggedy blue lined paper, the tart sweetness of spiced peaches flooded my mouth.

Dear Miss Johnson,

I have left this town, but I wanted you to know I did not mean to hurt you. I know the police are looking for who shot that man, but I'm not turning myself in. I don't think white people on a jury would care about a black mother's pain. They wouldn't understand how all the years of missing my baby girl hurt me. Evil as that man is they would still side with him because he's white. Perhaps it was Annika or all those other dead babies' spirits who put you in front of him to save me from one of God's greatest sins. I hope you can forgive me that your blood is on my hands. If Annika had grown up, I would have wanted her to be like you.

Love in Annika's memory,

Lawanda

I shuddered and sighed. "Annika," I whispered to the baby's spirit now clinging to me. "I could have lived without knowing this."

I sat for a long time on my aunts' porch, trying not to cry as I thought about what I should do next. I sat for even a longer time in Chief Atkinson's office, weeping as he read the letter.

"You did the right thing bringing this to me, " he said, sitting back in his chair.

"So do you have to find and arrest her?" I asked. "I don't want her to go to prison for hurting me. Isn't there such a thing as too much justice?"

Chief Atkinson looked at me deep and hard. "Maybe there is," he said.

We talked about how the other victims' families were doing, how some people were grieving well and others completely flying apart emotionally. When we were all out of memories and observations, Chief Atkinson said, "Grace, you go home and be a kid for a little while. The moral burden of Ms. Parson's letter is now mine."

I left, not knowing if the policeman or the little brother in him would win the discussion about what should or shouldn't be done about finding Lawanda. Deep in my heart, I placed all my bets on Belinda Atkinson's baby brother.

* * *

The night before the ceremony of remembrance and renewal, Shanta and I lay on a blanket of grass looking up and marveling at the star-encrusted canopy of darkness. We were quiet, wearing our shared silence like comfortable shoes, together in a way that only good and old friends can be.

"I'm leaving next week for school," Shanta said. She was speaking a truth I hadn't exactly wanted to face.

"Yeah, I know," I said, trying to keep the selfish sadness out of my voice. I wanted Shanta to stay, of course. She had been my best protector and guide, a generous womb and cradle for my spirits. But her destiny was calling and she, the math queen and goddess of three inch heels, needed to set out on her own journey.

"They say you will be fine," she said.

"I suppose."

"Nikki's having a girl, and she's going to name her after you." Shanta's voice was drowsy and distant.

I felt my cheeks burning. "Oh, come on ..."

"She admires you. She thinks you're brave."

"She hated me in high school."

Shanta laughed. "Grace, high school might as well have been another lifetime ago."

"That's the truth."

Shanta began to doze, but I kept studying the heavens, wondering if the stars were perhaps like incandescent tea leaves that could be read to tell my future.

Monroe had already counseled that college should perhaps wait a term until I was both physically and mentally ready.

"You need to give yourself over to your grief in order to fully heal." After some hesitation, he'd added, "but don't think, Rabbit, that this means you won't have work to do. Remember, you belong more to the next world than to this one. The ancestors will work you because that is your purpose. Dealing with the Gilmores was only the beginning of your spiritual journey out into the world."

"Am I supposed to be happy about this?" I had asked him, because I thought the spirits had worked my behind enough in the hospital and I wanted a real rest.

Monroe had laughed his best Skin Horse laugh, a laugh that is always tinged with sorrow and secrets. "When you are real, Grace, you will understand that your happiness will probably never be the issue."

I began to wonder what to do with the book of names and its terrible legacies. It didn't feel right to keep it on some shelf or in a drawer. I kept mulling this over until Shanta woke up. She turned over, and with eyes full of some other soul besides her own, said, "bury it in the bottle tree forest, because trees are a sign of spirits on their way to the land of the ancestors. They represent the persistence of life. They are signs and symbols that death is not the end."

"You want to come and help me do this?" I asked.

"No," Shanta-who-wasn't-Shanta said. "This is something you and your aunts need to do alone."

I know now how to listen. I know now how to obey.

So, this morning my aunts and I woke up early, just as the Hare's full moon was dying and the sun was being reborn. Dressed in the pink suits we had worn to Nana Grace's funeral, my aunts and I stood around the living room table, meditating on how the past had shaped this future.

"May all who have suffered find peace and solace," Casmil said as I wrapped the book with all its understated history of bloodshed and pain in a square of red cloth.

To the sound of their bright voices chanting prayers, I sealed the bundle close with twine, tying a knot for each victim. Eight rough navels of string represented Annika, Dymond, Effie Maria, Malcolm, Perry, Macy, Belinda, and my father.

"Come, baby," Peaches said, "we're almost done."

The book weighed heavily in my arms as we slowly walked up the road, shrouded in veils of morning mist. Birds, loud and playful, heralded our arrival at the grove of trees. The bottles gleamed bright as stained glass, and ancient eyes watched as Casmil handed me a spade. I fell to my knees and began to dig at the base of one of the biggest pine trees. The earth gave way easily, crumbling like good cake.

"We can help you," Casmil reminded me.

I paused and shook my head. No, I was a grown woman and this part was mine to do. The push and pull of my body, the raking in and out of my breath as the hole grew deeper, brought solace and the sound of children laughing.

When I was finished, and the book was entombed, I sat back on my legs, closed my eyes and listened. In the dim distance, where the land of the living meets the oceans of eternity, I could hear my father singing in a voice that was as deep and straight as mine is crooked and shallow:

And in the gardens of my heart,
Grace, I heard you calling me.
Now, I am fully here.
Now, I can go to the blue world under.
Daughter, I am going home.

WADE IN THE WATER

OVER A THOUSAND BLACK AND white folks from Vigilant and beyond came to the ceremony of remembrance and renewal, if for nothing else than to be nosy. Though I had arranged for everything to be catered, people still came with offerings of food. It was a memorial ceremony after all, and people believed that out of respect for the dead and those who were grieving, food had to be made and shared.

A well-dressed procession of women from every church in town arrived down to the beach with every kind of baked good known to man or woman: pound cakes worthy of the name, angel wing, coconut, red velvet, and bright-colored Kool-Aid cakes that were sure to make kids giggle and grown people reminisce about being children again. Somebody's mama prepared enough banana pudding to feed the next town over, and somebody's daddy brought a couple of fruit cakes so damp with brandy you could have gotten drunk just by smelling them.

Food-filled stomachs and hardened attitudes began to soften. People ventured to nibble around the edges of talking to each other over steaming plates bowed into the shape of crescent moons by huge helpings of Jambalaya, and red beans with rice. It's hard not to talk to somebody when there was fried catfish and crawfish etouffee.

"Is your mother and sister coming?" Joe asked.

We stood together, watching the Ghanaian drummers Monroe had hired set up.

I shrugged. "I don't think Mama or Jamila are coming."

"Evan? Did you invite him?"

I sighed. "Evan is where he needs to be, back home in Atlanta."

"He sent you any more flowers?"

"No," I said, looking at Joe like he had lost his mind. *No, no, flowers,* I thought, but he had sent the truth about Kadija in a letter. How he had all but abandoned her during her illness. How he had been away when she died. He had also sent me an apology and a promise of better days together.

I had accepted the apology, but I didn't know if I fully trusted his promise. *He'd abandoned her,* I thought. *Would it be any different with me?* But then there had been our first kiss to the rising notes of Coltrane before he left to go back home to Atlanta.

"Gracie," he had said, and my name in his mouth became like honey or maple syrup or apple butter or anything else that is sweet, brown and good. I knew I couldn't go anywhere until I had some of that.

As I'd imagined, the kiss began in the touch, the way his fingers gently stroked my arm like tendrils of a warm breeze. The chef in him made him patient. He just let things simmer until I fell into his arms and let his lips touch mine. As a moan of pleasure I meant to keep to myself escaped my mouth, all I wanted to believe was maybe someday there would be love.

"You're still sweet on him aren't you?" Joe asked.

"Smitten, yes."

"So, you gonna see him again?"

I laughed. "Why are you suddenly interested in Evan? You don't even like him."

Joe gave me a sheepish look and a he-he-he kind of laugh. "It ain't about me, Gracie. My mother won't leave me alone about this. And Shanta, well, she ain't going to tell your business."

It did sound about right that it was more his mama wanting to know than Joe being nosey.

"Tell your crazy mother that I might, and I'm stressing *I might* see Evan in the spring when I go to Spelman."

"She's not going to be happy with that."

"Well, tell Aunt Doris that's all she's going to get 'cause that's all there is."

* * *

When the sun went down in full bloom, leaving behind a sky strewn with petals of pink, orange and gold light, African drummers began a joyous beat of traditional music. People marched down to the lip of the lake, which was the luminous edge of the crossroads. Those who were called to dance, danced, until Monroe, in his deep and sonorous voice, chanted out the names of those who had been taken. Then he poured a libation, asking God and the ancestors to open all of our hearts to the wonders of forgiveness and grace.

Silence engulfed the crowd, and those of us who had been made family by the tragedy lit our candles and released our boats onto the water. Waves like small, eager hands accepted their rich gifts of memories. Moved by the spirit, Chief Atkinson's mother began to sing in a small, sweet voice, "wade in the water. Wade in the water, children. Wade in the water, God's going to trouble the water."

By the second stanza, we were all singing, even me with my voice. When we were done singing and crying and hugging each other, Monroe said, "perhaps Grace would like to end this with a blessing."

Perhaps Grace really didn't, because deep down a sliver of me still believed that justice this delayed was still justice denied. Like a flawed superhero, I'd fought evil with good and won, but in the end was that enough? I felt like I had nothing to say until I looked out at the brightly lit boats, floating like delicate flowers on the skin of eternity.

"All I have to say is this," I began. "I don't believe that the opposite of evil is just good, but rather, it is faith and hope and love, and the greatest of these ..." I paused and looked out at all of the people who were now my family. "But the greatest of these is love."

Acknowledgments

To God, who was at the beginning and will be at the end. To my ancestors, upon whose mighty shoulders I stand.

To my family, Gary, Nancy, John, Kathryn and Garth, for your unwavering belief and support. Much love to my favorite sister, Delphia, whose determination kept this novel from being three chapters at the bottom of my desk drawer. All my love to my nieces and nephew, Lauren, Mallory and Garrison. You are the hope of the future. To my mother's best friend, Marjorie Cash, thank you for holding in your heart the memory of my mother and for voicing the artistic dreams she had for me. Special thanks to my extended family, the Simpsons and VanCatledges, with a special shout out to Natalie, Aunt Pat and Aunt Rosie, who told me they believed in me when I most needed to hear it. To Nyla, the best dog a writer could have.

Special thanks and gratitude to those authors, editors, literary experts and poets who helped shape my novel: Barbara Shoup, Anita Diggs, Mat Johnson and Tim Tomlinson. Special love and blessings to the wise and amazing poet, Sharon Dubiago.

To my writer's posse who gave me sage advice, willing ears, incredible editing, hugs, laughter, wild and wonderful poems, kicks in the butt, huge cups of coffee, long lunches, bags of chocolate, and a whole lot of wine: Mark Bolanowski, Stephanie Feldstein, Robyn Ford, Lois Godel, Skipper Hammond, Karen Hildebrandt, Leslie

McGraw, Shelly Schanfield, Debbie Taylor, Pat Tompkins, Robbie Townsel, Sherlonya Turner, and the incredible writer and person, Dallas Walters.

To the Nicholas Bookstore Monthly Writing Group, who read *Act of Grace* first: Dan Alberda, Betsy Beckerman, Reena Worley and our extraordinary leader, Judy Schmidt. You were my very first group, and we are still going strong some 10 years or more later. I love you guys.

To my fabulous children's writers group (folks we really need a name) who helped shape Grace's voice: Gina Boldman, Joanna Brod, Jennifer Burchill, Paula Payton Gurrie, Mindy Krasner, Pam Patterson, Wendy Ratkowski and Jeff Wolf

To my Woman of Words Writers Group, thanks for your prayers, laughter and love: Jacquie Hall, Coralie Cederna Johnson, Jennifer Martin, Carol Richard.

To The Ann Arbor Writers Group, I found you during the worst time in my life; you took me in and helped me write myself whole again. New member or old, please know that you all are very special to me. Shout outs to: Cynthia Allar, Jeannie Ballew, Sandra Beal, Rebecca Biber, Mat Bilton, Bob Brill, Courtney Conover, Connie Cohn, Syd Bridges, Adrianna Buonarroti, Fritz Freiheit, Dan Gilbert, Noelle Goodin, Donnelly Hadden, Skipper Hammond, Ellen Halter, Joanna Holt, Keith Hood, Jeff Jackson, Ray Juracek, Roxann Keating, Ron Kelley, Terry Linden, Rochell Maithot, Pran Mukherjee, Beth Neal, Patrick McHugh, Jose Mojica, Beth Neal, John Perry, Kay Posselt, Sarah Rigg, Louis Smith, Sonja Srinivasan, Kate Stone, Edd Tury, Elizabeth Van Ark, David Wanty, Tammie Williams.

To my African-American women writing group, thank you for your support and excitement: Tahira Naeem, Soheila Naeem, Angela Verges and Tory Williams.

To the staff and authors I worked with at the Callaloo Writing Workshops (2007, 2008), the Hurston/Wright Writers' Week Workshop (2003) and The Split Rock Mentoring Program for Writers, a heartfelt thanks.

To the Speculative Literature Foundation, heartfelt thanks for the award of your 2009 Older Writers Grant.

To the Peninsula Writers Group, thanks for the peace and fellowship I found at your great writers retreats.

To some of my first readers and quilting buddies, Mary Shue and Karen Morehead, thank you for your time, friendship and fabric.

To photographer, Beth Neal and my hairdresser, Nesa Malcheff, many thanks for helping me feel confident.

Last, but certainly not least, love and endless gratitude to my publisher and editor, Tieffa Harper. Ti, you and your team are nothing but amazing. After a year of rejection after rejection, I thought my novel was never going to find a home. Thank you from the bottom of my heart for giving Grace a chance to get out in the world.

If I have forgotten anyone, please charge it to my head, and not my heart.